"*Gossamer* is a tend...
—Tere... ...ng
...*Your Touch*

"Beautifully written and very touching . . . If you're looking for something a little different from the norm, this is the one to read." —*Old Book Barn Gazette*

"Outstanding and unforgettable." —*Bell, Book & Candle*

"A moving and emotional love story."
—*All About Romance*

"*Gossamer* is an incredible diamond." —*Affaire de Coeur*

MORE PRAISE FOR THE NOVELS OF
## Rebecca Hagan Lee

"A wonderfully charming story of friendship, love, and commitment . . . A must-have for anyone who enjoys intelligent, well-developed characters and a fresh sense of humor interwoven throughout the story." —*Romance Reviews Today*

"Sparkling romance and passion that sizzles . . . Lee taps into every woman's fantasy."
—Christina Dodd, *New York Times* bestselling
author of *Danger in a Red Dress*

"Engaging . . . Fans who relish an emotional, character-driven plot will find Rebecca Hagan Lee's latest story enticingly fulfilling." —*Midwest Book Review*

"A charmingly clever romance deftly seasoned with wit and graced with some delightfully unforgettable characters."
—*Booklist*

*Titles by Rebecca Hagan Lee*

# A
# WANTED MAN

*Rebecca Hagan Lee*

BERKLEY SENSATION, NEW YORK

**THE BERKLEY PUBLISHING GROUP**
Published by the Penguin Group
Penguin Group (USA) Inc.
375 Hudson Street, New York, New York 10014, USA

USA | Canada | UK | Ireland | Australia | New Zealand | India | South Africa | China

Penguin Books Ltd., Registered Offices: 80 Strand, London WC2R 0RL, England
For more information about the Penguin Group, visit penguin.com.

A WANTED MAN

A Berkley Sensation Book / published by arrangement with the author

Berkley Sensation Books are published by The Berkley Publishing Group.
BERKLEY SENSATION® is a registered trademark of Penguin Group (USA) Inc.
The "B" design is a trademark of Penguin Group (USA) Inc.
For information, address: The Berkley Publishing Group,
a division of Penguin Group (USA) Inc.,
375 Hudson Street, New York, New York 10014.

ISBN: 978-0-425-26729-5

PUBLISHING HISTORY
Berkley Sensation mass-market edition / August 2013

PRINTED IN THE UNITED STATES OF AMERICA

10  9  8  7  6  5  4  3  2  1

Cover photo by Claudio Marinesco.
Cover design by George Long.
Interior text design by Kristin del Rosario.

ALWAYS LEARNING                                         **PEARSON**

*This book is dedicated to my readers
who have waited patiently for my return to the American
West and who wanted to know what happened
to Will Keegan from* Gossamer.

*And to the men and women who dedicate their lives
to fighting the monsters who traffic in human misery
wherever it occurs.*

*Thank you for the work you do.*

# *Prologue*

*❦*

CORYVILLE, CALIFORNIA
SEPTEMBER 22, 1874

Will . . ." She came to him in the deep of the night. Calling his name. Slipping out of her silk nightgown and into his bed while he slept. She came as she always did: wanton and naked and wanting him. She came to him as she had nearly every night since they had left Hong Kong for California.

And Will welcomed her. As he had always welcomed her. Mei Ling was his. The girl he had loved at sixteen. The woman he continued to love. He held her close, absorbing the warmth of her body, inhaling the intoxicating scent unique to her—jasmine and Mei Ling. Tangling his fingers in her long, silky black hair, Will kissed her. Deeply. Thoroughly. As if he could never get enough of kissing her. She was young and beautiful, full of joy and life and love for him.

She broke the kiss long enough to smile down at him. Staring up into her dark, almond-shaped eyes, Will saw his love reflected in them. Pulling her deeper into his embrace, he reversed their positions. Her dark hair fanned across his pillow. Mei Ling closed her eyes. He kissed her lips. Her cheek. Her nose. Nibbled at her earlobe, teasing the pearl earring she always wore with the tip of his tongue before moving on to kiss the delicate skin at the corners of her eyes.

She sighed. Her pleasure was a breath that hung like incense in the air between them. Heating them. Will's heart expanded in his chest. His blood, hot and thick, roared through his veins, filled with his love for her. He watched her in the glow of the lamplight, memorizing her features, before he leaned forward to kiss her again.

"Will . . ." she whispered his name, then reached up and looped her arms around his neck, drawing him to her, into her. In an embrace as close as it was possible for two lovers to be.

Will ached for her. Burned with his love for her.

Until she opened her eyes and he found himself staring down into Elizabeth Craig's extraordinary blue-green eyes. Will recoiled. As Will watched, Mei Ling's delicate features started to blur. The shape of her eyes, the slope of her nose, the curve of her lips, the color of her eyes began to merge with the delicate features of another woman—a woman he saw most every day.

WILL AWOKE IN A COLD SWEAT.

He was afraid that history was repeating itself. Afraid that he was coveting what belonged to the man who was closer to him than a brother. Afraid that he was falling in love with James Cameron Craig's wife . . .

For the second time in his life . . .

# Chapter One

❦

*"Virtue is the only firm ground for
[friendship] to stand upon."*
—THOMAS FULLER, 1654–1734

SEPTEMBER 23, 1874

What's this?" James Cameron Craig looked up as a folded piece of fine ivory linen paper slid across his desk.

"My resignation." Will Keegan stood squarely in front of James's desk.

*"What?"* James arched his eyebrows in query as he stared up at his closest friend.

"It's my resignation, Jamie. Effective immediately," Will repeated in a determined voice. "I'm leaving Craig Capital."

He stood before his best friend, the president and heir to Craig Capital, Ltd., a banking and investment firm based in Hong Kong that James's father had built and that Will had worked for since his graduation from university. Six months later, James had graduated as well and joined the family business as a junior clerk. Will had become his supervisor and trainer.

They had learned the business together from the ground up.

James had become president upon his father's early retirement and they had all settled into a good life in Hong Kong.

They might have stayed in Hong Kong forever if James and his wife's infant daughter hadn't died. James's grief over Cory's death had been almost unbearable, but he'd been strong enough to survive it. Mei Ling hadn't. She had grieved herself to death, and neither he nor James had been able to save her.

With his wife and daughter gone, Hong Kong had held too many sad memories for James. He had needed a change. A new challenge. So he had brought the firm to California. As vice president of Craig Capital and James's closest friend, Will had followed, and together they had increased the firm's holdings, investing in mining, timber, shipping, real estate, and ranching.

Now he was breaking up the partnership he and James had shared for more than a dozen years. And he wouldn't be swayed by friendship or sentimentality.

"You can't leave," James told him. "We're friends. Partners. You've been with Craig Capital as long as I have. Longer. I wouldn't know how to run it without you." He lifted the folded sheet of paper and thrust it back at Will. "You might as well take it back, because I refuse to accept it."

Will ignored the letter of resignation, letting it fall to the floor between them. The letter was a formality. It didn't matter whether Jamie accepted it or not. It wouldn't change his mind or the fact that he was leaving. "You don't have a choice, Jamie. I've made my decision."

"Without consulting me? Without so much as a word about what's bothering you? What happened, Will? What's brought this on?"

"There was no need to consult you, Jamie. I'm a grown man—older than you, in fact—"

"By what? Four or five months?" James scoffed.

"And perfectly capable of making decisions. It's time—actually long past time—for me to leave Craig Capital and Coryville and strike out on my own. I need to go where I'm needed. Where I am wanted. I can't ride your coattails and shelter beneath your wings forever, you know." He managed a grin for Jamie's benefit.

James shook his head. "That's bloody rubbish and you

know it. You've never ridden anyone's coattails, least of all mine, and as for sheltering under my wings . . ." He sputtered in frustration, searching for the right words. "That's a bloody joke! We've worked together more than fifteen years and been friends since our school days. I don't understand what's prompted this sudden decision, Will, but whatever it is, we can fix it. Have you received a better offer? I'll match it. I'll surpass it." He raked his fingers through his hair. "Craig Capital needs you. Hell, *I* need you. And what's more, I want you here helping me run the firm we've built. You're as much a part of this venture as I am. Dammit, Will, you're my partner. I'll do whatever it takes—make whatever changes need to be made—in order to keep you happy. . . ."

Will took a deep breath, then slowly exhaled. "That's the thing, Jamie: There's nothing you can do to keep me happy." He smiled, but the smile didn't reach his eyes, and Jamie wasn't fooled. "Because I haven't been happy for a while."

James slammed his palms down on top of the desk, shoved his chair back, and stood up, facing off with his dearest friend over the expanse of the massive oak desk. "That's utter rot, too! Why, just yesterday . . ." He thought back to the previous morning, when Will had joined him, his wife, Elizabeth, and their four adopted daughters—Ruby, Garnet, Emerald, and Diamond—fondly known as the Treasures, at the breakfast table. Will had been laughing at the Treasures' antics the same as he did nearly every morning, indulging Ruby's whims, gently teasing Garnet and Emerald, and spoiling baby Diamond. He hadn't seemed unhappy or eager to resign from Craig Capital and leave Coryville. He'd seemed perfectly content sharing Elizabeth and the Treasures with James, praising Elizabeth for her patience in putting up with James and the Treasures. James recalled Will jokingly declaring that Elizabeth was welcome to leave the morning oatmeal wars and all the chaos behind, throw caution to the wind, and run away with him. *Oh, Christ . . .*

"This hasn't anything to do with Craig Capital, has it?" James pinned Will with his gaze.

"No, it's personal."

James took a deep breath and breathed a name he hadn't spoken aloud in more than a year. "Is it about Mei Ling?"

A muscle began to twitch in Will's jaw. He let out a deep breath. She was there between them once again, the ghost in the room, refusing to relinquish her hold on either one of them. "Do you ever think about her, Jamie? Dream about her?"

"No." James bit out the word, dismissing the thought along with the possibility. "Not anymore. I finally made my peace with her."

"Then you've forgiven her?"

James raked his hand across his forehead. He didn't want to think about Mei Ling. He didn't want to remember her or the pain she'd caused or how much he'd loved her. She was dead. And in his past. His future lay with his new wife, Elizabeth, and the life they'd forged from the ashes of his old one. But neither could he lie. Not to Will. "I can't say I've managed to forgive her completely for what she did, but I've come to terms with it. I've learned not to dwell on the past anymore and to let sleeping dogs lie. If I happen to think of her, I remember the love. I remember the joy and the happiness we shared, not the agony."

Will nodded. "You've come a long way, my friend." He met James's earnest gaze. "California's been good for you."

"Not California. Elizabeth. I owe it all to her and the Treasures. They saved me." James had begun rescuing the unwanted daughters of Chinese families shortly after Mei Ling died. He had started with Ruby, and by the time he met and hired Elizabeth Sadler to be his daughters' governess, he had added Garnet, Emerald, and Diamond to the family. He and Elizabeth had married a little more than a year ago, and James loved her as fiercely now as he had when he'd tumbled head over heels in love with her.

"And for that, I am truly grateful," Will told him. "Beth is a wonderful woman. I'm happy for you, Jamie."

"But . . ."

Will squeezed his eyes shut and let out a mirthless little laugh. "I am singularly unlucky when it comes to affairs of the heart."

"We can't choose whom or why we love," James reminded him. "It chooses us."

"Don't I know it?" Will gave another ironic laugh. "And what I wouldn't give to change it."

"Does she still haunt you, Will?" Will's love for Mei Ling had never been a secret. He and Will had both grown up in Hong Kong. Will had been the only son of a pair of protestant Scots-Irish missionaries, and James the only son of a former East India Company officer who had married the daughter of a Scottish banker, and founded Craig Capital, Ltd. Will had been there when Mei Ling had been sent to Craig House as concubine for the noble son of the house. They had both fallen in love with her. But she'd been sent to James, and Will had stood by his friend's side when he'd gone against tradition, the wishes of his parents, and the British community and married her. Although he'd never expressed his feelings or given James any reason to doubt his friendship or his loyalty, Will had worn his heart upon his sleeve. And Mei Ling had made the most of it, toying with Will's affections as only a woman who knew she had the love of two men could do.

Will had borne her reckless disregard for his feelings in true gentlemanly fashion. He'd been James's best friend through it all, and had continued to love Mei Ling long after James had ceased to do so.

"She comes to me in dreams, Jamie."

"God's mercy, Will!"

"Yeah, well, I pray for it, Jamie, but so far my prayers have gone unanswered. I seem to possess the singular talent of falling for your wives." He looked Jamie in the eye, refusing to flinch when James swore louder and harder.

*Wives. Plural. Mei Ling and Elizabeth.*

Jamie tried to take Will's admission in stride, tried to smile. "We wouldn't be friends if we didn't share a majority of the same likes and dislikes, and we wouldn't be business partners if we didn't possess the same general goals and ambitions. . . ."

Will's forced smile matched the one James was wearing. "You have another partner, Jamie," he said softly. "One infinitely more dear to you than any affection you hold for me."

"Will . . ." James reached out a hand.

Will shrugged it off. "I'm no good at hiding my feelings." He made a wry face. "I never was. And it's only a matter of time before Beth notices. What kind of friend would I be to either of you if I allowed my unwanted, unbidden, and unrequited feelings to cause Beth any discomfort or embarrassment? It's time I moved on, Jamie, and made a life for myself—away from you and Beth and the Treasures."

James didn't argue. "What do I tell them?"

Will gave him a blank look.

"What do I tell my wife and girls? Elizabeth and the Treasures are very fond of you, Will. They're bound to notice the empty chair at the breakfast table and wonder where you've gone and when you're coming back."

"Tell them I love them and that I've gone home to visit my father," he said.

"Hong Kong? You can't be serious." The thought of returning to Hong Kong for any reason—even to visit his mother and father, was anathema to James.

"I am," Will admitted. "My sisters have married and moved on. They have husbands and children. My father's been alone since Mother died, and he isn't getting any younger or stronger. It's time I played the prodigal son and returned to the fold to help him."

"You're no more suited to the life of a missionary than I am."

"Maybe not," Will agreed, "but it's a life I know and a place where I can be of service and where I can start over."

"I can't see you following in your father's footsteps. I don't mean this as an insult, but ministering to the poor and spreading the gospel is a waste of your education and your talents."

"I don't need to minister to the poor or preach the gospel to be of service. The missions need money, and I'm quite good at making it and raising it."

"Yes, you are, and that's why you're vital to Craig Capital."

"Jamie, my mind's made up."

"What about our ventures? With you gone, who is going to take over the special project we've worked so hard to put together?" James glared at him across the oak desk. "Or are you prepared to walk away and abandon that as well?"

"No." Will bit out the admission. "I'm not prepared to abandon our special project." Their project was something he and Jamie had dreamed up together. It had nothing to do with Craig Capital, but would be funded by the two of them. Will had agreed to fund the San Francisco part of the operation, while James and Elizabeth handled the Coryville and northern California operation. "But neither am I prepared to stay here and rain havoc on our friendship." He glared back at James. "I recommend Jack O'Brien take over the project. He's my assistant. He knows the plan. That will clear the way for Peter Malcolm to assume the role of head of operations in the San Francisco office. Jack is more than able to take over the special project in my absence. He's the one I had in mind and the man best suited for the job."

James snorted in disgust.

"What have you got against Jack O'Brien?"

"I don't have anything against Jack. I like Jack, but he's not the man best suited for the job. You are." James held up a hand to forestall him when Will would have protested. "Hear me out. I need a man I can trust implicitly."

It was Will's turn to snort in disgust. "You trust the man who just admitted he's afraid of falling in love with your wife?"

"Yeah, Will, I do," James told him. "I trust you implicitly. I trusted you with my first wife and I trust you even more with my second one."

"Then you're a better man than I am, because I don't trust myself."

"You should," James said. "Because you're as trustworthy and honorable as the day is long. So you loved my wife. I was away on business half our married life. Did you act on those feelings? Did you seduce her? Or allow her to seduce you?" He stared at Will. "Did you take her into your bed, Will?"

"No. Of course not!"

"Why didn't you?" James asked. "You loved her. You wanted her, and you had every opportunity."

"Because she was your *wife*, Jamie. And I may make a habit of falling in love with them, but I don't make a habit of seducing other men's wives. Especially when the woman I love happens to be in love with my closest friend."

"Then what the devil has changed?" James was practically shouting, his blue eyes shooting sparks at him. "So you're afraid of falling in love with Elizabeth. . . . I was scared spitless at the idea of falling in love with her—of falling in love with anyone again—and I did it anyway."

"Dammit, Jamie, you don't understand!"

"What? That it hurts? That it hurts for you to be around us? I understand pain, Will. I watched you struggle with your feelings for Mei Ling for years. Did you think I was blind to the pain you were feeling? Did you think I didn't feel guilty because she was sent to me instead of to you? Did you think I enjoyed seeing you want what I had, then struggle with guilt for being human and feeling a bit of envy from time to time? Did you think I enjoyed seeing the pain in your eyes when I couldn't bring myself to look at her or forgive her when I knew she needed it so desperately? When I knew it was killing her? Killing you? Killing all of us?" James sucked in a ragged breath. "Open your eyes, Will, because what you're feeling is double-edged. It cuts both ways. I understand your need to get away. I understand your need to do penance, but you don't need to sail halfway around the world again for that," James told him. "If it's distance you need from me and Elizabeth, why not work from the city instead of Coryville? Use the San Francisco office. Put whoever you want in charge of day-to-day operations and oversee him along with our new enterprise. I can't do it. I've got my hands full here and have no desire to travel back and forth to the city to check on Jack or Pete Malcolm or anyone else."

"All right." Will's sudden capitulation came as a shock—to him and to Jamie.

"All right?" James required confirmation.

"All right, Jamie." Will couldn't keep a note of self-disgust out of his voice. The truth was that he didn't want to abandon their venture to go to Hong Kong. That city held as many painful memories for Will as it did for James, and although he loved his father, ministering to the man's flock held no particular appeal for him either. "I'll go to San Francisco. I'll assume responsibility for the special project we're about to launch and the Craig Capital office. And I'll run it as I see fit, with no argument or interference from you."

James laughed. "I can't promise not to argue," he admitted. "But I'll draw up papers transferring the ownership of the San Francisco operation to you. You'll get no interference from me." He reached out and offered Will his hand. "Fair enough?"

Will shook the hand Jamie offered. "Fair enough."

## Chapter Two

≈≈≈

> *"A good cause makes a stout heart and
> a strong arm."*
> —PROVERB

SAN FRANCISCO, CALIFORNIA
FEBRUARY 6, 1875

Will Keegan opened his eyes and stared at the ceiling of his bedroom in the Silken Angel Saloon. His head ached from the pall of bluish smoke that lingered in the saloon, produced by the hundreds of cigars and cigarettes his customers smoked each night. The half bottle of brandy and the pot of coffee he'd drunk, the loud conversation, and the music from the slightly out-of-tune piano also contributed to the pounding behind his eyes.

He'd dreamed the dream again. Dreamed that he was back in Hong Kong with Mei Ling, whose features blurred, merging once again with Elizabeth's. Will groaned.

The tinny drone of a piano, the beat of the drums, and the cacophony of dozens of voices speaking different dialects of Chinese, including the only two he could understand—Cantonese and Mandarin—drifted up from the first floor of the saloon and through the open window from Dupont Street. The Silken Angel occupied a large lot at the corner of

Washington and Dupont. It was the last saloon in the Occidental section of town between Jackson Square and the
entrance to Chinatown.

He had chosen the lot and built the building for just that
reason. A saloon was the perfect front for the special project.
The construction of any other sort of building might have
raised suspicions and alerted the tongs, but no one gave
another San Francisco drinking establishment a second
thought.

Will squeezed his eyes shut and gritted his teeth against
the splintering pain in his brain. It was early. The soft light
of the Saturday morning barely penetrated the heavy fog, but
the clouds of moisture hanging over the city did little to muffle
the noise. He had lived here for nearly four months and
worked longer, later hours than he'd ever worked in his life,
but he couldn't seem to get used to the constant din. Coryville
and the chaos that was breakfast with James and Elizabeth
and the Treasures was an oasis of blessed silence compared
to this. The mining camps in the High Sierras were quieter
than this. And it would only get worse.

Today marked the beginning of the Chinese lunar year. In
a few hours Dupont Street and the streets along the waterfront
would be filled with more discordant sounds—parades, fire-
works, bells and horns, bamboo flutes, cymbals, drums,
including the hundreds of toy *bolang gu*, the pellet or rattle
drums sold by street vendors, as well as the squeals of live
pigs that would be paraded through the narrow city streets as
the residents of Chinatown welcomed another Year of the Pig.

As a boy in Hong Kong, he had loved the pageantry of the
dragon parades and the noise of Chinese New Year, but as a
man suffering from a painful head and too little sleep, he
found it another challenge to overcome. But it was early yet,
and Will hoped that a mug of the strong, scorching-hot brew
that passed for coffee and a heaping spoonful of willow bark
elixir would ease his head enough to allow him to grab
another hour or two of sleep despite the drum banging and
the cymbal crashing and the amazingly clear mezzo-soprano
voice growing closer and louder by the minute.

" 'Sowing in the morning, sowing seeds of kindness. Sowing in the noontime and the dewy eve . . .' "

Recognizing the anthem, Will rolled to his side, reached over, grasped the window sash, and shoved the window down to block the sound of the Salvationist crusading for women's suffrage or temperance or some other cause. He'd heard hundreds, perhaps thousands of hymns, and had heard the psalms quoted and preached an equal number of times over the course of his life. Some hymns he liked, some he didn't, but Will had never heard this one until he'd come to live in the city. He hadn't known anyone had put the psalm to music. Now he knew every word and note of the song, the anthem of every Salvationist in San Francisco. It grated on his nerves like no other.

Closing the window silenced the tinny piano, but not the singing.

It kept coming . . . growing closer and louder. . . .

"Not again." Will sat up, raked his fingers through his hair, grabbed the silk dressing gown at the foot of his bed, flipped the bedcovers aside, and stepped into his boots.

She was inside the building. Inside his saloon . . .

Will didn't know who had let the crusader slip through the doors of the Silken Angel, but there would be hell to pay when he identified the culprit.

He didn't mind religious fervor. He'd grown up with missionaries and had been surrounded by it. His father was minister of the First Presbyterian Church of Hong Kong, his mother had preached the gospel according to John Knox on her deathbed, but a little religious fervor went a long way, and Will was rapidly reaching the end of his patience.

The construction of the Silken Angel Saloon had become a clarion call for every follower of William Booth's philosophy in San Francisco—and their numbers seemed to be multiplying daily. A year ago, you could count the San Francisco Salvationists on one hand, but the past few months had brought boatloads—all looking to save the city—particularly the Barbary Coast—from itself and eternal damnation.

Will didn't object to the goal, but he certainly objected to the methods. Between visits from the Salvationists and the

Women's Suffrage and Temperance League, he'd had to replace three bar mirrors, two plate-glass storefronts, a case of whiskey, two tables, and half a dozen chairs. All of that in addition to the breakage caused by the usual assortment of rowdy customers.

He'd nearly reached the bottom of the stairs and was in the midst of shoving his arms into the sleeves of his dressing gown when the soprano reached the refrain.

" 'Bringing in the sheaves. Bringing in the sheaves. We shall come rejoicing, bring—' "

He hurried down the remainder of the stairs and collided with the figure standing at the foot of them. The girl looked up, widening her eyes in surprise at the force of the impact. He recognized the look of astonishment and fear as her ugly black boots lost purchase on the polished oak floor and she wobbled backward.

Reacting instinctively, he reached out, grabbed the girl around the waist, and hauled her against his chest. The air left her lungs in a whoosh of warm breath.

"Oh!" came her muffled exclamation. Her hat had been knocked askew and her face was buried in the hair on his chest, revealed by his open robe.

Will held her fast until he was certain she was in no danger of falling, then set her down on the floor and released his hold.

She sucked in a breath.

"Please . . ." Will held up his hand. "Don't sing anymore."

A startled look crossed her face. "I wasn't going to sing."

"Thank God," he murmured beneath his breath.

"I was going to scream." She didn't look up, but continued to stare at his bare chest as if mesmerized by the sight.

Staring down at the top of her head, Will pulled the silk edges of his robe together and knotted the belt. "Don't do that either."

"I most certainly will!" she warned, still staring at the bit of flesh left exposed by the wide lapels of his dressing gown, a frown marring the area between her eyebrows. "If the situation warrants it."

"It won't," he muttered. "As long as you don't sing."

She looked up at him then, her gaze narrowing in a warning that matched her frown. "What's wrong with my singing voice? I'm told it's quite pleasant. And how dare you manhandle me this way?"

Her eyes were blue. Cornflower blue fringed by thick dark lashes and framed by eyebrows that were a dark reddish brown. A tiny sprinkling of lighter reddish-gold freckles dotted her nose. Her hair, beneath her awful military-gray bonnet, matched her eyebrows. "Would you rather I allowed you to tumble to the floor?"

"No. Of course not," she replied. "I thank you for saving me from that, but if you hadn't come charging half-clothed down the staircase as if the building were on fire, I wouldn't have been taken unawares or thrown off balance in the first place."

"You're blaming me?" Will was taken aback by her audacity. He stood nearly three inches over six feet tall in his bare feet and was solidly built, while the top of her head barely reached his chest despite the two-inch heels on her boots. She was a tiny, auburn-haired spitfire of a girl standing toe-to-toe with a man practically twice her size.

A man whose hands, he recalled, were large enough to span her waist.

Yet she refused to be intimidated.

"Who else *is* there to blame?" she countered, glaring up at him. "You charged into me."

"That's because I didn't expect to find you standing at the bottom of *my* stairs," he told her. "I thought you'd be wreaking havoc in the saloon."

"Why?"

"Because that's what all you Salvationists and Women's Suffrage and Temperance women do." He looked down at her, searching for an umbrella or parasol—the weapon of choice of nearly all the female crusaders. "You wreak havoc on private property. You sing at the top of your lungs while you smash bottles of liquor and mirrors and plate-glass windows."

"I've never smashed anything in my life!" She was indignant at the very idea.

He gave her a wry look. "You must be new to the soul-saving business."

"I've been a member of the Salvationists for nearly three months."

"I don't recall seeing you before. Who sent you to the Silken Angel?"

"No one sent me," she told him. "I came on my own."

Will snorted in derision. "How long have you been in San Francisco?"

"Two days."

He snorted again. "In town two days and you manage to find your way from Mission Street to my establishment." He looked down at her. "I don't believe it."

"It isn't that difficult," she told him. "The Salvationists warned us about Sydney Town and the Barbary Coast on the journey and explained that most of San Francisco's disreputable establishments are located near the waterfront. I came by ship. I disembarked along the waterfront. Returning to it was simply a matter of going back the way I came."

She was fairly boasting of her ability to navigate a strange and often dangerous city on her own, and Will was impressed in spite of himself. "Who the devil *are* you?"

She stiffened her spine and drew herself up to her full height. "I'm Julia Jane Parham. Who the dev—" She caught herself before she uttered the oath, took a deep breath, and regrouped. "Who are you?"

Will bit the inside of his cheek to keep from grinning from ear to ear as the little spitfire's temper got the best of her. "William Burke Keegan," he answered, offering her his hand to shake. "My friends call me Will."

Julie slipped her gloved hand into his much larger one. The fabric of her glove did nothing to dampen the jolt of electricity that sparked when she touched him. Lifting her chin a notch higher, she spoke in her best proper governess voice. "Mr. Keegan."

He gave a wry shake of his head. "So that's how it's going to be."

"I'm sure I don't know what you mean," she replied in the same tone of voice.

"You know *exactly* what I mean, Miss Parham." Will was astonished at his uncharacteristic rudeness. He had been brought up to be a gentleman and had always exhibited gentlemanly behavior and extended ladies every courtesy, but something about Miss Julia Jane Parham and her ugly gray Salvationist uniform and equally atrocious black boots set his teeth on edge.

"I most certainly do not!"

"I meant that we both know where we stand." Will bent at the waist and retrieved her tambourine.

Taking a step closer, Julie reached for the instrument that was standard issue to Salvationist recruits.

Will shook his head and held it out of her reach. "Stay there," he ordered, before turning on his heel and heading toward the grand parlor that was home to the poker and billiard tables, roulette wheels, bar, and the stage used by singers and dancers hired to entertain the customers.

"Wait!" She stopped him in his tracks.

Will looked over his shoulder at her, raising his eyebrow in silent query.

"Where are you going?"

"Into the saloon."

She moved as if to follow him, but Will waggled a finger at her. "No ladies allowed."

"What are you going to do?"

"What you're supposed to be doing." He flashed her a wicked grin. "Collecting on behalf of the Salvationist movement, contributing to its fight against sin."

Will strolled into the grand parlor, tambourine in hand. The room was nearly empty. There were fewer than a dozen customers, five of whom—Adams, McNamara, Dennison, Littleton, and Royce—were engrossed in a poker game that had begun the night before. Will smiled as he approached the table. He greeted each player by name before he thrust the upturned tambourine at the closest man.

"Hey, Keegan," Dennison protested, "what the hell? Did you just roll out of bed?"

"Yes, I did, and I'm taking up a collection." Will tapped him on the shoulder with the tambourine, frowning at the racket it made.

"You have a run of bad luck or something?"

Will shook his head. "It's protection money."

All five cardplayers looked up from their cards. "Who do you need protection from?" Adams asked. "Rival business owners?" He laughed at his own joke.

" 'Bringing in the Sheaves.' "

Reaching into his stack of cash, Adams dropped a silver dollar into the tambourine. "Ante up, boys."

The other four players followed suit. Will thanked them, then made his way around the saloon, soliciting donations of protection money to keep the Salvationists at bay.

He returned to Julia Jane Parham with thirty-one dollars and twenty-five cents in coins and currency in her tambourine. He let her have a good look at the money, but kept a firm grip on the instrument and the cash. "I managed to collect a little over thirty dollars in contributions for your group."

"Oh, how lovely . . ." She reached for the tambourine.

Will lifted it above her reach. "Not so fast. I want a guarantee that there'll be no singing or saloon smashing by your group of soul savers for at least a month."

"A month?" Julie widened her eyes at the notion. "That's bl—"

*"Business."*

"You collected thirty dollars in under"—she glanced at the big clock hanging on the wall above the second-floor landing—"ten minutes." She did some quick arithmetic. "That works out to be three dollars a minute. There are one thousand four hundred and forty minutes in a day. Thirty days in a month . . ." She looked at him. "That works out to be . . ."

He couldn't miss the gleam in her eyes. "A good deal more than I'm willing to pay."

"But you've plenty of money. You collected thirty dollars in ten minutes. . . ."

"Thirty-*one* dollars." He stared down at her. "We're all suffering from aching heads. We were feeling generous."

"But . . ."

"My dear Miss Parham, eight dollars is more than the average man earns in a fortnight. That's fifty-seven cents a day. The offer on the table is thirty-one dollars and twenty-five cents for a month free of singing and smashing." He narrowed his gaze and firmed his mouth. "Which roughly works out to be over a dollar a day. Double the average workingman's wage. Take it or leave it."

"A week," she countered.

He quirked his brow at her once again. "Surely you jest. . . ."

"Two weeks." She fluttered her eyelashes at him. "That's more equitable."

"A bird in the hand is worth two in the bush."

"A week and a half."

"The bird in the hand is about to become another bird in the bush. . . ."

Realizing he was quite capable of carrying out his threat and that she was about to lose money the Salvationists needed in order to continue ministering to the city's less fortunate, Julie capitulated. "Very well."

Will bit the inside of his cheek once again to keep from smiling. Little Lady Spitfire didn't like losing. Neither did he. So he decided a bit of clarification was in order. "Very well what?"

"I'll accept the bird in the hand." She forced the words out.

"In return for what?"

"A month free of singing and smashing by Salvationists at the Silken Angel."

"I'd like that in writing," he said, knowing he was pushing his luck, but curious to see her reaction.

"Absolutely not!" She didn't disappoint him. "My word on the matter should suffice, and it's my word or nothing."

Will lowered the tambourine and presented it to her. "Agreed."

Taking the cash and coin, Julie turned away from Will and stuffed the money into the inside pocket of her uniform jacket.

He stepped back, allowing her a moment of privacy to secure her cash before he spoke. "All right, Miss Parham, time for you to go . . ."

Julie deliberately misunderstood. "I haven't seen the rooms upstairs."

"That's right."

"Why not?" she protested. "The Silken Angel is a first-class business establishment with public rooms above stairs." She gave him another sharp look from beneath her lashes. "Or so I've heard."

"I don't know where you got your information, but my upstairs rooms are open only to the *male* public." He returned her glare with a look of appraisal. "You don't qualify."

She moistened her lips with the tip of her tongue. "I'm curious."

"I'll bet you are," he drawled, in a voice husky with meaning.

"And *I'll* bet the rooms are marvelous."

"You would win that bet," he said, "if you were a gambling sort of woman. If the Salvationists allowed such a thing." He shot her a speculative look. "The rooms are marvelous. Compared to what you've been subjected to on Mission Street, I've no doubt they are palatial. But my rooms are open only to males. Unless I miss my guess, you're a lady."

"What if I were new to San Francisco and desperate for a roof over my head?" The tambourine clattered as she propped her hands on her hips.

"You have thirty-one dollars and twenty-five cents in your pocket, and the Russ House Hotel is down the block. Their rooms are almost as marvelous as mine. You'll be fine."

"I am in desperate need of employment, and I've heard that you allow females to *work* above stairs."

"You were misinformed," Will said. "And I don't believe you're desperate for work. You're a missionary. They may pay you only a pittance, but they furnish room and board and see that you have plenty of work to keep you busy. Idle hands and all that . . . And even if it were true, I'm sure your crusading would keep you too busy to hold down a real job. You have thirty-one dollars and twenty-five cents in your possession, and in any case, you don't qualify."

"It's Salvationist money," she protested. "Not mine."

"You're a Salvationist. It's yours if you need it. Unless, of course, you were forced to take a vow of poverty when you joined the movement . . ."

"I'm a missionary, not a nun. And in any case"—she used his favorite phrase—"the Salvationist movement welcomes members of independent means and charitable contributions."

"I'm delighted to hear it," Will replied. "Now, be a good little girl, Miss Parham, and take our generous charitable contribution back with you to Mission Street or the Russ House and stay out of saloons—especially my saloon." He shouldn't touch her. He was a gentleman and there were rules against such behavior, but since he'd already broken most of them, Will ignored the edict warning him not to make contact with any part of her person. And he did his best to ignore the frisson that ran up his arms as he took her by the shoulders and gently turned her around and nudged her toward the front door. "There are plenty of souls for you to save in the city without invading saloons. This is no place for a young lady."

"What about the young ladies upstairs?" She turned back to face him.

"What young ladies? This isn't a convent or a boarding school. As far as I know, there are no young ladies upstairs," he said. "Only me."

"Surely, you don't . . ." She blushed to the roots of her hair and began to sputter. "I mean . . . this is a saloon. . . . There must be females. . . . I never imagined that a man would . . ."

He was sure there were a great many things a gently bred young lady never imagined. What went on above stairs in most of the other saloons and bordellos in San Francisco was just the beginning. And Will had no doubt that she *was* a gently bred young lady, despite the fact that she'd dared to enter his establishment. He'd seen the look of fascination on her face when she'd found herself pressed against his naked chest. And although she seemed completely unaware, Will recognized the spark of electricity that arced between them.

There was no mistaking that jolt of sexual awareness, just as there was no mistaking her vocal inflection. Miss Julia Jane Parham was a proper English miss who had undoubtedly grown up among the cream of society. She had no business marching around the Barbary Coast unescorted—no business marching through this part of town at all, escorted or otherwise. She might be wearing military-style dress and soldiering for God, but that mannish, unbecoming frock was no protection from the dangers of San Francisco's waterfront. What the devil were the Salvationists thinking to turn an innocent loose on the city streets? To send her into saloons— and worse? Were they that bent on finding new converts to do God's work?

He didn't much like the idea of sending her out onto the city streets alone either, but he couldn't keep her at the saloon. The best he could do was get her out of here before the bulk of his customers began arriving. If the Salvationists weren't worried about sending a lamb into the lion's den of iniquity that was San Francisco, he wouldn't worry about it either. "You never imagined what, Miss Parham?" He watched her, a teasing light in his eyes. "That a man might *live* above his place of business?"

"You live upstairs?"

"I do."

"Alone?"

Will tapped her on the nose with the tip of his index finger. "That, my dear Miss Parham, is none of your business. . . ."

"Saving souls from a life of sin and degradation is my business," she informed him.

"Then go about your business elsewhere." He turned her around and headed her toward the front door once more. "There's no one upstairs but me, and my soul is long past saving."

## Chapter Three

❧❦❧

*"I am a kind of burr; I shall stick."*
—WILLIAM SHAKESPEARE

Without quite realizing how it happened, Julie found herself standing on the rough boardwalk outside the Silken Angel Saloon. Will Keegan gave her a jaunty little wave as he pulled the heavy wood-and-glass doors together and turned the key in the locks, locking his customers in and her out.

The word *closed* was lettered in bold black in English and the Chinese equivalent on the milky glass for the public to see. A small sign tacked to the doors advised deliverymen to go around back. Julie realized that when the doors were closed, the Silken Angel was closed. Following the advice left for tradesmen, she headed toward the alley that led to the back of the saloon.

"Clever girl," Will Keegan murmured when she arrived in time to have the back door closed in her face and locked as well. "But not quite clever enough."

A sign above a bell at the back door read: RING BELL FOR SERVICE. Julie reached up to do so, only to find the clapper had been removed. She recognized his triumphant chuckle moments before he lifted the blue checked curtain covering the small back-door window and held up the clapper. "Clever and resourceful. But like I said, not quite clever or resourceful enough . . ."

"You had an unfair advantage," she called, raising her voice loud enough to carry through the door.

"Insider knowledge," he called back. "And I intend to keep it, just as I intend to stay inside and keep you outside."

"You can't keep me outside forever."

"I can try," he told her. "And get high marks for the effort."

Julie stamped her foot in a show of frustration. She hadn't come thousands of miles in search of her friend to be thwarted the first day of her search. Turning on her heel, Julie lifted her skirts and hurried back through the alley to the front of the Silken Angel.

The doors were still locked. She rattled the handles anyway, then banged her tambourine against her hip. "You haven't heard the last of me, Mr. Keegan," she promised.

"I have until the end of the month," Will replied.

"I promised not to sing *inside* your establishment," she announced. "I didn't promise not to sing *outside* it." Taking a deep breath, Julie began singing at the top of her lungs, " 'Bringing in the sheaves, bringing in the sheaves. We shall come rejoicing, bringing in the sheaves. . . . ' "

"Don't you know any other songs?" he called out.

"Of course," she called back ever so sweetly, "but I also know that this one is your favorite."

She thought she heard him laugh, but she couldn't be sure above the sound of the tambourine. So she increased the volume of her song before stomping her way down the boardwalk toward the Salvationist headquarters on Mission Street.


"YOU GONNA STAND THERE STARING OUT THE WINDOW ALL day, Keegan?" Littleton called. "Or you gonna pull up a chair and join us?"

Will stayed at the window watching until Julia Jane Parham was safely out of sight and out of earshot before turning to face his cardplaying regulars. "Thanks, but no thanks, gentlemen. Now that I've bought a little peace and quiet, I'm going back to bed for an hour or two."

"You bought?" Royce reminded him. "We anteed up into that psalm singer's tambourine."

"I saw your five and raised it by twenty," Will told him. Which meant the remaining seven customers contributed the rest—including the change Jack, the bartender, had left lying on the bar.

"You put in twenty dollars?" Royce asked.

"I did." Will nodded. "And it was worth every penny, Royce."

Royce scratched his head. "This place will be swarming with every psalm-singing, umbrella-swinging, vote-wanting female in the city once word gets out that you paid one of them to go away."

"Maybe. Maybe not." It would be interesting to see whether Julia Jane Parham kept her word or if she made a return visit before the month was out.

"It could get a mite expensive if it does," Royce warned good-naturedly. "But I reckon you can afford it."

"I can as long as you keep playing poker here every Friday and Saturday night."


THANKS TO WILL KEEGAN, JULIE HAD MORE THAN MET HER daily collection quota.

It wasn't a set rule, but the Salvationists encouraged each member do his or her best to raise enough money to buy one soul a day's worth of food. Julie's contribution would help buy food and pay for shelter for dozens of needy souls. She had succeeded in her first attempt in soliciting donations because Will Keegan had collected the money for her, but Julie had failed miserably in her attempt to make it to the second floor of his saloon—the floor almost every saloon in town reserved for the working girls.

Julie sighed. She supposed it was too much to ask that after joining the Salvationists and traveling thousands of miles from home, she would find her friend on her first foray into the city's saloon districts. Or that she would find her in the nicest saloon she'd come across.

While the other Salvationist recruits had joined the movement to minister to the sick and needy while spreading William Booth's message throughout the world, Julie's motives had been less altruistic. She had joined in order to secure passage on a ship bound from Hong Kong to California and to gain entrance to San Francisco's infamous Barbary Coast without drawing attention to her search for her dearest friend. In Julie's experience, ladies were protected and barred from all but the safest and most mundane of places, while lady missionaries were allowed to work and live in the most exotic and notorious locales. Julie had managed to find herself a sponsor and been recruited into the Salvationist movement in order to keep the vow she'd made to her family housekeeper.

Lolly had lived and worked in Parham House for as long as Julie could remember. She had come to keep house for Julie's father, Commodore Lord Nelson Parham, a widowed naval commander, and to take care of his infant daughter. La Ling had lost her husband and his parents when cholera swept through their village. Only she and her baby, Su Mi, survived. When she recovered, Lolly had sought work in the city and been hired first as wet nurse for Julie, and then as housekeeper to Commodore Parham. Julie's first attempts at imitating her father's crisp British aristocratic pronunciation of La Ling's name had come out as "Lolly," and Lolly she had remained.

Julie and Su Mi had suckled at the same breast and had grown up as close as any two sisters—with one exception: Julie was the English daughter of a wealthy naval commander. Su Mi was the daughter of Chinese peasants. With her father and his family dead, responsibility for Su Mi's welfare had fallen to her mother's brother. As head of the family, her uncle had arranged Su Mi's marriage to a man who had brought her to California. Su Mi's uncle had trusted the young man and believed him honorable when he promised to marry Su Mi as soon as they arrived in California. But word had reached Hong Kong that the man who was to be Su Mi's husband had sold her to a woman, along with three other would-be brides, to be used as prostitutes in San Francisco.

There was nothing new in the story. Girls were bought and sold as brides, as concubines, as prostitutes, and as domestic servants in Hong Kong and the mainland of China every day. Females served their families in any way they could, just as sons supported the family as best they could. It was a tradition as old as time in China. The only thing new about it was that this time the girl sold into slavery was Su Mi, and Julie had promised her friend's mother she would find Su Mi and bring her home.

Julie had chosen the Silken Angel because it was new and clean and seemed to cater to a higher class of customers than the other saloons she'd skirted along the way. The name on the sign had drawn her: THE SILKEN ANGEL. It sounded like Su Mi—refined and elegant—and Julie found that entering it hadn't been nearly as daunting as the prospect of entering the others. Su Mi spoke proper English and was well educated. Surely she would be found in a place where gentlemen who valued such things sought pleasure. . . .

*As far as I know, there are no young ladies upstairs. Only me.*

Will Keegan's words drifted back to her. Julie hoped he was telling the truth. She hoped there weren't any girls working above stairs in the Silken Angel. But if what he'd told her was true, why have rooms upstairs that only men were allowed to frequent?

Her father belonged to a gentleman's club in Hong Kong, where he drank and dined several times a week when he was in port. His club kept rooms available for its members and valets hired to attend them. A gentleman could look upon his club as a home away from home. He could rent a room or a suite of rooms at the club for a nominal fee by the night, the week, the month, or on a quarterly or an annual basis, to live there or to use as his base of operations for business. Perhaps the Silken Angel operated in a similar fashion. While it appeared to be primarily a drinking and gaming establishment, might it also provide lodging for customers who frequented it? Will Keegan lived there. Surely other gentlemen might live there as well.

The members of the Salvationists she'd spoken with following her arrival had assured Julie that every saloon between the Embarcadero and Van Ness Avenue had girls working above stairs. She hoped the Silken Angel proved to be the exception. San Francisco was full of saloons that catered to the lower classes, and they weren't the only establishments to do so. There were boardinghouses and bordellos on nearly every block to accommodate the large numbers of sailors, soldiers, miners, railroad workers, cattlemen, gamblers, Chinese, and ne'er-do-wells and drifters of all nationalities and walks of life.

Will Keegan was the proprietor of a saloon. Julie didn't like to think of him compounding his sins by dabbling in the flesh trade. She wanted him to be above that sort of commerce in human misery. Because there was something about the Silken Angel that appealed to her.

Although she wouldn't admit it to anyone but herself, Julie was frightened. She was alone for the first time in her life, and filled with trepidation at the thought of entering a bordello. If men could be shanghaied from waterfront saloons and pressed into naval service, wasn't it possible for lone women to disappear from city streets and be pressed into service in the hundreds of bordellos and cribs hidden among them?

Somehow, saloons seemed safer. In a rough, wild city like San Francisco, with bars and saloons on every corner, the Silken Angel and its handsome, dark-haired, brown-eyed, chiseled-jawed owner made her feel safe. She particularly liked the color of his eyes—not the dark brown of melted chocolate, but the sparkling golden brown of expensive sherry. She found his clean, masculine smell, his wide, hard chest, the way he'd closed his arms around her to keep her from falling, and the cleft in his chin equally appealing.

Julie had been completely confident of her eventual success when she'd joined the Salvationists and paid for her passage to America. She had been born and brought up in Hong Kong.

She knew the Chinese, knew their languages and customs. She knew about ports and waterfronts from her father, but San Francisco was proving to be much larger and more intimidating than she'd anticipated. She had spent only one night there, but she'd hated the women's dormitory at the Salvationist headquarters.

After spending her entire life in a fine house with a room of her own and servants and her weeks at sea in the private cabin she'd paid for, Julie was accustomed to privacy. The notion of sharing space with strangers was as foreign to her as the notion of providing every missionary and rescued soul with space of their own was unheard-of to the Salvationists. The women's dormitory was one large open room that had once been a warehouse and was now crammed with rows of beds, each made up with two sheets, one rag-stuffed pillow, and a scratchy woolen blanket. There were wooden chests at the foot of each bed to store belongings, and pegs on the wall to hang things. There were no locks on the trunks or on the doors. Missionaries didn't require privacy. They were not supposed to have anything to hide. Besides, missionaries didn't pilfer through one's belongings or take what didn't belong to them.

There were no dressing tables, no screens, and no armoires.

The dormitory had a large iron stove at one end of the room for heat and a washroom at the other end of the room. The washroom contained a washbasin and pitcher, one tin hip bath, one full-length mirror, and a pump that supplied cold water. Hot water had to be heated in kettles on the stove and carried to the basin or the hip tub.

The privy was outdoors behind the mission.

Upward of thirty single women occupied the dormitory at any given time. There were no servants. Everyone was expected to make their own beds, carry their own water, empty their own basin, tend the stove to keep the fires lit throughout the chilly nights, and arrange for their own laundry service.

Single male Salvationists occupied a dormitory one building over from the women's dormitory, as the two were separated by a central building that housed the kitchen and dining facilities and rooms assigned to the married couples. Julie hadn't seen the inside of the men's dormitory, of course, but she suspected it had a similar setup as the women's dormitory.

The two meals she'd eaten at the mission had consisted of soup and bread, and porridge and bread. They were hot and filling, but had nothing more to recommend them.

The servants at Parham House lived better than the missionaries at the Salvationist headquarters. She hadn't slept more than a couple of hours the night before and didn't expect to sleep any better tonight. She was exhausted, but she couldn't get used to the sounds of other women in the room—the rustling of bedclothes, the creak of other beds, the coughing, the whispers, the prayers. As she lay in her bed staring at the ceiling, Julie fought back the hot sting of tears as she thought about her room in Parham House far away in Hong Kong. She longed for her comfortable bed and soft sheets and silk coverlet, for the warmth of the coal fireplace, and Lolly, who was as constant as the rising of the sun. Julie thought of her father sailing the HMS *Gallant* to faraway ports of call, and wished that he'd been home, that Lolly could have prevailed upon him to search for Su Mi instead of her.

Remembering Will Keegan's words, Julie thought longingly of a private room at the Russ House Hotel.

She had turned the thirty-one dollars over to Mrs. Rowland, the secretary in charge of collections, but she wasn't destitute without it. Secreted inside the pocket of her corset cover were documents verifying her status as an account holder at the First British Bank of Hong Kong and a letter of credit from the bank president guaranteeing her the right to draw upon her account in any amount up to ten thousand American dollars. She didn't have to live in the dormitory. She had inherited her mother's portion of her family's fortune. The Gramercys were as aristocratic and wealthy as the Parhams, and upon her twenty-first birthday, Julie had become a young lady of independent means, a fact that meant she had little in common with the majority of her fellow Salvationists and nothing in common with the desperate women they fed and clothed and housed.

As strange as it seemed, the time she'd spent with Will Keegan was more stimulating and more enjoyable than any she'd spent with her fellow Salvationists during the journey or since her arrival in San Francisco.

While she did her best to make friends and to fit in, the truth was that Julie wanted nothing more than to wake up in her own bed in her own room at home and discover that her journey and the reason for it were all a bad dream.

Until that happened, there was nothing for her to do but to screw her courage to the sticking place and continue her search. With courage enough, she would not fail.

She had made a solemn promise to Lolly, and Julie intended to keep it.

The Salvationists had provided her with a mission, a place to stay, and valuable information about the city and its inhabitants. She would use what she'd learned from them to carry out her search for Su Mi.

As far as she knew, there were no rules against a member of the Salvationist movement joining other organizations with similar goals—like the Women's Suffrage and Temperance League.

What she couldn't do through the Salvationists she would have to do on her own. . . .

# Chapter Four

*❦*

*"When we are planning for posterity, we ought to
remember that virtue is not hereditary."*
—THOMAS PAINE, 1737–1809

The monthly meeting of the San Francisco Saloon and
Bordello Owners' Association met on Wednesday, nearly
a fortnight after the beginning of the Chinese New Year in
the basement of the Lotus Blossom, one of the nicest of
Madam Li Toy's boardinghouses. The association, made up
of a dozen or so saloon and bordello owners, had been formed
three months earlier in order to protect independent business
owners from the gangs, or fighting *tongs*, made up of Chinese
members of the criminal underworld seeking to control all
gambling, opium, prostitution, protection, and enforcement
in the city.

The Kip Yee and Gee Kong tongs specialized in the extortion and intimidation of business owners and the theft of
shipments of goods. The aim of the fighting tongs was to force
the independent operators out of business and to assume possession of their establishments.

Will had formed the association of the San Francisco

Saloon and Bordello Owners during the building of the Silken Angel. Representatives from the Kip Yee and the Gee Kong fighting tongs had paid him repeated visits to demand money in exchange for protection from the other neighborhood tongs they had been hired to destroy in a power struggle to acquire more territory in Chinatown. There were benign tongs that served as cultural and social outlets for their members and fighting tongs that were the enforcers and assassins for the criminal tongs. Because members of the Chinese community often belonged to cultural and criminal tongs, Will seized the opportunity to learn the hierarchy of San Francisco's criminal underbelly—and to find out who allied with whom—by forming the association of business owners operating in the seamier parts of Chinatown and greater San Francisco.

He sold the saloon and bordello owners on the idea of strength in numbers. Individual businesses might not be able to withstand the change in ownership the tongs were forcing on them, but an association made up of business owners united in a common cause might.

There were half a dozen fighting tongs vying for control of San Francisco's lucrative liquor, flesh, opium, and gambling trades , and Will needed to know which ones wanted control of which operations. To that end, he'd begun keeping track of the visits tong members paid to the businesses operating on Dupont Street, recording the dates of the extortion demands and the payments. He started with his own business and expanded his ledgers to include the businesses closest to the Silken Angel. At the first meeting of the association, Will shared his information with the other business owners. By the close of the first meeting, he found himself appointed treasurer of the association, responsible for the account ledgers. He was so good at keeping the ledgers that several of his fellow association members had asked him to help with their books—particularly the businesses with imports to track.

Imports were the topic of discussion for this morning's meeting. Li Toy, the most notorious and prosperous madam in Chinatown, had purchased a shipment of girls from the

Kwangtung province in China. A select few of the girls would work at Li Toy's boardinghouse, and the others would be sold at auction to the highest association bidder. Today's meeting had been called to inform the other members of the association of the time and place of the auction. Shipment arrivals and auctions were kept as quiet as possible to avoid theft at the hands of Kip Yee and his men or the leaders of the other mercenary fighting tongs seeking to strengthen their power.

Li Toy was anxious about the shipment and speaking rapid-fire Cantonese in a shrill, high-pitched voice that had earned her the nickname "Madam Harpy" among the Chinatown locals. Will struggled to follow her mixture of singsong English and Cantonese as the madam related the times, dates, and places of her payments to tong collection men and to San Francisco policemen, attorneys, and judges for him to record in the ledger.

They did not discuss the particulars. Li Toy wouldn't reveal the names, ages, or home villages of the girls from Kwangtung province until the auction. Will jotted that information down in a separate, private ledger he kept locked in the safe at the Silken Angel. That ledger documented everything he learned about the girls Li Toy and the other members of the association imported, including the amounts paid for each and the names of the buyers who purchased them at auction. The private ledger was Will's way of tracking as many of the girls who inhabited second-floor bedrooms and cribs throughout Chinatown as possible, as well as those who were sent to the mining camps or sold to pimps and madams in other cities. The members of the association knew he made notes during auctions, but they had no idea how much he detailed, and Will meant to keep them ignorant of it by using an almost indecipherable form of personal shorthand he'd perfected during his time as a clerk at Craig Capital. His health and welfare depended upon it, as well as the health and welfare of the girls whose names and personal information were written inside his ledger.

Li Toy looked tiny and fragile, although she was anything but. She had survived famine and disease, transportation from

China, and years as a prostitute before becoming a madam. She owned houses of pleasure and a series of long, narrow, one-story shacks called "cribs" that were sparsely furnished and divided into two curtained compartments. The cribs had three solid walls and a door set with bars that resembled the door of a jail cell. There were cribs throughout the city and in high-country mining camps as far away as Seattle and Gastown, across the border in British Columbia, housing two to six girls apiece. Every crib girl wore a black silk blouse banded by a row of turquoise embroidered flowers that was the traditional costume of prostitutes. They were allowed to wear black silk trousers in cold weather, but most of the time the girls in the cribs wore blouses only and were required to show themselves at the bars of the door and call out to customers night and day.

Arriving in San Francisco shortly after the gold rush, Li Toy catered to the common man and had clawed her way to the top of her profession. Any empathy she felt for the girls who worked for her was buried along with the girls who displeased or disobeyed her. As far as she was concerned, China was full of girls. What did it matter if three or four disobedient and stupid ones disappeared from San Francisco each month?

Reaching out, she poked Will in the arm, and he realized that while he'd been woolgathering, Li Toy had been seeking information about a solution to a different threat to her enterprises. "How much?"

He blinked, then fixed his attention on Li Toy. "How much what?"

She showered him with a flurry of foreign-devil insults, disregarding the fact that in America, she was as much a foreign devil as he was, before repeating her demand. "How much you pay to shut down mission?"

"I didn't pay to shut down the mission," Will told her.

"You paid to stop 'Bringing in the Sheaves,'" Li Toy insisted. "How much?"

Will frowned. He'd managed to put a temporary halt to the constant barrage of "Bringing in the Sheaves." But if Li Toy knew he'd paid to keep the Salvationists from invading the Silken Angel, he'd bet that she also knew exactly how much he'd paid. "Thirty-one dollars."

She gave him a knowing nod. "For how long?"

"One month."

Li Toy cackled in delight. "In two weeks, you have to pay another thirty-one dollars to keep the mission singing away. *I* offer to pay man thirty dollars to shut mission up permanently."

*"What?"* Will sat up straighter in his chair, giving the madam his undivided attention.

"You paid thirty-one dollars to stop singing for one month." She pointed a finger at him. "I offer thirty dollars to stop nosy missionaries from interfering with business and asking questions forever."

"To whom?"

"Policeman," Li Toy replied. "He needed money to pay Lo Peng. I need relief from nosy missionary girl. I paid him to quiet her."

Lo Peng was a fighting tong leader and the owner of a string of opium and gambling dens. Will fought to keep the unease roiling in his stomach from spilling over into his conversation with the madam. "Quiet her how?"

"However." Li Toy gave an elegant shrug of her silk-clad shoulders. "I do not care."

Unease quickly became dread. "You cannot dispose of a missionary without someone noticing," Will replied in a calm, businesslike tone, despite the fact that the hair on the back of his neck was standing up in alarm.

Li Toy gave a derisive snort. "Foolish girls disappear every day in Chinatown. By the time nosy girl is missed, auction will be over. My girls will be working in my houses and other girls will be sold." She gave Will a meaningful look. "I help you, too. I get rid of fire-haired missionary; you buy upstairs girls for the Silken Angel."

Will looked the madam in the eye. She was all business, cold, calculating, and without a hint of compassion. "No need to do murder on my account. I was already planning to purchase a few girls from you for several wealthy gentlemen who prefer to remain anonymous—*if* they're quality merchandise. These men want brides and only the best will do."

"I buy only the best," Li Toy told him. "All young virgins."

Will forced himself to smile. "According to you. But as far as I can tell, you keep the young virgins for yourself and foist the used merchandise onto everyone else."

Li Toy cackled in delight once again. "You pay me top dollar, I sell *you* all my virgins and keep experienced girls."

Will played along, shaking his head as if he were surprised by her offer. "I won't be buying any girls—inexperienced or otherwise—and neither will anyone else if you're in jail for soliciting an assassin."

Li Toy narrowed her dark eyes at him, her expression shrewdly calculating. "No need to worry about Li Toy. I not go to jail." She smiled. "Not when association pays money to police."

Will lifted an eyebrow, then glanced at the ledger filled with numbers representing the names of San Francisco policemen. City officials, police, and judges were assigned numbers the first time they accepted a bribe from an association member. Will saw that the payments recorded were the usual amounts. "Who do I need to pay?"

"No one," Li Toy told him. "I take care of it myself."

"I see." Will's eyes had been opened since he'd established the Silken Angel. The men and women who operated businesses on the Barbary Coast did not adhere to the rules to which he was accustomed—rules governing gentlemanly business practices. Will knew that corruption existed in polite society as much as in any other society, but it was usually kept quiet. Cheating at cards and in business was ungentlemanly, and cheats were shunned. Gentlemen adhered to a code of honor, and men who did not were not accepted in polite society. Will had spent most of his adult years in banking and finance, and in his experience, dishonest bankers soon succumbed to the lack of clients. Not so along the Barbary Coast. The corruption among city officials was blatant and pervasive. The rules and codes of conduct of polite society did not apply, and no vice was beyond the pale.

In Chinatown, no one flinched at the idea of hiring an assassin to put an end to the inconveniences caused by crusading missionaries, temperance leaders, or women fighting for the right to vote. No one gave a second thought to bribing police and city officials or was surprised to discover that those same men were subject to bribery. Everyone had a price, and merchants greasing the wheels of justice and commerce considered it a business expense. No one complained when the police broke the laws they were supposed to uphold or looked the other way when others were breaking them, because everyone understood they were paid to do so. Li Toy was right: Nobody cared about Chinese prostitutes—not even the Chinese men they were originally brought in to service. But Chinese men did not like to share. They preferred their own concubines or second wives to take the place of the wives they'd left behind. The only Chinese men in San Francisco who visited prostitutes were those too poor to afford wives or concubines. The overwhelming majority of the customers who frequented saloons and bordellos were American and European men.

Will was very much afraid that no one would worry about one fewer missionary girl, either. He cleared his throat. "If you've taken care of the matter, there's no need to concern myself with extra protection to keep missionaries from causing trouble."

Li Toy laughed once again, and the sound of it made Will uneasy. "No trouble from missionaries. No 'Bringing in the Sheaves.' Extra protection needed only to keep fighting tongs away from basement of the Jade Dragon on Friday night."

# Chapter Five

*"Boldness be my friend."*
—WILLIAM SHAKESPEARE

Two days later, Julie Parham shivered as she made her way along the rabbit warren of streets and alleys that made up Chinatown. She was headed for what was known as the Chinese "red light" district—the area between Stockton and Montgomery streets, north of Sacramento—dressed as a peasant in a tunic and trousers and black cotton shoes she'd purchased from a street vendor for a dollar and fifty cents.

Feeling conspicuous in her Salvationist uniform and aware that the locals were tight-lipped and suspicious of a "foreign devil" missionary who spoke perfect Cantonese, Julie had exchanged her woolen dress for this costume.

She'd rinsed her hair in a mixture of cold black coffee and vinegar to darken it, plaited it into one long queue that hung down her back, lined her eyes with kohl to elongate them, darkened her eyelashes and brows with a mixture of lamp-black and beeswax, and had even gone so far as to stain her face, neck, and hands with finely ground rice powder tinted yellow. There was nothing she could do about the color of her eyes, and her cosmetics wouldn't fool anyone in bright sunlight or beneath the glow of lamps or candles, but San

Francisco was perpetually wreathed in fog and mist, and with a conical straw hat covering her head and shading her face and no sun to speak of, she found that she could pass among the locals with little fear of discovery as long as she kept her eyes humbly downcast. Julie had worn her disguise on three consecutive days, but she couldn't relax her diligence. The slightest mistake might give her away.

Her ugly Salvationist dress had protected her from the more unseemly elements and characters in the Occidental sections of the waterfront, proclaiming her a missionary and acting as a shield against unwanted advances from all but the most jaded and depraved of men, but it was of little use in Chinatown, where it was met with suspicion and disdain.

She reveled in the freedom the costume provided, but she missed the warmth of the gray wool and the extra protection from the damp and cold afforded by the undergarments needed to support her wool dress. Her tunic and trousers were comfortable and liberating, but the chill cut through the fabric like a hot knife through butter.

Julie bit her bottom lip to keep her teeth from chattering as she hurried down the makeshift boardwalk to the next boardinghouse.

It had taken her almost a week to work up the courage to approach the saloons situated around the perimeter of Chinatown, and another few days to cross into Chinatown, where saloons were replaced by gambling houses, opium dens, boardinghouses or parlor houses, and cribs where many of the Chinese girls who came to San Francisco worked— willingly or unwillingly—as prostitutes. Julie didn't approach the boardinghouse from the front, but went around to the side entrance. Carrying a single willow basket in her guise as Chinese peasant, rather than the double baskets suspended from a shoulder pole that were currently outlawed by a city ordinance, Julie presented herself at the back and side entrances of establishments, pretending to be a laundry worker collecting soiled linens.

She had learned her first week in San Francisco that entering disreputable establishments through the front door while wearing a gray wool Salvationist gown was guaranteed to get one unceremoniously escorted out the door and off the premises. She barely managed to whisper Su Mi's name to the girls in the front parlor before the madam's hatchet men had ushered her out the door. And her second week in San Francisco had taught her that missionary "ladies" were not allowed entrance to the back and side entrances of disreputable establishments either. Especially missionary ladies asking questions about Chinese girls. She'd been forced to wait outside the establishments in order to question customers entering and exiting the premises about Su Mi under the guise of soliciting donations for the mission. Unfortunately, that had lasted only as long as it took for the customers to complain and for her to be escorted away from the area. She had been threatened, intimidated, spit upon, and shoved off the plank walkways and into the street.

No one looked twice at Chinese laundry workers collecting or delivering linens. They were permitted access to all the boardinghouses and a few of the cribs lining the streets and alleys.

Chinese laundries were plentiful in San Francisco. Most operated seven days a week; all she had to do was find one that needed the business she promised to bring it. She began by befriending the laundry girl who collected the linens used in the female dormitory at the mission. After that, it was a simple matter of paying Zhing Wu a better-than-average price to keep quiet and to look the other way while Julie took her place at the boardinghouses, and eliciting a promise that Zhing would do any laundry Julie brought back and never question its origin.

The ruse worked like a charm. As it turned out, Zhing Wu hated collecting soiled linens and clothing from the Chinese-owned boardinghouses. She was rare in San Francisco: a free Chinese woman. The young widow of a mine worker, Zhing Wu had come from the interior of China to work for her father-in-law at the laundry he'd established on the far end of Washington Street, past the ladders that led to the underground housing derisively known as the Dog Kennel. Zhing

Wu was terribly afraid of being kidnapped by the madams in the boardinghouses. She was especially afraid of being kidnapped by the notorious Li Toy, who owned a dozen or more boardinghouses, brothels, and cribs. Zhing was terrified by the possibility that Li Toy or one of the other madams might force her into becoming a *baak haak chai*, a Cantonese term that meant "one of a hundred men's wives."

Julie couldn't blame Zhing Wu. Li Toy's name was enough to put the fear of God in all but the most hardened Celestial. From what she'd learned during her two weeks in San Francisco, Li Toy was not a person one wished to have as an enemy.

Julie had spent three days collecting laundry, from the boardinghouses on Dupont Street to the brothels lining both sides of Montgomery and Stockton streets, slipping silently into the back and side entrances during the midmorning hours and going from room to room, retrieving dirty linen while making quiet conversation with the girls working in the houses, asking as many questions as she dared about Su Mi. Did anyone know her? Had anyone traveled from Hong Kong to *Gum Saan*, the Cantonese term for California, with her? Or heard her name mentioned?

None of the girls she'd questioned so far admitted to knowing anything about Su Mi, or admitted to even having heard her name. But there were dozens of brothels in Chinatown left to investigate, along with the second-floor businesses in the saloons surrounding Chinatown on streets lined with cheap cribs, as well as Li Toy's establishments like the Lotus Blossom and the Jade Dragon.

Julie knew the likelihood of anyone from the mission recognizing her was slight. Her Salvationist sisters preferred patrolling the businesses in San Francisco proper, leaving the waterfront dives to the Women's Temperance League members and mysterious Chinatown to the men brave enough to tackle its maze of narrow, dirty alleyways. Julie didn't blame them. She'd lived in Hong Kong all her life and spoke fluent Cantonese and Mandarin, and still found Chinatown and the Barbary Coast surrounding it daunting. The people and the sounds of the area were as familiar to her as the faces of her loved ones, but Chinatown and the Barbary Coast were worlds away from the closed sedans and coaches she'd traveled in and the walled gardens of home.

Taking a deep, steadying breath, Julie made her way to the back entrance of the Lotus Blossom. Fridays were busy days for Zhing Wu. On Fridays she made two visits to the brothels on Montgomery and Stockton streets, picking up soiled laundry in the mornings and delivering clean laundry in the afternoons before the brothels began teeming with customers. She began with the Lotus Blossom at the top of Montgomery and ended with the Jade Dragon at the bottom.

Balancing her willow basket on one hip, Julie knocked on the back door of the Lotus Blossom and called out in singsong Cantonese, "Wu's laundry pickup."

Someone peered through the peephole drilled in the back door, then slid the bolt, allowing Julie entrance. She stepped inside. "Dirty laundry, please," she called out in her singsong voice.

In minutes, piles of soiled sheets, towels, and female garments and accoutrements began appearing outside the doors. All the garments were similar. There was nothing to distinguish one corset, silk stocking, nightgown, or sheer robe from the others. The embellishments and embroidery were identical—nothing special, nothing personal. Julie had hoped to find something—a nightgown or handkerchief—bearing Su Mi's exquisitely detailed embroidery, but so far all she'd collected was dirty bed linens, bathing flannels, and shockingly revealing dressing gowns and blouses. No outer garments and no drawers. Women in the brothels and parlor houses wore sheer robes or opened blouses during working hours, but were required to leave their nether regions uncovered. There wasn't a pair of drawers or a tunic and trousers to be found.

Zhing Wu had tried to prepare Julie for the immodesty she'd find in the brothels, but she'd been scandalized nonetheless. Nothing could prepare an innocent young lady for the sight of a Chinese brothel. The first day she'd arrived early and had had to struggle to keep the shock off her face and her eyes downcast. It had gotten a bit easier in subsequent days, but Julie feared she'd never get over the sight of girls lounging about with breasts and nether regions bared, or covered in robes so transparent they provided no coverage at all—or worse—entertaining grunting, groaning men behind curtained alcoves or closed doors.

The thought of shy, modest little Su Mi trapped in such a place haunted Julie. Her desperation to find her friend was growing with each passing day.

Reaching for the closest pile of laundry, Julie stuffed it into her willow basket and whispered to the girl in the doorway in Cantonese, "Do you know of a girl from Hong Kong? A girl named Su Mi? Is she here?"

The girl shook her head. "No Su Mi here."

"Are you sure?" Julie persisted, scooping an armload of dirty linen from the girl in the next doorway and pushing it into the basket. "She left Hong Kong for the Flowery Flag Nation almost three months ago."

"No Su Mi here today," the second girl told her. "No Su Mi here yesterday. No Su Mi here day before yesterday."

Julie heaved a sigh.

"Why you care?" the first girl asked. "No one else care about poor China girls in here."

"Su Mi is . . ." Julie thought for a moment. She and Su Mi couldn't pass for blood sisters, not upon close scrutiny, but she could be family. "Su Mi is the daughter of my father's—" She searched the word for *housekeeper*, but what came out was *wife*.

"Poor Su Mi." The second brothel girl clucked her tongue and shook her head in sympathy. "Nobody to look for her except Wu's big-footed laundry girl, Jie Li."

Julie absorbed the insult, but she couldn't keep from glancing down at her feet. They were small compared to most Englishwomen's, but she supposed they appeared enormous when compared to the tiny feet of the China girls. "Perhaps, but Wu's big-footed laundry girl won't stop looking until she finds Su Mi."

"If Jie Li don't stop looking and asking questions, Jie Li

will get herself and all Lotus Blossom girls in big trouble with Madam Li Toy," the first brothel girl said as a third girl shoved laundry into Julie's basket.

"I don't want to cause the Lotus Blossom girls any trouble," Julie said. "I just want to find Su Mi."

"Girls not always stay in *Dai Fow* parlor houses," the third girl whispered, using the Cantonese term for San Francisco.

"What?" Julie gasped.

"Ignorant laundry girl," the third girl chided. "Bad girls sent to mining camps and little towns. Very bad or ugly girls sent to cribs."

"Or *auction*." Pronouncing the word in a tone filled with dread, a fourth girl stripped the sheets off her cot and shoved them at Julie. "As rich man's concubine."

*"Auction?"* The girls' demeanor and the way they pronounced the word showed how much they feared the humiliation and shame of being displayed and sold in that manner. The sound of it sent a shiver of dread down Julie's spine. "Bad girls are auctioned off?"

The first girl nodded. "Bad girls and virgin girls."

Julie's heart began to pound. "Where?" Su Mi's uncle had arranged her marriage to the scoundrel who had sold her into slavery, so Julie doubted she was still a virgin, but she was fairly certain that shy, modest Su Mi would have put up a fight when her tunic and trousers were taken away. Or her needlework. Su Mi was an artist when it came to elaborate and intricate embroidery. It was her passion. If anyone attempted to take her needlework, Su Mi would have fought like a tiger. Julie knew Su Mi, knew her friend would have fought to protect her needlework and clothing, but would have been docile and pleasing with her husband, the way she'd been taught, no matter what he did or how badly he treated her. Was it possible that Su Mi had been auctioned and sent somewhere outside San Francisco? How would Julie ever find her in the land beyond the city's boundaries? San Francisco was big, but California was so much bigger. . . . Julie sucked in a breath she felt as a stabbing pain deep inside her chest.

A shrill voice carried up the stairs from somewhere below. The girls tensed at the sound and began tossing their dirty linen in the basket.

"Quick! Quick! Go!" The first girl hefted the basketful of laundry and thrust it into Julie's midsection. "Madam coming."

But Julie refused to be hurried until she had an answer to one of her questions. "Where do they hold the auctions?"

"This time at the Jade Dragon," the first girl whispered, pushing Julie toward the back door.

Julie paused in the doorway. "When?"

"Tonight."

"Thank you," Julie whispered.

"No thank me." The girl shoved Julie through the door with all her might. "Go!"

## Chapter Six

*"It is not in the stars to hold our destiny
but in ourselves."*
—WILLIAM SHAKESPEARE

Julia Jane Parham had gone missing.

Will Keegan raked his fingers through his hair in extreme frustration. He sat at a table in the grand parlor of the Silken Angel, a cup of coffee and a bottle of Irish whiskey at his elbow. Nobody had seen the flame-haired missionary or heard the dulcet tones of "Bringing in the Sheaves" on the streets of Chinatown in three days. Not since Wednesday, when Will had learned Li Toy had hired a San Francisco policeman to quiet her.

He'd spent the past three days making discreet inquiries all over town to no avail. Will had made a personal call at the mission in his guise as a respectable officer of Craig Capital, Ltd., and made a sizable contribution to the mission's indigent fund in order to inquire about Miss Parham, but no one seemed to know where Miss Parham had gone or recall exactly when they had last seen her. It was as if she'd fallen off the face of the earth. And Will was very much afraid that despite his best efforts to prevent it, she had done just that. Lifting the whiskey bottle, he poured a healthy shot into his coffee, then recorked the bottle, got up from the table, and carried it to the bar, where he handed it to the barman.

"Put this away for me, will you, Jack?" He gave the other man a rueful look. "We've a busy night ahead of us, and I'll need a clear head on me in order to deal with Madam Harpy."

"If you say so." Jack flashed a smile. "Personally, I wouldn't blame you for downing the whole bottle. Madam Harpy is right. Her screeching can peel the paint off the walls, that's for sure. And she looks at us as if she'd relish cutting our livers out with a spoon and serving them to us as mince on a plate."

"I had a more obvious bit of anatomy in mind," Will said.

Jack snorted with laughter. "That, too."

"I don't think she has a very high regard for men in general, and she holds a particularly low opinion of us white devils," Will continued. "Fortunately, she uses chopsticks. I wouldn't trust her with cutlery."

"I wouldn't turn my back on her chopsticks, either. I'll wager she sharpens the ends."

"You'd win that wager," Will told him. "But not the ones she uses to eat; it's the ones she wears in her hair. I've heard they're deadly." According to local gossip, a stab through the jugular was Li Toy's favorite method for dispatching troublesome girls.

"Saints preserve us," Jack muttered, hurriedly crossing himself for the blasphemy before replacing the whiskey bottle on the mirrored shelf behind the bar. "Just looking at the woman gives me the willies. She's cold."

"It's her inscrutable face," Will replied, enjoying the familiar banter.

"There's nothing inscrutable about Li Toy's face. It's got hatred, cruelty, and greed written all over it."

"Let's hope her greed is stronger than her hatred or her cruelty." Will walked over to the table and retrieved his mug of coffee.

"Amen to that," Jack seconded. "Drink your coffee, boss, before it gets cold. You'll need it to keep your blood pumping if you don't want to lose parts of your anatomy to frostbite wrangling with Madam Harpy."

Will chuckled in spite of himself, then did as his head barman and trusted friend ordered and took a sip of his coffee. "I would appreciate it if you didn't mention pumping, willies, blood, and Madam Harpy in the same sentence."

Jack laughed out loud. "Done, boss."

"Speaking of which . . ." Will paused long enough to glance around the room. There were few customers this time of day, and they were occupied at the billiard or poker tables. Nobody was paying close attention to the conversation between the saloon owner and his head barman. But it never hurt to be cautious. Will swallowed another mouthful of whiskey-laced coffee. "Is everything ready for tonight?"

"The rooms are made up and ready, and the old man sent word that they will be here tomorrow night in time for the evening performance. What about you? Are you ready?" Nobody expected new girls to go to work the first night—not at the Silken Angel—but by tomorrow night, everyone in town would know there were new girls on the second floor of Will Keegan's saloon.

"As I'll ever be." Will sighed.

Jack nodded. "It's a nasty business we're in now. Not like Craig Capital, where everything is aboveboard and tidy and the numbers all add up at the end of the day."

Will stared at him. "Any regrets about leaving that world for this one?"

Jack O'Brien had followed his older brother, Murphy—a detective with the Pinkerton National Detective Agency—to America. As the youngest son of a devout Irish Catholic family, Jack had been destined for church life, but found he and the priesthood didn't fit. He'd left the seminary at St. Patrick's College in Dublin before taking his final vows and made his way from Ireland to the Comstock Lode in Nevada, where Murphy was working a case. Jack had been hired by the Pinkertons' Denver office and had spent several months helping his brother by working as a barman in a saloon in Queen City before moving on to San Francisco. Will had met him while on business in the city and hired him as his personal secretary at Craig Capital, Ltd. Jack spent four years working there with Will and proved himself time and time again. He was smart, ambitious, hardworking, and entirely trustworthy. He'd thrived at Craig Capital and would have been the de facto manager of the San Francisco office in Will's absence instead of Peter Malcolm, but he had jumped at the chance to work with Will on his latest venture.

Jack smiled. "I knew those few months of tending bar and managing the rowdies at the Queen City Saloon and Opera House would come in handy." He met Will's serious look with one of his own. "Truth is, I don't like the idea of you going into the dragon's lair on your own. I'd feel better if I was going with you."

"I would, too," Will admitted. "But we don't want to change the way we do things. You've never accompanied me before. And I need you to handle things here."

"I know," Jack agreed. "Just as I know that what we're doing here is worth the risk."

"If we're lucky and Madam Harpy proves greedy enough, we should have a half dozen or so new girls to fill those upstairs rooms and keep the troupe busy."

"And speaking of upstairs, why don't you head up there and catch a few winks, boss? It's going to be another long night for you, and you look like the devil."

Will squeezed his eyes shut. His eyes felt dry, gritty, and bloodshot, and the idea of grabbing a few hours of sleep before the auction was tempting.

"I'll keep watch over the saloon and an ear out for any word about our little grain-gathering missionary," Jack said.

Will shot Jack a cautioning glance.

Jack acknowledged the warning look by reassuring Will that he wasn't telling tales out of school. "The word is out all over Chinatown that our little friend spent her first two weeks in town poking her nose into the saloons, parlor houses, and boardinghouses, asking questions and trying to incite rebellion among the China dolls."

Will choked on his coffee.

"You didn't know?"

"Not that she had progressed from psalm singing to incit-ing rebellion in Chinatown."

Jack frowned. "That's the word going around. But I think the rebellion claim is exaggerated."

"Oh?"

Jack nodded. "I think the owners are claiming she's incit-ing rebellion in order to get rid of the little psalm singer." He looked at Will. "I'm surprised you haven't heard. She's made quite a name for herself in the short time she's been in San Francisco." Jack shook his head in bemusement. "I'm amazed she hasn't paid us a return visit, despite the fact that her month isn't up yet."

"If only she would," Will muttered. What he wouldn't give to hear her singing "Bringing in the Sheaves" and banging on her tambourine about now.

Jack laughed. "Why? So you can pay her another thirty dollars to go away again?"

"So I'll know she's alive," Will told him.

"*What?*" Jack was taken aback by Will's matter-of-fact statement.

"Li Toy hired a policeman to quiet the missionary girl going about town singing 'Bringing in the Sheaves.' And she's not paying for a month of silence. She's paying for permanent silence." He looked at Jack. "And I'd rather not have that guilty knowledge on my conscience."

"Jaysus!" Jack's broad County Clare brogue came through loud and clear when he swore. "What are you going to do?"

"Nothing until the auction ends and we take possession of our merchandise." Will shook his head as if to clear it. "Busi-ness has to come first. Once we get the ladies settled in, I'll do what I've been doing for the past two nights."

"Which is?"

"Prowling the streets and alleys of Chinatown after we close, poking *my* nose where it doesn't belong, looking for information as to the whereabouts of our little Salvationist," Will told him.

"No wonder you look like hell."

"Yeah, no wonder." Will raked his fingers through his hair,

then crossed over to the bar and set his empty mug on the polished wood. "As far as I can tell, our little songbird isn't at the mission."

"Aw, no . . ." The brogue was broader.

"Oh, yes," Will said. "Nobody has seen her in three days, and I have no idea which of the policeman on Li Toy's payroll was paid to *quiet* her."

"What are you thinking?" Jack asked.

"I'm praying I can come up with some answers, and that they don't come too late."

"She's not your responsibility," Jack reminded him.

"She's an innocent, Jack," Will retorted. "A babe lost in the woods. I'll stake my life on it."

"You start asking questions about Madam Harpy and corrupt police and you *will* be staking your life on it."

Will shrugged his shoulders. "Can't be helped."

"What about the Salvationists?" Jack demanded. "Are they doing anything to find her?"

"Not yet."

Jack frowned. "But she's one of their own."

"And they sent her out to minister to the needy," Will replied. "As far as they're concerned, she's in the city performing missionary work. God will protect her."

"But you feel differently. . . ."

"I feel responsible."

Jack nodded. He was well aware of his boss's resolution. The Silken Angel Saloon was the product of that resolution. "Watch your back," Jack warned.

Will gave a genuine smile. "That's why I have you," he retorted. "I can't do everything. Watching my back is *your* job."

## Chapter Seven

❧

*"Wrongdoing can only be avoided if those who are not wronged feel the same indignation at it as those who are."*
—SOLON, 6TH CENTURY B.C.

Julie peeked out from beneath the burlap sacks stacked atop two large beer barrels in the far corner of the cellar of the Jade Dragon. The room was dank and dusty, filled with the pall of cigar smoke, the scent of exotic oils, and the sickly sweet-smelling residue of opium that clung to the clothing and hair and skin of the recent visitors to the Washington Street opium dens. The cellar was large by San Francisco standards, with a raised dais illuminated by footlights at one end and a small bar, a concession to the white men attending the auction, set up along the western wall. The remainder of the space was taken up by tables and chairs.

The room was packed with men of all shapes, sizes, ages, and nationalities. The sound of deep voices, the shuffle of feet, and the scraping of tables and chairs sent the mice sharing the cover of the burlap sacks with her scurrying for newer, safer hiding places. She did her best to bite back a squeak of dismay when one of them crawled over her hand, and failed.

The man sitting alone at the table closest to her turned in her direction.

Julie clamped a hand over her mouth, sank down on her

bottom, pressed her back against the wall, and willed herself to become invisible. She was playing a dangerous game, and while she hadn't suffered the consequences of her actions yet, she knew there would be consequences. There always were. And they could be deadly. Struck for the first time by the enormity of what she'd done, Julie wriggled up the wall just far enough to take another look around. She gritted her teeth against the sharp prick of pins and needles in her feet. She'd been huddled on the floor in the cold, damp corner so long her feet were numb. Running was impossible, walking unlikely. If discovered, she feared she'd be reduced to crawling past the guards at the entrance and praying for divine intervention.

There was no other way out.

She'd discovered that unpleasant truth when, acting on impulse, she'd hefted a box from the bed of the wagon parked in the alley and followed the two men carrying identical boxes into the cellar of the Jade Dragon.

It took a moment for her eyes to adjust to darkness inside the cavernous room, but once they did, Julie quickly realized she was trapped. Her heart pounding at her foolhardiness, Julie set the box on the nearest table, whipped off her straw hat, replaced it with a man's black cap she'd kept tucked in the waistband of her trousers, and slipped behind two large beer barrels in the darkest corner seconds before Li Toy's henchmen returned to the wagon for more supplies.

She hadn't been able to see what they were doing from her hiding place, but she knew from their conversation that they were tasked with the chore of setting up a makeshift bar on the near wall. She'd listened to the two men arguing over who had left the box of whiskey sitting on the table and cursing white foreign devils whose sense of entitlement demanded that they be able to drink.

With their tasks complete, the two men withdrew to the entrance to stand guard at the doorway.

Unable to escape with Madam Harpy's hatchet men guarding the door, Julie settled into the darkness to wait for what came next. She closed her eyes, intending to rest them for a moment, but she must have dozed, because she was awakened suddenly by the sights and sounds and scents of people filing into the room.

Horrified by the thought that she'd allowed her exhaustion to overtake her good sense, Julie held her breath and took another peek at the action in the cellar. She was rewarded with her first look at Li Toy, the infamous madam whose name struck terror in the hearts of Chinatown residents—especially the laundry girl, Zhing Wu, and the girls trapped in Li Toy's brothels. Julie was surprised to find that the woman in the long yellow silk cheongsam was tiny—tinier than Su Mi, and Julie stood head and shoulders above her best friend. Seeing Li Toy up close and in the flesh, Julie found it hard to believe the small, middle-aged woman a few feet away was lethal when crossed. She looked like someone's kindly aunt or grandmother, and she dressed like Lolly in the traditional mandarin-collared, narrow-skirted embroidered silk dresses slit up the front to allow easier movement. Julie studied the embroidery on the yellow silk. It was well-done, but it didn't bear any of the hallmarks of Su Mi's exquisite needlework.

Julie exhaled. That didn't mean Su Mi hadn't come in contact with the notorious madam, only that she hadn't decorated the madam's cheongsam. She turned her attention back to the woman wearing the dress. If worse came to worst and she was discovered, Julie believed she could hold her own against Li Toy, provided she could overcome the uncomfortable sensation in her feet and legs. The guards were another matter. But if everything followed the plan she'd formed after finding herself trapped in the cellar, she'd pick up a tray of dirty cups and glasses, keep her head down and her eyes averted, and slip through the crowd when the auction ended. That was her plan. Julie hoped it worked. But she couldn't worry about that now. She had to focus on the matter at hand.

The auction.

Li Toy stepped onto the dais, clapped her hands. "Gentlemen!" Her voice was a high-pitched shriek. "Now business time." She clapped her hands together again, and two of her minions lit the footlights along the perimeter of the raised dais, raised the wicks to their highest positions, then stepped back as another underling led a young Chinese girl onto the stage.

Julie couldn't swallow her gasp at the sight of the poor girl. During her fortnight in San Francisco, Julie had seen many shocking sights. She'd seen the inside of brothels and girls imprisoned in cribs. She had seen Chinese females with bared breasts call out in broken singsong English at all hours of the day and night, "Lookee, nice China girl. Come inside, please." She had witnessed men and women openly engaged in sexual congress before the uncovered windows of the establishments lining both sides of China Alley between Jackson and Washington streets—a sight that convinced her that spinsterhood had much to recommend it and intimacy with a male had none.

None of those horrors prepared her for the sight of a young Chinese girl standing before a crowd of rapacious men and two or three seemingly heartless women; the girl wearing a short opened blouse and nothing else, her hands bound at the wrists behind her back so that she was unable to cover herself and preserve her modesty. Julie's heart went out to the poor girl. She fervently prayed Su Mi hadn't had to endure this public degradation.

"Bid now for number one girl!" Madam Harpy ordered the men seated at the tables. "Ah Fook, handsome young virgin from Kwangtung province." Using a polished black-lacquered walking stick, Li Toy poked the girl in the thigh. "Stand up straight," she snapped in Cantonese, before turning back to the audience. "Bid start at five hundred American dollars."

Julie pressed her face against the beer barrel, unable to watch as several men rose from their seats, walked to the dais, and began intimate examinations of the girl.

"Five hundred dollars!" came the first bid.

"Six hundred!"

"Eight hundred!"

"Eight hundred twenty-five!"

Seated at his table near the back corner, Will jotted quick notes in a ledger by the light of a small lamp as the bidding grew feverish: *Girl number one, Ah Fook, virgin from Kwangtung province. Approximately sixteen years of age.*

"One thousand dollars." The sound of Will's firm voice carried above the din.

Li Toy grinned. "One thousand one time. One thousand two times. One thousand three times." She clapped her hands. "Sold. Mr. Will Keegan, the Silken Angel Saloon."

*Will Keegan. The Silken Angel Saloon.*

Ignoring the pain in her legs and feet, Julie shifted her position, peered through the gap between the barrels, saw that the light shining from the small lantern on the table was brighter than it had been earlier, and recognized Will Keegan as the man seated at the table closest to her corner making notations in a ledger. Julie gasped, the air leaving her lungs in a rush as she recalled William Burke Keegan's assurance that there were no girls upstairs in the Silken Angel Saloon. That *he* lived upstairs. *Alone.*

And she'd believed him. *Trusted* him.

Fury swept over her like a tidal wave. Julie clenched her teeth to keep from screaming her outrage. He was either a liar or the living arrangements at the Silken Angel Saloon were about to change.

Will Keegan had just purchased a woman at auction for one thousand American dollars.

But that wasn't the worst of it. Ten more women—girls, really—were auctioned that evening as Julie sat hidden in the dark corner behind the beer barrels. Ten more girls were paraded almost naked onstage in front of the foot lamps. Ten more girls were poked, prodded, and pinched while being inspected as merchandise.

Will Keegan purchased seven of them. Without giving them more than a cursory glance. Without leaving his table. Without inspecting the merchandise.

Hugging herself, Julie pulled her knees to her chest, gagging as anger and nausea and regret threatened to swamp her.

She, who prided herself on being a good judge of character, had made a mistake.

He was a liar and a scoundrel. He wasn't a gentleman.

And she was a fool for believing otherwise. Julie felt the sting of betrayal like bitter quinine on her tongue.

She wanted to scream. She wanted to stand up and confront the beast masquerading as a gentleman, to bear witness to his perfidy. She wanted to run. She wanted to soak in a steaming-hot bath to rid herself of the sounds and sights and smells of the Jade Dragon, soak until she felt clean again, then curl up on her bed, pull the coverlet over her head, and forget everything she'd seen and done since she'd come to San Francisco, but she sat frozen in place, determined to stay to the bitter end. To see what happened after the auction. To see what happened to the girls . . .

Julie pinned her gaze on Will Keegan and waited for her opportunity to escape. . . .

"How we do?"

Will looked up from his ledger as Li Toy approached his table. He waited until the other attendees began filing out the door before replying. "You're a few thousand dollars richer. I'm a few thousand dollars poorer."

Li Toy laughed. "You charge ten dollars and keep girls on their backs at the Silken Angel, you make that money back in no time."

Will narrowed his gaze at the madam. Her shrill laugh grated on his nerves. He had to steel himself to keep from flinching when Li Toy leaned over and placed her hand on his shoulder.

"Ten dollars?" He didn't like to think how long it would take the girls to earn a thousand dollars apiece one customer at a time. "You must be joking."

Li Toy shrugged her shoulders. "The Silken Angel is very nice. You charge twenty dollars."

"Is that your going rate?"

"For very nice house," she replied. "Ten dollars top price for the Jade Dragon and the Lotus Blossom."

Will tapped the ledger with the end of his pen. "And all your other parlor houses . . ."

Li Toy laughed again and gave him a playful shove. "You know better than that. Ten dollars for parlor houses Jade Dragon and Lotus Blossom. Five dollars for boardinghouses. One dollar for nice cribs. Twenty-five cents for cheap cribs."

He'd never seen evidence of there being any nice cribs. "And auctions?"

"You tell me," she said. "You pay me seven thousand dollars. Now. In cash."

Will smiled. She was testing him. There were formalities that must be observed in order for the sales to be finalized. He knew it and she knew it. Reaching into the inside breast pocket of his jacket, Will pulled out his wallet, removed seven thousand-dollar banknotes, and stacked them neatly on the table before him for her to see. "I believe the contracts require me to make payment to the young ladies in question."

Will didn't consider the contracts legal or binding, but the Chinese merchants who imported the slaves from China demanded that each girl sign a bill of sale or indenture for five years and willingly accept cash payment for their services. That meant the money must be placed in each girl's hand before she signed the documents. After signing the contract, the girl immediately gave the cash to the person who arranged her sale. Because there were laws forbidding the importation of Chinese women for purposes of immorality, the contracts afforded the buyer legal protection from prosecution for trafficking in slavery.

Li Toy gave him an unwilling nod. "You pleased with auction?"

"I don't care for the process," he told her. "I would have paid you fifteen thousand for the lot to avoid it."

"And have other buyers say you Li Toy's favorite gentleman?" She shrugged. "Then nobody come to Li Toy's auctions no more."

"If I buy your entire shipment you won't need to arrange auctions," Will pointed out.

Li Toy shrewdly narrowed her gaze at him. "If Keegan not like competition, why you want so many girls? You building a parlor house to rival Li Toy's?"

"I have a very exclusive clientele," Will said. "Gentlemen visit the upstairs of my saloon in order to meet the brides they pay me to find. Those gentlemen can't afford to risk disease. They prefer untried partners and pay handsomely for opportunity to be first. As a consequence, I'm always in the market for virgins."

"You crazy, Keegan," she scoffed. "You no need new virgins. You can keep the same one for years. Men not know the difference."

"These men know the difference," Will told her.

She relaxed. "Then I sell you more girls."

Will nodded.

"For now, tell me how much I make tonight."

"Seven thousand from me and two thousand for the other four." He scratched some numbers in the ledger. "Minus the twenty-five hundred you paid for them equals sixty-five hundred."

"Minus more expenses," Li Toy added.

"How much more?" Will asked.

"Two hundred fifty dollars for miss expenses."

"*Miscellaneous* expenses?"

Li Toy nodded.

"Sixty-five hundred minus two hundred fifty dollars equals six thousand two hundred fifty dollars," Will answered.

"Profit?"

He nodded.

She clapped her hands together. "Very nice for me."

"Indeed." The idea of paying Li Toy a princely sum for seven of her unfortunate countrywomen made Will's blood boil.

The madam laughed once again. "For you, too," she reminded him. "You get seven lovely Celestial virgins for your gentlemen who pay top dollar."

"According to you."

"According to Hong Kong broker, but I inspect girls myself." Li Toy shook a finger at him. "I *guarantee*."

"What, no *Chinese* physician?" Will emphasized the fact that Chinese madams generally used Chinese physicians because they could be bribed and controlled more easily than American doctors. Chinese doctors understood the trade and profited from it. They weren't terribly interested in rescuing the unfortunate victims of prostitution.

"Physician cost money."

"I believe the contracts specify a physician."

"Bah!" She dismissed his concern. "You no good business-man, Keegan. Why pay doctor when you can inspect girls yourself before you buy?"

Will did his best to erase the mental image of Li Toy inspecting those poor girls. The knowledge of what they had endured to come to California was sickening. These women—most of whom were little more than girls—had been betrayed at every turn: first by their families who sold them to the "bride" brokers, who in turn shipped them to California in the company of men whose job it was to break them to the idea of a life of prostitution and slavery. Then they'd arrived in San Francisco and been handed over to this vile little woman, who stripped them of their clothing and their personal modesty and sold them at private auction to the highest bidder. In this case, Will knew his ends justified the means, but the burden of guilt he carried for buying human beings weighed heavily on his Knoxist conscience.

"They'll need clothes," Will said.

Li Toy held out her hand. "Four dollars apiece."

Will shook his head. "You try this ploy every time we do business," he chided the madam. "They were wearing clothing when they docked. They didn't come into port naked, and I can't very well parade them through Chinatown the way you had them dressed, can I?"

"New tunics and trousers cost four dollars apiece," she insisted. "You owe me."

"What happened to their other tunics and trousers?" he demanded.

"Filthy rags." She shuddered. "I burned them."

"If you burned their clothing instead of having it laundered, you're responsible for replacing it." He looked Li Toy in the eyes. "I just paid seven thousand dollars for these young women. I am not paying for new tunics and trousers in addition to that. The way I see it, you owe *me* twenty-eight dollars."

Li Toy cackled in delight at his response. "You learn fast, Keegan. You better businessman than I thought."

Will closed the ledger. He wanted to laugh at the irony of the situation. He was an investment banker by trade. During his years with Craig Capital, Ltd., he'd made good investments and amassed a tidy fortune. He could buy and sell Madam Harpy a dozen times over, but the illiterate Chinese madam was complimenting him on beating her out of twenty-eight dollars' worth of clothing for seven women for whom he'd paid seven thousand dollars. Of course, any price was worth it, but Will was aware of the irony all the same. "I'm just a saloon keeper," he told her. "Certainly not the businesswoman you are."

Li Toy gave him a conspiratorial smile. "I like you, Keegan."

He couldn't say the same. Lifting a shot of the whiskey from the bottle he'd brought with him, Will gave her a mock salute. "Then I'm a fortunate man."

"You pay too much money for worthless girls, you know."

"Perhaps." He took another sip of his drink. "But it's only money. . . ."

"*Only* money?" The concept was sacrilege to a woman like Li Toy. In her world, money was everything. "You one crazy foreign devil."

"Perhaps," he drawled once again. "But I believe the ladies are worth it."

"Bah!" She waved a dismissive hand at him. "These girls no different from any other *loungei* girls."

"I beg to differ, madam." He stared at the little woman.

Li Toy lifted one thinly plucked eyebrow.

Will smiled. "These girls are *special*. They're *my* girls. And I'd like them dressed and delivered to me inside the hour."

# Chapter Eight

S he's gone." Will glanced over at the corner several minutes after Li Toy left the cellar to secure clothing for his purchases and to see that they were readied for delivery. "You can come out now."

Julie sucked in a breath. If he thought she was going to stand up and present herself to him, he was drunk or mad or both.

"I know you're behind the beer barrels," Will continued. "I heard you rustling around back there earlier in the evening. I don't know who you are or what you're doing here, but if you're one of Kip Yee's men, tell him the auction is over, the merchandise is sold, and any attempt he might make to seize it would be foolhardy and unsuccessful."

Julie stayed frozen in the corner.

Will stood up and stretched, then turned his back and took a moment to straighten his notebook and the ledgers. "Are you going to stay there and hide or make the most of your chance to escape? There's only one way in and out of here. If you're going to flee, might I suggest you do it while my back is to you? Before Li Toy returns with her bodyguards." He paused a moment, listening to the rustling behind the beer barrels as the stowaway scrambled out of his hiding place.

"No need to thank me," he called after the figure scurrying through the cellar door. He raised his glass in a private salute, refilled it, and returned to his seat at the table. "Consider it my good deed for the day." Will hoped it didn't turn out to be his only good deed of the day. He had purchased seven girls, removing them from the life of degradation and hardship Li Toy had planned for them. His purpose was to guarantee them a better life. These girls hadn't come to America for the opportunities it afforded them. Almost to a woman, they had come unwillingly. They'd traveled thousands of miles away from everyone and everything they loved to be enslaved for someone else's gain. Will clenched his teeth and firmed his jaw at the idea. Just because they hadn't come willingly didn't mean these young women should be denied their piece of the American dream.

"I brought unworthy girls." Li Toy entered the cellar followed by the seven young women he'd purchased, all properly clothed in trousers, tunics, and shoes. Two hulking hatchet men she'd employed for her protection brought up the rear. She marched the girls to Will's table.

"Contracts? Bills of sale?" Will glanced at the madam.

Li Toy clapped her hands and one of her hatchet men removed a bundle of papers from the sleeve of his tunic and handed them to the madam, who placed them on the table. "Here."

Will pulled the contracts and the bills of sale in front of him, opened his ledger, and dipped his pen in the ink bottle. He looked at the first girl. "Name?" he asked in English.

The girl didn't reply until Madam Harpy translated his question into Cantonese. "Ah Lo."

Will wrote her name in the blank space on the indenture contract, then handed her a thousand-dollar banknote, which she handed to Li Toy in response to her impatient prompting. He recorded the amount of money he'd paid the girl in the place allotted for that purpose, then handed her the pen and watched as Ah Lo made her mark at Li Toy's urging.

He repeated the process with Ah Fook, Ah Woo, Ah So, Ling Lau, Ling Yee, and Ling Tsin. When he finished, Will paused long enough to take a sip of his whiskey in hopes of erasing the bad taste in his mouth. He had drawn up and signed hundreds of contracts during his tenure at Craig Capital, all of them fairly negotiated to suit the needs of all the parties involved.

There was nothing fair about the contracts binding these young women to him. The contracts, drawn up by the madam, were slanted in the purchaser's favor. The documents secured the rights to each woman's body for a term of five years in order to repay the sum of money paid for them. The women were entitled to purchase their freedom at the end of service, but there was little likelihood of that happening, since they did not receive wages and there were penalties for missing work and for escaping or attempting escape. Three months of service were added to their indenture for any attempt at escape, and a month was added for each day of work missed due to sickness—including days of the month the women endured their menses. If they had menses. Will's heart ached as he looked at the two youngest girls, sisters Ling Yee and Ling Tsin, who at eight and seven years of age had yet to reach puberty. He couldn't fathom the sort of man who would choose to slake his passion on a female child. And yet Will knew those depraved individuals existed. And what was worse was knowing that he had probably crossed paths with more than one of them on any number of occasions.

Taking the pen from little Ling Tsin's fingers, Will dipped it in the ink pot and recorded their names and ages on the bill of sale. The deal was done.

It was time to take the girls to the Silken Angel Saloon.

AFTER MAKING HER ESCAPE FROM THE BASEMENT OF THE Jade Dragon, Julie hurried to Wu's Gum Saan Laundry to retrieve her Salvationist dress, but the business was closed and locked, and Julie had been unable to wake Zhing or her father-in-law without drawing attention to herself and waking

Wu's neighbors. She had no choice but to leave her missionary costume where it was. Unfortunately, that meant she wouldn't be able to return to the room she'd rented at the Russ House Hotel dressed as a Chinese laundry girl, or return to her cot in the women's dormitory at the mission. She had no place to stay—unless she could find a way inside the Silken Angel Saloon before Will Keegan led the girls he'd bought at the auction to his place of business.

But fear of discovery kept Julie confined to the shadows at the rear entrance of the saloon. On Friday night the place was a beehive of activity, with men coming and going along the side alley and through the opened front doors. Julie listened to the music of the slightly out-of-tune piano, the low rumble of voices, and the occasional roar of laughter while she waited for her chance.

Shivering in the cool night air, Julie shifted her weight from one foot to the other, doing her best to ignore the dampness seeping through her cotton shoes and socks. Her feet were as cold as blocks of ice, and she longed for the warmth of her ugly missionary boots. But wearing boots with her tunic and trousers in her disguise as a laundry girl might have aroused suspicion in Chinatown and brought questions she would rather not answer, so she had reluctantly left them behind.

She had only herself to blame for the impulsiveness that had led her to Li Toy's cellar. She could be safely tucked into bed at the hotel or sleeping in the dormitory with her fellow female missionaries—not that the women sharing her dormitory cared where she slept as long as it wasn't in the male dormitory. Salvationists were free to come and go as they pleased and to seek lodging elsewhere. Her bed was hers until she informed the head of the mission that she no longer needed it. In her desperation to find Su Mi, she'd once again acted without thinking, and it was going to cost her more time spent hiding in the miserable damp and cold of night in San Francisco.

Hearing the sound of approaching footsteps, Julie suddenly realized she was not alone in the darkness behind the Silken

Angel. As she watched, Will Keegan came up the lane at the side of the saloon, leading a line of girls. She counted the figures as they passed a stone's throw away from her hiding place. Keegan had purchased seven girls. Julie counted six and wondered what had happened to the seventh unfortunate girl, before she spied Keegan shifting a bundle in his arms. It took her a moment to realize there were white-stockinged feet in black cloth shoes sticking out from the bundle, and that those little feet belonged to the seventh girl, who appeared to be sound asleep in Will Keegan's arms.

The door opened before he could knock, and the barman Julie had seen during her visit to the saloon ushered them inside. "What took you so long?" he asked. "I was beginning to worry you'd run into trouble at Madam Harpy's lair, or been waylaid by the Kip Yees or some other tong."

"We didn't cross paths with any tong members that I could tell on the way home," Will answered. "There was one hidden away in the cellar during the auction, but I sent him back to his master with a warning that attacking our little group would be a mistake."

The barman blew out the breath he'd been holding. "Jaysus, Will, but you took a risk doing that. What if he'd taken that as an invitation to intercept you?"

"He didn't."

"What delayed you?"

Keegan shook his head. "Li Toy. The contract process took longer than I anticipated. The girls were half-naked. I had to wait for Madam Harpy to produce clothes for them to wear. Then we lost a bit of time when the little one collapsed."

The barman took the child from Keegan. "From hunger or exhaustion?"

"Probably both."

"I wonder how long it's been since she had anything to eat."

"You can bet she didn't get anything to eat at the Jade Dragon," Will said. "I would be surprised if she's had more than a cup of boiled rice since she left the ship."

"Poor mite," the barman murmured, brushing the little

one's hair with his chin. "And she's not the only one. I'll wager they are all hungry and feeling lost and abandoned."

Will nodded. "You would win that wager. She *was* abandoned. And so were her two sisters and her cousins. Their parents sold them." He sighed. "I hope they did it to give the girls a better life, but I'm afraid it was simply an opportunity to rid themselves of unwanted girl children who had to be fed. I imagine all these girls feel lost and abandoned." He thought of his friend James Craig's four little Treasures, all of whom had been abandoned as infants. "Now here they are amidst barbarian strangers." Will rubbed a hand over his eyes in a classic gesture of weariness. "But at least Ling Tsin and her sisters and cousins will have food to eat, milk to drink, and a better chance of survival."

"Mary and Joseph." The barman groaned. "I didn't think to order milk." He glanced down at the little girl, then over at Keegan. "I'll have to send someone to locate the milkman and ask him to put us on his morning route."

"Not cow's milk," Will told him. He and James had learned that lesson when Jamie first adopted his eldest daughter, Ruby. Cow's milk was difficult for starving children to digest.

Jack was baffled. If not cow's milk, what milk was there? "What then?"

"Goat. Find a goatherd and order goat's milk. Or have someone bring a nanny goat and milk her. This is the first time we've ever rescued little girls, Jack. There was no way you could have known to order any kind of milk. We're a saloon, not a nursery." He frowned. "And the milk can wait until the morning. What they need most are meals, baths, and beds." The girls they'd rescued on their previous missions had all been older.

"What about a doctor?" Jack asked. "Should I send for him? They'll need health inspections."

Immigrants from China were supposed to receive health inspections before they were allowed to disembark from their ships, but Will knew that wasn't always the case. When money changed hands, the inspectors often looked the other way, allowing all but the sickest females to enter the country. "That can wait until tomorrow, too," Will told him. "They've been through enough poking and prodding for now."

"And the little ones?" Jack asked. "Do we bed them down with the older girls or put them in rooms of their own? I didn't expect children. . . . I prepared for older girls."

"I know," Keegan agreed. "I wasn't prepared for children either, or the sight of grown men salivating at the prospect of deflowering them. . . ." He shuddered, then met the other man's gaze. "The second floor of a saloon is no place for innocent little girls, but I couldn't leave them behind."

Jack clapped Will Keegan on the shoulder in a friendly gesture. "I couldn't have either. Not with her. Come on; I've got coffee on, and water heating in the kitchen for tea and baths."

"Food?" Will asked hopefully. His stomach was rumbling. The eggs and bacon he'd eaten at breakfast had long since disappeared. And eating or drinking anything at the Jade Dragon that he hadn't brought with him was out of the question.

"I've got a pot of soup and Cantonese vegetables with chicken and rice from Ming's kitchen simmering on the stove."

"Bless you, Jack."

Keegan ushered his charges ahead of him, then followed them inside.

Julie's mouth watered at the mention of Cantonese vegetable chicken with rice. She hadn't eaten anything since tea and toast for breakfast. Her stomach growled, and she pressed her hands over it in a feeble attempt to muffle the sound. Her goal was to get inside the Silken Angel Saloon. It seemed perfectly logical to start with the kitchen. . . .

## Chapter Nine

*"Curiosity is one of the forms of feminine bravery."*
—VICTOR HUGO, 1802–1885

She came to him in a dream for the first time in weeks. Will woke up, heart pounding and skin damp with perspiration, afraid that the face and form he knew so well would be the blend of Mei Ling and Elizabeth that had driven him from Coryville and proximity to Jamie's new wife. But this time she came with Mei Ling's face and form and Li Toy's cackle. Mei Ling, the gentle girl he had loved for so long was gone. In her place was a woman who taunted him for his foolishness in thinking that he could drive her out of his heart by purchasing a harem of concubines. For believing that he could save them when he could not save her . . . For trying so hard to save *them* when he hadn't tried hard enough to save *her* . . .

Will sat up amid the tangle of twisted bedsheets, turned to the side, and placed his feet on the floor. He leaned forward, elbows on knees, and cradled his face in his hands until the pounding of the blood rushing through his veins subsided and his erratic breathing calmed. His head told him that the dream was a result of an evening spent buying human beings—buying girls—at the Jade Dragon, but his heart . . .

He had bathed in steaming-hot water after dinner, washing

away the stench of the auction, doing his best to wash away the stain of what he'd done, but it hadn't been enough. It wasn't the first time he'd purchased girls at auction and it wouldn't be the last—although he fervently hoped it would be the last time he would ever see children forced onto the auction block and displayed for the prurient pleasure of grown men.

Will shuddered, remembering. His reaction following the first two auctions had been much the same. The hot bath and the whiskey he'd consumed afterward hadn't been enough to make him feel clean or to keep the dream away. Will rubbed his hand over his chest. He inhaled deeply, then slowly exhaled.

Just when he thought the dream was gone, it returned anew. Fortunately James's wife, Elizabeth, hadn't played a part in this newest incarnation. The woman in tonight's dream had brown eyes, Mei Ling's features, and Li Toy's laugh.

With his hands shaking so badly, Will didn't bother lighting the lamp, but reached out and grabbed his dressing gown from the foot of the bed.

He shoved his arms into the sleeves, tied the sash at his waist, and stood up to retrieve his trousers from the trouser press. He stepped into them and pulled them up his legs and over his hips, buttoning the top as he searched beneath the edge of the bed with his right foot for his slippers. Unable to locate them, Will gave up the search and padded barefoot across the room.

A lamp on the wall opposite his bedroom door burned low, illuminating the landing and a portion of the hallway. Another lamp mounted on the wall halfway down the hall illuminated the remainder.

Closing his bedroom door behind him, Will stepped into the hall and made his way toward the bedrooms along the right-hand side of the corridor. The Silken Angel Saloon had eight upstairs bedrooms, three on one side of the hallway and four on the other. Will's bedroom was located at the east end of the hall and included a sitting room and a small washroom. A larger washroom with two basins and a full-size bathtub occupied the space at the opposite end of the hallway, past the landing at the top of the stairs. Fitted into an alcove between Will's suite of rooms and the nearest single bedroom was a large armoire that held linens and towels, toiletries, and other female necessities.

When the saloon opened for business later today, there would be chairs positioned beside each of the seven bedroom doors for the men posted there. Not to keep the girls in. It was almost unheard-of for any bound prostitute to escape or attempt escape. The contract forbade it. And even though the girls were illiterate, Will knew Madam Harpy had read and explained the contract to them item by item. Li Toy had a reputation for striking fear in the hearts of the girls she smuggled into the country. No, Saturday nights were the saloon's busiest. The men posted by the bedrooms were there to protect the girls from the unwanted attention of curious downstairs customers who might be tempted to wander upstairs.

The fact that girls occasionally occupied the upstairs rooms was not a secret. Since it was impossible to keep their presence hidden, Will made certain that Li Toy, the tong leaders, and his saloon customers understood that the girls were housed in the Silken Angel only as long as it took their intended "husbands" to come claim them.

Early in the planning stage of the operation, Will and James realized that saving female infants and toddlers like James's Treasures was far easier than attempting rescues of young women who had value to the men and women who had purchased them. Infant and toddler females were often unwanted, abandoned, and discarded like refuse. The same could not be said of girls purchased for the purpose of prostitution.

After analyzing several plans, Will and James had based their rescue operation on the American Underground Railroad abolitionists had created to smuggle black slaves from southern slave-holding states to safety in the north and Canada using trusted associates and safe houses as stops on the "railroad." The plan was not without flaws and was a constant work-in-progress, but it was the best they had. The safe houses and identities of the conductors on the Silken Angel railroad were closely guarded secrets, known only to Will, James, and Jack O'Brien. The identities of the men who pretended to be husbands come to claim their brides were also kept secret for their protection and for the protection of their "brides."

Will tapped lightly at the first door on the right, then eased it open and peeked inside. One glance told him that at least two of the other bedrooms would be empty, the beds unoccupied. Inside on the single bed, huddled together like puppies in a litter, were little sisters Ling Yee and Ling Tsin and older sister Ling Lau. He and Jack had put the Ling sisters in adjoining bedrooms so the two youngest girls would be close to their older sister. Will had purposely left the adjoining doors open so Ling Yee and Ling Tsin could move back and forth between their bedrooms and that of ten-year-old Ling Lau. He wasn't surprised to see that sometime after he had bidden them good night, the little ones had crowded into bed beside their sister.

Smiling in spite of himself, Will quietly closed that door and moved on to the next one. He opened it. The coverlet on the bed had been thrown back and the sheets were mussed, but the room where he'd tucked Ling Tsin into bed was empty. He entered the room, walked across to the connecting door, and stepped inside the third of the adjoining bedrooms. He expected to find Ling Yee's bedroom empty, but there were two girls curled together on the bed. He thought they might be Ah So and Ah Woo, but he couldn't be sure. They might just as easily be Ah So and Ah Fook, or Ah Woo and Ah Fook. The room assigned to Ling Yee was now home to two of her cousins, but without a much closer look, Will couldn't tell which two.

The girls all bore a remarkable resemblance to one another. Not that he found that surprising. While listening to Li Toy bark instructions to them in their native tongue during the contract signings, Will had learned that they were family. His group of seven girls was two sets of sisters, first cousins to one another, who had been sold to Chinese "bride" brokers by their parents, whose farms had been devastated by drought.

In danger of starving, unable to feed themselves, their live-stock, and all their children, the parents had decided to keep their sons and sell their daughters for cash that would enable them to buy the rice and grain they needed to survive.

Will wondered whether the girls' parents felt as guilty about selling them as he did about buying them. He wondered whether his motives were as pure as theirs, or whether it mattered. The girls' parents had sold them to pay debts and to keep the rest of their families from starving. Will was fighting to keep from drowning. They were trying to save their families. He was trying to save himself. And still he dreamed of Jamie's wives. . . .

Continuing his check on his charges, Will exited Ling Yee's bedroom through the main door and moved to the last room at the back of the building on the south side of the hall, which belonged to Ah So. He knocked on the door, then gently eased it open. He expected it to be empty, expected Ah So to be the sister sharing the bed with Ah Woo or Ah Fook in Ling Yee's bedroom, but the room was occupied. Ah So was in bed. Her back was to him, the coverlet on the single bed pulled up close over her shoulders and neck, and unlike the other girls, this one had made use of the feather pillow, curving her left arm around it and hugging it to her face. She seemed different somehow, maybe taller than he remembered, despite the fact that she was curled into a tight ball in the center of the bed. Will stared at the covers. Not just taller. Taller and curvier. He frowned, amazed at the ability of a simple Chinese tunic and a pair of cotton trousers to hide a woman's assets. And yet, he'd seen her uncovered at the auction. He'd seen all of them uncovered at the auction, and he didn't remember feminine curves on any of them. Will closed his eyes, then opened them once again. Maybe he was just recalling the way the younger girls had looked. If he remembered correctly, Ah So was about fifteen. She had to be a bit curvier than her sisters and cousins, who had no curves at all.

Leaving Ah So's room, Will moved across the hall to the other bedrooms. These rooms had been assigned to Ah Woo,

Ah Fook, and Ah Lo, respectively. He knocked softly, then pushed the first door open, unsure of what he would find.

Ah Lo, the eldest of the seven at seventeen, sat up in bed as he opened the door.

"Shh." Will put a finger to his lips, then quietly retreated, closing the door behind him. In the room next door, Ah Fook was sound asleep alone in her bed. Ah Woo's bedroom was empty. The mystery was solved. It seemed Ah Woo had tiptoed across the hall to join the Ling sisters. She was sleeping in Ling Yee's bed.

With the girls all safe and tucked into bed, Will gave serious thought to returning to his, but, afraid of what his dreams might bring, he turned and headed downstairs.

He stopped briefly at the bar for a bottle of the hair of the dog that had bitten him after he and Jack had gotten the girls settled and into bed last night, then headed to the kitchen to put a pot of coffee on to boil.

Entering the kitchen, Will grabbed the coffeepot from its customary place on the stove. He primed the kitchen pump and, after checking to make sure Jack had measured the coffee and crushed an eggshell into it to keep the coffee grounds from floating to the surface, filled the pot with water. He set the pot on a rear burner, stirred the banked coals to life inside the stove, and added more coals from the scuttle to the firebox. His stomach rumbled, and Will checked the warming oven on the range for biscuits or bread and found it empty. The soup and the chicken and vegetables and rice from supper were also gone, the pots and pans left beside the sink. Glancing at the regulator clock on the wall, he saw that it was still too early to send to Ming's or one of the other kitchens along the street for something to eat, but the bakeries on Fillmore Street should be open for business in a half an hour, and the milkman would soon be making his rounds through the neighborhood.

His chore done, Will turned to pull a chair out from the kitchen table and discovered a dirty bowl, a spoon, a pair of wooden chopsticks, and an empty bar glass on the table. Seemed he wasn't the only one who'd worked up an appetite last night. Jack had polished off the last of the soup and chicken and rice and vegetables. Grabbing a clean mug from the overhead cabinet beside the sink, Will shoved the dirty dishes aside, pulled the half-empty whiskey bottle from his bathrobe pocket, sat down at the table, and waited for the coffee to boil.

Jack exited his rooms some ten minutes later and joined Will in the kitchen. "You're up early this morning. Coffee smells good. Is it ready yet?"

Will stood up as his second in command entered, then walked to the stove, grabbed a towel, and hefted the coffeepot. "You're just in time."

Jack snagged a mug from the cabinet and set it on the table along with the sugar bowl. "Apparently not."

Will frowned as he filled the mugs with the steaming brew. "Come again?"

Jack sat down at the table across from Will and nodded toward the dirty dishes. "Save any for me?"

"I didn't leave those there," Will told him. "I thought you did."

Jack shook his head. "I'm afraid not."

They looked at each other. "If it wasn't me," Will continued, "and it wasn't you, who was it? Kitchen help?"

Jack looked at the dirty pots and pans stacked beside the sink. "Kitchen was clean when Luis left last night." He added a spoonful of sugar to his coffee, then offered the bowl to Will. "One of the ladies, perhaps?"

"I don't think so." Will waved away the sugar bowl, then added a splash of whiskey to his coffee before offering the bottle to Jack. "Hair of the dog?"

Jack grimaced. "No, thanks." He rummaged around the kitchen pantry until he located a tin of biscuits. Retrieving a plate, Jack arranged the shortbread on it and set it on the table between them to share with their coffee.

Will corked the whiskey bottle and put it aside. "The ladies are all upstairs in their rooms."

"I left the soup and the chicken and rice in a covered bowl in the warming oven before I turned in," Jack said.

"Somebody ate it." He met Will's gaze. "It had to be one of the girls."

"The older girls are still in their beds." Will reached for a biscuit. "I know because I checked before I came downstairs. I don't believe any of them would leave the second floor without permission."

Jack knew it was unlikely, but he had to ask: "What about the younger ones?"

"The little ones can't reach the stove, much less handle a pot of soup. And while they were changing bedrooms upstairs, sleeping two and three to a bed, I don't think they would have ventured this far alone at night." Will took a bite of his shortbread.

"They are sleeping two and three to a bed?" Jack shook his head.

Will nodded. "Ling Yee and Ling Tsin were bunking with their sister, Ling Lau." Will washed the shortbread down with a swallow of coffee before explaining, "And Ah Woo and Ah So were sharing Ling Yee's bed. Wait a minute . . ." He paused. "Ah So was in her bedroom alone. And so were Ah Lo and Ah Fook." He looked at Jack. "How many girls was that?"

"Eight if you count Ah So twice," Jack confirmed, grabbing a shortbread for himself.

"I bought seven girls," Will said. "I brought seven girls home with me. Someone else was sleeping in Ah So's bed."

"So who's number eight, and where did she come from?" Jack asked.

"I don't know," Will admitted, "but I'll wager it's the same someone who helped herself to a bite to eat."

"You said there was a stowaway hiding in the corner of Li Toy's basement during the auction," Jack recalled. "A Kip Yee man."

"A person I *assumed* was a Kip Yee man," Will corrected. "What if it wasn't a Kip Yee man at all, but another girl from the auction? One trying to escape? One who followed us home because she had no place else to go?"

Jack set his coffee cup on the table with a thump. "You

said you left her sleeping upstairs. . . ." He looked over at Will.

"Yes. In Ah So's bedroom, with her face hidden by a pillow and the covers pulled up to her neck."

"Why don't we go find out who she is?" He got to his feet.

Will joined him, setting his mug aside and pushing his chair back from the table to stand up. "Yes. Why don't we?"

They heard the distinctive click of the front door latch unlocking before they reached the main salon.

"Damnation!" Will swore when they reached the door and found it standing ajar.

Jack hurried outside and onto the boardwalk, but whoever had slipped out of the Silken Angel Saloon at the crack of dawn was lost in the interminable fog that rolled off the San Francisco Bay, muffling sound and obscuring all but the closest buildings. "She got away." he announced unnecessarily as he returned to the main salon. "I lost her in the fog."

Will gritted his teeth so hard a muscle in his jaw twitched from the strain. "Could you tell if it was a girl?"

Jack shook his head. "Man. Woman. Great hairy ape. I couldn't see a damn thing."

A sense of foreboding sent Will racing back up the stairs. "Check the girls," he yelled to Jack. He opened Ah So's bedroom door first. The bed was neatly made, the coverlet pulled tightly over the mattress and the single feather pillow. There was no sign that the bed had ever been occupied. If he hadn't seen the figure sound asleep, Will would have sworn he'd imagined the whole thing. He stood in the doorway trying to puzzle it out.

"The girls are safe." Jack placed his hand on Will's shoulder. "All seven."

"Did you . . ."

Jack nodded. "Yeah, I checked to make sure they were breathing."

Will exhaled the breath he'd been holding. He'd prayed he was overreacting, but it wasn't uncommon for the tongs or disgruntled competitors to threaten a rival's business by doing away with the new merchandise. There had been instances where men from the warring tongs had gone into the cribs and suffocated, strangled, or cut the throats of the girls as a warning to the owners.

"Find anything?" Jack asked.

"Just that." Will pointed to the dresser.

Jack followed Will's lead and spotted several coins on top of the dresser. Stepping inside the room, Will walked over, scooped the coins off the furniture, and counted the money. One dollar and fifty cents American to cover the cost of one night's food and lodging, as posted on the sign on the wall at the foot of the stairs. He weighed the coins in his palm. "Whoever it was wasn't one of Li Toy's girls." He looked at Jack. "They don't have access to money. Li Toy collects the fee in cash before customers go upstairs or enter the cribs, and issues them a token. The only way one of her girls could have gotten this much money is if a customer gave it to her."

"And she was able to keep it hidden from Madam Harpy and her coworkers," Jack added. "She left money to pay for the use of the bed and for the food she ate, so she wasn't here to steal."

"The correct amount of money," Will pointed out. "Which means she knew how much we charge for a meal and one night's lodging, or she was capable of reading the posted rates."

"How many languages are represented?"

"English, French, Spanish, and Chinese." Will named the most frequent languages spoken in the Silken Angel Saloon. The gold rush of 'forty-nine had brought an influx of humanity from all parts of the globe that had all but overwhelmed the original Spanish settlement. The result was a cosmopolitan city with a variety of languages. The common men spoke their native languages with a range of dialects, some of which Will had a rudimentary vocabulary in and comprehension of. With the exception of tradesmen, almost no Chinese ever entered the saloon, but the Silken Angel routinely posted signs using Chinese characters.

"So our guest could be male or female and one of several nationalities," Jack mused.

"That's the sum of it," Will agreed, "except that I have the distinct feeling that our unexpected guest was female." He couldn't distinguish much about the figure sleeping in Ah So's bed except curves. Will remembered the curves and the slender arm hugging the pillow. "What man would sleep alone when there are two or three of-age females sleeping next door?"

"Other than you?" Jack asked.

Will shot him a withering look. "Other than me."

"Me, of course," Jack said, easing the tension they were both feeling and the rush of adrenaline that came with fear.

"Of course," Will acknowledged Jack's teasing. "Present company excluded. Any idea?"

"Not unless you're wrong about her being a female . . ."

"I don't think so."

"But it's possible?"

Will nodded. It wasn't likely, but theoretically it was possible.

"Then we're back to your Kip Yee man," Jack said.

Will paced the length of the room, stopping at the locked second-floor window. "Maybe," he conceded. "But would a Kip Yee man leave girls purchased at auction as prostitutes unmolested?"

"He would if Kip Yee dictated that the merchandise remain untouched."

"True. But why leave them?" Will paced back to the door. "If the object was to remove them from the Silken Angel and install them in one of the tong's establishments, why leave them behind?"

"Maybe the object of the exercise wasn't to take them tonight," Jack suggested. "Maybe he was simply reconnoitering the layout of the building, seeing if gaining entrance was possible. . . ."

Will looked over at Jack. "Which brings up the question, how the devil did he get in?"

"The saloon was open for business until two a.m., Will," Jack reminded him. "And you and I were preoccupied with getting the girls settled into their rooms and fed. He could have walked in the front door and stayed hidden somewhere until we locked up and went to bed."

"Then crept into the kitchen and helped himself to a meal while a former Pinkerton detective slept a few feet away."

Jack smiled. "While an *exhausted*"—he paused long enough to emphasize the word—"former Pinkerton detective slept a few feet away. I was probably snoring loud enough to wake the dead. And in fairness to our intruder, he'd have no way of knowing I was once a detective. Or your assistant at Craig Capital. As far as our sneak thief is concerned, I'm simply a barman."

"It's a brassy move just the same," Will said. "Whoever it was had to know there were two grown men in the place. He had to know he could have been discovered at any moment. By the girls. By you. Or by me."

Jack scratched his head. "Could be an act of desperation."

Will disagreed. "Desperate men don't leave money behind."

"Then it has to be Kip Yee replying to your message."

"I'd believe that if our intruder hadn't availed himself of a meal and a few hours of sleep." Will raked his fingers through his hair. "It just doesn't feel right. And I don't know that Kip Yee received my message."

"True," Jack agreed. "But you do know that by now, the tong knows the auction went off without a hitch and that you purchased a large portion of the merchandise they meant to steal. And if they know that, they're likely to retaliate. The gossip around Chinatown had it that Kip Yee wanted Madam Harpy's cargo. Badly."

Will considered the implications. "You're right, Jack. This must be the tong leader's way of letting me know that he can get to me—get to us—get to the girls—anytime he pleases." He looked at Jack. "At any rate, one thing is certain. . . ."

Jack winced.

"We need better security," Will concluded.

## Chapter Ten

> "When it is obvious that the goals cannot be reached,
> don't adjust the goals,
> adjust the action steps."
> —CONFUCIUS, 551–479 B.C.

Julie was breathing hard and soaked to the skin by the time she made it to Wu's Gum Saan Laundry on Mission Street. Zhing Wu greeted her as soon as Julie entered the lean-to shack, where Zhing was pulling clothes from the rinse water and wringing them by hand.

The lean-to belonged to Zhing. She'd built it herself from her meager earnings. She worked in the laundry with her father-in-law, cooked and cleaned and ran errands for him, but she'd never felt comfortable sharing his living space. Craving privacy, she'd built her lean-to on the opposite side of the laundry, away from Wu's slightly larger lean-to. It allowed her to be close enough to her father-in-law to see to his needs, but afforded her a measure of independence and privacy for the first time in her life.

"Jie Li, you're all wet. Where have you been?" Zhing demanded in her native tongue, her voice high and tight with strain. She called Julie by name, but gave it the Cantonese pronunciation. "I have been so worried since I woke up and saw that you did not come back for your ugly mission dress." She tossed a rolled-up shirt into a basket to await hanging, dried her hands on a towel, and pulled a bamboo screen away from the wall and positioned it so it would catch heat from the stove. "Get out of wet clothes while I make you some tea."

"I was trapped in the cellar of the Jade Dragon," Julie told her.

Zhing Wu shuddered. "How did you get trapped in that evil place after you collected dirty laundry and brought it to my husband's honorable father?"

Julie stepped behind the screen, toed off her cloth shoes, and began peeling off her wet socks and trousers. "I went back late yesterday afternoon to deliver the clean linen and got trapped." She hung her black trousers on the top of the bamboo screen, then placed her white socks beside them. She stood shivering in her tunic, waiting for Zhing to toss her a towel.

"You don't deliver clean linen to cellar of the Jade Dragon." Zhing whisked Julie's wet trousers and socks off the screen and replaced them with a dry towel. "You don't go in the Jade Dragon to deliver. You knock on back entrance door and give to girl who answers."

Julie took a deep breath. "*You* don't go in the Jade Dragon to deliver. *I* take the linens inside and put them in the cupboard for the girls."

"You do too much," Zhing scolded. "You spoil *loungei* girls."

"Don't call them that," Julie objected. "It's vulgar." The term was one of the commonly used Cantonese words for *prostitute*, but literally translated, it meant "woman always holding up her legs." "Besides . . ." Julie paused long enough to pull her sodden tunic over her head and drape it over the screen. "But for the grace of God . . ." Never overtly religious, despite her affiliation with the Salvationists, she was compelled to make the sign of the cross before undoing the length of cloth she used to bind her breasts and placing it on the top of the screen beside her tunic. She dried herself and wrapped the towel around her.

Zhing was waiting with a long flannel robe and slippers when Julie stepped from behind the screen. "What does that mean, Jie Li?"

Julie lifted an eyebrow in query. "What?"

" 'But for the grace of God.' "

"It means that the gods have favored us by not allowing us to become one of the unfortunate girls who live and work at the Jade Dragon," Julie translated.

"The gods may not always favor you, Jie Li," Zhing reminded her. "Not if you go into the Jade Dragon."

"I have to find my friend," Julie told her. "I have to know if Su Mi is trapped in that life. I had to see the auction for myself." She looked over at Zhing. "I had to know if she was there."

"Was she?" Zhing asked.

Julie shook her head. "No."

"Then you risk much for nothing, Jie Li. If you are caught, Wu and I may suffer for helping you." She placed a pot of tea and a cup on the small kitchen table, along with a bowl of noodles and chopsticks, and urged Julie to sit. Glancing at Julie's pile of wet clothes, Zhing clucked her tongue. "Clothing will not dry this morning." Retrieving the tin box she kept hidden under a floorboard near the stove, Zhing reached inside for the coins needed to buy Julie a new set of clothes. "I go to tailor shop to get you more Chinese clothes."

"Not this morning," Julie told her.

"What will you wear?" Zhing asked.

"My gray wool uniform dress."

Zhing sighed. "Today you go out as an English lady instead of a laundry girl?" That meant that Zhing would have to collect the day's dirty laundry from the boardinghouses without Julie's help.

Julie swallowed a mouthful of noodles. "I have to do missionary work today."

Zhing dragged a bathtub from beneath the kitchen table and positioned it near the stove, pulling the bamboo screen around it to shield it from the drafts. "I'll heat water. For English lady costume, Jie Li must bathe and wash hair."

Zhing Wu had helped Julie transform herself into Jie Li, the laundry girl, and back to Julia Jane Parham, missionary, several times over the past few days. The transformations were equally time-consuming. One required cosmetics and hair color; the other required the removal of cosmetics and hair color. Both meant more work for Zhing. Julie paid her well for her assistance, but she couldn't help feeling guilty for increasing Zhing's workload instead of decreasing it.

But Zhing didn't seem to mind. She enjoyed Julie's company. They were close in age, and Zhing appreciated Julie's offer of friendship and the opportunity to practice her English, and was genuinely grateful for the extra income she earned, which allowed her to purchase little luxuries for herself and for Wu that she would not have been able to afford otherwise.

Julie finished her bowl of noodles, drained the last of her tea, and got up from the table to help Zhing with the bath preparations, pumping water to add to the large pot Zhing kept on the stove to boil water.

Running a laundry was hard, hot, backbreaking work, but the one by-product was plenty of soap and hot water. Julie had brought bars of her favorite soap to use in her bath and for Zhing to use on her laundry. Zhing's lean-to wasn't much of a house when compared to the walled mansion Julie called home. It wasn't nearly as nice as the Russ House Hotel or as large as the mission dormitory, but because it functioned as a laundry, it had water from the city's wells delivered right to the kitchen pump. And unlike the women's dormitory at the mission, the only two women who shared it were Zhing Wu and Julie. "When you go to the apothecary shop for Wu, would you get a better temporary dye for my hair for my laundry girl disguise? I'll need it and my disguise tonight." Julie poured a final pail of water into the pot on the stove as Zhing beckoned her to the sink. Julie pulled her hair forward and bent as Zhing pumped water over it. "I'll leave you money to purchase enough for me and for Wu." The fact that Zhing's father-in-law dyed his hair to hide the silver strands in his queue was a closely kept secret Zhing had confided to Julie the day before, when she'd offered Julie the use of his dye. It was, Zhing assured her, better than the coffee-and-vinegar concoction Julie used, easier to apply, and did not run like bootblack, but could be washed out with soap and water and a vinegar rinse. "Why need disguise tonight? We do not collect or deliver laundry at night. And why you pay for Wu's hairdressing when you already help at laundry for free?"

"I have something I need to do tonight and I can't do it in my mission dress. And I don't want Wu to run low on hair dye," Julie managed to reply despite the water cascading over her head, "and wonder why."

"Wu won't question. He looks the opposite way."

Julie's heart began to race. "You told him about me?"

"No need. He already knew you are 'Bringing in the Sheaves' girl who wears China clothes and works in laundry." Zhing's answer was matter-of-fact as she rinsed the last of the soap out of Julie's hair, twisted it to wring out the water, and handed Julie a towel.

Julie wrapped her hair in the towel, then helped Zhing fill the bathtub for her bath. "Did he ask why?"

"I told him you help us to earn favor from your gods." Zhing emptied a pail of boiling water into the tub.

Julie poured two more pails of cold water into it and Zhing added another pail of boiling water and peach-scented bath salts. Testing the temperature of the water with her big toe, Julie slipped the flannel robe off and climbed into the bath tub. She leaned back, letting her head rest against the rim, and slid down until the water reached her shoulders. Closing her eyes, Julie allowed the hot water to soak away the aches and pains and the bone-chilling cold that had accompanied her early morning journey through the thick fog.

The thick fog that had facilitated her escape from the Silken Angel Saloon. She'd come very close to being caught. Too close. It was sheer luck that the sound of the bedroom door softly closing woke her from a deep, dreamless sleep. She'd managed to slip quietly out of bed and tidy the room, because she'd crawled into it fully clothed after helping herself to the leftover soup and chicken and vegetables she'd found on the kitchen range. Making her escape from the saloon had been almost as frustrating as waiting for her chance to slip in. But nothing was as frustrating as knowing she'd failed to rescue the girls Will Keegan had purchased at the auction.

After making her way from the kitchen, through the main salon, and up the stairs to the second-floor bedrooms, Julie had found the girls from the auction sleeping soundly. She'd planned to get in and out of the Silken Angel Saloon without Keegan being the wiser. She intended to liberate the unfortunate girls right from under his nose. She'd planned to lead them out of bondage, out of the Silken Angel Saloon, and out of Chinatown to the mission, but to her dismay Julie discovered she wasn't as resolute as she thought she'd be. Julie was cold and wet, hungry and tired, and her resolve had fallen victim to her need for food, shelter, and sleep. "Wake up, Jie Li!" Zhing touched her shoulder. "You cannot be lazy here."

*Lazy?* Julie opened her eyes and realized she'd fallen asleep again. She was burning her candle at both ends as Jie Li and Julie; working as a laundry girl, collecting dirty clothes, delivering clean ones, hauling pails of water to and fro, and keeping up with her everyday missionary chores and the duties to which she'd been assigned was exhausting for a young lady who had never done anything more strenuous than ride horses and garden. It seemed as if she fell asleep every time she closed her eyes. "Sorry."

"Finish bathing before the water gets cold, Jie Li. So I can help you dress before I leave to collect dirty laundry."

Julie did as Zhing Wu asked and bathed in record time, scrubbing her face and neck, arms, and hands, washing away all traces of Jie Li. Exiting the tub, she removed the towel from her hair and reached for a comb while Zhing laid out her undergarments.

Pulling on stockings and garters, drawers and petticoats, chemise and corset seemed strange after the freedom of her peasant clothes. Julie sucked in a deep breath as Zhing tugged on her corset strings, and held it while she tied them. Julie barely breathed as she smoothed her camisole over her corset. When she was finished, Zhing dropped the gray wool dress over her head. Julie fastened the brass buttons on the military-style jacket that covered the plain sleeveless bodice, pinned her hair into a smooth bun at the nape of her neck, placed her gray bonnet on her head, and tied the ribbons beneath her chin. Turning to Zhing, she asked, "How do I look?"

"Like an English missionary girl in an ugly dress," Zhing replied in Cantonese as she handed Julie her brushed and polished black boots.

Julie sat down on a kitchen chair to put them on. They weren't as comfortable as her black cloth shoes, but they were warm and dry and sturdy—exactly what she'd wished for when she was standing in the cold outside the Silken Angel the night before.

"Don't forget your cloak." Zhing took Julie's gray wool cloak off a peg on the wall and handed it to her.

"Thank you, Zhing," Julie said. "I don't know how I'd manage without you." Reaching into the pocket of her cloak, she removed a small leather purse and handed Zhing two ten-dollar gold pieces. "Will this be enough for a new tunic and trousers and shoes and the hair color?"

Zhing nodded. "More than enough, Jie Li. I'll bring your change when I bring your clothes. Where will you be?"

"I'll be at the mission later this afternoon, or the Russ House," Julie told her.

"Be careful, Jie Li," Zhing told her as Julie walked to the door. "And keep hat on and hair covered in Chinatown."

Julie paused, her hand on the door latch, puzzled by Zhing's order. "Why? Didn't all the dark stain wash out?"

Zhing nodded. "Dark stain is all gone, but so is safety."

Julie frowned. "I don't understand."

"Chinese girls not the only treasure in Chinatown," Zhing told her. "Fiery hair is of great value to Chinatown madams."

Julie sighed. The red hair that had been the bane of her existence since childhood was of great value in Chinatown? Zhing had given her another reason to despise it—and one more thing to worry about in her search for Su Mi. . . .

## Chapter Eleven

*"I am contented with the violence of my own
character; it draws a line for me between
friends and enemies."*
—LADY HESTER STANHOPE, 1776–1839

Sowing in the morning, sowing seeds of kindness. Sowing
in the noontime and the dewy eve . . .'" The words of the
hymn announced her arrival moments before Julie stepped
onto the boardwalk outside the Silken Angel Saloon.

Seated on a chair in the main salon, Will Keegan looked up
from his breakfast of steak and eggs and coffee and saw Julia
Jane Parham in all her tambourine-banging, psalm-singing
glory through the newly cleaned gold-lettered plate-glass window. Will was so relieved to see her he was willing to overlook
the fact that her visit was premature. There was a week left in
the month. Miss Parham had violated their agreement.

He smiled to let her know there were no hard feelings on
his part.

She smiled back. Right before she began the refrain of that
infernal song: " 'Bringing in the sheaves, bringing in the
sheaves, we shall come rejoicing, bringing in the sheaves. . . .' "
Right before she dropped her tambourine on the boardwalk
and raised a parasol with a silver knob handle.

"No!" Will shouted, jumping to his feet, overturning the
table and his breakfast in the process.

The sound of the table and his breakfast dishes and cutlery crashing to the floor was drowned out by the sound of the plate-glass window in the main salon shattering. Glass flew everywhere. Shards of it littered the floor and covered the tables and chairs nearest the window. Will watched as Julia Jane Parham raked her battered parasol along the bottom edge of the windowframe, dislodging the remaining bits of glass. Retrieving her tambourine from the boardwalk, she hitched up her skirts, flashing shapely ankles and calves in the process, and climbed through the open storefront. Glass fragments crunched beneath her boots as she made a beeline for the bar.

"Are you crazy?" Will roared, grabbing her around the waist and lifting her off her feet as she swung her parasol at his head. He ducked, narrowly avoiding being bashed in the face. She missed his head, but she connected with the crystals dangling from one of the wall sconces and a bottle of whiskey sitting on the bar. She sent the whiskey bottle skidding down the polished mahogany bar and into three glasses. The whiskey and the glasses sailed off the end of the bar and crashed to the floor in a spray of spirits and broken glass. "You could have been sliced to ribbons! What the hell do you think you're doing?"

"As much damage as possible!" she shouted back, wriggling in his grasp, trying with all her might to smash the rows of liquor bottles lining the shelf in front of the mirror behind the bar.

The saloon was empty at this time of morning, but it wouldn't stay that way for long. Not with Julia Jane wreaking havoc on the place. They were sure to draw a crowd of onlookers and a constable or two. An angry red-haired Salvationist wielding a parasol was hard to miss. The last thing they needed was to provide the residents of Chinatown with fodder for the gossip and rumor mills. He didn't want Li Toy or members of the Kip Yee tong or any other tong nosing around, or for the police to come calling. Until he learned whom he could and whom he couldn't trust, Will didn't want members of the San Francisco Police Department anywhere near the Silken Angel.

Not with Julia Jane Parham on the premises.

Holding her in a viselike grip with one arm, Will wrested the parasol from her grasp with his other arm and tossed it aside before she could do any more damage to the saloon or to him. "I can see that," he replied. "What I want to know is why?"

"I should think you would know why!"

"If I knew why, I wouldn't be asking."

She kicked at him, and her booted foot connected with his shinbone.

"Ouch! Dammit! That hurt!" He yelped.

"Let me go!" she ordered. "Or I'll do worse!"

She smelled like peaches. Peaches and good Irish whiskey. The combination was surprisingly complementary and highly intoxicating. Will found it hard to keep from dropping her, with all her thrashing about, and it was difficult to protect himself from her boot heels when all he could think about was how good she felt and how good she smelled. He resorted to threats. "If you don't stop wiggling, I'm going to drop you."

"Drop me onto my feet and I'll stop wiggling," she told him, kicking out once again, hoping to connect with more bone and sinew.

Will managed to avoid her kick, but several chairs and a table were overturned in the process. "You kick me again and I'll turn you over my knee and give you the paddling you deserve."

"You wouldn't dare!" Julie sputtered, more incensed at being held so easily than she was at his threat.

"Try me."

She was spoiling for a fight and rebelled against being thwarted, but Julie recognized the steel in his voice. She'd met her match in Will Keegan. He was serious, and she didn't doubt for a minute that he would do exactly what he'd threatened. "Put me down at once!"

"I'll be happy to," he told her. "If you agree to live up to your promise not to smash the place and behave."

She continued to struggle against him. "That promise is no longer valid."

"Oh?" He grunted when she elbowed him in the ribs. "Why not?"

"I made that promise because I thought you were a *gentleman*," Julie informed him.

"I accepted it because I thought you were a *lady*," Will retorted.

"I *am* a lady."

"Prove it by behaving like one," he challenged.

Instead of meeting his challenge, Julie offered one of her own: "When you prove that you live alone above your place of business."

Will remained silent.

Julie was triumphant. "I was a fool to believe you were a gentleman. I should have trusted my instincts. I knew I was right. I knew you were lying about living alone upstairs. I knew that wasn't the case at all."

"It was very much the case," he retorted. "At the time. And I'm as much a gentleman now as I was then."

"I wouldn't boast about it," she told him. "It doesn't speak well of your character."

"And going back on your word and wrecking my saloon speaks well of yours?"

"My motives are pure," she argued. "Yours are not."

"I doubt that," Will shot back, his tone dripping with sarcasm. "Are you going to keep your promise and behave or not?"

She declined to answer.

Will heaved a sigh. She didn't weigh that much, but he was beginning to tire, holding her off the ground while she struggled to free herself. She was testing his strength as well as his patience. "I'll take that as a no. And since you don't appear inclined to honor your promise, I guess we'll stay as we are awhile longer."

"Since you don't appear inclined to release me," Julie pitched his words right back at him, "I'm going to scream bloody murder, and I promise I'll have every constable in the district swarming around you in minutes."

"Scream away, my lady," he invited, calling her bluff, praying she didn't call his. "And when the constables get here, I promise to let you explain why you broke my window, vandalized the grand parlor, and attacked my person without provocation."

"Without *provocation*?" She huffed. "I assure you, Mr. Keegan, that I had plenty of *provocation*. Seven thousand dollars' worth of *provocation* . . ."

He looked down at her. Her ugly gray bonnet was askew, the bow beneath her chin partially untied, and the brim shielding her face covered with slivers of glass. There were more splinters clinging to her cape and dress. And although it didn't show on the dark gray wool, Will knew her garments were stained with whiskey. A line of tiny blood droplets beaded along a small scratch on her cheek. Her blue eyes shot sparks at him, nearly singeing him with the heat of her wrath. "That was you last night? Behind the barrels?"

"Of course it was me," she informed him.

Will was as alarmed as he was stunned by her admission— so alarmed the hair on the back of his neck stood on end. "Have you lost your mind? Do you know what might have happened to you if you had been found out?"

"The same as those poor unfortunate girls, I suppose."

"You should be so lucky." He snorted. "I brought seven of those girls home with me."

"You *bought* seven of those girls," she reminded him. "You purchased them like cattle."

"That's what has your dander up this morning? That's what sparked this display of missionary zeal . . . ?"

"Of course." Julie smirked at him. "I'm a missionary. Missionary *zeal*, as you call it, is one of the requirements."

Will glanced at the damage in the main salon. "I call it wanton destruction, and I'm heartily sick of it."

"I could say the same of you," she told him. "After three weeks in San Francisco, I'm heartily sick of men like you. . . ."

"Men like me?" He arched an eyebrow in an elegant gesture made up of equal parts query and haughtiness.

"Gentlemen who become *pimps*."

Surprised that she knew the word and stung by her use of it, Will nearly made good on his threat to drop her amid the liquor and the broken glass. "Is that what you think of me?"

"What else should I think? You purchased women at an auction. You brought them to your saloon." She paused to gather her thoughts before continuing. "I can only assume that like so many other men in San Francisco, you intend to profit from their misery, to prey upon poor ignorant Chinese peasant girls and use them to . . . to . . ."

"To what, Miss Parham?"

"To . . . to slake *your* passions." Julie gasped for breath as she felt the muscles in his arm tighten involuntarily. Her face flaming with indignation and embarrassment, she snapped, "And I'll thank you to remember that as far as you're concerned, it's not *Miss* Parham; it's *Lady Julia*."

Her sudden disdain for him sparked his temper. "I'll thank you to remember that this is the United States of America. We put an end to British rule. We're a democratic republic with little use for aristocratic titles. Here in my saloon, it's Miss Parham or Miss Julia. *No ladies allowed*." His words were a reminder of her earlier visit to the Silken Angel, when he'd refused to risk her reputation by allowing her inside the main parlor.

"Yes, of course," Julia replied in her most proper, aristocratic English. "But I seem to recall hearing that the United States of America had *abolished* slavery." She gave him another of her proper little British smirks. "How wonderfully *democratic* of you to find a way to circumvent that law in order to purchase Chinese females as chattel for your personal pleasure." She glared at him. "And how dare you preach American civics to me when, judging by your accent, you are as British as I am!"

"Not anymore," he informed her. "I became an American citizen when I immigrated to this country." Will bit the inside of his cheek to keep the muscle there from twitching. He was annoyed as hell, but he couldn't ignore the fact that he found her incredibly alluring. He was drawn to the little spitfire like a moth to a flame. And like the moth, he'd have his wings singed if he wasn't careful. There was no doubt about it: Julia Jane was maddening. Intelligent, courageous, daring, beautiful, and absolutely maddening. She was different, and that intrigued him. She wasn't coy and she didn't resort to feminine wiles to get her way. She didn't cry or plead or cajole. She stood her ground like a bare-knuckled prizefighter and gave measure for measure every bit as good as she got. After years spent in the company of docile Chinese women—after years spent mooning over Mei Ling—Will found that refreshing and stimulating. "You seem awfully interested in my personal pleasure, Miss Parham," he drawled, to see how she'd react. To see whether he affected her as much as she affected him.

"I am not!" she exclaimed. "My interest in you is purely professional."

"Liar," he whispered close to her ear. "Methinks the lady doth protest too much. Your interest in me is completely personal. It's neither pure nor professional."

Julie's heart began a rapid tattoo. He was too close. She could smell the citrus-and-sandalwood scent of his shaving soap. It mingled with the smell of the liquor, tickling her nose, imploring her to investigate. He was holding her too closely. She could feel his breath on her neck and the shell of her ear, feel the heat of his body as he gripped her below her bosom. Having him pressed against her, having him surround her, made it hard to breathe and impossible to think of anything but pleasure. It took all the concentration she could muster to keep up with the conversation and be able to form coherent sentences. "You are the liar. I don't care a morsel about your personal . . ."

"Passion?" he suggested. "Pleasure? *Desires?*"

Julie shivered in his arms as warmth spread through her. "Nature," she squeaked in a voice that sounded nothing like hers. "My sole concern is for those poor unfortunate girls you purchased and installed on the second floor of your establishment."

Will loosened his grip enough to slip his arm beneath her jacket. He felt the boning of her corset through the wool covering her bodice, pictured the whalebone cupping her breasts, and remembered the curves beneath the coverlet in Ah So's bed. If she was the one who had hidden behind the barrels at the Jade Dragon, was she also the one who had raided his kitchen larder and slept beneath his roof? "How do you know where they're installed?"

She hesitated a moment before she answered. "Everybody knows the second floor of a saloon is reserved for the girls who entertain the male customers."

"For your information, Miss Parham, I don't slake my passions on poor unfortunate Chinese girls." Will didn't know why he volunteered that bit of information. Maybe it was because he didn't like the idea of her thinking he was a monster who bought and raped young girls and children. "I save them for willing young ladies with red hair and blue eyes. . . ."

Her legs went weak. "Oh."

Will held her tighter, keeping her upright and against him. "Yes, 'oh,'" he murmured.

Caught up in Will's presence, Julie found it nearly impossible to think of anything except the feel of Will Keegan surrounding her—the way *she* felt in his arms. Until she met him, she'd never engaged in any manner of verbal sparring with a member of the opposite sex. But something about him spurred her on. Something about Will Keegan intrigued her. Excited her. He was big and handsome and nearly twice her size. He was unscrupulous and a trafficker in human flesh. She should be terrified. But she wasn't terrified. She was exhilarated and fascinated and thrilled. And she discovered she liked playing with fire—as long as he was holding the torch. As strange as it seemed, when she was with him, Julie felt safe and reckless, and entirely secure in the knowledge that he wouldn't allow her to get burned. "You bought them for someone's pleasure," she accused. "If not your own."

Will didn't like the idea of her not believing him any more than he liked the idea of her thinking he was a lecher. "Did it ever occur to you that I bought them in order to give them better lives than the ones they would have with Madam Harpy? Did it ever occur to you that I bought them to keep other men from buying them?"

Julie was ashamed to admit that the thought hadn't occurred to her. She had done the very unmissionary, un-Christian, uncharitable thing and automatically believed the worst of him. "No. Did you?"

He nodded.

"Let me go," she said softly.

Will hesitated.

"I promise to behave," she added. "And not to smash anything else."

He loosened his grip and let his arm drop to his side, then took a step backward, putting the proper distance between them.

"What are you going to do with them?"

"I'm not going to *slake* my passions on them or strangle them in their sleep or cut their throats or sell them to anyone else," he assured her. "I'm not going to rent them out."

She looked up at him. "Then what?"

"I'm going to keep them safe from the people who would harm them," he admitted.

"Why should I trust you?" she asked. "When you lied to me before."

Will looked her in the eye. "I didn't lie to you. There weren't any girls upstairs."

"Only because you hadn't bought them yet," she countered. "What about now? What will I find if I go up the stairs this morning? Are the rooms still empty? Were you alone up there last night?"

"I was alone in my bed last night." His voice was low, melodic, tempting. "As you well know, since you spent the night in the bedroom down the hall from mine."

She *had* spent the night in the bedroom down the hall from his last night, but she wouldn't tell him that. Not yet. Nor would she overlook the fact that he'd chosen to evade. "You didn't answer my question, Mr. Keegan."

"You either trust me or you don't, Julia Jane."

"You *bought* human beings."

"Would you rather I had left them to Madam Harpy's tender care?" he asked.

"No, of course not."

"Then you agree they're better off today than they were last night?"

"That depends on where they are today, and with whom."

"They're safe from the person who would do them harm," Will reminded her. "As are you, for the moment."

She was clearly surprised. "Who would harm me?"

Will frowned at her, then turned to look at the damage she'd done to the grand parlor. "That depends on how many saloons you've smashed and how many questions you've asked, how many people your singing has annoyed, and how many girls you've tried to rescue. . . ." He paused for effect. "There could be hundreds of people in Chinatown alone." He hoped he was exaggerating, hoped there weren't hundreds of angry purveyors of vice out to silence Julia Jane Parham. He didn't know whether there were more; he knew of only one. And it was only fair that he warn her.

"I haven't smashed any saloons, done any singing, or tried to rescue any girls," she protested.

He shot her a wry look. "All evidence to the contrary."

Julie had the grace to blush. "Except here today."

"I hope not," Will said. "Because you've already made one powerful enemy. And believe me, this one is enough."

"I may not believe you're a gentleman, entirely," Julie began, "but I don't believe you would do me harm."

Will gave a short laugh. "Damned with faint praise once again."

She tried again. "I'll pay for your window."

"My window is the least of your concerns," Will told her. "The gossip around Chinatown is that Madam Harpy wants to quiet your singing."

Julie pretended to misunderstand his meaning. "What has that woman got against my singing?" she demanded to know. "And who is she to criticize? She's got a voice like a screech owl."

"She doesn't like the song you sing. And she doesn't like the questions you ask."

Julie pulled herself up to her full height and began brushing the bits of glass from her cape and from her dress. "As you pointed out, this is the United States. Free speech is a right guaranteed by the Constitution."

"In theory, yes. In reality, no," he said. "It may be in San Francisco, but Chinatown isn't the United States. Not yet."

Reaching over, Julie bent down to get her broken parasol. "I'll take my chances."

Will placed his foot on the umbrella. "Your chances aren't very good. Not when she's hired a professional to kill you."

Julie felt the blood drain from her face, and her knees shook so badly she lost her balance. She would have fallen if Will hadn't reached out to steady her. "She hired someone to *kill* me?"

"That's what I've heard."

"From whom?"

Will didn't answer.

"From whom?" she repeated. "Where did you hear this? Who told you?"

"Li Toy."

*"Dear Lord."* Julie lost her fight to stay on her feet and sat down hard on the chair Will shoved at her. "She told you she hired someone to kill me?"

"Yes."

"I don't believe it."

"You either trust me or you don't."

"I don't mean you," Julie said. "I mean the situation. If she admitted to you that she hired someone to kill me, it should be a simple matter of going to the police, telling them what you told me, and letting them take care of it."

Will didn't mince words. "The police intend to take care of it. They intend to take care of you for Madam Harpy. At least, one of them does."

"The police?" Her teeth began to chatter.

Will walked to the bar, stepped over the broken glass and puddle of whiskey on the floor beside it, and grabbed a clean glass and a bottle of brandy from the row of bottles in front of the mirror. He poured a measure of brandy into the glass and carried it back to Julie. "Here," he said, pressing the glass against her lips, "drink this."

She drained the glass, coughing and sputtering as the liquor burned a path from her mouth to her stomach.

"Better?" he asked when her coughing subsided and color returned to her face.

"Yes, thank you." Julie's voice was very small, her words very polite as she looked up at him. "Do you know who?"

Will shook his head. "It could be anyone."

"I can't believe a policeman would . . ."

"Agree to eliminate a problem for a notorious madam?" Will finished her thought. "And accept payment for doing so? By now, you must realize this city is filled with corrupt police, politicians, and city officials . . ." Will told her. "Get out of San Francisco. Go home. Madam Harpy's reach is long, but if you leave here and lie low, if you stop asking questions and stop poking your nose into other people's affairs, there's a chance Li Toy might call off her dog and forget about you."

"I can't. I can't go home. Not yet. Not until I've done what I came here to do." She looked up at Will.

He read the trepidation in her eyes. She was afraid, but not for herself. Her fear was for someone or something else. Will wanted to shake her. Or take her in his arms and keep her there until he knew she was safe. "Is what you're trying to do worth your life?"

Julie handed Will her glass, then pushed to her feet. "Is what you're doing worth your immortal soul?"

"Touché." He acknowledged her point. "But our odds are different. My risk is minimal. I lost my soul a long time ago."

"I believe in redemption," Julie said. "I'm a Salvationist."

"You may be one of them," he conceded. "You may be the best of them. But being a Salvationist doesn't mean they'll protect you."

She turned and walked back across the broken glass and through the empty windowframe. "They don't have to, Mr. Keegan." Julie managed a tremulous smile. "I can take care of myself."

# Chapter Twelve

❧

*"Faith in oneself is the best and safest course."*
—MICHELANGELO, 1475–1564

What a mess! Who would think one little lady could do so much damage with a frilly little umbrella?"

Will turned from the front window to find Jack O'Brien behind the bar. "I would. Now that I've seen Typhoon Julia in action."

Jack laughed at the appellation. "*Typhoon* Julia?"

Will glared at him. "Or its near equivalent. Where the devil were you? And how did you get in here without my hearing you?"

"I was coming up from the wine cellar when I heard glass breaking." Jack shrugged his shoulders. "Call me a coward, but I decided to wait until the firestorm ended before I put in an appearance. I wasn't all that keen on giving her another target or adding fuel to the flame. I knew you were here and I was sure you could handle the situation."

"That makes one of us," Will replied, although if truth be told, he had handled the situation and enjoyed every minute of it. "How long have you been standing there?"

"Long enough to catch Miss Parham's exit through what's left of our window."

Will arched an eyebrow in silent query.

"You were concentrating so fully on her departure you wouldn't have heard a brass band march into the saloon. I'm considerably quieter." Jack smiled. "I take it she went back on her word and broke her promise to you."

Will grinned. "Along with everything else."

Jack let out a whistle of admiration. "She managed to put the temperance sisterhood to shame. You must be so proud. . . ."

Will welcomed Jack's tongue-in-cheek humor. "Strangely enough I am. I'm in need of a new front window, a new place setting of Meissen china and bar glasses, liquor, and replacement crystals for the wall sconces, but it took a great deal of moral courage for her to do what she did. And I find that quality in a woman quite admirable."

"From what I've seen, Miss Parham is a young lady to be admired," Jack agreed. "She's a lot stronger than she looks, and she has a devil of a redhead's temper." Grabbing a broom and a dustpan, he began sweeping up the glass around the bar. "What set her off?"

"The fact that we have upstairs guests."

"That would do it." Jack bent down and began to pick up the largest pieces of the broken bottle and the bar glasses. "She is a Salvationist, after all. 'Tis a crying shame about the whiskey, though." His brogue was strong, and his inflection made it seem as if the loss of the whiskey were far more serious than the purchase of the seven Chinese beauties sleeping one floor above them. Though how they could sleep through the racket Julia Jane had made was anyone's guess.

Will laughed. "That was an accident. She was swinging for my head," he explained as he began righting tables and chairs that had been knocked over during Julia Jane's struggles. "The whiskey bottle got in the way."

Jack nodded. "It's good to know she wasn't on a mission to destroy our store of liquor."

"She *was* on a mission to destroy, and the bar was a target, but not because she believes alcohol is the devil's brew as the temperance women do. She willingly drained the brandy I gave her when her teeth began chattering and her knees gave out," Will elaborated. "Her mission was to smash as much glass and inflict as much interior damage to the Silken Angel as she could."

"Glad you were able to save the bar mirror and all the display bottles, which is more than I can say about our last encounter with the Women's Temperance League."

"Luckily I managed to get an arm around her before she reached the bar."

"You were taken unawares the last time glass breakers came to call. This time you knew what to expect."

"And whom to expect," Will admitted. "I heard her singing a block away."

"That must have been a relief," Jack said. "After the past few nights . . ."

Nights Will had spent searching for her after learning Li Toy had hired someone to kill her.

Will couldn't deny it. He gave Jack a wry smile. "It was such a relief, she was brandishing her parasol outside the window before I realized what she intended." He shook his head. "I'm amazed she was able to break the window, and I can't believe I didn't see this coming. . . ."

"She gave you her word," Jack reminded him. "You believed her."

Will glanced at the damage Julia Jane had inflicted. "Imagine me trusting a missionary. . . ."

Jack laughed, well aware that Will and his two older sisters had grown up in Hong Kong with Scots-Irish Presbyterian missionary parents. He put down his broom, then walked over and clapped his boss on the shoulder. "Live and learn, boyo. Live and learn."

Will smiled. "We'll have to move our plans back a few hours while we take care of the debris left by Typhoon Julia."

Jack nodded. "We'll manage."

"When Luis comes in, send him around to Montgomery Street Glass to order a new storefront," Will directed. "Thicker this time."

"Any changes in style or lettering?" Jack asked.

"No," Will answered. "Same lettering. Same gold leaf. They have the particulars. Ask them to send white canvas and some workers to hang it until the window is ready for installation. And ask them to send the bill for it to Miss Julia Jane Parham in care of the Salvationist mission."

Jack looked stunned. A gentleman did not demand payment from a lady for any reason. And Will Keegan was every inch a gentleman. "Will . . ."

"She said she'd pay for the storefront." Will thought for a moment, then came to his senses. "Never mind. I'll take care of the storefront." He turned to Jack. "And I'll take the matter up with Miss Parham later. . . ."

That discussion wouldn't go well for Miss Parham. Jack had seen that determined glint in Will's eyes before. Will Keegan had earned his reputation for being an iron-fisted negotiator, making thousands of dollars for Craig Capital, Ltd. "Should I warn Miss Parham of the impending negotiations?" Jack joked. "Or should we simply install a fence around the new window?"

"And give her another challenge to overcome?" Will retorted.

"It's either that or leave the canvas in place."

"Lumber would be a better option," Will deadpanned. "I was thinking shutters might be a good idea. The canvas would save us money replacing storefronts, but what we'd save there, we'd lose in whiskey. There would be no protecting our liquor from temperance women or drunks or even our thirsty guests, and no privacy or protection for our other enterprises from enemies with sharp knives or a pair of scissors. And think what we'd have to pay out in additional security. . . ."

The two men exchanged looks. Sometimes you simply had to find the humor in a situation. The stakes were high. For them. For Julia Jane Parham. And for the seven young women upstairs. The fact that an intruder had spent the night in a bed upstairs had played a major part in their decision to hire additional men to help protect the occupants of the second-floor bedrooms. "I see your point."

"Where do we stand on that issue?" Will asked.

"Since we dare not go to the police for help, I wired my brother, Murphy, for suggestions when I went to order milk and breakfast this morning," Jack told him. "Then I wired the Pinkerton agency requesting that the men on Murphy's list be assigned here until further notice." Anticipating Will's next question, Jack continued. "I haven't received the reply from the Denver office yet."

"I thought the Pinkertons maintained an office in San Francisco."

"A small one," Jack replied, "but we've no way of knowing if it's been compromised. Better to go with out-of-towners until we know who we can trust."

"Agreed."

Jack fixed Will with a hard stare. "Speaking of trust, did you tell Miss Parham about the threat to her safety?"

Will's mouth hardened into a grim line. "I did."

"How did she take the news?"

"She found it hard to believe the police department is filled with men willing to sell themselves and their guns to a notorious madam for cash."

"She didn't believe you?"

"She believed me," Will said. "She didn't believe the city constables were less than trustworthy. . . ."

"But you convinced her otherwise? She realizes she's in danger?"

Will recognized the concern in Jack's voice. He shared it. The threat to Julia Jane was real. If Li Toy wanted Julia Jane dead, her life was forfeit. It was simply a matter of time. "She seemed more concerned about my immortal soul than with her mortal life. She assured me she could take care of herself."

"What are you going to do?" Jack demanded. "You can't run this place, meet with Malcolm at Craig Capital every Tuesday, and walk the streets at night keeping watch for Miss Parham. You have to sleep sometime. . . ."

"That's another reason we need extra security," Will replied. "Miss Parham may believe she can take care of herself. She may not mind risking her life, but I do."

"So you're going to become her guardian angel?" Jack guessed.

"I wouldn't mention that around Typhoon Julia if I were you." Will handed the broom and dustpan back to Jack.

"Your secret is safe with me."


THE ACTIVITY GOT UNDER WAY IN EARNEST ONCE THE workmen from Montgomery Street Glass installed the canvas. Jack supervised the workers and hired extras to help with the cleanup while Will saw to the care and feeding of the girls.

Speaking to them in Cantonese, Will detailed the plans for the evening and what they might expect. He explained that the two men sitting on the chairs on either side of the landing were there to protect them, and that they were to tell him if anyone attempted to accost them in any way. He assured them that he wouldn't hurt them or allow anyone else to hurt them. He explained that they would all be staying together in one room for the remainder of their stay at the Silken Angel, and that their stay was temporary.

Reading the expressions on their faces, Will realized they didn't believe a word of what he was saying. They didn't trust him. And Will couldn't blame them. He had witnessed some of the torment they had endured while in Madam Harpy's dubious care, and could only imagine the hell they had endured on the journey from Hong Kong. The fact that their previous captors were all Chinese should have helped him earn a measure of trust, but these girls were too wounded by the betrayals they had endured to trust the white foreign devil who had witnessed their humiliation, then purchased them and brought them here.

And Will was honest enough to admit that he had given them no reason to trust him. Or anyone else in the Flowery Flag Nation. It would take more than food and a soft bed and a few hours of tender care to earn their trust. Or help them learn to trust.

With one exception.

Little Tsin. She had fallen asleep in his arms as he carried her from the Jade Dragon, trusting him to keep her safe while she slept. Trusting he wouldn't drop her or abandon her or hurt her. Will couldn't ask for a greater demonstration of pure trust than that. Every time she looked at him with her big brown eyes, Will was struck by her resemblance to Jamie's daughter Garnet, who wore her heart on her sleeve for everyone to see. Reaching over, he picked up her empty bowl. "Would you like more porridge?"

Tsin froze. She didn't move a muscle or utter a sound of protest. She just watched in silence as he removed her bowl and seemed to will herself to disappear.

The other girls were just as quiet. Everything stopped. Whereas minutes before the kitchen had been filled with the sounds of breakfast—with the soft clinking of spoons against pottery bowls and the sounds of mugs thudding against the surface of the table and the rattle of the older girls' teacups against their saucers—now there was deafening silence.

Long accustomed to the chaos at Jamie and Elizabeth's breakfast table, where four little girls made enough racket to put the New Year celebrations to shame, Will couldn't believe seven girls could create such profoundly deafening silence. It was as if they were all bracing themselves for whatever came next, as if the removal of Tsin's bowl signaled the end of the endurable and the start of the new humiliations to follow.

Will walked to the stove and added another spoonful of rice porridge to Tsin's bowl, then returned to the table and set it down in front of her. Her face lit up as she picked up her spoon and plunged it into the sweetened mush. When he refilled her mug with the milk Jack had ordered from the local goatherd, she gave him a rapturous smile. He smiled down at the little one, then spoke to the other girls. "There's plenty of congee for all of you. You may have more if you'd like, and more tea and milk."

In Will's experience, the girls lately arrived from China were always hungry. Most had suffered starvation at home from the famine and the drought, and received only minuscule rations of rice and endured seasickness on the voyage to California. He and Jamie had learned that a diet of rice or oatmeal porridge or noodle soup or plain noodles with bits of chicken and vegetables worked best for the first few days to avoid stomach upsets. Other foods—meats and fruits, fried offerings and pastries—were introduced gradually. He took a risk by providing the goat's milk to children who had probably never drunk anything but rice or soy milk, but the little ones were in desperate need of the rich nutrition goat's milk provided. Although, he'd never purchased girls this young at auction before, Will knew Jamie's little girls loved the taste of goat's milk.

Will had ordered the congee prepared thicker than the way it was normally eaten in China. There the porridge was little more than watery gruel, but Will had grown up eating porridge made from oatmeal and preferred it to the rice version. Unfortunately, oatmeal prepared the British way was almost unheard-of in Chinatown, and entirely unheard-of in Mr. Ming's kitchen, where he and Jack ordered most of their meals. Thick rice congee, sweetened with honey and goat's milk, was as close as he could come to the traditional Irish oatmeal on short notice and with a Chinese cook. He smiled down at Tsin, then grinned when the other six offered their bowls for refills in the Chinese girls' version of Charles Dickens's story of *Oliver Twist, or The Parish Boy's Progess* that was music to his ears: "More, please."

## Chapter Thirteen

❧❧❧

*"If you want to be found,*
*stand where the seeker seeks."*
—SIDNEY LANIER, 1842–1881

They're here," Jack announced late that afternoon as he opened the door to Will's private office.

Will looked up from his paperwork. "The Pinkertons or the players?"

"The players," Jack replied. "They came to the back door in an Empress gin delivery wagon."

Will shook his head in awed admiration. "You have to love the old man's ingenuity."

Jack agreed. "We'll have to order some Empress gin labels and distill a few bottles in the event any of our regular customers ask for some."

"Knowing the old man, he distilled a few bottles of his own and brought them to us," Will said.

Jack grinned. "I'll be sure and ask him."

"You do that." Will's grin matched his friend's. "Where are they?"

Jack delivered his status report: "I took the players up the back stairs. The ladies are in five of the rooms and the gents are guarding them. Our seven girls are in your sitting room. The old man is having a drink at the bar."

"What about the Pinkertons? Did you hear from them?" Will asked.

"We got a wire from the Denver office. They're sending men, but they won't arrive until late tomorrow afternoon."

Will did his best not to show his uneasiness at that bit of information, but couldn't bite back his groan or fool Jack.

"We could try the San Francisco office," Jack suggested. "It's a risk, but . . ."

Will shook his head. "It's a bigger risk than I'm willing to take. If corruption permeates the city government and police, how do we know it hasn't pervaded the Pinkerton agency in San Francisco?" He looked at Jack. "Were there any names on your brother's list from the local office?"

"No," Jack replied. "None of the agents Murphy knew to be absolutely trustworthy were assigned the San Francisco office."

"Then the risk is too great," Will decided. "We'll move forward with what we have tonight. If the old man's finished his drink, ask him to come in so we can finalize the plans."

Jack nodded. "I'll send him in."

"Has any of your bar help arrived?"

"Luis and Ben."

"Leave one of them to work the bar. I want you here when I meet with the old man so we can go over the final details," Will told him.

"You've got it." Jack turned to the door. "I'll go get him."

Jack returned a few minutes later with an elderly gentleman blessed with the visage, stature, and charm of a leprechaun, and with enough cunning and talent to dwarf a colossus. Born Humphrey Osborne, the old man had celebrated seven decades of life. He was a colleague of Father Francis Paul, the priest at St. Mary's Catholic Church near Portsmouth Square, with whom Osborne had gone to seminary. But Osborne hadn't remained a priest. He'd left the Church after twenty years to tread the boards as an actor. And he'd never regretted his decision. The Church had been his family's choice for him. Osborne loved the pageantry, but had never cared much for the religious dogma. He preferred the works of Shakespeare and Marlowe and Sheridan, of Molière and the classical Greek comedies and tragedies.

"Hello, Will, my boy." Osborne greeted Will with a handshake and an embrace, his voice a charming Irish lilt. "It's good to see you again."

"It's good to see you again, Sir Humphrey," Will replied, using the courtesy title the former priest had adopted when he took to the stage. "Thank you for coming. I realize Saturdays are one of your busiest performance nights and that doing a favor for us is costing you box office revenue."

"Not to worry, my boy," Sir Humphrey assured him. "Your generosity has made it possible for our little troupe to take a Saturday busman's holiday now and then without worrying about the finances. We are in your debt."

"Not at all, Sir Humphrey," Will answered. "You've more than paid your debt to me with your discretion, loyalty, and talent."

Sir Humphrey scratched his grizzled head. "On that I am afraid we must agree to disagree, my boy, for you gave a poor troupe of performers a home and a place to earn our living."

Will had met Sir Humphrey a year earlier, when the traveling troupe of the Empire Players had spent three weeks in the mining camps of the High Sierras and Coryville, performing Shakespearean comedies and tragedies in the camps and in the Coryville Town Auditorium. During the final week of the tour, James Craig had hosted the troupe in the Coryville Hotel, and while sharing dinner one evening, Sir Humphrey confided that while he loved traveling, he was old enough to crave a softer bed and a permanent home.

Will had offered the leader of the Empire Players a vacant San Francisco coffee warehouse he had purchased as an investment and financed the renovations needed to turn the vast warehouse into a theater and apartments for the actors. He had originally intended to rent the space to the players for a nominal fee, but he'd reconsidered and decided to give the theater to Sir Humphrey when he'd built the Silken Angel Saloon and realized the thespians could be of help with his special project.

And Sir Humphrey had never failed him. An abolitionist to the core, he and his players had come during the two previous missions, and the members of the troupe hadn't breathed a word about their performances at the Silken Angel Saloon.

Will knew that he and Jack wouldn't have been able to accomplish everything they had if it hadn't been for the help of the Empire Players. And he was grateful.

"What do you need us to do, my boy?" Sir Humphrey asked.

Will gestured for Jack and the elder gentleman to take a seat while he detailed the plan for the evening. "First, we need men who look like Pinkerton detectives. . . ."

When Will finished explaining the plan, Sir Humphrey rubbed his hands together in delight. There was nothing he loved more than a good theatrical. "With or without real weapons?"

Will was taken aback by the question. Surprised that a former priest would think to ask about weapons—real or otherwise.

"Real," Jack replied before Will could. "We've got a safe full of cash, a small fortune in liquor, and a canvas for a front wall."

Sir Humphrey nodded. "Set decoration, my boy," the wizened little man said to set Will's mind at ease. "Weapons on make-believe Pinkerton men create the illusion of force. I couldn't help but notice your storefront met with another unfortunate accident."

Will gave him a wry smile. "One we affectionately call Typhoon Julia."

"So . . ." Sir Humphrey grasped the situation. "The little missionary went back on her word."

Will was genuinely taken aback. "You heard?"

"Of course," Sir Humphrey told him. "San Francisco may be a city, but it gossips like a small town." He stood up and wiped his hands down the front of his trousers. "I'd better start unloading the costumes and props." He glanced at Jack. "If you don't mind, I'd like to borrow one of your men. We don't want the customers to see the Pinkertons unloading a liquor wagon in work clothes."

Jack stood up and headed for the door. "I'll get Luis to help."

"Good," Sir Humphrey pronounced. "Good. Start with the case of Empress gin I brought for the bar." He looked at Will. "We'll be wanting a nip of gin to quench our thirst after the manual labor. . . ."

## Chapter Fourteen

*"Audacity augments courage."*
—PUBLILIUS SYRUS, 1ST CENTURY B.C.

Returning to the Russ House Hotel after an afternoon spent meeting donors to the Salvationist mission work at the Christian Ladies' Benevolent Society tea, Julie couldn't shake the feeling of being followed.

Glancing over her shoulder once again at the city policeman down the street, Julie ducked inside a store with the sign, EVANGELINE DUMOND, DRESSMAKER AND MILLINER, two doors up from the Russ House Hotel. Pretending to browse the latest selection of Parisian fashions, Julie did her best to convince herself that if the person following her was male, he would avoid the inside of a dressmaker's shop like the plague.

Selecting a ready-made jade-green serge walking dress and a matching green bonnet with a netted brim from a display near a willow dress form, Julie slipped into one of the two curtained alcoves the shop owner used as dressing rooms and tried the dress and the deep half bonnet on for size. The dress was an inch too long, so Julie added another stiff starched petticoat and a pair of high-heeled boots to compensate for the length. She accessorized her new frock with a matching short cape, gloves, and a brown false fringe and curls for her hair. Affixing the hairpieces to her dark auburn hair, Julie stared into the mirror mounted on the wall and debated her color choice of jade green.

She wanted to blend in instead of standing out, and she decided that the man following her wouldn't be looking for a missionary in a fashionable and expensive Parisian-style walking costume. Although there was no rule against it, no one expected Salvationist missionaries to be people of independent means. The idea that missionaries were poor was an erroneous but pervasive myth, and the Salvationists contributed to the myth by insisting their female missionaries wear ugly gray dresses and black boots that bore no resemblance to anything stylish or fashionable.

After deciding to wear her new purchase of the green dress and carry her other purchases of a brown-and-camel-striped silk day dress with all the necessary accessories—including a black wig with a straight-cut fringe and hair that hung down her back that she thought would work with her laundry girl disguise. After quickly plaiting the wig into a long queue, Julie had her Salvationist dress wrapped in brown paper along with her new day dress and accessories, then placed her new green bonnet on her head and her old gray bonnet and black wig in a hatbox. She glanced out the front window and saw the San Francisco city constable leaning against the post of a gas street lamp surveying the boardwalk up and down and across the street, watching the late-afternoon shoppers. With her heart racing, Julie gathered her belongings and hurried into the nearest hansom cab.

"The Russ House Hotel, please," she directed.

"Miss, the Russ House Hotel is two doors down," the driver told her. "It's hardly worth a fare when you can walk it."

"I have purchases," Julie answered. "I prefer to ride. And I'll double your fare."

The driver heaved a put-upon sigh. "It's your dollar."

Clucking to his horse, the driver pulled out into traffic and drove Julie ten or so feet to the front door of the hotel. He parked his cab in line behind three or four others and waited for the hotel doorman to open the door for his passenger.

Scooping her packages into her arms, Julie leaned forward in order to exit the cab. Through the window in the door she saw the doorman conversing with the city policeman who had followed her from Mission Street, and quickly called out to the driver, "Driver, I just remembered I've other errands to run."

"Where to?"

Julie had to stop and think. She didn't minister to the affluent citizens of San Francisco and knew only a few places in town where ladies shopped or dined with regularity. She needed to come up with someplace she would be safe. Oddly enough, her first thought was the Silken Angel Saloon and Will Keegan, despite the fact that she had done her best to destroy it only hours ago. It was the one place in all of San Francisco where she felt safe, and Julie suspected the only reason for that was Will Keegan. Her second thought was Wu's Gum Saan Laundry, but it lay in the heart of Chinatown, and Chinatown had become more dangerous than ever for her. And her presence at the laundry could be hazardous for Zhing and Mr. Wu. She couldn't go back to the mission dressed as she was; nor did she want to. The mission offered basic shelter and necessities, but she doubted the Salvationists could keep her safe, even if they could bring themselves to raise a hand against another human being in order to protect her. The most Julie thought they might do was send for the police, and the police might be her greatest enemy. Julie bit her bottom lip as she considered her options. She couldn't go to the Silken Angel. She couldn't go to Wu's. She wouldn't go to the mission. "Ghirardelli Chocolate Company."

The cabbie laughed. The chocolate shop was a favorite of San Franciscans, especially young ladies. It was one of the few places in town where they could go unescorted and enjoy chocolate confections and pastries and the most delicious cup of hot chocolate in the city. "Corner of Greenwich and Powell. Right away, miss."

Julie hazarded a nervous glance toward the front entrance

of the Russ House as the cabdriver announced her destination
but the policeman didn't appear interested in the cab and was
pointing toward the dressmaker's shop.

She said a heartfelt prayer of thanks as the cab merged
smoothly into the late-afternoon traffic and headed for Ghirardelli's without incident. Sitting back against the seat cush-
ions, Julie forced herself to breathe normally as she tried to
calculate how far it was from the hotel to the chocolate shop.
As long as she was alone in the cab, she was safe.

But the ride didn't last very long, and before she knew it
the cab had pulled up to the front of Ghirardelli's. Julie waited
for the cabbie to open the door and lower the steps before
alighting from the vehicle. He helped her down and gathered
her packages for her while she got out money.

Julie met his gaze as she handed him his fare and a generous tip. "Would you consider returning for me in half an
hour?" she asked.

"I'll wait for you, miss, if you're willing to pay the half-hour
fare," he told her.

Julie stuck out her hand. "It's a bargain, Mr. . . ."

"Winston." He took her hand in his and shook it. "Miss?"

"Burke." Not willing to give her real name, Julie said the
first name that popped into her head, then remembered where
she'd heard it. *William Burke Keegan. My friends call me Will.*
"A pleasure to make your acquaintance, Mr. Winston."

"The pleasure is mine, Miss Burke." He doffed his hat to
her. "You may leave your packages in the cab. I won't be
accepting any other fares until I see you safely home."

"Thank you, Mr. Winston." She smiled at him, then shivered as the wind coming off the bay seemed to cut right
through her. "Shall I have them bring you a hot chocolate
while you wait?"

"That would be most kind of you, miss, and greatly
appreciated."

"Consider it done," she assured him. "I shall return in one
half hour."

"Take your time, miss. There's no rush. I'll be here when
you're ready to leave."

The cabbie was as good as his word. He was waiting when Julie emerged from the chocolate shop exactly one half hour later with a box of chocolate pastries and three tins of chocolates. The pastries were for Julie's breakfast, but the tins of the exquisite chocolates were meant as gifts. Mr. Winston jumped down from his vehicle to pull out the steps and open the door to hand her into the coach.

"Thank you for the hot chocolate, Miss Burke," he said. "It was most welcome, and took the edge off the chill of the evening."

Julie was gracious. "These are for you as well." She handed him a tin of chocolates. "With my gratitude."

"Thank you, miss." The cabbie was genuinely touched by her thoughtfulness. "Where would you like to go?"

"Back to the Russ House Hotel."

"As you wish." Mr. Winston climbed up to his seat, clucked to his horse, and began the short trip back to the hotel.

Julie let out a sigh of relief when the coach rolled to stop and the hotel doorman opened the coach door. The policeman who had followed her from Mission Street was gone. She directed the doorman to collect her packages and have them delivered to her room while she paid and thanked the cab-driver once more.

"Anytime you need a cab, miss, you have Turner there"—he pointed at the hotel doorman—"send for me."

"I'd be pleased to, Mr. Winston," she promised.

He waved good-bye and doffed his top hat to her. Julie waved back, then turned and entered the hotel.

She walked through the lobby and stopped at the front desk to collect her room key from the desk clerk. Hotels in the West routinely collected keys from guests when they left their rooms, returning the keys for the night upon request. "I would like the key to my room, please."

The desk clerk stared at her. "I'm sorry, miss, but are you registered here?"

Remembering that she was wearing dark brown hairpieces and the deep half bonnet to hide her red hair, Julie quickly rephrased her request. She was getting good at lying, perhaps too good. Julia Jane Parham prided herself on always telling the truth, no matter what the consequences, but now . . . The fact that her fabrications were growing more elaborate and easier to concoct was cause for concern. She promised herself she would do something about it. But not as long as her safety depended upon her quick wits. "Forgive me," she told the desk clerk. "I'm Jane Burke. I've come to join my cousin, Miss Parham. She wired me with instructions to come here and ask for the key to her room."

"That's quite all right, Miss Burke. You may share a room with your cousin, but you must sign the hotel register in order to do so."

"Of course," Julie agreed. "But I should like a room of my own, if that is possible." She knew the room next to hers was vacant. "Perhaps one that connects to Miss Parham's . . ." She dropped the suggestion hoping the desk clerk would pick up on it.

"As it happens," the desk clerk began, "the room next to Miss Parham's is available. It doesn't connect, but it's right next door." He collected the key from the eighth box in the row of open cubicles mounted behind the desk and held it out to her. "Room eight. Up the stairs to the right."

Julie took the key he offered. "Thank you."

"Thank *you*, Miss Burke, and welcome to the Russ House Hotel."

"I left packages with the doorman," Julie remembered.

"We'll have them sent up to your room."

"Thank you again." She turned toward the stairs.

The desk clerk stopped her. "Miss Burke?"

Julie turned back to the front desk. "Yes?"

"The girl from Wu's Gum Saan Laundry delivered Miss Parham's laundry this afternoon." He lifted a package wrapped in thick brown paper from behind the front desk. "Would you please tell her it's here?"

"Why don't you give it to me?" Julie suggested, reaching for the package. "I'll see that she gets it."

"That's most considerate of you, Miss Burke, and just so you know, we have a 'no Celestials' policy at the Russ House.

If you would be kind enough to remind Miss Parham to ask one of our employees to collect her laundry from Wu's, rather than have the China girl come to the hotel to deliver it. We have a reputation to maintain. We cannot have Celestials running about the hotel. It upsets our guests."

"I see." Her words were clipped and precise as Julie struggled to mask her anger. "My apologies, sir. I'm quite certain Miss Parham was not aware of your hotel policy. She would never purposely upset your guests—or upset the Chinese laundry girl by asking her to trespass where she isn't allowed." She took the package out of the clerk's hands and carried it upstairs.

Her packages arrived shortly after Julie entered her room. After accepting them and tipping the bellman, Julie closed and locked the door behind her, then collapsed on the bed. What was she going to do now? She'd become three people— Julie Parham, Jane Burke, and Jie Li, the laundry girl. She was paying for two hotel rooms, and she couldn't leave either one of them dressed as Jie Li. And Zhing Wu couldn't come to the hotel and act as a lady's maid to transform her into Jie Li or back into Julie. How was she going to get back to Chinatown to search for Su Mi? Or to the Silken Angel Saloon to rescue the seven girls trapped there? How was she supposed to accomplish what she'd come to San Francisco to accomplish?

Julie wanted to pound the mattress in frustration and scream into the pillows, but what was the use of a temper tantrum if there was no one around to witness it? She needed to think, needed to find a way to return to the Silken Angel. . . .

Getting up from the bed, Julie changed out of her green dress and bonnet and removed her brown hairpieces. Opening her packages, she took out her Salvationist uniform and reluctantly put it on. She had to make an appearance sometime, and she might as well use it to retrieve her room key.

Dressed as a Salvationist missionary, Julie left room number eight and went out the back exit, walked around the hotel, and entered through the front doors before approaching the desk to request her room key.

The front desk was empty when Julie rang the bell. The desk clerk came out of the back, discreetly wiping his mouth with a napkin he then surreptitiously tucked inside his trouser pocket. She had purposely waited until the middle of the man's supper break to interrupt him. "Good evening, Miss Parham."

"Good evening, Mr. Bishop," she returned the greeting. "May I have my room key, please?"

"Yes, of course." He pulled the key from the room box on the wall behind the front desk and held it out to her.

"Would you happen to know if my cousin has arrived?"

He nodded. "She checked in a little while ago. She is in the room beside yours. Haven't you seen her?"

"How could I, Mr. Bishop?" she asked, "when I've only just returned from the mission?"

"Oh. I didn't realize . . ."

"That's quite all right."

"I gave her your laundry."

"You gave my laundry to my cousin?"

He nodded. "The China girl from Wu's laundry delivered it for you. I had it here behind the desk and Miss Burke offered to take it to her room in order to save me a trip up the stairs. I also made your cousin aware of the hotel's 'no Celestials' policy."

Julie arched one elegant eyebrow at him and put a questioning note in her best Queen's English voice. "A 'no Celestials' policy? What, may I ask, is that?"

Bishop explained the hotel's policy barring Orientals from entering the hotel.

"I contracted with Mr. Wu to provide laundry services," Julie told him, pretending ignorance of a bigoted and blatantly biased policy. "How will he be able to meet his obligations? I cannot take a carriage to Mr. Wu's. The alleys are too narrow. And I'm not inclined to walk to Mr. Wu's and carry my laundry back when I'm paying him to deliver it."

"Of course not, Miss Parham!" He sounded shocked, although he was most likely very much aware of her mission work. "Chinatown is no place for a lady. Especially the rabbit's warren of alleyways where most of the Chinese laundries—including Wu's"—Julie noticed that Mr. Bishop refused to honor Wu by attaching the courtesy title of "Mr." to his name—"are located. If you will come to the front desk whenever you need laundry services, we will see that a bellman is sent to collect it and take it to the laundry of your choice. When your laundry is ready, we'll send someone to collect it for you. With this system in place, there is never any need for one of our guests to come in contact with an Oriental. We at the Russ House Hotel strive to make our guests' stays as comfortable and trouble-free as possible. As I explained to your cousin, Miss Burke, we simply can't have Celestials running about the hotel. Our guests find it objectionable."

Julie pinned the desk clerk with a look. She wondered whether, if she complained to the hotel's owner, he would eliminate the desk clerk she found objectionable. "I apologize for my ignorance, Mr. Bishop." She said the right thing, in the right tone of voice, without meaning a word of it. "I grew up in the Far East, where Celestials, as you call them, work as house servants in my home. I do not find their presence a nuisance. I did not know I was the exception, rather than the rule, in San Francisco."

"Now you do," Mr. Bishop said.

"Yes," Julie agreed, "now I do." Taking the key from him, she turned on her heel and went upstairs to her room.

After spending three-quarters of an hour shuttling belongings from one room to the other, separating what might belong to Julie Parham and what might belong to Jane Burke into two rooms that gave the appearance of being fully occupied, Julie returned to her original room, locked the door, slipped off her missionary dress, hung it in the armoire, and lay down on the bed to rest her eyes.

## Chapter Fifteen

*"I am escaped by the skin of my teeth."*
—JOB 19:20

Someone was in her room.

Julie awoke with a start to discover she had fallen asleep dressed in everything except her dress.

Her heart was pounding as if she'd run a race, her senses heightened in awareness as she tried to figure out what had brought her out of a deep, dreamless slumber. Everything seemed to be just as she'd left it, but something had awakened her.

And then she heard it.

The sound of quiet rustling and footsteps.

Barely daring to breathe for fear of discovery, Julie lay as still as death, afraid to move. She held her breath. Her lips moved in silent prayer, but the rest of her didn't. She lay in the darkness listening as a stranger rifled through her belongings, thankful that she'd put the bundle of laundry Zhing Wu had left for her in the other room.

Moving as quietly as possible, Julie eased off the bed. The soft creak of the bedsprings was deafening to her ears. She half expected the intruder to grab her, but his back was turned and he was busy rummaging through the dresser drawers, flinging silk stockings and delicate garters about the room, scattering her underthings.

Her pulse beat a rapid staccato.

Sneaking a peek over her shoulder, Julie saw that his back was still turned, his focus on the chest of drawers. It was now or never. Summoning all her courage, she slowly, carefully inched toward the door.

"Where do you think you're going, Miss Parham?" he hissed a moment before he grabbed her by the back of the neck and yanked.

Julie grabbed for the knob and jerked the door open a few inches. "Help! Somebody!"

Placing his white-gloved hand against the door, the intruder slammed it shut. Julie barely registered the sound of it echoing through the hotel corridor before he locked an arm around her waist.

Acting on instinct, Julie flung her head back and connected with his face.

Yelping in pain, he reacted, hurling her toward the bed. She bounced off the side of it and hit something hard. Or something hard hit her. She rocked back, momentarily stunned. It took her a moment to comprehend the fact that he'd hit her with his fist. She shook her head, tried to focus, and saw stars before he grabbed a handful of her petticoat, lifted her off her feet, and threw her back on the bed, facedown.

And held her there. With one hand against her head and his knee in her back, he pressed her face against the mattress while he fumbled for something just out of reach. . . .

Struggling to breathe, her lungs burning, realizing he was smothering her against the feather bed, Julie fought, twisting and bucking, trying to dislodge him, until she managed to turn her face to the side. She inhaled, sucking precious air into her lungs. . . .

"Oh, no, you don't!" he growled, trying to subdue her, his breathing as labored as hers.

Fighting like a wildcat, Julie wriggled free, then rolled onto her back and reached out her right hand, searching for something, anything, to use as a weapon as he balled up his fist. Julie vowed that she was going to do whatever she had to do to survive. She was not going to allow this man to take her life. Not today. Not ever.

Feeling the smooth, cool surface of the Ghirardelli's chocolate tin, Julie latched onto it and swung with all her might, clouting him on the side of the head. Reaching up, he managed to take hold of her wrist, twisting it until she cried out in pain and let go of the chocolates. The tin bounced off the bed and hit the floor with a clatter.

Her attacker grabbed hold of her throat, shoved her hard against the mattress, and squeezed, cutting off her air once again.

"Hey! What's going on it there?" Someone pounded on the wall separating her room from room four. "Some of us are trying to sleep. Keep it down!"

Realizing that the assault was loud enough to disturb the neighboring guests, Julie's attacker froze.

Seizing the opportunity, knowing it was her last chance to save herself and Su Mi, Julie clawed at his hand, managed to grab hold of his little finger and bend it backward. He eased his grip on her throat and reached for something in his boot.

Julie gulped in a breath, then wasted no time in rolling off the bed once again.

Breathing hard, but breathing, Julie stumbled toward the door, pulled it open, and yelled, "Fire!" It came out as a croak. Inhaling as deeply as she could, Julie tried again. He grabbed her skirts to pull her back inside. Refusing to let go of the door, and bracing herself for whatever came next, Julie kicked out with all her might and connected with his knee. Hearing his grunt of pain, she made another attempt at escape. Ignoring the agony in her throat and her wrist, she stumbled into the hall. "Help! Fire!"

Her shout sounded loud in her brain, but it was barely audible. A mere whimper, but it was a sound. Suddenly her attacker burst out of the room and shoved her to the side.

She saw the flash of the blade a moment before he stabbed her. The pain seared through her shoulder as her would-be assassin hurried down the hall toward the stairs.

Julie pressed herself against the door to number eight, fumbling with the ribbon around her neck that held the key to Jane Burke's room as blood ran down her arm and over her fingers, staining her neck and the muslin of her corset cover.

Finally managing to unknot the key, Julie gritted her teeth against the pain, leaned heavily against the door, and shoved the key into the lock. She turned the knob and practically fell into the room.

Dizzy with blood loss , Julie jerked the key out of the lock, then closed the door and relocked it. She leaned against it, marshaling her strength before she pushed away from it and began undressing. Hands shaking, shoulder and wrist throbbing, she unbuttoned the waistband of her petticoats and let them fall to the floor. Standing in her corset, corset cover, boots, and stockings, Julie ripped the paper off the laundry bundle lying on the foot of the bed and reached for the long cloth and began winding it around the top of her corset cover as tightly as she could manage, hoping the cloth would help stanch the flow of blood from the wound in her shoulder. She thought she might faint from the pain and the exertion, but Julie knew that if she did, she would die here. Operating on a combination of terror and determination, she forced herself to pull the tunic of her laundry girl disguise over her head. She sat down on the bed, but her fingers were trembling so badly she couldn't manage the laces of her boots. Giving up, Julie worked her trousers over her boots, tugged on the drawstring, then stood up and retrieved her black wig from the hatbox from Madam Dumond's. Biting her bottom lip till it bled, Julie managed to pin her hair atop her head and secure the black wig, which she had braided into a queue. She completed her look with one of the hand-painted conical straw hats street vendors hawked to tourists as Chinamen hats.

She'd left her tinted rice powder at Wu's, but found a stub of a kohl pencil in the bottom of her reticule. She thought she would line her eyes with it using a tiny mirror and the sliver of moonlight coming from the window, but one eye was rapidly swelling shut and the other had a bleeding cut above it.

With her face battered and bruised, there seemed little point in trying to disguise her eyes. At night and in her present state, no one could tell they were blue. Dropping her pencil on the dresser, Julie decided it was time to go.

Unlocking her door as quietly as she possibly could, Julie eased it open and slipped through it. She paused long enough to relock it and pocket the key. There was no going back. Only forward. Taking a last look around to make sure the hallway was deserted, she headed for the back stairs and the service entrance as fast as she dared, walking at a brisk pace, keeping her head low, praying she could make it to her destination before anyone noticed her.

It was late. Past the Chinese curfew. According to the city ordinance, any Chinaman or Celestial woman caught on the city streets past the hour of midnight was subject to a fine or arrest or both. Going out as Jie Li was a risk, but it was a risk Julie had to take. She had no choice but to walk. And if she hurried, she might make it before her strength or her luck failed her.

Julie hurt all over. But she didn't stop. She was gasping for breath, but she didn't slow her pace. She kept walking—away from the Russ House, past the Salvationist mission and the women's dormitory, right to the only place she felt safe.

The Silken Angel Saloon.

# *Chapter Sixteen*

❧❧

*"Let us run into a safe harbor."*
—ALCAEUS, C. 625–C. 575 B.C.

Hey, Keegan, you missing one of your little China dolls?"
one of the regular poker players called out as Will
walked by.

It was a few minutes before closing, and Will was
exhausted and doing his best to persuade the regulars it was
time for them to leave and go home so he could lock the front
doors. Jack had already called for the last liquor orders before
closing and the saloon girls had called it a night an hour
earlier after a long, busy evening.

Sunday through Thursday, the Silken Angel operated as a
rather staid, conservative establishment in much the same
way as a British gentleman's club. Men came to socialize,
drink, play billiards or poker, or try their hands at roulette or
faro. It was a quiet, expensive saloon where members of the
upper class relaxed and conducted business in the absence of
saloon and dance hall girls whose sole objective was to convince men to buy them drinks or to pay for a dance.

Two nights a week—on Fridays and Saturdays—the atmosphere of the Silken Angel mirrored that of the dozens of
other drinking and gaming establishments in San Francisco.

It was filled with saloon girls soliciting drinks and dances from customers while the piano player banged out lively popular tunes. The card and billiard rooms were packed and the balls were clattering around the roulette wheels at a steady pace. Along with all that activity were customers who purchased tokens granting them access to the second floor and the four women occupying the bedrooms. None of the men were seeking Chinese brides and none of women were prostitutes—Chinese or otherwise. The men buying tokens were "bridegrooms" carefully chosen by Sir Humphrey Osborne and Father Francis from members of the Empire Players stock company, students studying for the priesthood at St. Mary's Seminary, and a network of the underground Silken railroad conductors. The ladies were actresses, carefully chosen friends, and crusaders brought in by Will and James and Elizabeth to help with the rescue work. There was every appearance of a thriving weekend upstairs business, but it wasn't real. There were no ladies of the evening upstairs, only ladies willing to play a part and games of chess or checkers or engage in intellectual discussions with gentlemen for a few hours. Even James's staff in Coryville took turns in the roles. The Treasures' governess and several teachers at the Coryville Training Academy had spent the weekend helping. A good many of the amateur actors and actresses were teachers, one or two were distinguished journalists, and all of the men and women involved in the drama were abolitionists dedicated to the rescue of San Francisco's poor, unfortunate Chinese slave girls.

And so the weekend bustle at the Silken Angel seemed perfectly normal, but most of it was a carefully orchestrated ruse designed to hide the true nature of the venture. Will made sure his customers knew that the girls he purchased at auction were off-limits to everyone except the men who had asked him to find them wives. In this case, he let it be known that the youngest girls were sisters of the brides who would be joining the bridegroom's household. The new *husbands* were an essential part of the carefully cultivated fiction. They existed for Li Toy, the members of the San Francisco Saloon and Bordello Owners Association, and the tongs. The story Will told of finding Chinese brides for well-to-do bachelors wanting the exotic, rather than the ordinary, gave him the touch of authenticity he needed to convince Madam Harpy his invitation to her auctions was mutually beneficial. It provided Will with the nefariousness he needed to operate on the fringes of the underworld. They viewed him as a procurer, rather than the matchmaker he professed to be.

The participants weren't random choices. They were part of the expensive, elaborate plan Will and James had spent the past year organizing and implementing. There was a great deal of money at stake and the work of the amateur players was crucial to the success of the rescue missions; everyone took it seriously.

Sir Humphrey and the female Empire players who had pretended to be working prostitutes all evening had quietly gone home the way they had come, through the hidden entrance at the back of the saloon, using the gin wagon to return to the theater after a successful evening's performance. The male actors pretending to be the evening's bridegrooms also departed quietly through the private exit, while Will and Jack escorted the seven girls to safety in Coryville. Other players and legitimate customers departed in ones and twos through the front doors, as patrons were wont to do after a long evening of drink and entertainment.

The actors pretending to be Pinkerton detectives were still on duty and staying the night. They would be handsomely rewarded for their time and devotion to their craft when the real Pinkertons arrived. Until then, they were working in shifts, guarding the grand parlor and the bar and the doors of the upstairs rooms until the ruse ended, taking turns sleeping in the cots Jack had set up in Ah So's former room.

The only other people left in the saloon with Will and Jack were the regular poker players who spent a large percentage of their waking hours at the Silken Angel. One of whom had just asked Will about the Chinese girls.

"Not that I know of, Royce," Will replied. "Why do you ask?"

"I just saw one slip past the parlor door."

Will was instantly alarmed. "Are you sure?"

"Sure I'm sure," he retorted. "I haven't had that much to drink, and I know an Oriental when I see one."

Will closed his eyes, gritted his teeth, and prayed for the patience for which he was well-known. "Are you sure it was a Chinese *girl*?"

"Looked like a girl," Royce told him. "From the brief glance I got. But I wouldn't bet on it. Could have been a boy or a little man, but definitely wearing a Chinese getup with black leather boots."

"Chinese girls don't wear black leather boots." Will knew there were no Chinese girls upstairs. He and Jack had just spent the past six hours moving them from the Silken Angel through the underground tunnels that began in the wine cellar and wound their way through the city. It had been a long, exhausting journey. They had taken the girls into the tunnels as a group, but had been forced to pair them off because the tunnels were too narrow in places for them to walk in anything other than twos. The tunnels were badly lit and claustrophobic, and little Tsin, separated from her sisters for the first time, had cried during the entire trip, and no amount of cajoling or bribing or promises from him that she would see them again as soon as they reached their destination had stopped the steady flow of tears. It had torn at Will's heart and made his head ache.

"I thought that was odd, too," Royce remarked. "But, hell, this is San Francisco. It's cold and damp. Could be she's tired of having wet, frozen toes, or she likes boots. I don't know. I only noticed because I was expecting to see those little cloth shoes and white stockings."

"Was she heading upstairs or downstairs?"

"I didn't notice that," he admitted, glancing at his cards. "It was my deal."

Will understood. Cards came first. After all, Royce was a professional cardsharp. "Thanks, Royce. I'll check it out." He looked at the other players. "We're closing in a few minutes. Of course, you're welcome to stay and play, but the doors will be locked and the bar closed until eight a.m."

A city ordinance declared that all saloons and bawdy houses within the city limits close by four o'clock in the morning and remain closed until eight in the morning if they were open to the public for breakfast. If the saloons chose not to serve breakfast, they were required to remain closed until ten.

"We paid for half a case of sipping whiskey to see us through until breakfast before Jack shut down." Dennison shuffled the cards, passed the deck over to McNamara for the cut, then began to deal. "He's gone to the storage room to get it." He nodded toward the door that led to the wine cellar and the storage rooms. "We know where the glasses are. We'll serve ourselves."

Will nodded. "The Pinkertons will be on duty," he told them. "The coffee is on the stove and the mugs are behind the bar. I'm going to see if I can find our mystery girl."

Jack came out of the storage room carrying a wooden box with six bottles of whiskey in it. He set the box on the table beside the poker players' table. "What mystery girl?"

"The little China doll I just saw sneaking around," Royce answered without looking up from his cards. "Came in the front doors and went that way." He pointed toward the entry to the grand parlor. "Could have been heading up the stairs," he reasoned. "Or toward the back to Jack's place."

The regular poker players knew the layout of the Silken Angel Saloon almost as well as Will and Jack did. They had been coming to the saloon since it opened—had come to view the construction and offer suggestions even before it opened—using it the same way they would use a gentleman's club: to play cards and drink and smoke cigars all night without interruption. They made use of the bar and the kitchen and the facilities attached to Jack's apartment, and occasionally the washroom upstairs, but they never rounded the bar or helped themselves to the liquor without paying for it, and they never ventured into the wine cellar and storage rooms. Those areas were off-limits to customers, and the poker players respected Will's rules. They weren't interested in flirting with saloon girls or finding Chinese brides, their only diversions were good whiskey and cards. They knew Will had bought girls at auction on two previous occasions and knew the Silken Angel was a temporary rest stop before the girls began their lives with their husbands elsewhere. The regular poker players knew that the only time ladies were present upstairs was Friday and Saturday nights and, since Jack and Will were the only staff members who granted tokens, the clientele was very exclusive. The only time Chinese girls were upstairs was immediately after an auction. If they suspected the upstairs business was a sham, they gladly kept it to themselves in order to retain the privacy and the privileges afforded to them at the Silken Angel.

Jack looked to Will for confirmation. "I didn't see her," Will said.

"But it could be the same one. . . ."

Will gave an almost imperceptible nod of his head. "You search the downstairs. I'll take the upstairs."

"She's not in the wine cellar," Jack said. "I just came from there. I would have seen her on the stairs, and I locked the door behind me."

"Search the kitchen and the rest of the downstairs," Will instructed. "She may be hungry again and looking for food. I'll lock the front doors and look around upstairs." Glancing at the poker players, he offered an explanation. "We had an intruder last night who helped herself to some food and an empty bed. She may have returned."

Jack frowned, trying to relay coded information to Will with the poker players none the wiser. As far as they knew, Will's new China dolls were still upstairs. "I moved Ah So into a different room and set up the cots for the Pinkerton agents in that room." It wasn't a lie. Jack had moved Ah So through a web of tunnels and onto a private CCL railway car that would take her to Coryville and a different bedroom. Not that Jack thought it mattered to the regular poker players, but you couldn't be too careful in a city where the walls had ears.

He needn't have bothered. The only reply from the poker players was a grunt and a comment that there were a lot of desperate Chinese girls in San Francisco.

Will acknowledged Jack's message, then turned and headed toward the front doors. He noticed something unusual as soon as he left the grand parlor and approached them. There was a smear of blood on the wallpaper just inside the entry. It looked as if someone had leaned against the wall to rest and left blood behind. There had been a great deal of scattered glass after Julia Jane's tirade. One of the workmen removing the remains of the front window, installing the canvas, or cleaning up the debris might have cut himself earlier.

Reaching out, Will touched a drop. It was fresh. Too fresh to have been left there earlier in the day. Pushing the front doors closed, he locked them and pocketed the front door key, then rattled the handles to make sure they were secure before he vaulted the stairs to the second floor, following the trail of blood droplets all the way up. He reached the second-floor landing and cautiously made his way down the dimly lit corridor. The chairs outside the bedroom doors were empty, the actors pretending to be Pinkerton agents having all turned in for the night. Will knocked on the door of Ah So's former bedroom, opened it, and stuck his head inside. "Good job, gentlemen," he congratulated them. "The saloon is closed. All the customers except the five regular poker players have gone home. I discovered fresh blood on the floor and on the wall on the way up here. Anyone wounded and bleeding?" He looked around, but the three men occupying the room seemed to be fine.

"No, sir," one of the men answered.

"Have you seen anyone other than me, Jack, and your colleagues up here?"

"We haven't seen anyone," another one offered.

Will nodded. "Well, feel free to make use of anything you need. You'll find extra toothbrushes, tooth powder, and shaving supplies in the hall closet. If we don't have what you need, we'll get it." Will indicated the door to the closet. "Well, good night, gentlemen, and thank you again for your excellent work tonight. See you in the morning." Will closed the door and walked to the washroom at the end of the hall. He gave a courtesy knock, then opened the door.

It was empty. As was the hall closet Will checked as he walked by. After searching the six other guest bedrooms and finding them unoccupied, there was only one more place to look.

Will took a deep breath and opened the door to his suite of rooms. He had left several lamps burning, and at first glance his room looked as empty as the others, but there was a spot of blood on the floor beside his bed. He looked closer and saw other drops of blood leading to his private washroom, where the door he'd closed before going downstairs for the evening was standing ajar, and a pair of small black leather boots lay on the threshold. The owner of the boots, wearing black trousers and a white tunic, was lying facedown on the washroom floor, feet still in the boots, a straw Chinaman's hat hanging by its ties resting on the back of the tunic.

Crossing to the washroom threshold in two strides, Will leaned forward and took hold of the intruder's arm. "Who the devil are you and what are you doing in my room?"

The interloper let out a cry of pain and curled into a tight ball.

Instantly regretting his rough handling, Will gentled his voice and asked, "Where are you hurt?"

The person on the floor—male or female, it was impossible to tell from behind—groaned in reply.

Kneeling on the floor, Will untied the strings holding the hat in place and tossed it to the side. Easing his hands beneath the person's torso, he gently rolled the body over and got the shock of his life.

"Oh, Christ!"

One eye was swollen shut. The other had a bleeding cut above her eyebrow. Her face was bruised, her lips cut and swollen, and her hair was inky black, but there was no mistaking the sprinkle of golden freckles decorating the bridge of her nose. "Julia Jane!" Cradling her against his chest, Will scooped her up and carried her out of his bedroom to the landing at the top of the stairs. She was so pale her bruises stood out like India ink on an alabaster surface and there was fresh blood seeping through the fabric of her tunic. "Jack!" he bellowed. "Bring bandages. Ice if you have it. Cold water if you don't—and hurry!" Turning on his heel, Will carried her back to his room and laid her atop the counterpane on his bed, yanking his pillows from beneath the covers and using them to prop her up as he began unfastening her tunic, searching for the source of the blood. "Julia Jane? It's Will. Can you hear me?"

She tried to open her eyes. One eyelid fluttered open. The other stayed closed. "Will?" Her voice was a rough, barely audible whisper. *"Keegan?"*

"That's right," he assured her. "It's Will Keegan, and you're safe with me. I won't let anyone hurt you."

Julie tried to smile, but couldn't. Her bottom lip was split and cut where she'd bitten it. "Too late," she whispered. Tears leaked from the corners of her battered eyes, rolling into the hair at her temple, and she began to shake with reaction.

Will shoved her tunic open and discovered blood saturating a long strip of fabric awkwardly wrapped around her torso and tucked into the top of her corset. "I'm so sorry, Julia Jane. So damned sorry this happened to you."

"Not your fault," she managed.

"The hell it isn't." Will worked as he talked. Reaching down, he slipped his hand beneath his mattress and pulled out the knife he'd hidden there, then began carefully slicing through the bloody cloth, dropping strips of it on the floor as he removed it. "I knew the danger. I should have gone with you. I should have insisted on taking you to a hotel and making sure you were safe." He peeled two layers of red-stained fabric away before he revealed a nasty stab wound a couple of inches deep and about four inches long—the classic mark of a wound where the assailant jabbed the knife in and sliced when he withdrew it. A steady trickle of blood leaked from the injury. Pulling the rest of her makeshift bandage from beneath her, Will pressed it against her shoulder, applying pressure to staunch the bleeding

She moistened her lips with the tip of her tongue, wincing at the discomfort. "I should have listened."

"Can you tell me what happened?"

Julie lifted her hand and gestured toward her neck and shoulder. "He tried to kill me."

"Who tried to kill you?" Her words filled him with a rage he'd never felt before. It was different from the moral outrage he felt over the hundreds of innocent Chinese girls who were brought to California by the promise of freedom who found themselves enslaved, humiliated, brutalized, and often murdered. This rage was primal—and personal. Someone had hurt her. Leaning closer, Will recognized the bruising on her throat and neck. Someone had tried to kill his Julia Jane by strangling her. Someone had put his hand around her throat and attempted to extinguish her life.

Julie rolled her head from side to side against the pillow. "I don't know," she croaked. "A big man." She took a deep breath. "Is it bad?"

Will clenched his jaw so tightly he was in danger of cracking his teeth. His brave little missionary who dared to go where angels feared to tread was crying . . . and her silent tears tore at him like nothing else had ever done. "Not too bad."

"There was a l-lot of b-blood." She struggled to speak.

He was no doctor, but he knew enough to recognize shock when he saw it. "You'll probably need a few stitches. . . ." She blanched, turning paler by the second.

Afraid she might faint, Will wisely changed the subject. "Did he attack you on the street?"

"No," she whispered. "My room."

"At the mission?" As far as he knew, she lived in the women's dormitory at the Salvationist mission. How the hell had a man gotten in there? What kind of operation were those people running?

"No," she managed "Russ House Hotel." Reaching up with her good hand, she tugged from her tunic a key suspended from a ribbon. The number six was painted on the tag.

He knew it didn't matter, knew it hurt her to talk, but he couldn't stop himself from asking, "You took a room at the Russ House?"

"Needed privacy."

He looked at her costume and realized the women's dormitory at the mission couldn't offer the sort of privacy she'd need to transform herself into a Chinese girl. "Someone tried to kill you at the Russ House?" Will didn't attempt to hide his shock. The Russ House was one of the finest and safest hotels in San Francisco. Until he moved to San Francisco, it was where he'd stayed whenever he was in the city. It was still Jamie's favorite hotel. Will was appalled. "How did you get here from the Russ House?"

"Walked."

His horror worsened. "Like that? Past curfew? In your condition? Are you mad?"

Julie nodded, then moaned. The sound of her pain and the reason for it shot through him, touching every raw nerve in his body. "Jack!" Will bellowed once again, glancing over his shoulder at the door. "Where the devil are you?"

The urgency in Will's voice carried down the stairs and sent Jack scurrying into action. He came barreling up the stairs carrying a pail of cold water, ran down the hall, and came to a sudden halt in Will's door. "I'm here!" He took a moment to catch his breath after running up the stairs and saw the figure lying propped up on pillows in Will's bed. "Sweet Jaysus!" Jack exclaimed. "You caught her."

"I didn't catch her," Will told him. "I found her. On the floor."

"You think she's our intruder from the other night?"

"Without a doubt."

"Who is she? And what the devil happened to her?"

"Someone did their damnedest to kill her." Will turned to look at his friend and colleague. "Lock the door, bring the ice, and take a closer look, Jack."

"No ice." Jack closed and locked the bedroom door, then walked over to Will's shaving stand and poured cold water from the pail into the washbasin. He grabbed a clean flannel face cloth from a shelf and dropped it in the basin. He snagged the towel hanging on the hook and threw it across his shoulder, then lifted the basin and brought it over to the bedside table.

Leaving the compress on her shoulder, Will wrung the face cloth out and placed it against Julie's swollen eye before Jack set the china bowl down on the table.

She sucked in a breath and let it out in a hiss as the cold water stung. "I must look like Quasimodo."

"Shh," Will soothed as he gently washed the blood from her face. He carefully pressed the soft cloth against her swollen flesh, using the cold water to help ease the pain. "I know it hurts. I'm sorry for that, but I need to wash away the blood so I can see the damage."

She whimpered at the word *blood*, but she had to know she was covered in it.

Jack watched Will ministering to the battered figure on the bed and was struck by the tender note in his voice. He spoke to her the way he'd spoken to little Tsin, soothed her in the same voice he'd used to soothe the frightened child during the long trek through the tunnels. Jack didn't recognize this girl, but there was something familiar about her. He took in the black hair, the tunic and the trousers, the black leather boots, and the tears leaking from her good eye—her good *blue* eye—and put the pieces of the puzzle together.

"Good lord, it's Typhoon Julia!"

# Chapter Seventeen

*T*yphoon Julia?" Julie's question came out in a harsh, painful-sounding whisper. "You call me *Typhoon* Julia?"

Will nodded. "Affectionately, of course."

She managed the ghost of a tiny smile. "Of course."

Jack stepped forward and bowed. "We haven't been formally introduced. I'm Jack O'Brien, born in Dublin in the auld sod, most recently from Chicago and Silver City, Nevada. Now San Francisco."

"Julie Parham," she murmured. "Late of Hong Kong, now San Francisco."

Will and Jack exchanged meaningful looks. She'd introduced herself to Will as *Julia Jane Parham*, not Julie Parham, and hadn't breathed a word about growing up in Hong Kong. Will was honest enough to admit that the fact that she'd introduced herself to Jack as the less formal, less forbidding Julie rankled more than he liked. He wasn't honest enough to explore the reasons for it. *Not yet.*

They were from the same British Crown colony, after all, and might have crossed paths on occasion. She might have even been a day student at the Presbyterian mission school.

His parents' school. Though the island was packed with souls, the British community was insular, and far smaller than the Chinese one.

"A pleasure, Miss Parham," Jack said.

Julie winced as her split lip made itself known. "The pleasure is mine, Mr. O'Brien."

"Under other circumstances, perhaps. Not under these." Will looked down at her and frowned, then dabbed at the bead of blood on her bottom lip. "You're from Hong Kong?"

"Born in London." She spoke around the flannel cloth as he continued to blot her lower lip. "Grew up in Hong Kong."

"Any relation to Commodore Lord Nelson Parham?" Will asked. He didn't know the commodore intimately, but he had been introduced to him at one of the Craigs' parties. A young lieutenant during the Black Sea campaigns of the Crimean War, Commodore Parham had been awarded a captaincy for saving his ship and his crew. He had risen through the ranks of the Royal Navy and been awarded his current rank. Commodore Parham's name and flagship were well-known in Hong Kong.

She looked alarmed. "Father."

"Does your father know that his daughter is our Typhoon Julia?" Will asked.

Julie didn't answer.

"All right," he conceded. "That can wait." He dipped the face cloth into the bowl of water once again, wringing out the excess, then tenderly bathing Julie's battered face. "I have a more important question. . . ."

Julie braced herself.

"What in Hades have you done to your hair?"

She sagged with relief. "Wig," she managed.

*"Thank God."*

Julie looked up at him, fixing her undamaged eye on him.

"I was afraid this was permanent." He lifted a strand of jet-black hair.

"No," she whispered.

"Then let's get rid of it." Will ran his hands over her black hair and began removing hairpins. After locating all the pins,

Will removed the wig and revealed her glorious red hair, freeing it from its confines by raking his fingers through it to separate the strands. "That's much better," he said when he finished.

"That explains her hair. What's she doing dressed like a Chinese peasant?" Jack was pretty sure he knew the answer, but the detective he had once been had to ask the question.

"Can you think of a better way to move around China-town?" Will folded the face cloth and placed it over Julie's swollen eye, then handed Jack the basin. "We need more water."

Jack carried the bowl into Will's washroom and poured the rusty-colored water down the sink drain, then refilled it with fresh water from the pail he'd brought up from the kitchen. From the looks of the flannel and the stained water, she'd bled enough to cause concern, and was still bleeding. "She needs a doctor."

"I agree," Will said to Jack before turning to Julia. "I'm going to send someone for a doctor friend of ours."

Julie rolled her head from side to side against the pillow. "No doctor."

Will brooked no argument. "Yes, a doctor. My needlework is atrocious and you may have internal injuries Jack and I aren't equipped to handle." He pressed the damp cloth against her lips. "Dr. Stone is trustworthy. He has a practice here in the city, and he's affiliated with a company owned by a friend of mine. He'll keep your secret."

She looked up at him. "Will you?"

"You know the answer to that, Julia Jane." Her name sounded like a caress on his lips. "Or you wouldn't be here. After the havoc you wreaked this morning, you would have to be crazy to come back, unless you knew I wasn't a danger to you. And you're not crazy. Foolhardy, perhaps, but not crazy."

She closed her good eye, then slowly opened it. More tears rolled from the corner of it, over her cheekbone, and into her hair. "You're right. I knew I'd be safe here, because you didn't hurt me when I wrecked your saloon."

He grinned, showing a dimple in one cheek, and touched the end of her nose with the face cloth. "Why would I hurt you? What's a little broken glass between friends?"

He said *friends*, but the look in his eyes suggested a more intimate association.

Jack coughed. "About a hundred dollars."

Julie would have smiled at his dry wit if her guilty conscience hadn't plagued her ever since she'd wielded her parasol against the Silken Angel Saloon's front window. "I promised I would pay for it," she managed in a raspy voice. "And I will."

Will shot Jack a dirty look. "Not to worry. We have insurance. Right, Jack?"

"Right," Jack agreed. "Cost us a blooming fortune, but we secured it after our second broken storefront."

"That's all that matters." Will took a deep breath. "Now, Miss Julia Jane, have you any objections to Dr. Stone seeing you dressed like this?"

"Yes," she said.

"Then you'll have to trust me to get you out of your tunic and trousers into something more conventional," he said.

"All right." She was so tired and battered and bruised, she'd trust him to do anything.

He couldn't tell through the discoloration and the assortment of cuts and bruises on her face, but he thought she was blushing.

"Buck up, Julia Jane," he said. "I promise not to look at the interesting bits."

"Speak for yourself," Jack teased, winking at her.

Julie raised her uninjured arm to cover her eyes.

"What's this?" Will asked, touching the fabric wrapped around her wrist.

She flinched.

"Does your wrist hurt?"

Julie cradled her wrist and nodded. "He twisted it when I hit him with the chocolates."

Jack wasn't sure he'd heard her correctly. "Did you say *chocolates*?"

"In a two-pound tin from Ghirardelli's." It hurt to talk, hurt to swallow, but Julie was compelled to tell Will and Jack what she couldn't tell the police.

"You were planning to eat two pounds of Ghirardelli chocolates?" Jack was astounded. She was such a slim little thing.

"I was planning to give them to friends as *gifts*."

The spark of annoyance in her barely audible voice brought a smile to Will's lips. She was badly hurt and scared, but the man who attacked her hadn't touched the fire inside her. Brave, idealistic Julia Jane was still there. "Ignore Jack and go on."

"I bought the tins of chocolate this afternoon." Julie frowned, recalling that it was after midnight. "*Yesterday* afternoon. I left one on the chest at the foot of my bed. The man in my room was trying to smother me. I reached out, felt the tin, and hit him on the side of the head with it. He twisted my wrist until I let go. Then he put his hand around my throat and squeezed." She stared down at the blood staining her hand. "I couldn't breathe, but I twisted and turned until I managed to get him to loosen his grip so I could breathe. But I had tied my room key to a ribbon I wore around my neck, and I think he got hold of it. I could feel it cutting into my neck when I was trying to breathe." She fixed her good eye on Will.

The matter-of-fact way she said it sent chills down his spine. He didn't want to think about how close she had come to losing her life, didn't want to think about how close her assailant had come to permanently extinguishing the spark that was Julia Jane, instead of temporarily dampening it. But Will couldn't show the mix of terror and relief and gratitude he was feeling, so he praised her instead for clouting her attacker. "Clever girl." Will continued his inspection of her, recognizing the abrasions on her neck and the bloodied ribbon. "Let's take a look at your wrist."

Julie nodded. Her wrist was swollen and marked with bruises in the shape of a man's thumb and forefinger. The man who had attacked her had had to exert a tremendous amount of pressure in order to cause that bruising. But Julia Jane had been fighting for her life, and she'd refused to let go of the only weapon she had. Will held her arm in a tender grip and studied the damage. "I think it's broken," he said to Jack. "But I'm not sure." He looked up and raked his finger through his hair in an angry gesture. "If it's not broken, it's badly sprained."

Jack agreed. "It needs to be set if it's broken, and tightly bandaged if it isn't."

"We'll leave that for the doctor to determine." Will looked down at Julie. "Try to keep that arm as still as possible, and maybe we can limit the damage and minimize the pain until the doctor gets here."

Because he and Jack both knew it was going to hurt like hell if the doctor had to set it.

Will turned to Jack. "I'm going to need your help. Is there anybody else we can send for Dr. Stone? Luis? Ben?"

Jack shook his head. "Nobody here except the poker players. It will have to be one of us."

"I'm not leaving her." Will was firm.

"Then it will have to be me," Jack said. "How are we going to explain a young lady being here in your room? Besides the obvious?"

"I don't want the obvious," Will said. "We have her reputation to consider." He gave the question a moment's consideration. "Any suggestions?"

"Nobody has to know who she is or that she came to the Silken Angel dressed like that," Jack said. "If we get her out of her Chinese garb we can say we found her and create a fiction to support it."

"We could leave her in her Chinese garb and say we found her," Will pointed out. "Without the fiction."

"A white girl dressed like a Chinese peasant? With a British accent to boot? Care to explain that one?"

"No." Will was adamant. "Either way, the doctor is sure to think she's a saloon girl. Especially with the beating she's taken. I just hope he doesn't think I'm capable of this. It would make our continued association difficult."

"He knows better," Jack replied. "And the fiction is better than him knowing who she really is."

Will turned to Julie. "Agreed?"

He didn't think she would answer, but she finally did. "Agreed."

"All right, Jack, let's finish converting this Chinese peasant into British aristocracy." He looked at her.

"I'm sure that is going to be more like trying to turn Quasimodo into Esmeralda," Julie murmured sotto voce.

"What's that?" Will smiled, the single dimple in his cheek finally making a return appearance.

"You heard me."

"So I did," Will agreed. "Brace yourself; I'm afraid this is going to hurt. . . ."

"*Everything* hurts."

"I'll do what I can to minimize the pain."

Julie bit her already bitten lip.

Jack passed Will the folded flannel face cloth.

Will placed it against Julie's lips. "Bite on this," he urged as he carefully worked her tunic over her head and down her arms, taking special care not to touch her shoulder or jostle her injured wrist. "I'm going to have to cut this off," he told her, staring down at her very pretty corset embroidered with tiny rosebuds. And stained with blood splotches.

"You wear a corset under your peasant garb?"

Julie closed her eyes. "Of course not. I wore binding because Chinese peasant girls don't wear corsets."

"*You're* dressed as a Chinese peasant girl and *you're* wearing a corset."

"For the same reason you're cutting it off. I was wearing my undergarments when I was attacked. The wound in my shoulder prevented me from unlacing," she explained. "I used my binding to stanch the blood. . . . And I wore my corset because I couldn't go without anything. . . . But corsets p—" Realizing she was having a conversation about her intimate apparel with a man, she abruptly broke it off.

But she'd provoked Will's curiosity. "Corsets what?"

She heaved a weary sigh. "Push up and display. I needed

the opposite in my peasant costume in order to make me look like a boy."

Will stared down at her, and Julie swore the temperature in the room rose a few degrees. "I hate to be the one to disappoint you, Julia Jane," he told her, "but nothing is ever going to make you look like a boy."

She tried to frown and failed. "It does when I bind them—when I pull the binding tight enough. But I couldn't do it by myself with my wound—" She broke off again.

"Or Quasimodo," he added, in a husky voice.

Heat flared between them as Julie stared up at him.

"Turn your back, Jack," Will ordered.

Jack let out a good-natured groan, but he turned his back without argument or further protest.

"Close *your* eyes," Julie demanded, her whisper a bit louder.

"I can't close my eyes," Will protested. "If I'm going to cut your corset off and check your wound, I need to see what I'm doing."

"You promised," she reminded him.

Jack snorted. "Nice try. But she's got you there, boyo."

Will kept his eyes open while he sliced her corset off, but closed them and worked by feel, to pull it away from her flesh. He immediately discovered that was an erotic torture of its own. His eyes were closed and he couldn't see the flesh he was uncovering, but his brain supplied an assortment of images of breasts—stark white or cream-colored or slightly darker hued and showered with freckles like gold dust, and crowned with strawberry-colored or pink-tipped or dusky rose areolas and nipples. He did his best to control it, but each brush of his fingers against her warm, soft skin brought a fresh image. Will clenched his jaw against the almost overwhelming urge to press his palms against her breasts as he ran the flannel over her, bathing her, washing the blood away from her wound. He ached to feel the weight of her breasts and run the pads of his thumbs across the sensitive tips. He smelled the scent of her peach soap. It clung to her skin and the muslin of her corset and his body, guided by his heightened sense of smell and feel and his too-vivid imagination, reacted in the predictable manner. Will sucked a breath in between clenched teeth, suffering the tortures of the damned playing blindman's buff with Julia Jane Parham's delectable flesh. He ached to taste her. All of her. Every part of her.

Will heard rustling sounds and tiny whimpers, felt the mattress give slightly, and although he knew the whimpers indicated pain, his imagination painted other images.

"You can open your eyes now," she said.

Will opened them to find Julie primly clutching her discarded tunic against her chest, covering the interesting bits. She was sitting where he'd propped her, against his pillows and on top of the quilted coverlet and sheets on his bed. He could see the beginnings of a large bruise forming on her left shoulder where the edges of her tunic failed to cover everything. Leaning closer, Will reached under the ends of her shirt and carefully traced the contours of the large mark where her blood was seeping into the tissue.

Julie cried out at his touch.

Recognizing her distress call, Jack turned around to see what was wrong and watched as Will spied the contusion forming on her right shoulder. She flinched when he touched that one, but she didn't cry out. He turned his attention back to her left side. "What happened here?"

"I was trying to get away," she said "He grabbed me and threw me against the bed."

Will's eyebrows knitted together and his face seemed to darken with fury. "Your ribs are bruised, but I don't think he cracked any," he told her. "Did you get a look at him at all?"

Julie shook her head, She was weary. The rush of terror that had kept her pain at bay was gone, and her strength had all but disappeared. "No."

"Any impressions?" Jack asked.

"Big. Strong. Tall," she remembered. "Not as tall as Will or you, but tall. He wore white gloves. And something on his coat cut me. A button, maybe. His breathing was labored. I hit him with the tin of chocolates and kicked him in the knee. I think he was limping when he left the hotel."

"Policemen wear white gloves," Jack commented.

"And sharp-edged badges," Will added.

"Badges that might produce a cut like that one above her eye," Jack continued, "if she was struggling and he held her against it."

"That narrows the list of suspects," Will remarked wryly as he untied the laces of her ugly missionary boots and pulled them off her feet, along with her plain white stockings and beautifully embroidered garters. He dropped her shoes and stockings on the floor beside his bed and turned his attention to the drawstring of her trousers. "Just how many bribable policemen are there in San Francisco?"

"I've no idea, but we know Madam Harpy paid one," Jack reminded him. "One. Singular."

"We know she *said* she paid *a* policeman," Will corrected. "She could have paid a dozen. All we need to do is find one with a bruised face, wearing white gloves and walking with a limp." Will couldn't keep the sarcasm out of his voice. He undid the knot at her waist, and gestured for Jack to lift her up. "Close your eyes, Jack."

"After you, my friend," Jack retorted, lifting her hips off the bed high enough to allow Will to take off her trousers with a minimum risk of exposure.

"Jack." Will bit out his friend's name, carefully enunciating it.

Jack obeyed.

"You, too," Julie demanded. He did as she bade and squeezed his eyes shut, but not before he caught sight of the fact that there was nothing beneath her trousers except Julie

Clutching her tunic to her chest with her bad arm, Julie did her best to cover the thatch of copper-colored curls decorating the vee at the juncture of her thighs by gripping the opposite edge of the quilt in her other hand, and tugging i over her womanly parts.

Will bit back a groan. As if having images of her naked breasts in his mind weren't enough, he now had a vivid menta picture of the enticing red curls hiding the entrance to para dise. He wanted to cover her hand with his and guide he fingers to the secret place within. He wanted to watch her pleasure herself, to teach her the motion if she didn't know how, and then he wanted to pleasure her with his hand and his mouth and tongue before burying himself to the hilt inside her warm, welcoming sheath and making hot, slow, tender love with her.

Tamping down the raging libido, Will forced himself to remember that his needs were secondary to hers, and that his erotic fantasy was a private flight of the imagination of which she was entirely unaware. And she was no doubt innocent of the sexual congress that took place between men and women. Although how she could remain innocent of the intimacies in which men and women indulged while navigating the dark underbelly of Chinatown was a mystery worth investigating. But she'd blushed as she pulled at the quilt, and in his experience that was a sure sign the young lady lacked practical knowledge of the ways of the sexes.

And no matter how Julia Jane felt about engaging in a little sexual exploration with him, she was in no condition to do so. Right now, she needed the attentions of a qualified physician more than she needed the burden of a fully aroused saloon owner sniffing at her skirts.

Will dropped her trousers on her lap, then pulled the covers from beneath her. Julie held on to her corner of the quilt and her modesty.

"You can put her down, Jack."

Jack placed Julie on the bottom sheet, and Will quickly flipped the bedclothes over her bare legs.

She settled back against the pillows with a heavy sigh.

Will opened his eyes. Julie was still clutching her tunic to her chest. "Have you any idea where we can get a ladies' nightgown?" he asked Jack.

Jack opened his eyes and lifted an eyebrow in query. "At a dressmaker's," he answered. "But they won't open until ten."

"We can't wait that long," Will said. "You've got to summon the doctor before the shops open. She's in pain."

"Then we'll have to improvise," Jack replied. "Have you a nightshirt?"

Will snorted in disgust. "Do I look like the sort of man who wears a nightshirt to bed?"

"No," Jack conceded. "And neither do I."

"I do wear dress shirts every night in the saloon," Will remembered. "Silk dress shirts long enough to cover the essentials and preserve her modesty." Walking over to his armoire, Will opened a drawer and took out a silk shirt, then returned to the bed, unbuttoned the top two buttons, and dropped it over Julie's head. He straightened it as best he could without jostling her and gently turned the cuffs and rolled up the sleeves.

Julie sagged against the pillows, the last of her energy spent.

"She's ready," Will pronounced before turning to Jack. "Go get the doctor."

# Chapter Eighteen

※

*"Wisdom, compassion, and courage are the three*
*universally recognized moral qualities of men."*
—CONFUCIUS, 551–479 B.C.

Dr. Galen Stone, a rather spare, stoop-shouldered man,
world-weary and older than his years, confirmed much
of Will's layman diagnosis as he examined the girl Will
Keegan told him he and Jack O'Brien had found beaten and
half-conscious on the boardwalk outside the Silken Angel
Saloon when they were locking up.

She had a badly bruised throat and neck, a sprained wrist,
a bruised rib or two, and a nasty little stab wound. The stab
wound, high on her shoulder, wasn't life threatening by itself,
but the puncture could spawn infection or fever or both. In
addition to her other injuries, her face was a mass of lacera-
tions and bruises.

There was no mistaking the fact that someone had tried
his damnedest to kill her. Documenting the damage done to
her, Dr. Stone thought it was a miracle that the person hadn't,
and that she hadn't suffered more serious injuries.

Shortly after arriving, he'd sent Jack downstairs to boil
water and tear strips of linens for bandages. Will stayed with
the doctor, not because he was necessarily better suited for the

job of doctor's assistant, but because he refused to leave the girl's side.

The laceration above her right eye required five stitches. The cut on her bottom lip took two. Because the young woman was in considerable pain from the beating she had taken, Dr. Stone had opted for a dose of chloroform to induce sleep during the suturing, instead of using a local anesthetic to numb her lip and browbone.

Will Keegan had hovered at his shoulder like a mother hen with one chick while he administered the chloroform. And once the patient had fallen asleep, Keegan had watched him sew up the cuts, insisting that he use the tiniest stitches his aging fingers could manage, insisting that the scars the cuts would leave be all but invisible.

"I suture cuts, Will," Dr. Stone snapped while sewing the delicate skin of her bottom lip. "I don't do ladies' fine embroidery."

"Maybe you should. We don't want her looking like Dr. Frankenstein's monster," Will snapped back, referencing Mary Shelley's novel.

Dr. Stone was no fool. He knew there was more to the story than Keegan and O'Brien had told him, but he also knew that they were completely honorable men. Dr. Stone suspected Keegan might be on pins and needles because he worried that the doctor might not believe the story he and O'Brien had told him—might believe Will was capable of brutalizing the girl in his bed. Stone knew that was nonsense. Will Keegan had never hit a woman in his life. He'd sent for him to care for the sick and injured Chinese girls who stayed at the Silken Angel Saloon on two previous occasions. Keegan and O'Brien trusted him and had complete faith in his discretion. Dr. Stone respected that, and believed that any information they withheld from him made no difference in the young woman's care and was most likely concerned with the protection of her identity and reputation.

The way Keegan was hovering over her, Dr. Stone surmised that she might be one of Will's lady friends or one of his stray lambs. Dr. Stone knew Will's compassion wasn't limited to the Chinese, but extended to abused women of all races and backgrounds.

Dr. Stone sympathized.

By the time he'd met James Cameron Craig and William Burke Keegan, nearly five years ago, Galen Stone's promising career as a surgeon had been in shambles. James Craig had financed his move to San Francisco, and Will Keegan had given him the opportunity to help the unfortunate women who found themselves caught in the harsh, ugly world of prostitution. His introduction to Jack O'Brien had come later, after Will hired Jack as his assistant at Craig Capital, Ltd. Jack had helped Stone create a new identity and set up his current very prestigious and very profitable practice among the most affluent of the city's citizens.

Very few people knew that Dr. Galen Stone had once been known as Dr. Grandon Stonemeyer, whose career had been anything but prestigious or profitable. After earning a reputation as a fine surgeon, he'd been recruited into the Army of Northern Virginia and attached to Lee's command. He'd been performing desperate surgery behind enemy lines when Lee surrendered to Grant at Appomattox Courthouse, and Stonemeyer had spent several months in prison as a guest of the Unites States government. By the time the Union army discovered that he was a noncombatant physician instead of a rebel traitor, his reputation was in tatters and his career as a surgeon was over. His prison sentence had cost him everything—his wife, his unborn child, his home, his practice, his reputation. He drank to numb the pain of the deaths of his wife and unborn son and ended up in Chicago, where he'd set up a women's clinic. And where he'd twice been jailed for distributing contraceptive devices and providing information on birth control. He'd also performed surgery and treated venereal diseases, and cared for victims of botched abortions in the heart of Chicago's Tenderloin district.

James Cameron Craig had advertised for a doctor interested in relocating to California to start a medical practice in the newly established town of Coryville. William Burke Keegan had accompanied Craig on the journey to Chicago to interview him.

Dr. Stonemeyer hadn't been Craig's first choice, but Craig had watched him perform an emergency cesarean procedure on one of his clinic patients when his assistant had interrupted the job interview and dinner at Craig's hotel to summon the doctor back to his clinic. He had saved Mrs. Jorgensen and her son and been offered a position with the company on the condition that he change his name and give up the drink. Coryville was a new California town populated by veterans of both sides of the War Between the States, as well as Chinese and European immigrants, and miners and lumberjacks and laborers from all over the globe. It was the height of Reconstruction, and Coryville couldn't run the risk of polarizing its population for one side or the other by hiring a rebel doctor who had served time in a federal prison. And the town couldn't afford to hire a doctor whose usefulness would be limited, if not ruined, by alcohol or the delirium tremens caused by the heavy use of it.

It had taken months for Stonemeyer to kick the bottle, and he'd learned after wiring James Craig that Craig had hired his first choice to become doctor for the town of Coryville. But he'd kept his word to Dr. Stonemeyer and hired him to be the company physician in San Francisco, and helped him establish his practice as Dr. Galen Stone.

Keegan and O'Brien kept his secrets. And he kept theirs. But there were times when Dr. Stone's curiosity plagued him.

Like now.

"She bears a remarkable resemblance to the girl they're calling the 'Bringing in the Sheaves' girl," he said as he watched Will Keegan smooth a stray red curl off her forehead.

"You think so?" Will countered.

"From what I've heard, she fits the description."

Will lifted an eyebrow in cautious query. "What description is that?"

"Red haired, blue eyed, fair skinned, with a sprinkling of freckles." Dr. Stone looked over at Will from where he was busy cleaning and suturing the girl's shoulder wound. It was easier for him to dress her wounds because she was sleeping, but it necessitated Will lifting her into sitting position and holding her there while Dr. Stone worked.

"That description would fit most any girl of Irish, Scottish, or English extraction, Doctor," Will said.

Will was glad that Julia Jane was unaware of the indignities her modesty suffered. When the doctor finished stitching and dressing her stab wound and treating her other cuts and bruises, he examined her for signs of forced sexual contact. For now, Will thought it best that Julia Jane remain ignorant of that particular examination.

Dr. Stone looked over the rims of his half-spectacles at Will when he concluded the exam. "She fits the description of the missionary much better than the description of the profession to which I first thought she might belong."

"What profession is that?" Will asked.

"The oldest one," Dr. Stone admitted. "But this young woman is a virgin. A real one. Not an advertised one from the brothels. She's never had sexual contact—forced or otherwise—with any man."

Will heaved a sigh of relief. "She didn't mention him trying to force himself on her during the attack," he told the doctor, "or succeeding. He was more concerned with killing her. But I don't suppose rape is something a young woman would generally discuss with a man who's not a relative or physician."

"You would be amazed at the things a young woman won't discuss with her physician," Dr. Stone admitted. "I'm surprised she allowed you and Jack to undress her."

"We had to," Will told him. "She couldn't continue to wear what she had on when we found her." He told the truth. Julia Jane couldn't let the doctor see her in her Chinese peasant girl disguise and keep her identity safe. The doctor was completely trustworthy, but he was human, and as apt to reveal information about her as anyone else. And at present, her China girl disguise was the best and safest one she had. "We were perfect gentlemen. Jack turned his back and I closed my eyes. And as far as I know, neither one of us peeked."

"You are both to be commended for that and for being

good Samaritans and souls of discretion. So tell me, Will, were all her cuts inflicted by her assailant or did she suffer a few while she was wrecking your saloon?"

Will met the doctor's unwavering gaze and smiled. "How is she, Dr. Stone?"

"Barring complications from infection or fever, she should make a full recovery," he said.

Will knew the doctor meant his words to be reassuring, but Will wasn't reassured. "How likely is she to suffer from infection or fever?"

The doctor shrugged his hunched shoulders. "There is no way for me to tell yet. We bathed, disinfected, and stitched the stab wound and cuts, so infection should be kept to a minimum, but fever is always a possibility—especially in this damp climate."

"What do we do for her?" Will asked.

"Cold compresses for the bruising. And willow bark dissolved in water for fever." He looked at Will. "You can get it at the pharmacy. I will write you a prescription for it. Or you can get it at the Chinese herbalist's, if you prefer. I'll leave a bottle of laudanum for pain, but use it sparingly. It's highly addictive. . . ."

"What do we use if we can't use the laudanum?"

"Brandy," the doctor told him. "It numbs a good deal of the pain and is less addictive than laudanum. Trust me; I used it to great effect for a number of years."

"I do trust you, Doc."

"As for the rest . . ." He shook his head. "Her bruises will heal in their own time. In the meantime, she must stay here and rest."

Will nodded. "Looks like I'm out of my room and my bed for a while. Thanks, Dr. Stone." Reaching into his pocket, Will pulled out a few bills and pressed them into the doctor's hand. "I appreciate it."

The doctor nodded. "You are welcome, Will. Take good care of our little missionary girl. Send for me sooner if her fever rises or if you need me for anything else. Otherwise I'll see her in a few days."

Will met the doctor's gaze again. "I will."

"Get some sleep. You'll the scare the girl to death looking like you do." He patted Jack on the shoulder as he walked past him toward the door. "I don't want you as a patient, too." Dr. Stone turned in the doorway. "I probably shouldn't say anything, but I owe you, Will. I owe all of you—you and James and Jack. I know where my loyalties lie, and I know there are too few good men doing good in the world. So watch your back. I got the description of the missionary girl from the police commissioner." He shrugged once again. "He has a special interest in seeing that she doesn't cause a certain little businesswoman any more trouble."

"Thanks, Galen, and if you happen to treat a policeman with a limp resulting from a kick in the knee, I need to know about it." Will shook the doctor's hand. "Jack has a cab waiting for you out back."

Dr. Stone turned back toward the hall, calling over his shoulder, "Don't bother to see me out; I know the way."

WILL AND JACK TOOK TURNS SITTING WITH HER.

She slept most of the first day. Will repeated what Dr. Stone had told him—sleep was good; sleep was necessary; sleep was healing—over and over as he sat at her bedside.

Will was sitting in a wing chair near the bed on the evening of the second day when Julie awoke briefly.

"Hurt."

Will opened his eyes and sat up on his chair as she rasped out the single word.

"Here." Will reached for a glass of water and poured into it a teaspoon of laudanum the doctor had left. Moving from his chair to the edge of the bed, Will sat down beside her, anchoring the sheet in place at her chest, preserving her modesty as Julie thrashed against the bed linens.

"Hurt," Julie muttered. "I *hurt*."

"I know," Will answered, shifting his position, supporting her head and shoulders as he placed the rim of the glass against her lips. "But you must stop thrashing about the bed," he told her, "or you might do damage to your shoulder or your wrist or both."

She wrinkled her nose in distaste as he presented the glass. "I'm wet and cold." She shivered involuntarily.

Will placed his palm on her forehead and discovered that her forehead was dry and hot. "Drink this," he urged. "It will make you feel better."

"What is it?"

"A little laudanum in water to help with the pain so you can rest," he told her. "Drink it all down like a good little girl and I'll get you a dry shirt and another blanket to keep you warm."

"Hate laudanum," she complained.

"I'm delighted to hear it," he said. "Used properly, laudanum is highly effective as a painkiller; unfortunately people who like it too much often develop a habit for it," he explained. "But Dr. Stone ordered it to help ease your pain. He says it's good for you. So drink it." He bumped the glass against her lips once again, taking great care not to make contact with the stitches in her bottom lip.

Julie grimaced and tried to refuse the medicine, but Will gave her no choice. Tipping the glass, he forced Julie to drink—or to drown.

"One must take the good with the bad, Julia Jane," he reminded her. "Dark and light. Yin and yang. That's the way life works."

Julie drained the glass, then blinked up at him. "Will?"

"Yes?" He set the glass on the bedside table and eased Julie back down on the pillows, then stood up, turned his back to her, and crossed to the front of the room. He closed the window he'd opened while she was feverish, then retrieved a fresh shirt from his armoire and a clean towel from his shaving stand and returned to her side.

Folding the covers down to her slim hips, Will unbuttoned the silk shirt she was wearing as a substitute nightgown. *His* silk shirt. He tucked the towel inside the shirt, arranging it over her bosom, hiding her breasts from view before he gently eased the damp shirt she was wearing off her shoulders, down her arms, and out from beneath her.

*"Will?"* Julie opened her eyes.

He recognized the urgency in her whispered query and looked at her face. It was grayish green beneath the bruising, and the drops of perspiration on her forehead seemed to have tripled. "I'm here." Reaching for the washbasin, Will fished the flannel out of the water once again, wrung the excess out, and took a step toward the head of the bed.

"Ill." Julie rolled to the edge of the bed, braced herself on her elbow and forearm, hung her head over the side, and spewed the laudanum he'd just forced her to swallow across the tops of his shoes, then began to cry.

"Shh, don't cry, Julia Jane," Will soothed her, pressing the cool flannel cloth onto the back of her neck as she hung her head over the side of the bed. "It's all right. Don't cry, sweetheart; you can't help it when you're sick." Glancing down at the vile-smelling concoction she'd spewed onto his shoes and the bedside rug, Will doubted that they would ever be the same. It didn't matter. Rugs and shoes could be replaced. Julia Jane Parham could not. She was one of a kind.

Julie groaned again.

Recognizing the look of distress on her face, Will scrambled to grab the washbasin as Julie was ill once again. He held her head as her retching dissolved into a fit of dry heaves and eventually subsided, then carefully wiped her face and neck with the damp cloth.

The stench filling his nostrils nearly overpowered him. His stomach roiled and contracted in protest. Will fought to keep from disgracing himself as he slipped his feet out of his shoes and left them on the soiled rug while he padded in stocking feet splattered with the contents of her stomach across the room to empty and rinse out the washbasin in the washroom sink.

He returned to her side and helped Julie lie back against the pillows, then poured her another glass of water from the carafe on the table and offered it to her.

"No more." Julie clamped her mouth closed to keep him from forcing her to swallow more medicine.

"It isn't laudanum," he told her. "It's warm water. To rinse your mouth."

Julie relented. She rinsed her mouth and spit in the basin Will held for her. The effort it took exhausted her. Her teeth began to chatter as she lay back against the pillows. Will carried the basin to the washroom, emptied it and rinsed it out once again, and refilled it with fresh, clean water from the pitcher Jack had brought up earlier.

He pulled the single sheet up to Julie's chin, then unfolded the coverlet at the foot of the bed and draped it over her, tucking it with the sheet tightly around Julie's shoulders.

"Cold," she murmured.

Will bent at the waist and peeled off his soiled socks, balancing first on one foot and then the other, before dropping his socks onto his shoes and rolling them both up in the stained rug. Walking to his armoire, he opened a drawer and took out a fresh pair of socks, then crossed to the fireplace and stirred back to life the coals he'd banked. One look at Julie told him she was suffering fever and chills in equal measure. Her eyes were closed and her teeth were chattering.

Will's heart went out to her. He knew from experience that as soon as she succeeded in getting warm, she'd become too hot, and as soon as she succeeded in cooling off, she'd be chilled to the bone. Leaving her long enough to walk down the hall to the linen closet, Will retrieved another blanket, took it back to his bed, and spread it over Julie.

"Whoa!" Jack entered the room half an hour later with a fresh pot of coffee and barely made it over the threshold. "How can you breathe in here?" he demanded of Will, who sat on the chair beside the bed, reading aloud to Julie, who was sound asleep and buried beneath a mound of covers.

"I'm not sure I *am* breathing," Will admitted.

"Between the heat and the stench . . ." Jack set the pot of coffee on the table beside the wing chair and walked over to open the window. "I think the paint is sliding off the walls. Aren't you hot?"

"As a sinner in Hades." Will closed the book and looked up at his friend. "I feel like a pig on a spit, but she's having chills."

"Saints preserve us!" Jack exclaimed. "It's going to be a long night."

Will nodded. "She threw up the laudanum. All over my shoes and the rug. She's in pain, but the medicine makes her ill."

"Drag the rug into the hall. I'll have Ben come collect it."

"We'll have to use brandy for the pain," Will told him. "And hope for the best."

If the course of this evening followed the course of the previous one, it would be one long night of piling on covers and building up the fire to warm her, only to open the window, pull off the covers, and bathe her with cool water in order to get her temperature down.

Over and over again.

And with the fever came the nightmares. She tossed and turned, thrashing about, reliving the attack, crying out for help. Shouting, "Fire!" while Will held her to keep her from doing further damage to herself as did her best to escape.

After her struggling to get away from him, Julie collapsed in Will's arms and cried tormented, piteous tears, repeatedly calling out for Su Mi, begging Su Mi to stay alive until she could find her and take her home.

The cycle continued through the night—fever, bad dreams, tears, chills—until she finally fell sleep.

"Poor girl. I'll sit with her for a while. Go downstairs," Jack ordered, already shedding his jacket and rolling up his shirtsleeves to combat the overwhelming heat in the room. "Get some fresh air. Walk around. Get something cold from the bar. Cool off."

Will stood up. "If she wakes . . ."

"I'll send for you," Jack said, repeating the assurance he'd repeated every time Will left the room. "Is she still having bad dreams?"

"Yes, and the brandy I've been forcing down her for the pain is no better than the laudanum. The pain may be diminished, but the nightmares seem to be worse." He glanced from Jack to the girl on the bed. "Maybe I should stay. . . ."

"I don't think so, boyo," Jack told him. "You need to get out. The heat in here is almost intolerable."

Will had to agree. He'd been drenched in perspiration off and on for hours. "Maybe I'll walk down to that little shop on the way to the wharf. Gino's or Giovanni's—the one that sells those Italian ices. Or Ghirardelli's for chocolate ice cream. Something cold and soothing for her throat."

"Why don't you get one for yourself?" Jack suggested. "I don't think she's up to it yet, but your throat must be raw. I heard you reading from down the hall. You've been at it for hours."

"It keeps me from dozing by the fire," Will admitted, peeling off his sweat-soaked shirt, exchanging it for a fresh one he took out of his armoire. Snagging his tie from the back of the chair, he draped it around his neck.

"Why are you fighting so hard to stay awake, Will?" Jack asked. "You need to sleep while she does. You need to get some rest."

"I'm bone-tired. I'm afraid I'll fall into a deep slumber." *And that might bring dreams of Mei Ling. Or worse, of Elizabeth.* Haunted dreams he hadn't the strength to fight.

"Don't be afraid," Jack teased. "That's the best kind of slumber."

"What if she wakes up and needs something?" Will frowned down at his dwindling supply of clean shirts before removing another one from the drawer and placing it atop the armoire for Julie. She would need it if her chills were followed by another bout of fever. "Her voice is a whisper. I'm not sure I could hear it."

Retrieving the gold cuff links he'd removed earlier when he'd rolled up his sleeves in order to seek relief from the heat, Will shoved them through his cuffs. He picked up his discarded waistcoat and jacket.

Jack gave Will a look of patent disbelief. "Trust me; you'll hear her."

"Are you certain?"

Jack gifted him with another look of disbelief. "You've been listening to the girl breathe for two days, Will. You'll hear her."

Will exhaled his relief. It was unlike him to be uncertain or to worry over situations beyond his control. Needless worrying wasn't part of his nature. He was deliberate. And decisive. He planned for the best possible outcome in any situation, did his best to eliminate the unknowns, and trusted that he could handle anything unexpected that might arise. Will had never been given to second-guessing himself. He had always been secure in the knowledge that he'd done his best, and his best was better than most.

But he was worried about Julia Jane. And Will was honest enough with himself to admit that his worry stemmed from his feelings of general helplessness. He hadn't been able to prevent his little missionary from making enemies, and despite his warning, he hadn't been able to protect her from those enemies. When it came to protecting her, he had been useless, just as he'd been useless to prevent what had happened to Mei Ling, and the guilt he carried was eating away at him.

"I'll relieve you in an hour or so," Will told him.

"Take your time," Jack replied. "Put in an appearance in the grand parlor. Our regulars are beginning to wonder what's become of you. Get acquainted with the Pinkerton detectives."

"They've arrived?" So much had happened since Julie had taken her parasol to his front window on Saturday morning, Will had all but forgotten that he had wired Denver for Pinkerton agents he knew to be completely trustworthy, the only agents Murphy O'Brien had included on the list he had sent to his younger brother for consideration.

"Earlier this afternoon on the Denver train," Jack confirmed. "I gave them their duty assignments and arranged their schedules. I also took the liberty of paying the previous 'Pinkertons' and releasing them from their obligations."

"Thanks, Jack." Will extended his hand in friendship. "I couldn't have managed without you."

Jack grinned. "That's why you hired me, Will. To handle the things you need help handling. Or things you don't wish to handle."

"Speaking of which . . ." Will paused for effect. "If I am not mistaken, there is a meeting of the San Francisco Saloon and Bordello Owners' Association Wednesday morning at the Lotus Blossom."

"You are not mistaken."

"How would you like to go in my stead? To represent the Silken Angel Saloon?"

"I would be delighted to go in your stead, Will, but I am sure that my presence there would not be tolerated or allowed."

Will knew where the conversation was headed, but he was enjoying this bit of sparring with Jack. It was comfortable. It was normal. It was the way the two longtime friends and colleagues dealt with the strain of their dangerous endeavors. "How so?"

"The name of the organization whose meetings you are obligated to attend is the San Francisco Saloon and Bordello *Owners'* Association. You are the owner. I am but a barman in your employ."

Will chuckled. "And a finer barman never lived."

"And don't you forget it," Jack warned.

"I'm not likely to," Will retorted. "Not with you reminding me at every turn."

"You're already deciding how to handle Madam Harpy's presence at the meeting on Wednesday." Jack was serious.

"How am I going to sit beside the woman and pretend everything is business as usual when I know she ordered *that*"—he spit out the word as he nodded toward the bed—"done to that girl lying in my bed?"

"I don't know," Jack told him. "But I've no doubt you will do whatever you have to do to manage it. Because as far as Madam Harpy is concerned, it *is* business as usual. *Ugly, deadly* business," he added. "And, Will?"

"Yes?"

"Do me a favor and get one of those Italian ices when you take your walk. But leave the hunt for Typhoon Julia's assailant for a later time." Jack knew as well as Will did that the beat cops tended to congregate at a coffee shop next to the Italian ice shop on the wharf. "You are exhausted and in no shape to confront anyone. And I prefer you free and in one piece. I'm sure Typhoon Julia would agree."

"He won't keep the marks she gave him much longer," Will protested. "I need to locate him now, while he still has them."

"There's no guarantee he still has them," Jack argued. "And you've a better way of finding him than prowling the streets at night."

Will muttered a curse beneath his breath. "Madam Harpy."

"'Fraid so," Jack commiserated.

"I don't know if I can stay in the same room with her without revealing my contempt for her."

"Too bad," Jack reminded him. "Because she's going to want to demonstrate her particular fondness for you."

## Chapter Nineteen

❧❧❧

*"All truths are easy to understand once they are
discovered; the point is to discover them."*
—GALILEO GALILEI, 1564–1642

Someone was reading aloud. Julie lay with her eyes closed
and listened to the cadence of the voice. It took her a few
seconds to identify the owner and the story he was reading.
It was Will Keegan, and he was reading Victor Hugo's *Hunchback of Notre Dame* in French.

"Interesting choice." Her voice was stronger. It wasn't back
to normal yet, but she was no longer relegated to a mere
whisper.

Will closed the book and looked over at her. Her eyes were
open, although it was impossible for her to open her swollen
and bruised eye completely. "My library here is limited. But
you knew the work, so I assumed that meant you liked
Romanticism."

His voice was hoarse, and from his place in the story, Julie
suspected he must have been reading aloud for quite a while.
Reaching up, she traced the sutures above her eyebrow with
her fingers and grimaced. "I enjoyed the story, but I never
aspired to resemble Quasimodo."

Will set the novel aside and gave her a reassuring smile.
"Dr. Stone had to sew you up in a few places."

She wasn't normally vain, but the thought of being scarred for life frightened her. "On my *face*?"

He heard the alarm in her voice and read the panic in her uninjured eye. "And your shoulder."

"Oh." Julie reached up to touch her shoulder and felt a bulky bandage beneath the silk of the garment covering it.

"It took ten stitches to close the wound," Will explained. "But not to worry: Dr. Stone was very careful. He took tiny stitches. If there is a scar, it will be all but invisible."

"You said he sewed me up in a *few* places," she reminded him. "How many others?" She gingerly circled the area around her swollen eye and cheekbone, searching for more sutures.

Will slid to the edge of his chair, leaned over, and gently ran the pad of his thumb over her lower lip. "Here." He touched the first stitch, and then the other one. "And here."

His gentle touch sent a shiver of longing—or perhaps *belonging*—through her. Something about this particular man made her feel special. As if he saw something in her that no one else had ever seen.

Julie ran the tip of her tongue across the wound. "That's all?"

"That's all," he confirmed, gently stroking the area between her bottom lip and her chin. "You bit through it."

*"Oh."* That frisson of awareness shot through her once again. There was no doubt about it: Will Keegan made her feel sensations she'd never felt before. She smoothed her fingers through her hair and noticed the new bandage on her wrist. "Is it broken?"

Will shook his head. "I'm happy to say that my diagnosis was incorrect. He twisted it enough to sprain it. Not enough to break it." He made a face. "I'll wager it hurts the same, though."

She tried to smile, but couldn't quite manage it. "Only a bit." She glanced over to his shaving stand. A length of toweling was draped over the mirror. "Thank you for that. I must look a fright."

Will had covered the mirror after shaving that morning to prevent the light from the lamps and the fire from reflecting off it and into his eyes as he sat reading. He hadn't thought to cover it to keep Julia Jane from waking and seeing herself, but he was willing to let her think it. "You look like a beautiful, brave, and clever woman," Will told her. "You look like a survivor."

She blushed once more, and this time the brighter reddish-pink color was visible beneath the dark red-and-violet bruising. "You look tired, Mr. Keegan."

He shrugged his shoulders in a graceful gesture. "I've been unable to claim my bed."

"For how long?" she asked.

"Four nights. Beginning with the night you arrived," he answered.

She was stunned by the sacrifice he'd made on her behalf. He had given her his bed and his bedroom, and the other upstairs rooms were occupied by the Chinese girls. Where was *he* sleeping? Other than on that terribly uncomfortable-looking wing chair. "I've been in your bed three days?"

"I was happy to give you the loan of it." He smiled, the dimple forming in his cheek. "And under the circumstances, I think it more fitting that you call me Will." His warm sherry-colored eyes twinkled. "We have shared a bed, after all."

"Concurrently?"

"I'm afraid not," he admitted. "To my very great disappointment, I was a complete gentleman and respected your privacy." It wasn't the absolute truth; there had been moments when he'd held her when she was caught in the throes of fever and nightmares. He'd glimpsed different parts of her body over the course of her illness, but he and Jack had done their utmost to protect her modesty. And although he'd been present when Dr. Stone had conducted the intimate examination of her to determine whether she had been violated, the doctor had covered her lower half with a sheet to ensure her privacy, and Will had voiced his appreciation for Stone's thoughtful gesture.

"Thank you for giving me the loan of your bed and bed-chamber, and for taking care of me." She stared up at him. "I presume you've tended to my . . . personal . . . needs."

"I didn't do it alone," he told her. "The doctor treated your wounds. Jack and I simply saw that you received the care and the rest your body needed in order to begin healing. We took turns sitting up with you."

"You *and* Jack?" She was mortified by the idea that two men had seen to her most intimate needs without her knowledge. It was bad enough to think of Will Keegan tending to her alone, but to have his barman tend to her as well . . .

His eyes twinkled once more. "I gave you my word I wouldn't peek. I honored it. Jack did as well."

"Weren't there any women available?"

"I'm afraid, Miss Parham, that you chose to collapse after hours in a business and a residence inhabited entirely by bachelors." A half smile played on his lips. "I thought you'd want us to keep your secret and preserve your reputation as well as your well-being."

"There were ladies at the mission . . ." she ventured.

"And saloon girls here during working hours, but we didn't know who was trustworthy and who wasn't," he said. "And it's safer for you if we keep your presence here to ourselves."

"What about the Chinese girls you purchased?"

He shot her a strange look. He thought about denying that the girls were ever in residence, but decided to tell the truth. "The girls are no longer here. They left a few hours before you arrived."

"Where did they go?"

"Someplace where they won't become prostitutes. Someplace where they'll be free of Madam Harpy and anyone else who wants to prey on them."

"Oh." Julie couldn't keep the note of disappointment out of her voice.

"You sound dismayed I didn't succumb to my baser instincts and 'slake my passions' on the Chinese girls." He was chagrined by her inability to accept that he had no designs on the Chinese girls.

"It's not that," she murmured. "I know better than that now. I know you only want the best for them. . . ."

"Since when?" he demanded.

"Since I—" Julie caught herself in time. Before she admitted that she trusted him and felt safe when she was with him. Before she admitted that she liked him and believed he was special, that he was the kind of man she'd thought he could be when he'd carefully checked her for injuries after finding her on the floor of his washroom. When she realized that the only reason she'd taken her parasol to his storefront had been because she was so angry at him for buying the Chinese girls. "Since I woke to find you reading *The Hunchback of Notre Dame* to me in French."

"I'm glad to know that my appreciation for Monsieur Hugo's novel and my classical education have changed your opinion of me." Will couldn't keep the sarcasm out of his voice.

She didn't flinch outright, but the barb found its mark. *"Vous parlez très bien français,"* she said.

*"Merci,"* he said. "My father would be pleased to know his French lessons weren't wasted."

*"Je suis désolé que j'ai mal jugé vous,"* she said softly.

Will recognized how hard it was for her to apologize for misjudging him. "Why were you disappointed to learn the girls are no longer here?"

"I wanted to speak with them."

"It wouldn't have done any good," Will told her. "You could barely speak at all, and they don't speak English."

"No matter," she assured him. "I speak Can—" Julie could have bitten her tongue off at the slip. It was no secret that the Salvationist movement did its best to teach its missionaries Cantonese and Mandarin, but it was rare to find a missionary who spoke the languages like a native. When she'd hit upon the idea of becoming Jie Li, the laundry girl, she'd thought it best to keep her ability a secret so no one would suspect that Julie Parham and Jie Li were one and the same.

*"Cantonese?"* He pinned her with a penetrating look. "And Mandarin, perhaps?"

She looked down at the coverlet and began pleating it between her fingers.

"You mentioned that you grew up in Hong Kong," he continued. "Most British citizens in Hong Kong have a working knowledge of Cantonese. If only to instruct the servants."

"What do you know of Hong Kong?" she asked, without meeting his gaze.

"A fair amount," he told her. "I grew up there."

She looked up at that. "You grew up in Hong Kong?"

"Imagine my surprise when a girl from the old neighborhood shows up at my door, masquerading first as a missionary and then as a Chinese peasant girl," he said, with more than a touch of irony. "The missionary smashes my saloon window because she despises me and everything for which I stand, and the Chinese peasant, half-strangled, stabbed, and bleeding, comes to me for sanctuary." Will gave her that mysterious half smile once again. "Forgive me if I'm a little confused and intrigued by the contrast."

"I'm *masquerading* as a Chinese laundry girl," Julie told him. "I joined the Salvationists. I *am* a missionary, even if I lack the normal missionary zeal."

"My storefront window begs to differ."

Julie couldn't help but smile, despite the two stitches in her lip. "I'm also masquerading as my cousin, Jane Burke."

*"Burke?"* He lifted one brow in query. "Have you a cousin named Jane Burke?"

"I haven't any cousins at all," she replied, her voice weakening, becoming hoarse.

"May I ask how you chose the surname?" he asked.

"You know how," she said. "I became Jane Burke when I realized a policeman had followed me from the Christian Ladies' Benevolent Society tea to the Russ House the night I was attacked."

More intrigued than ever by the fact that she had chosen his middle name as the surname for her new identity, Will reached over, poured her a glass of water from the carafe on the bedside table, and handed it to her, encouraging her to continue. "You went from being Julia Jane Parham to Jane Burke at the Russ House?" He shook his head. "How did you manage that?"

Julie took several sips of water, thanked him, then handed him the glass and picked up the thread of her tale where she'd left off. "You said Madam Harpy hired a *policeman* to kill me. When I realized one had followed me from the Christian Ladies' Benevolent Society tea, I ducked into the shop of Evangeline Dumond, dressmaker and milliner, two doors up from the hotel, and changed from my Salvationist dress into a lovely and very fashionable jade green serge walking dress and a matching green bonnet with a netted brim Madam Evangeline had made up, along with brown false fringe and brown sausage-curl hairpieces beneath my bonnet to hide my red hair. Then I purchased additional hairpieces in blond and black, and another ready-made gown, and hired a cab to take me to the hotel. But when I got there the policeman was talking to the doorman, so I had the cabbie take me to Ghirardelli's."

He had to smile at that: a woman fearing for her life fleeing to San Francisco's premier chocolate shop. "And after Ghirardelli's?"

"The cabbie took me back to the hotel." She looked up at Will. "I thought I was safe, because the policeman was gone by the time I returned, but . . ."

"He didn't leave," Will guessed. "He was waiting in your room when you entered."

"No," she said. "Because I entered Jane Burke's room."

"What did you do after you entered Jane's room?" he asked, completely caught up in her account of what happened to her.

"I spent nearly an hour arranging, rearranging, and moving my belongings from Julie Parham's room to Jane Burke's room, making certain all the Salvationist things were in Julie's room and that Jane Burke's room contained the new dresses, my laundry girl disguise, and enough of my regular clothing and personal items to make it seem that the room was occupied. And I didn't see anyone." She pinned Will with her gaze. "I was in both rooms. Nobody else was in either room."

"How did he get in your room?"

"I don't know," she told him. "I fell asleep, and when I woke up, he was there."

"In Julie's room?" Will asked, following her logic and separating her identities.

"Yes," she replied. She began to shiver in reaction. "He was in Julie's room." She looked up at Will. "I thought my disguise would protect me, but it didn't fool anyone except the desk clerk."

"Maybe. Maybe not." Will was thoughtful. "He might have simply chosen Julie's room first. Had you not been there, he might have gone to Jane's next. How many people know about Jane Burke?"

"Not many. I created her on the spur of the moment because I didn't want to give the cabbie my real name. And then, when the hotel desk clerk didn't recognize me as Julie, I told him I was Julie's cousin, Jane Burke, and asked for a room."

"Nobody else knows that Jane is Julie's cousin?" he asked.

"Nobody."

"You're sure? Was there anybody in the lobby who might have heard you tell the desk clerk?"

"No. There wasn't anyone else in the lobby," she recalled. "The only person I told was the desk clerk."

"Are you certain?" He was relentless. "Is there anyone or anything you left out?"

"No," she insisted. "I've told you everything."

"Except who Su Mi is and why you followed her here."

# Chapter Twenty

❧

*"Act honestly and answer boldly."*
—DANISH PROVERB

*Su Mi?"* Julie tried to sound surprised and innocent, as if the name were unfamiliar to her, but Will Keegan knew better.

"Yes, Su Mi," he replied. "The name you've been crying out in your sleep for the past three days. The person for whom you've been searching."

She was so surprised she couldn't speak. Julie opened her mouth to deny that she might have uttered Su Mi's name in her sleep, but no words of denial came out. Her mouth was a swollen, perfect *O*.

Will watched a mix of emotions cross her face—fear, denial, shock, resignation. "That's why you've been running around Chinatown pretending to be a Salvationist and a laundry girl, isn't it?"

His voice was so gentle and understanding Julie couldn't pretend any longer. "I cried out for Su Mi?"

He nodded. "You were feverish and in pain. Either the willow bark or the laudanum or the trauma brought on the nightmares. In them you called out for Su Mi. In English and in Cantonese." He raked his fingers through his hair and managed a wry smile. "That's how I knew you spoke more than a few words of Cantonese. That's how I knew you were fluent in the language."

"As are you," she whispered. "Apparently."

Will inclined his head in her direction, but didn't confirm or deny her suspicion before changing the subject. "Who is Su Mi, and what is she to you?"

Julie took a deep breath, reluctant to give up any more of her secrets.

So Will took the bull by the horns. "You won't be going anywhere for a while," he told her. "Not with a fever, a stab wound, a badly sprained wrist, a black eye, and a battered face." He didn't spare her feelings in naming her injuries. "I'll wager you're as weak as a kitten. And at any rate, you can't go out as Julia Jane Parham, Salvationist missionary, even if the doctor deems you able to walk around—and he isn't ready to do that yet. You can't run around Chinatown dressed in your Chinese laundry girl disguise, and your Jane Burke disguise won't work no matter what color wig you put on as long as you bear identical marks from the beating Julie Parham took." He stared at her, his light brown eyes boring into hers. "Face it, Julia Jane: You can't leave my bedchamber until you've healed, and that will take *weeks*—not days."

She sucked in a breath that sounded suspiciously like a sob, but Will didn't relent. He couldn't. He had to make her understand that she had to trust someone—and she'd chosen to trust him or she wouldn't be tucked into his bed right now. "Can Su Mi afford to wait? Does she have weeks to spend waiting for you to be well enough to find her? Or do you have compatriots among the Salvationists helping you search?"

"No Salvationist compatriots," she admitted after allowing long, silent moments to pass while she weighed the consequences of telling him about Zhing Wu's help in her quest to locate Su Mi.

"Are you going to let pride prevent you from finding your friend?" He fought to keep from giving in to the frustration he was feeling at her stubborn refusal to tell him everything.

"You need my help, Julie. I'm willing to give it, but I have to know what I'm looking for and what I'm up against."

"Su Mi—" She broke off and quickly turned her head so he wouldn't see the tears forming in her eyes. *Dear God! Su Mi.* If one of Li Toy's henchmen had done this to Julia, what might happen to Su Mi at the hands of similar men? How was she ever going to find her in time to save her now?

"Su Mi?" Will repeated.

"Su Mi is our housekeeper's daughter." She spoke so softly Will had to strain to hear her.

"And?"

"Three—no, four months ago, her maternal uncle arranged her marriage to a young man from a suitable family. Su Mi's uncle paid the dower, signed the contracts, and gave her into the hands of her husband-to-be, who was bound for the Flowery Flag Nation. The marriage was to take place when they reached California. Su Mi was thrilled to be given to a young, handsome, and prosperous man, thrilled to become his bride. But weeks later, we heard that the young man Su Mi was to marry had taken three other brides with him to California. We learned that he wasn't a bridegroom, but a bride *broker*, and that he was selling the girls he had pledged to marry into slavery in California.

"Su Mi's uncle is terribly distraught at the idea that he arranged for his niece to become a *longei*." Julie deliberately used the word she'd chided Zhing for using, because she knew Will would understand how desperate the situation was for Su Mi. "And Lolly, our housekeeper and Su Mi's mother, is devastated. She made me promise I would come here and find her daughter. I couldn't refuse," Julie admitted. "Lolly was my wet nurse before she was our housekeeper. Su Mi and I grew up as close as or closer than sisters." She looked up at Will. "She's *family*."

"Why you?" Will demanded. "Where is your father? Why didn't he come after Su Mi?"

"He would have if he'd known about it, but he's aboard his ship and at sea. The fleet is patrolling international waters off the coast of mainland China," she explained. "With Papa gone, there was no one to do what had to be done except me. So I joined the Salvationists and came to San Francisco to find Su Mi."

Will's heart lodged in his throat. Julia Jane Parham, a mere slip of a girl, had promised to find her close friend and surrogate sister, even though doing so meant traveling thousands of miles to a foreign land and the worst part of an international city in order to search. In a city like San Francisco, filled with hundreds of Chinese prostitutes, it was like searching for a needle in a haystack. There were girls in private households, girls in parlor houses and boardinghouses and brothels, and hundreds of girls confined to the public cribs.

Julie had barely scratched the surface. Northern California cities like Sacramento and Stockton also had large populations of Chinese prostitutes, and the northern mining towns had their own communities catering to prostitution.

Trying to locate one lost girl amid hundreds was a Herculean task for anyone, especially a lone young woman, even if she had more courage and determination than a battalion of soldiers.

Swallowing the lump in his throat, Will lifted her hand from its resting place on the bed. "You don't have to carry your burden by yourself, Julie," he said softly. "Jack and I are here and we can help you. You're not alone anymore. . . ."

"I wasn't entirely alone," Julie told him. "I had Zhing Wu."

"Who is Zhing Wu?" Will wanted to know.

"Zhing is the widowed daughter-in-law of Mr. Wu, the owner of Wu's Gum Saan Laundry. She collects and delivers laundry to the Salvationist mission. That's where I met her."

"And where you got the idea of disguising yourself as a laundry girl." Will immediately grasped the nature of the relationship.

"I tried to gain entrance to the boardinghouses and the parlor houses in Chinatown by going as a missionary, but they wouldn't let me in."

"Whoa. Hold it." Will held up his hand to stop the flow of words as he got a vivid mental image of Julia Jane Parham wrapped in moral outrage and dressed in her Salvationist uniform, marching up to the front door of the Lotus Blossom or the Jade Dragon and ringing the bell. "Tell me you didn't march up to the front door of the boardinghouses and parlor houses in Chinatown."

"Of course I did," she replied, confirming his worst fears. "At first. I managed to get inside a few houses, but they threw me out. And the others barred their doors against me. Then I noticed that the laundry girls were allowed inside where I was not, so I struck a bargain with Zhing Wu."

Will groaned. "What kind of bargain?"

"I pay Zhing to let me collect and deliver laundry in her place." She waited for Will to chastise her for taking advantage of the Chinese girl. He didn't, but Julie felt she should justify her actions anyway. "The money I give her helps her and Mr. Wu, and the work I do at the laundry helps as well."

Will turned her hand palm up, then ran the pad of his thumb over the calluses marring her tender skin. Her hands were those of a lady who had lately been performing manual labor. "You've been helping in the laundry because laundry girls are allowed in every business and residence in the city." Will was awed, once again, by her determination and her ingenuity. Julia Jane was willing to do whatever she had to do to find her friend.

"Not every business," she said.

"For example?" He expected her to name another one of the city's brothels, but Julie's answer surprised him, and Will had thought he was long past surprise.

"The Russ House Hotel."

"What about the Russ House?"

"Laundry girls aren't allowed inside the Russ House," she answered matter-of-factly.

Will frowned. "Then who does the laundry?"

"One of the Chinese laundries, but the Russ House requires that the laundry girls or laundry men come to the back of the hotel and ring for a bellboy. The bellboys collect the laundry and hand it over to the laundry girls at the back door. And when the laundry girls deliver the clean laundry, they ring for the bellboys, who collect and deliver it to the guests' rooms so the laundry workers never set foot in the hotel or violate its 'no Celestials' policy."

"The Russ House Hotel has a 'no Celestials' policy?"

"Yes."

"You're certain?"

"Very." Julie nodded, then removed her hand from Will's massaging grasp in order to cover a yawn. "The desk clerk explained the policy to me quite clearly, first as Jane Burke and then as myself."

"Mmm." Will lapsed into deep thought.

Julie yawned once again.

This time Will noticed. "I've tired you out."

She didn't demur or dispute his statement, but slid down beneath the covers.

Will reached out and fluffed her pillows for her. "Go to sleep. We'll talk again later. And don't be afraid. I'll be here to keep you safe."

Julie closed her eyes and sighed as Will Keegan lifted her hand once again and pressed a gentle kiss on a callus on her palm, followed by a similar kiss on the tender lump on her forehead. "Will?"

"Hmm?"

"Can you help me find Su Mi?"

"I don't know," he answered honestly. "But I keep a private ledger with the names of the girls Li Toy and the members of the San Francisco Saloon and Bordello Owners' Association have bought or sold at auction since I've been here."

That roused her a bit. "A ledger? Su Mi may be listed in it!"

"She might," Will said. "But the names in the ledger are only a fraction of the girls coming into port. . . . There are many others I know nothing about. Not to mention the girls who di"—he caught himself before he reminded her that any number of girls died at sea and never made it to port—"didn't dock in San Francisco, but went to other ports."

"But you'll look in the ledger? You'll try to find her?"

"I promise I'll do everything in my power to find her for you."

# Chapter Twenty-one

*"Never promise more than you can perform."*
—PUBLILIUS SYRUS, 1ST CENTURY B.C.

The regular monthly meeting of the San Francisco Saloon and Bordello Owners' Association took place in the basement of the Lotus Blossom.

Will Keegan sat at a table with the association ledger open, pen in hand, waiting for Li Toy to appear and for the meeting to start. If this meeting followed the course of the others, the madam would boast about the success of the last auction and announce the estimated date of delivery for the next shipment of girls from Kwangtung province and, if he was lucky, the name of the ship arriving in port.

Will doubted he would be *that* fortunate. Madam Harpy played her cards close to her chest. She hadn't revealed the name of the ships in the past. Providing too much information might reveal the names of the ship's captains willing to smuggle girls from China, and a leak to the tongs from within the owners' association would be disastrous for her. The fact that she had to hire men to protect her from the tongs was particularly hard for the madam to swallow. The tongs liked to charge saloon and bordello owners forty dollars per girl in protection fees to prevent the girls from being stolen for ransom, and they charged the establishments' customers another forty dollars a month to keep from being assaulted, robbed, or beaten after each visit. Li Toy refused to pay the tongs who were trying to take over her business unless it was absolutely unavoidable. But she couldn't prevent her customers from regularly doing so. She spent her protection money on paid hatchet men hired to protect her and guard her assets—including her best customers—from street thugs paid by the tongs who would rob them of their purses and their purchases.

She arrived ten minutes late for the meeting, resplendently dressed in a pale lavender cheongsam. "Apologize for lateness. Unavoidable problem with new employee from another house. Must change dress before coming here."

Her admission surprised Will, who had never heard Li Toy apologize to anyone for anything. The fact that the ruthless little madam changed her dress before the association meeting brought an ironic smile to his lips. In some ways, the madam was no different from any woman he'd ever known. A portion of her six-thousand-fifty-dollar profit from her last auction had undoubtedly gone to increase and enhance her wardrobe.

One might say it was tradition for Li Toy to appear at the first San Francisco Saloon and Bordello Owners' Association meeting following each successful auction dressed in new finery. Will didn't know whether it was meant to signify an increase in her profits or to announce that a new cargo of girls was on its way.

Apparently, Li Toy appreciated beautiful clothes the way Will's mother had appreciated pretty shoes. Constance Grace Keegan had been a missionary to her core, married to a missionary, who believed in God, John Knox, hard work, sacrifice, and lovely, well-made shoes. His father used to say that in his mother's case, there should be an eleventh commandment forbidding the worship of shoes. Yet his father had indulged his mother's weakness for elegant footwear. Where other mothers might covet a new bonnet or a new dress to wear to church, his mother hadn't objected to wearing cast-off dresses sent to the mission by society ladies, or a refashioned bonnet, as long as she had the most fashionable shoes to wear with them.

Will supposed Li Toy enjoyed showing off her new dresses at the association meetings the way his mother had enjoyed showing her new shoes off at Sunday services by shortening her skirts just enough to allow her shoes to be seen and admired—even envied. His mother never boasted, never said a word, but everyone in the church knew Mrs. Keegan was wearing new shoes.

Will grinned at the incongruity of comparing Constance Grace Keegan to the ruthless madam Li Toy. John Knox or God or both would surely strike him dead for it.

"You like?" Seeing Will's grin, Li Toy sidled up to him.

Will swallowed his smile. Jack had teased him for months about Li Toy's penchant for him. And he had found it humorous, but there was nothing funny about the way Li Toy was looking at him now. Or the way she was preening in front of him. "The color is very becoming."

"That mean you like?" She pirouetted to give him a full view of the dress.

He knew she was fishing for compliments, but praising her for her looks was beyond him. Li Toy might have been pretty once, but that was at least two decades before he was born, and while Will had sympathy for her struggles to survive squalor and starvation in China, and humiliation and depravity as a prostitute in California, he couldn't sympathize with or admire what she'd become. He thought of little Tsin and her sisters and cousins instead. Still, he knew better than to make an outright enemy of her. "The dress is lovely."

She smiled at him, showing teeth stained from chewing betel nuts. She wore a lotus blossom in her hair, adorned with lavender-colored tassels that matched her dress. Her usual decorative chopsticks were missing. "I wear just for you, Keegan."

The tips of Will's ears turned red, though to his credit, he didn't blush like a schoolgirl, or show his embarrassment in any other way. Several of the other saloon and bordello owners snickered at Li Toy's obvious flirtation, and, hearing them, Madam Harpy rounded on them like a falcon diving for a mouse. "Why you laugh? Because Keegan likes? Bah! You no gentleman like Keegan. His women special."

A frisson of something akin to fear mixed with dread spread over him from top to bottom as his words from the night of the auction came back to haunt him. Will distinctly remembered implying that the difference between Li Toy's girls and his was that she believed girls were worthless. He believed the seven girls he'd bought at the auction were special—worth every penny he paid for them and more. He believed they had great value—to him, to themselves, to the world.

The unintentional consequence of his revelation to Li Toy was that Madam Harpy liked him more because of it. And Will wasn't comfortable with her affection. He was, in fact, most uncomfortable and uneasy with it. Will shifted in his seat, tapped his pen against the table, and called the meeting to order.

Treating the association as legitimate made it easier for Will to attend to its business. This morning his attention was turned to the monthly reports of payments paid to different groups throughout the city who were on members' payrolls for a variety of reasons.

Opening his ledger, Will prepared to record the amounts. Although he was capable of writing in Chinese characters and was proficient with an abacus, he didn't reveal those talents to the members of the association, because he was supposed to be a normal English gentleman who wouldn't have those skills. "Old business," he announced, before glancing at Li Toy. "Ladies first."

Madam Harpy giggled.

The sound grated on Will's nerves. "Payments?" He struggled to make the one word sound more like an invitation to impart knowledge.

Li Toy listed a dozen payments to police, city council members, and judges, several bribes paid to Chinese merchants, and a number of payments to tongs who provided protection for ships' cargoes—legitimate cargoes. Will recorded the amounts in the ledger. What he didn't record were the names of any of the people she had added to the payroll in the past month, because Li Toy didn't name names of policemen or city officials. Or ship captains. She referred to them as numbers. Policeman Number Twenty-eight. Councilman Number Four. Businessman Number Fifty-three. Judge Number Eight, Captain Number Five, Port Authority Number Seven, etc.

Will was happy to note that the number of policemen on Madam Harpy's payroll had increased by only three since the previous month. But he was disappointed to learn that the only people she named were the tong members she despised, because the tongs demanded payment for every girl she owned, although they bore no part of the expense of purchasing or importing them. The money the tongs extracted from Li Toy was pure profit for them, and Madam Harpy hated them for it.

Hiding his dissatisfaction, Will carefully wrote down all the details Li Toy gave him before moving on to the next association member.

After listing the payouts, Will turned to the first page of the ledger and tallied the amounts from each of the association members. When he finished recording the entries, Will had filled three ledger pages.

He was making the final notations in the ledger when Li Toy made her announcement. "New shipment of girls coming in. Auction at nine o'clock at the Nightingale Song on Saturday night."

A round of groans and several protests went up from the association members. Saturday night was the busiest night of the week. Most of the businessmen spent their evenings at their places of business greeting customers and overseeing their employees. Saloons and houses of prostitution were packed with customers on Saturday nights, because Sunday was the Sabbath for most of the white barbarian devils, and a day of rest. The brothel owners and madams were glad that a good many of the white men woke up considerably poorer on Sunday mornings. No one wanted to leave a manager or a head bartender or a most trusted girl alone with the till or with an office safe filled with cash on Saturday nights. It was bad business.

While most everyone looked forward to the auction and the influx of new blood in the brothels and upstairs businesses, few owners looked forward to making the arrangements required in order have the houses run smoothly on the busiest night of the week. New girls were always popular. That simple fact often caused friction among the girls and clients alike. Clients believed the myth that new girls were less likely to suffer from disease, and variety, being the spice of life, added to the new girls' cachet.

All that meant money to the owners. Big money. And big headaches.

"Cannot be helped," she said. "Storms over ocean cause late shipment."

It wasn't much of an explanation, but like her apology for her tardiness, it was more of an explanation than Will had ever heard Madam Harpy make. And it was enough to mollify the majority of the association members, all of whom appreciated the uncontrollable nature of delayed shipments by sea, by rail, or by mule train. Theirs was a difficult city to reach overland, and the seven-thousand-mile voyage across the Pacific from the coast of China was long and equally hazardous, especially when nature made matters worse. The major storm season was still a few weeks away, but the ship captains delivering goods across the Pacific had already reported strong storms and early typhoons.

With the meeting adjourned, Will gathered up his ledgers, pens, and ink bottle and returned them to his leather satchel. He bade the other association members good-bye as they made their way to the door, then buckled his satchel and stood up to leave.

Madam Harpy halted him. "Wait, Keegan." She moved closer to him. "You remember to hire more protection for the Nightingale Song on Saturday night?"

"How much more?" he asked, wondering whether she

wanted additional protection from the missionaries or the tongs.

"Enough for tongs," she told him. "I no need protection from the missionaries now that I get rid of nosy 'Bringing in the Sheaves' girl for you."

He gave her a sharp look. "For me?"

"Yes, for you," Li Toy confirmed, giving him a coy smile.

"What did you do?" Pretending ignorance of the deed, Will dropped his leather bag onto the seat of his chair.

"I hear she break front window at the Silken Angel," she explained. "I look out for you. I tell my man to take care of her so she not make more trouble and more expenses for my *special* friend, Will Keegan."

"I don't know what to say," he told her. "I would like to express my appreciation to your man for taking care of that, but I don't know who he is."

"Better to say nothing," she advised.

Will raked his fingers through his hair in a show of frustration. He knew it was a long shot, but he had to try to get the man's name out of her. "I can't believe you would do murder for me. . . ."

"I do many things for you, Keegan." Li Toy said his name in a singsong voice, pronouncing it with the accent on the second syllable. "But I not do murder for you. Other man do murder." She held up her hands to show him there was no blood on them. "Girl gone. My hands clean."

Will gritted his teeth to keep from shuddering at the idea that a woman old enough to be his grandmother was flirting with him. It made his skin crawl with revulsion, but he couldn't show it. "Madam, in the eyes of the law, there's no difference between hiring someone to commit a murder and doing it yourself," he explained, to see how much she would admit.

*"Keegan."* Reaching over, Li Toy placed her palm against his shirtfront. "Not to worry about the law. The law not hurt Li Toy, but you nice to worry about your *special* friend."

"You're certain the law won't hurt you?" He put as much concern as he could possibly muster into his tone of voice, marveling at how much better he was as an actor than he would have thought possible. If the Silken Angel Saloon venture failed and he decided not to return to Craig Capital, Ltd., he could always call upon Sir Humphrey Osborne and ask to join the theater troupe.

At the moment, Will needed to figure out a way to extricate himself from Madam Harpy's unwanted attentions.

"The law not bother with Li Toy." She smiled at Will, showing her betel nut–stained teeth. "Li Toy has law in her sleeve."

Will met her smile with one of his own. If she noticed his smile was forced, she didn't show it. "I am relieved to hear it."

"You be at auction, Keegan," she instructed. "You buy new girls."

"I bought seven at the last auction," he protested.

Madam Harpy giggled. "You buy more. Make Li Toy rich."

"You're already rich."

She giggled again. "Make Li Toy richer."

IT TOOK A FEW MORE MINUTES TO EXCUSE HIMSELF, BUT Will finally managed to leave the Lotus Blossom. He had originally planned to go directly to Craig Capital, Ltd., but observing Li Toy had given him an idea. He had an errand to run before he made his weekly meeting with Pete Malcolm at the company's San Francisco office a day later than usual.

Will wound his way through the narrow streets to his destination, completed his task in good fashion, then walked two blocks to Montgomery Street, hired a closed cab, and instructed the driver to take a roundabout route to Craig Capital, where he made it to his office in time for a meeting he'd requested with Peter Malcolm.

Peter Malcolm met him in the foyer and the two men shook hands. "Good morning, Mr. Keegan. I received Jack's message and got started right away."

"Were you able to locate the documents I requested?" Will asked without preamble. He'd been away from the Silken

Angel for close to three hours, and he was eager to conclude his business and get back to check on Julia Jane. He wanted to be there for Dr. Stone's visit.

"I have them ready for you to review," Malcolm told him as they walked down the marble hall toward Will's office. "They're on your desk."

"Did you review them?"

"Briefly," Malcolm said. "I went over the financial statements. But I thought we would go over them together." He opened the door to Will's office and ushered his boss inside.

"How many times have we extended the loan?" Will picked up the stack of papers on his desk, then walked around behind it and pulled out his chair. He hadn't been in the office in over a week and Will was struck by how different it felt to be there. Everything ran smoothly at Craig Capital. After the hustle and bustle of the Silken Angel, it was hard to imagine that he'd once thrived in the quiet, serene atmosphere of this office, where the excitement of the day was the routine accumulation of money and assets.

"Six."

Sitting down on his comfortable desk chair, Will began to read, searching the documents for the particulars of the agreement. It was there in section three, paragraph four. Will breathed a sigh of relief. He wanted to right a wrong, but it had to be done legally.

"Did you send word to Phillip Iverson that he was in arrears with his payments?" Will asked.

Malcolm nodded. "We've sent notices for the past three months warning him that the note would not be renewed for a sixth time without a payment or partial payment from him."

"Did you inform him that we are calling the note as of today?"

"Yes. I sent a copy of Mr. O'Brien's suggestions to Mr. Iverson and the manager, and I wired notice to Iverson two days ago."

"Have we received payment?" Will looked up from the documents he was reading and over at Malcolm.

"No."

"Have we received any communication from Iverson? Any effort to enact Jack's suggestions or to meet his obligations?"

Malcolm shook his head. "I'm afraid not, sir."

Will frowned. "According to his financial statement, the business is turning a handsome profit, yet he's made no attempt to pay us what he owes. It doesn't make sense. Unless . . ." He flipped through several pages to the investigator's report. "Ahh, here it is." He looked over at Malcolm. "Mr. Iverson is low on cash. It seems he's been speculating on Wall Street and he's suffered a reversal of fortune. There's a recommendation that we not renew the note, because Mr. Iverson is no longer a good risk." The written recommendation was signed by Jack O'Brien and dated six months earlier. Will handed the pages over to Malcolm to review and witness. "Draw up the necessary documents transferring ownership, Pete. Post the notices in the *Chronicle*. I'll call a meeting of the employees for the end of the week so we can evaluate the staff and decide whom to keep and whom to release."

Malcolm nodded in agreement. "Do you want me to wire Mr. Craig?"

"No," Will told him. "I'll do it."

"Have you a buyer in mind?" Malcolm inquired.

"Me," Will explained. "I'm the buyer."

Will's announcement surprised him. "You?"

"Yes," Will confirmed. "Unless Jamie decides to take it off my hands and keep it as a Craig Capital asset. Meanwhile, I'm buying it for personal reasons, and I'm paying the fair market value, plus another ten percent. Calculate the amount and pay Craig Capital from my personal account."

"But, Will—I mean, Mr. Keegan," Malcolm protested, "you're a partner. The property can be yours for the payoff of the note, plus the Craig Capital commission. If you do it the way you suggested, you'll be paying more than necessary."

"I know, Pete." Will appreciated Malcolm's concern and his honest assessment of the transaction. "But I want it this

way. Send word to me at this address when the paperwork i
done." He handed Malcolm a slip of paper with his mailing
address written on it. "I'll come in and sign it."

"All right, Mr. Keegan."

"Thank you, Mr. Malcolm, for your expertise in this mat
ter, and for your diligent stewardship of Craig Capital, Ltd.
He offered his hand to Pete, and Malcolm took it in a firm
handshake.

"You're welcome, Mr. Keegan. Thanks for the opport
unity."

After bidding farewell to his manager at Craig Capital'
San Francisco operation, Will hailed a cab. He had more
errands to run and business calls to make before he would be
free to return to the Silken Angel and the girl who waited
upstairs in his bed.

## Chapter Twenty-two

❧❧❧

*"Pray that you will never have to bear all
that you are able to endure."*
—JEWISH PROVERB

Jack O'Brien delivered Julie's breakfast tray Wednesday
morning. She looked up when he opened the door to Will's
bedroom and was clearly disappointed to see him instead of
Will.

Pushing herself up against the headboard, Julie ran her
left hand through her hair, combing the tangles in a self-
conscious gesture. "Where's Will?"

Jack smiled. "Good morning to you, too."

Julie had the grace to blush, the color more visible now
that the worst of her bruises had gone from crimson red to a
lighter shade of bluish purple. "Good morning, Jack," she
said. "I apologize for my rudeness." She smoothed the wrin-
kles from the covers at her side. "But Will usually brings my
breakfast."

"Apology accepted." Jack brought the tray to the bed and
set it on Julie's lap. He took the cover off the plate of food,
then handed her a napkin and arranged her cutlery, placing
it within her reach, along with a mug of tea.

The smell of fluffy scrambled eggs, bacon, pan-fried pota-
toes, and a light-as-air biscuits made her mouth water.

"I brought your tea in a mug," Jack told her. "I imagine you prefer a teacup and saucer, but I thought this would be easier for you to manage. One lump or two?"

Julie saw that Jack had placed a small container of cream on the tray and several lumps of sugar on a saucer. "One, please," she replied. "And a bit of cream." She was thankful for the tea. Yesterday Will had brought a rather strong mug of coffee with her breakfast.

He added cream and sugar to her tea and handed her the mug.

She took a grateful sip. "It's perfect. Thank you."

Jack nodded. "You're welcome." He watched Julie enjoying her tea and added, "Will left for a couple of early morning meetings—one of which is at the Russ House. If you would like, I can send your key over to him so he can retrieve some of your personal belongings."

She brightened. "That would be wonderful." Reaching up, she took the key to room six from around her neck and handed it to Jack. "The key to the other room is in the pocket of my trousers." She looked up at Jack, then took a deep breath. "Tell him I hid money in the pole of the headboard in room eight."

Jack nodded. "Will would have asked you for the keys to both rooms himself, but you were sleeping and he didn't want to wake you. He asked me to see to your breakfast tray and take care of anything you might need."

Julie was able to make it to the washroom and the water closet on her own to tend to her urgent needs, but dressing in anything other than one of Will's dress shirts and his robe was impossible. She couldn't manage her bandages, bind her breasts, or don her corset on her own, and Julie couldn't bring herself to ask Will or Jack to help her. And she was in desperate need of a bath, but without help that was beyond her capabilities as well. She was bored, and sick of her own company. Embarrassed, she glanced up at Jack from beneath her lashes. "I could use a bath and something to wear, if you can spare someone to help me."

Jack frowned. "I don't have anyone here who can help you. I'll be happy to draw you a bath, but . . ." He shrugged his shoulders. "Well, I . . ." He sputtered to a stop. He and Will had taken care of her while she was unconscious, but she was awake now, and the situation was different.

Julie blushed again. "I understand."

"The doctor is coming to check on you this morning," Jack told her. "Maybe he can . . ."

"I would rather he didn't," Julie replied. She didn't remember the doctor. To her, he was a stranger. Will Keegan and Jack O'Brien might consider him trustworthy and a friend, but Julie intended to reserve judgment until she met him. "I would prefer to bathe before he gets here."

"After you eat your breakfast, I'll set a basin with warm water, soap, and a face flannel out for you to take a sponge bath," Jack offered, knowing it wasn't as satisfying as taking a real bath, but it was the best he could offer.

"I would be grateful." Julie gave him a genuine smile and began to eat her breakfast. A sponge bath was better than nothing, but she longed for the real thing. "If only Zhing were here . . ." She didn't realize she'd given voice to the thought until Jack repeated the name.

*"Zhing?"* He was curious.

"Zhing Wu," Julie clarified. "She works at Wu's Gum Saan Laundry. We became friends when she came to collect laundry at the mission. She helped me with my laundry girl disguise."

Jack was thoughtful. "Would she come here if I sent someone to get her?"

"Who does your laundry?" Julie finished her bacon and eggs and drank more of her tea.

"The Market Street Laundry," Jack replied. "Why?"

"Zhing works for her father-in-law," Julie explained. "He wouldn't allow her to come unless it's worth his while."

"So she'd need to be paid for her time," Jack concluded.

"Either in cash or laundry to wash."

"We can manage that." Jack refilled her mug from the small teapot on the tray, added a lump of sugar and a splash of cream to it, then collected her dirty plate and cutlery. "You and Will have gone through his shirts at an alarming rate."

He smiled at Julie. "Do you think your friend would be interested in doing Will's laundry?"

Julie nodded.

"Should I send a note to her at Wu's laundry asking her to come here?" Jack asked. "Or should I send a runner to fetch her?"

"She cannot read," Julie explained. "And today is Wednesday, so Zhing is out collecting laundry." She glanced at the mantel clock. "She should be making her way to the boardinghouses along Jackson Street about now, and from there she'll go back to Wu's. If you have a runner you trust, send him to Wu's and tell him to ask Zhing if she would be willing to make a most profitable collection at the Silken Angel Saloon for Jie Li. Ask her to come as soon as possible." She described Zhing Wu to Jack. "Please ask your runner not to frighten her."

"Of course." Jack promised. He already had the man in mind for the job—one of the Denver Pinkertons currently standing guard downstairs, a young man named Seth Hammond whom his brother, Murphy, had recommended as smart, dedicated, and trustworthy. "Will you be all right by yourself while I go downstairs and make the arrangements?"

Julie glanced around the room, gauging the distances she would have to negotiate to reach the necessary and the washroom and the sitting area. "Yes."

"Can I trust you not to try to leave or to damage anything while I'm gone?"

Julie was surprised. "I wouldn't dream of repaying your kindness or Will's kindnesses by damaging any more of his property. And even if I did"—she gave him a self-deprecating shrug—"I don't have a parasol, and I'm in no condition to swing one."

"No insult intended," Jack told her, "but I'm to look out for you when Will's gone, and I can't be in two places at once. Nobody else knows you're up here, and Will would never forgive me if anything happened to you."

Julie did her best not to sound too eager, but she couldn't contain her curiosity where Will Keegan was concerned. She wanted to know everything about him. "Why do you say that, Mr. O'Brien?"

"My name is Jack, remember, and I said it because it's true. Will didn't go to all the trouble and expense to help you and keep you safe just to have me allow you to slip out and come to more harm." Jack pinned her with a hard look.

"I gave you my word."

"You gave Will your word you wouldn't come back here singing and smashing, and now we're missing the front plate-glass window." Jack hadn't meant to be accusatory, but the words were out before he could stop them.

Julie knew what he said was true, but having Jack bring it up again when she was confined to bed and unable to do anything about it stung. "I promised to pay for the window," Julie reminded him. "And I will. The money I hid should be enough. I can pay Zhing and the doctor, and reimburse Will for the window."

Jack raked his fingers through his hair, frustrated by her lack of understanding of the larger scope of the danger all around them. "And the team of men we've had to hire to guard the place around the clock until the new window is installed? Are you going to pay for them, too?"

"*What?*"

She looked so stricken, Jack swore beneath his breath at his uncharacteristic bluntness and lack of manners, and immediately began to apologize. "Forgive me for being rude and tactless. I'm afraid my exhaustion is showing." He gave her a half smile. "There's no need for you to worry about anything. Will can well afford the window, the doctor, the Pi—the guards, and anything else that might come up." He paused. "I'm usually the soul of discretion, but you need to understand that this thing with Li Toy and her hired police-man isn't only about you. You may be her primary target at the moment, but you aren't the only one. And Will has been so concerned with protecting you, taking care of you, that he's let down his guard. He's not looking out for himself."

"He's a member of the San Francisco Saloon and Bordello

Owners' Association," Julie said. "He and Li Toy are associates. Why does he need to be on his guard?"

Jack shot her a disgusted look. "And here I thought you were a clever girl. . . ." He clucked his tongue. "Haven't you ever heard the old saying, 'Keep your friends close and your enemies closer'?"

"Is that what he's doing?" Julie asked.

Jack sighed. "You figure it out. I've said too much already."

"You're a good friend to him," Julie said softly.

"I try to be," Jack said. "But I'm afraid I'm bungling it badly right now, and I'd prefer not to have anything—especially a young woman—damage our friendship. We've known each other too long and too well for that."

"How long?" Julie asked.

She expected him to say he and Will were lifelong friends, so she was a bit taken back at Jack's answer. "Since he hired me. Four years ago." Opening the bedroom door, Jack set the breakfast tray on the floor in the hall outside to collect on his way out. When he finished, he filled the washbasin with water and laid out soap, face cloth, and towels for her. "In case you need it before the doctor arrives."

"I didn't realize the Silken Angel Saloon had been here four years."

"It hasn't," Jack told her. "I worked with Will at his previous venture. I came with him when he opened the Silken Angel." He opened the bedroom door. "Now I need to return to work before he fires me."

"What about Zhing?"

"I haven't forgotten," Jack told her. "I'm sending word to Will. He'll go get her."

❦

# Chapter Twenty-three

*"No pleasure is comparable to the standing upon the
vantage ground of truth."*
—FRANCIS BACON, 1561–1626

W ill left his meeting with Peter Malcolm at Craig Capital
and made his way to the Russ House Hotel to collect
Julie's belongings from her room.

He arrived to find the youngest and most impressive of the
Pinkerton detectives sitting in the lobby. He felt a jolt of dread
as his senses went on immediate alert. "Is everything all
right?"

"Everything is fine, Mr. Keegan," the young Pinkerton
who identified himself as Seth Hammond assured him. "Mr.
O'Brien sent me with this." Hammond handed over a room
key with the number six painted on the tag. The key was tied
to a woman's yellow hair ribbon—a ribbon stained brown in
places with blood. Will recognized it as the one Julie had
worn around her neck. Hammond handed Will a second key
with the number eight painted on the tag. "He asked me to
give you this as well and tell you that the person who occupied
that room hid money in the post of the headboard. That person
would also like you to find a laundry girl named Zhing who
works at Wu's Gum Saan Laundry and send her to collect the
laundry at your saloon."

Will understood what Jack was telling him. Julie wanted him to collect her belongings and money from Jane Burke's room, and then she wanted him to find her friend Zhing Wu. "Thank you, Mr. Hammond."

"Mr. O'Brien told me to stay and help you."

Will stared at the earnest young detective. "Do you speak Cantonese?"

"No, sir," Hammond told him. "Spanish, a little Swedish, and some French."

Will lifted an eyebrow.

"My grandmother is Swedish."

Will smiled at the detective. "I speak a little Gaelic, courtesy of my mother's mother. She lived with us when I was small." She hadn't left Londonderry with the rest of the family. The journey to Hong Kong had been too much for her. She'd stayed behind and moved in with her other daughter while Will and his two older sisters, Molly and Colleen, set off for Hong Kong with his parents, Francis and Constance Grace Keegan, for a new life as missionaries and teachers. Will surprised himself; he didn't usually volunteer information about his childhood to strangers. His only excuse was that he was tired, and everything about young Hammond shouted that he was trustworthy. Jack obviously thought so or he wouldn't have sent him with a verbal message, and Jack was a very good judge of character—every bit as good as Will was. "You don't speak Cantonese, so that means I should be the one to pay a visit to the Chinese laundry."

"I'll go with you, sir, if you don't mind," Hammond said.

So that was how it was. Jack had sent Seth Hammond to watch his back.

"There's not much call for Swedish in a Chinese laundry," Will said, a hint of humor in his voice. "But we could encounter a lumberjack or two with an ax to grind along the way, and if that's the case, I'll be glad to have you by my side."

Hammond laughed. "You won't regret it, sir."

Will met his gaze. "I don't suppose I will. But before we go in search of the laundry, we need to collect a few personal items from room number eight."

Will nodded at the clerk on duty as he and Hammond passed the registration desk, heading up the stairs to the second floor.

"Mr. Keegan?" the clerk called out. "Are you looking for a room?"

Will had business with the management of the hotel, but he preferred to wait a few days before tackling those issues, so he simply shook his head and continued up the stairs. "Visiting a friend."

Hammond shot him a speculative look.

Will shrugged. "Visiting *the room* of a friend," he clarified out of earshot of the desk clerk. Having stayed at the Russ House many times, Will was quite familiar with the layout of the hotel. Turning right at the landing, he made his way to room six and inserted the key.

The door swung open, and he and Hammond stepped inside and quickly closed the door behind them. The room was a shambles. Will had seen the damage done to Julia Jane, so he knew she'd fought hard for her life, but seeing her room this way—the coverlet pulled off the bed, pillows and her ugly missionary bonnet tossed on the floor, armoire door standing open, several ladies' gowns hanging inside it, dresser drawers opened, and her undergarments, stockings, and nightgowns strewn about the room. Bloodstains dotted the coverlet and rug; a smear of blood marked the wall by the door. A box of pastries lay upside down on the chest at the foot of the bed.

Will picked a stocking off the footboard, noted the embroidery, and tightened his fist around the delicate silk fabric before tucking it into his jacket pocket.

The first thing Seth Hammond decided upon seeing the room was that it didn't belong to a man. His second impression was that something bad had happened to the lady who had occupied it. He took a step forward and kicked a tin lying on the floor. Bending to pick it up, Hammond was surprised to find it contained two pounds of Ghirardelli chocolates. There was a small dent in the lid. Straightening, he showed the tin to Will.

Will traced the dent with his finger. "That must have hurt."

"Sir, if you don't mind my asking, what happened to your friend?"

Recognizing the look of astonishment on Hammond's face, Will replied, "Injured, but alive and safe."

Scanning the room once again, Hammond nodded. "Must have a guardian angel."

"I believe so, Mr. Hammond," Will told him. Retrieving Julie's suitcase from where it had fallen to the floor in the struggle, he began stuffing nightclothes and undergarments into it, topping it with three dresses he removed from hangers and folded.

Seeing Will's intent, Hammond picked a bonnet up off the floor and placed it in a hatbox he recovered from where it had rolled beneath the dresser. Inside the hatbox was a knotted black stocking. Lifting it, Detective Hammond heard the clink of loose coins. He unknotted it and saw that the stocking contained a good bit of money in coins. Whatever the motive had been for what took place in this room, it hadn't been robbery. No self-respecting robber would have left a stocking full of coins behind, or the silver-backed brush, comb, and mirror on the dressing table. Hammond dropped the stocking back in the hatbox with the bonnet.

Will picked up the brush, comb, and mirror along with a box of hairpins and finished packing, then closed and fastened the case. Ready to leave, he lifted the suitcase and started toward the door. "Let's check room eight."

Leaving room six, Will and Hammond walked down the hall and unlocked the door to room eight. They crossed the threshold and closed the door behind them. Scanning the room, they saw a pile of petticoats in the middle of the floor that looked as if the wearer had stepped out of them and left them where they lay. Looking closer, Will could see smears of blood on the waistband that confirmed what Julie had told him: She had managed to get into Jane's room and change into her laundry girl disguise.

Other than the petticoats and a few displaced items on the dresser, the room was untouched by the violence that had taken place next door. Julie's dresses were hanging in the armoire, and everything seemed to be the way she had left it, right down to the tin of chocolates on the dresser. "Jane's room is safe."

Hammond raised an eyebrow in query.

"My friend rented this room for her cousin," Will explained.

"Somebody changed clothes, but it doesn't look like anyone slept here." Hammond studied the bed.

"No," Will agreed. "My friend's cousin left with her. They are staying together where they'll both be safe." He felt a twinge of guilt for lying to the young Pinkerton, but Will felt that the fewer people who knew where Julie was, the better.

"I guess the cousin needs her clothes as well." Hammond gestured toward the armoire.

Will nodded, and the two men began gathering more gowns and stuffing them into a satchel. When they finished, Hammond gathered the luggage and turned toward the door.

"Wait." Will tapped the pole of the headboard closest to him, frowned, then walked around the bed and tapped the other pole. One was hollow. One wasn't.

Hammond paused, his hand on the doorknob.

"Let's not forget the hidden money." Prying the cap off the second pole, Will reached inside it, grabbed a ribbon, and pulled a cylindrical leather case out of the pole. He opened the case, saw that it was stuffed with cash, then closed it.

Will handed the satchel and the suitcase he'd packed to Hammond, then took the leather parasol case and the hatbox in hand. "We'll carry what we can to a cab I have waiting out front and send a bellboy for the rest."

Glancing around the room one last time, Will spotted the Ghirardelli chocolates on the dresser. Thinking Julie might want to keep them as a souvenir if nothing else, Will scooped up the tin, cradled it in his arm, and opened the door, Hammond on his heels.

"What do you think you're doing here?"

Will stood framed in the doorway, waiting for the hotel manager to demand to know what he and Hammond were doing in Jane Burke's room. But he saw that the hotel manager had someone else by the arm. "What do you think you're doing in the hotel?"

"Laundry girl," Will heard the girl say. "I come for missy's laundry."

"What missy is that?" The manager jerked the laundry girl away from Julia Jane's door and spun her around.

Hammond took a step forward to put an end to the hotel manager's manhandling of the girl. Will stopped him with a shake of his head "Not yet."

"Missy room six," the laundry girl answered, her voice rising in direct response to the grip the hotel manager had on her arm. He was a big barrel-chested man more than twice her size. He sported muttonchop whiskers and was dressed in a suit that befitted his position in the hotel. Beneath his suit coat he wore a white dress shirt and maroon tie held in place by a gold tiepin. Over his shirt and tie was a brocade waistcoat that did nothing to disguise his big belly.

He looked the epitome of a prosperous businessman. And a bully.

"You were warned," the manager told her. "This hotel has a 'no Celestials' policy. Now I'm sending for the police."

Will stepped forward into the hall. "Mr. Palmer, what's the meaning of this?"

Palmer, his face florid, wheezing with exertion, turned and saw Will standing in the hall in front of room number eight. "Mr. Keegan, how nice to see you again! I wasn't aware that you were staying with us."

"I'm not," Will told him. "I'm just visiting. What has happened? Why are you accosting that young lady?"

"Young *lady*?" Palmer scoffed. "She's no young lady. She's a Celestial I caught attempting to break into Miss Parham's room."

"From what I overheard, Mr. Palmer, the young *lady* is here to collect laundry from one of your guests," Will said.

"That's what they all say," Mr. Palmer replied. "But the fact is that Miss Parham was informed of our policy forbidding Celestials to enter the hotel proper, and this *laundry*"— he sneered the word—"girl was warned on a previous occasion. The police will have to be called, and as a result of Miss Parham's flouting of our rules and regulations concerning guest conduct, I will have to ask her to vacate her room and the premises—"

"I don't think so." Will stared at the other man.

Having worked up a righteous head of steam, Mr. Palmer was astonished that Will had the audacity to interrupt him. "I beg your pardon?"

"You should be begging this young lady's pardon, sir," Will told him, "as well as mine. I object to any man—especially a man of your stature and girth"—Will heard Seth Hammond's snicker behind him and Palmer's snort of indignation in front of him—"using his position of authority as well as his size to bully weaker individuals, especially females. So I suggest you release the young lady before Mr. Hammond and I are forced to remove you from the premises without benefit of the police."

"You can't do that!" Palmer exclaimed. "I am the m-m-manager of this establishment. The owner, Mr. Iverson, will hear of this outrage!" Palmer was so irate he was sputtering, his double chin was wobbling, and his muttonchop whiskers were vibrating.

"Mr. Iverson no longer owns the Russ House Hotel," Will explained.

"Since when?" Mr. Palmer demanded.

Will shrugged his shoulders. "I heard the news this morning. From what I gathered from the gentlemen discussing it over breakfast, a notice will probably appear in the *Chronicle* in the next day or two. It seems your Mr. Iverson has suffered a reversal of fortune and has neglected an outstanding note, and the owner of that note called it in. As a consequence, the hotel was sold." Will looked Mr. Palmer in the eyes. "Or so I heard." Will concocted the fabrications on the spot and felt no guilt in relating them to a bully like Palmer.

"Who bought the hotel?" Palmer asked.

"I wasn't privy to the entire conversation," Will said in his best businessman's tone of voice.

Palmer looked a bit panicky. "But you're certain your information is correct?"

Will nodded. "There was no doubt about that."

"What about me?" Palmer demanded. "Did you hear whether they were discussing changes in management?"

Will shook his head. "But I'm sure you'll be notified in due course. In the meantime, you might consider the effect your current actions could have on those of us unfortunate enough to witness them."

Palmer's florid face turned redder. "Are you threatening me, Mr. Keegan?"

"I wouldn't dream of it," Will replied in a deceptively calm tone of voice. "I'm simply pointing out the fact that the gentlemen I overheard discussing business this morning are frequent visitors to my establishment and often ask my opinion of the characters and behavior of local businessmen." His look and his voice hardened. "Now, if you would be so kind as to let go of the girl . . ."

"I would do it if I were you." Seth Hammond moved to stand beside him. He was an inch or so shorter than Will, but was equally broad of shoulder and well muscled, and gave the appearance of being quite capable of handling himself in any scrape.

Palmer let go of the laundry girl's arm.

Will smiled at her, hoping to reassure her, then watched as she rubbed her arm where Palmer had gripped it. The expression on her face told him she was frightened and leery of foreign white devils—especially when she was surrounded by three big ones. Speaking to her in a low voice and in Cantonese, Will sought to keep her from running at the first opportunity. "Are you Jie Li's good friend Zhing Wu?"

"You speak that heathen gibberish?" Palmer was too arrogant or too shocked to guard his tongue.

Zhing moved as far away from the hotel manager as the width of the hall would allow.

Hammond shook his head. "Mister, you don't seem to know when your presence is no longer required." He stared at Palmer until the hotel manager heeded his suggestion and stormed down the stairs to his office.

Zhing gave Will a shy smile before replying in her native tongue. "I come here looking for Jie Li. I haven't seen her in days. I was worried."

"No need to worry," Will assured her. "My name is Will Keegan. Jie Li is staying with me."

"Keegan?" Zhing stared up at him, her eyes wide with surprise. "You're Keegan?"

Will watched the play of emotions that crossed her face. She was clearly familiar with his name, if not his history with Julie. "I am."

"What is Jie Li doing at your saloon?" She narrowed her gaze at him. "Why did you let her stay after she broke your window?"

Will smiled. "You know about that?"

"Everybody in Chinatown knows about that. Why would you let Jie Li stay at your business when she smashed it?"

"Jie Li was injured. She came to me for help. I let her stay at my place of business, where she'd be safe," Will answered honestly.

"Is Jie Li hurt badly?" Zhing asked.

Will nodded. "But she's going to be all right. She asked me to find you for her," he added. "She wants to see you. Would you like to come with me and see for yourself?"

Zhing nodded. "I'll go to see Jie Li with my own eyes, to see if what Will Keegan says is true."

"Fair enough," Will agreed.

## Chapter Twenty-four

❧

*"Forget injuries; never forget kindnesses."*
—CHINESE PROVERB

Zhing Wu cried when Will opened the door to his bedroom and she got her first look at Julie's face. He didn't know whether she cried in relief at seeing Julie alive and reasonably well when the word in Chinatown was that the "Bringing in the Sheaves" missionary girl was no more, or from the shock of seeing Julie's battered face. Maybe it was a little of both.

"Zhing!" Julie lit up like the footlights on Sir Humphrey's stage at the Empire Playhouse on opening night. "Thank you for coming."

"Oh, Jie Li, he hurt you too much," she cried in a mixture of Cantonese and English often heard on the streets of Chinatown. She ran to Julie and tried to hug her, but was mindful of what Will had explained was a stab wound in her shoulder, and of her bruised ribs, and settled for a series of awkward pats on her shoulders and arms.

"Jie Li, I so worried about you." Zhing couldn't stop touching her. She touched a finger to the stitches above Julie's eyebrow, then skimmed her hand over Julie's sleeve, up and down several times, as if to make sure her arm was still inside it. Zhing patted Julie's hands and smoothed her hand over

Julie's hair. "Oh, Jie Li, your poor face . . ." And she began to cry again.

Helpless to prevent Zhing's tears, Julie looked at Will. "Do I look that bad?"

"Not to me," Will said. "To me you're as beautiful as a warrior queen. As brave and as strong as Boudicca . . ."

"Boudicca was defeated," Julie reminded him. "And died."

Will stared at her for a long moment, the expression on his face unreadable; then he winked at her. "And you didn't. See how strong you are? Stronger and more beautiful than any warrior queen."

"You are full of blarney, Will Keegan," Julie's voice was low and husky, still only a fraction louder than a whisper, but it had a note in it that made every cell in his body stand up and take notice.

"That I am," Will replied in a fair imitation of Jack O'Brien's Irish brogue, as low and as husky as Julie's whisper, but for an entirely different reason. "Perhaps you'd like a good taste of it. . . ." He fastened his gaze on the stitches in Julie's bottom lip. "When you're feeling better."

Julie blushed. And Will was able to distinguish it from the discoloration on her face.

Ignoring the rise in temperature between Will and Julie— or oblivious to it—Zhing dried her tears with the sleeve of her tunic and launched into an account of everything that had happened since Julie smashed the saloon window. "I leave laundry and go to hotel to look for you," Zhing told her.

"Oh, no." Julie was genuinely alarmed. "Please listen to me, Zhing: You mustn't go into the hotel ever again. It's not safe for you, and I don't want you to get into trouble with the hotel manager."

"It's not safe for you, Jie Li," Zhing reminded her, switching back to Cantonese. "But you're not to worry about me. I'll not get into trouble at the Russ House. The hotel manager will not bother Zhing anymore."

The way she said it made the hair on the back on Julie's neck stand on end. "Why not? You didn't do anything to him, did you?"

"Not me," Zhing assured her. "Mr. Will Keegan." Zhing looked at Will as if he'd hung the moon and the stars.

Aware of Will leaning against the doorjamb watching, Julie met his gaze.

"Thank you so much for finding Zhing and bringing her here."

"I didn't find her," Will said. "Zhing found me at the hotel." Moving farther into his bedroom, Will set Julie's suitcase on the table near the washstand. "I went there to retrieve some of your belongings. . . ."

Julie was so excited she was practically bubbling. "Thank you again."

Will held up her parasol case and the hatbox from Evangeline Dumond's shop. "I brought this and your new green bonnet."

She let out a sigh of relief. "Thank you for retrieving it. I only got to wear it once. Very briefly."

"You'll get to wear it again." He walked over to the massive armoire, opened the door, and set the hatbox and the parasol case on the top shelf. "They're right here if you need them. Your reticule and your black stocking are in the hatbox, and your dresser set is in your suitcase."

"You brought my dresser set? My comb and brush and mirror and hairpins?" Her voice was filled with awe, as if she couldn't believe he could be so thoughtful.

Will closed the armoire door. "Yours or Jane Burke's. I'm not sure which." He looked at Julie.

"Doesn't matter." She beamed. "We're identical."

"The doctor will be here in a little while. If you want Zhing to help you with a bath, you'd better get started. . . ."

Julie turned to Zhing. "Do you mind? I can't manage on my own."

"I'll stay and help Jie Li get ready for doctor," Zhing replied.

Will gave Zhing a smile, then crossed the room and disappeared into the washroom. Seconds later, Julie heard him pouring water into the tub from the buckets of hot and cold water Jack had brought up for her bath. Will came out of the

washroom. "I forgot to tell you that I brought a tin of chocolates from your room." He gave Julie another meaningful
look. "A slightly dented tin of chocolates from Ghirardelli."

"I meant the chocolates as a gift for Zhing. I got a tin for
her and a tin for the girls at the mission, and both were perfect
when I selected them. I'm sorry I dented it."

"I'm not," Will told her. "You can give Zhing the contents
and save the tin." He looked at Julie. "Because that one saved
your life, Julia Jane."

"I could send to Ghirardelli's for another tin." Julie had
chosen the tin because it was decorative as well as functional,
and Zhing liked useful, pretty things.

"I'll have Jack send Ben to Ghirardelli's for another tin,"
Will said. His warm smile made Julie's nerve endings sizzle.
"Now why don't you go enjoy your bath? I'll entertain the
doctor until you're ready to see him."

She returned his smile with one of her own as Zhing hurried into the washroom to prepare Julie's bath.


THE DOCTOR ARRIVED SHORTLY AFTER JULIE FINISHED HER
bath.

She had soaked in warm scented water for as long as she
dared, relaxing as Zhing carefully soaped and rinsed her hair.
The warm water helped soak away the aches and pains and
bruises better than a sponge bath ever could.

She was clean and feeling more like herself for the first
time in days. And she was grateful to Zhing for her help in
assisting her in and out of the bathtub and for washing her
hair, which Julie could never have managed by herself.

Once Julie was out of the tub, Zhing helped her towel off
before wrapping her wrist with a strip of muslin. They
emerged from the washroom to find a lovely sky blue cheongsam lying across the foot of the bed with a matching pair of
slippers.

"Oh, Jie Li . . ." Zhing reached out and fingered the silk
dress. "It's very nice. Very fine silk."

Long and straight with a fitted bodice that fastened in

front, the dress offered support that didn't bind or pinch and didn't require a corset. It was a dress she could manage by herself, and the slit in the skirt from ankle to knee made movement easy. Julie could dress herself without Zhing's help—even with an injured shoulder and bruised ribs. She slipped the dress over her head and sighed with relief. It fit like a dream, and gave her a measure of independence to move around the room in something other than Will's shirts and brocade robe.

"Much better than ugly missionary dress," Zhing pronounced as Julie stepped into the slippers.

"And the ugly black boots." Will tapped on the door, then opened it and stuck his head inside. "May I come in?"

Her hair was still wet, and Julie put a self-conscious hand up to feel it.

"Come in, Mr. Keegan," Zhing invited. She turned to Julie. "Jie Li, sit on chair by the fire. I comb your hair." The little laundry girl patted the ottoman at the foot of Will's favorite chair and motioned Julie forward. "Sit. Sit."

Julie sat on the ottoman. Zhing stood behind her and began to drag a comb through her hair.

"Thank you for the dress."

"You're welcome," Will said. "You couldn't wear your English dresses or the tunic and trousers. It seemed a good choice. I guessed at the fit." He'd had four nights and three days of taking care of her to memorize the contours of her body well enough to be able to select a cheongsam in her size. And seeing her in this one meant he'd be back to purchase more in every color of the rainbow.

Julie ran her hand over the fabric. "It's lovely, and it fits perfectly."

"It matches your eyes," he told her. "And even then, it's not nearly as lovely as the lady wearing it." Will couldn't keep his eyes off her. He'd seen lovelier women. He had been with lovelier women. But this woman made him want, made him dream, made his heart sing. He frowned. She made his heart sing? What poetic drivel was that? He would like to think it utter rot, except there were no other words to describe what she did, what he felt whenever he saw her. The romantic in him, the poet in him, had suddenly come to life, just as the dead heart that had occupied space in his chest for so many years had suddenly sprung to life. Julia Jane Parham, Jane Burke, or Jie Li, the laundry girl—whoever she was made him believe in possibilities . . . once again. . . .

"*Lovely?* Bah!" Zhing exclaimed, busily working the silver comb from the set he'd retrieved from Jane Burke's hotel room through Julie's thick, rich auburn hair. "Keegan, you no see how ugly cuts and bruises make Jie Li's face?"

"I see the cuts and bruises, Zhing," he said softly. "But I think she's beautiful in spite of them."

Zhing snorted in disbelief. "Maybe with lots of rice powder on her face," she speculated. "Not like this."

"No rice powder," Will said.

"It might help," Julie told him, glancing at the mirror in the washstand she had bravely—and somewhat foolishly—uncovered to see for herself the damage to her face that he and Jack had kept hidden from her. "Zhing is brutally honest."

"Zhing is entitled to her opinion, of course, but so am I, and you don't need rice powder."

"I look hideous, but I thank you all the same for the compliments and the dress, and for protecting me from the truth."

Will eyed her sharply, then grinned. "Should I be suspicious?"

"No. Why?"

"You're full of thanks all of a sudden," he told her.

"Maybe I've just realized how lucky I am to be alive, and how fortunate I am to have friends like Zhing and Jack and you." She looked at him from beneath her eyelashes in a flirtatious gesture he'd have labeled coy in any woman but Julia Jane.

He was silent for a moment. "Is that what you think we are? *Friends?*"

"Aren't we?" she asked.

"Only if you're willing to settle for less than what we might be . . ." Will crossed over to his favorite chair, leaned down, and gently traced the bruise on her cheekbone with the pad of his thumb. "I'm not."

*"Keegan . . ."* She sucked in a ragged breath, suddenly aware of the look in his eyes.

"My name is Will," he said softly. "And when these come out"—he touched the stitches on her bottom lip with the tip of his finger—"I thought we might explore the possibilities. . . ."

Julie looked up at him, her mouth forming a perfect *O*.

"I'll bring Dr. Stone up in about fifteen minutes," he said, eyeing Zhing's progress with Julie's hair. "Will that be enough time?"

Too bemused to formulate a reply, Julie simply nodded her head.

WILL WAS AS GOOD AS HIS WORD. HE ESCORTED DR. STONE upstairs and introduced Julie to the physician who had treated her on the night she'd run to the Silken Angel for shelter. Will averted his face while Dr. Stone conducted his examination, in order to allow Julie a measure of modesty, but neither he nor Zhing left the room.

Julie didn't say so at the time, but although she found Will's presence while the doctor examined her a bit disconcerting, she decided it was also reassuring. They may have begun their relationship on opposite sides of the street—on opposite sides of a tambourine, so to speak—but they had become friends . . . or associates . . . or something more. She wasn't sure what that might be at the moment, but she was quite certain she didn't want to settle for friendship either. She wanted the chance to find out what that something else might be. . . .

"You are healing quite nicely, Miss Parham," the doctor told her as he removed his stethoscope from inside the front of her bodice and moved to the back. "You had some infection around your stab wound, which accounts for your fever, but it's much better. There's no fever at present, and your lungs sound clear. No sign of pneumonia or pneumothorax." He folded his stethoscope, put it in his jacket pocket, and fastened the frogs on Julie's dress for her before moving on to examine her sprained wrist.

After unwrapping the fabric binding it, Dr. Stone tested her wrist, checking the swelling and moving it up and down and side to side to gauge the range of movement and her level of discomfort.

Julie winced, but didn't cry out as he manipulated the swollen joint.

"Bearable?" Dr. Stone asked. "Or unbearable?"

"Bearable," she answered.

He nodded. "Still using the laudanum I left for you in order to ease the pain and sleep at night?"

Julie shook her head. "No. Not since the first night. I don't care for laudanum."

Dr. Stone raised an eyebrow in query before glancing over at Will for confirmation.

Will nodded. "She doesn't," he added. "She expelled it when I gave it to her. After that, we gave up and settled for coffee and brandy."

Julie glared at Will. "You put brandy in my coffee without my knowledge?"

"Don't get your dander up with him, young lady," Dr. Stone interrupted. "He gave you brandy on my orders, in case you displayed an adverse reaction to the laudanum. Some folks do. And you appear to be one of them."

"Are you still putting brandy in my beverages?" Julie asked.

"I'm the doctor," Dr. Stone reminded her. "I'll ask the questions." He stared at Will. "Well? Are you?"

"Not unless she wants it," Will replied. "And she hasn't complained of pain since yesterday morning." He turned his attention to Julie. "Jack made a pot of tea for you this morning. So no. We haven't added brandy to your coffee since yesterday morning, when you said your shoulder hurt."

"Good," she told him.

"Very good," the doctor pronounced. "From now on, I recommend a hot soak in the bath to ease the aches and pains, and brandy if she asks for it." He smiled at her. "But I would rather you try to do without it."

Dr. Stone concluded his examination with a check of her stitches. He looked at the cut above her eye and the two stitches in her lip. "Well, young lady, you are well enough to get up and walk around. In fact, I encourage you to do so in order to keep the threat of pneumonia at bay, but not anywhere unsafe. But these"—he indicated her stitches—"must stay a few more days."

Julie groaned. The stitches were beginning to itch, especially those in her bottom lip, and she wanted nothing more than to be rid of them.

"I'll be back Saturday morning to take them out."

"I'll be counting the days," she promised.

Dr. Stone laughed.

Will didn't say a word aloud, but when his gaze met Julie's, the look in his eyes said he was anticipating the removal of her stitches as much as she was.

Before he left, Dr. Stone reminded Julie to get up and walk around. Unfortunately, there was nowhere for her to go that was safe, so Julie was confined to the upstairs and her own company for a while longer.

*Chapter Twenty-five*

❧❧❧

"A cat pent up becomes a lion."
—ITALIAN PROVERB

By Friday, two days after the doctor's visit, Julie thought she would go mad from boredom. Always an early riser, she paced the floor of her room like a lioness in a cage at the zoo, expanding her territory on the second day to include the second-floor hallway. She paced as Will slept. And her boredom grew. She'd finished reading *The Hunchback of Notre Dame* Will had started reading to her while she was unconscious, and had read Mrs. Shelley's novel as well, but the cache of books in Will's room was limited, and as far as she knew, there was no library or gentleman's smoking parlor in the saloon where she might find something else to read, and the downstairs was off-limits to her in any case.

The Silken Angel Saloon was open for business twenty hours of the day. It opened at eight o'clock in the morning for breakfast and locked the doors every morning at four. Will and Jack slept during the hours between four and eight, as did everyone else except the Pinkerton detectives, who stood guard over the grand parlor downstairs.

Bringing her breakfast tray the morning after the doctor's

visit, Will had encouraged her to do the same. "I know that this will seem queer to you, but we function in a world very different from that of the mission or of most legitimate businesses to which you are accustomed." He'd poured her a mug of tea, added a lump of sugar and a splash of cream, then settled down in a chair beside the bed with his mug of coffee. "We work at night and sleep a few hours before daylight. That is quite against normal instincts and every early morning axiom you've ever had drilled into your head. But it is the nature of the beast. Saloons provide evening entertainment for men who work during the day."

Julie looked at him. "I've read everything you have to read in this room, and if there's a library on the premises, it's not on this floor. I've checked."

Will bit the inside of his cheek to keep from laughing. "You're right. There is no library. Saloons aren't generally equipped with them."

"The theory being that a man may read and drink at home, but must frequent a saloon in order to be thoroughly entertained," she snapped.

"Ouch! My, aren't we being a bit waspish this morning?" He set the tray down on the table.

"That's generally the outcome when one's sleep is constantly interrupted by the pall of cigar smoke filling the atmosphere, and the sound of men's laughter and loud voices, the clink of glasses, the infernal sound of that wheel going 'round and 'round, and billiard balls bouncing against one another and the rails of the table," she grumbled.

"The same could be said of the sound of windows opening to air out the cigar smoke and letting in the noise of the streets of Chinatown coming to life every morning, as well as the infernal pacing up and down the hall and around this room," he shot back before downing a mouthful of hot coffee to clear the early morning cobwebs from his brain so he'd be better able to spar with her at the ungodly hour of eight fifteen.

"You can hear me pacing downstairs?" Julie was ashamed

admit to herself that she hadn't thought to ask where Will
ept now that she had taken over his bedroom. She knew Jack
ept an apartment downstairs next to the kitchen and assumed
Will was sharing it with him.

"You'll have to ask Jack about that," he told her. "I sleep
up here."

"Up here where?"

"Earlier in the week, I slept in that chair beside the bed if
I slept at all. For the past two nights, I've been sleeping in the
room next door." A wedge of her delicate lawn nightgown
was visible through the opening in her dressing gown, and
Will found himself watching the rise and fall of her breasts
beneath the thin, almost transparent fabric.

Recalling the single iron bedstead in the room she'd occupied while the seven Chinese girls were here, Julie suddenly
wondered how he managed to fold his six-foot-three-inch
frame onto the mattress of those small beds. "How on earth
do you manage that? Don't parts of you hang off the bed?"

Will waggled his eyebrows at her and gave her a wolfish
grin. "Not the essential parts."

Julie frowned. "Maybe we should switch rooms."

"We can't," he reminded her. "Because the room I'm sleeping in and the others like it were designed to look like sporting
rooms open to the male public. There are no locks on the
doors. So it wouldn't do to have a customer make his way up
here by mistake or by design and find you in one of those
rooms. My suite of rooms—the rooms you're currently
occupying—are private and have locks on the doors to
prove it."

"But I'm short and you're . . ." she protested.

*Aroused.* "Fine where I am."

"You couldn't possibly be," she insisted.

"You're right, Julia Jane, I'd be more comfortable in my
own bed, but it's occupied." He gave her a meaningful smile.

She blushed.

"And now my unguarded tongue has made you uncomfortable," Will said by way of apology.

"It's only fair. The beds in those rooms are much too small for you. I would know," Julie said, recalling the night of the auction.

He nodded. "Last Friday night, when the other girls were here."

"I was planning to convince them to follow me out of the saloon to freedom," Julie admitted.

"Imagine that," Will said with a touch of irony, "Julia Jane Parham leading a freedom crusade. Now eat your breakfast before it gets cold." He pulled out the chair for her and motioned for her to sit down on it.

"What about you?" she asked, a lifetime of proper table manners and mealtime etiquette burned into her.

"I've already eaten."

*"Oh."* Julie took a couple of bites of her scrambled eggs, then put her fork down.

"I thought you knew my morning routine by now. Break fast with Jack first thing."

"I do," she said. "It's just that . . ."

Will read the disappointment on her face and realized that she was lonely and bored. Her world had narrowed to the second floor of the Silken Angel Saloon, her contact with the outside world limited to four people—him, Jack, Zhing Wu, and Dr. Stone. "I breakfast with Jack so we can discuss business matters. But I wouldn't object to having my morning coffee with you like this every day."

"That would be nice." Julie's voice cracked, her eyes sparkling with unshed tears.

"Then we have a date," Will promised. Reaching over, he picked up her fork and handed it to her. "Jack would be dismayed to learn you didn't like his breakfast." He smiled at her. "It may not be haute cuisine, but his breakfast is considerably better than Mr. Ming's. Take another bite."

She did as he asked, swallowing forkfuls of fluffy eggs and bites of ham until she cleaned her plate and finished her mug of tea.

Will whisked her plate away and put it on the tray and turned toward the door. "I'll see what I can find for you to read."

"Thank you."

"And Zhing will deliver the laundry later this afternoon."

Julie nodded.

He paused in the doorway as another thought occurred to him, something that might help her pass the time. "Do you play cards?"

"I played in whist drives back home."

Will frowned. Whist was a trick-taking game for four people. He and Julie equaled two. "Do you play any other card games?"

She shook her head. "No."

"Any games at all?"

"Chess," she admitted reluctantly.

Will's eyes lit up.

And Julie groaned.

"You don't play well?" he guessed.

She looked down at her hands neatly folded in her lap. "It isn't that." In fact, she played an excellent game of chess. She and her father had played for as long as she could remember, but it wasn't a game she particularly enjoyed. It was something she shared with her father when he was home, and she treasured their matches for that reason, but the commodore had insisted she memorize chess moves the way she memorized multiplication tables and sheet music. Her father was proud of the way she played chess. *I taught her to play the way I intended to teach my son*, was his oft-repeated boast. Julie withered a little inside every time she heard it.

Will studied her. "You don't like chess."

She glanced up. "I *loathe* chess."

He knew from her expression and the way she said it that there was a story there. But he wasn't going to push her to reveal it. Not today. "Then I'll save the chess for Jack," he said with complete equanimity. "Tell me, is there anything you enjoy playing in your spare time—when you aren't psalm singing and smashing glass? Tennis, perhaps?"

She cracked a smile.

"Cricket? Badminton? Golf? Croquet? You swung your parasol as if you'd had a great deal of practice."

"No tennis," she said. "No cricket. No badminton. N⸺ golf."

He shrugged his shoulders. "It's just as well." He sighed "With your injured shoulder and sprained wrist, you'd be n⸺ match at all." He snapped his fingers. "How abou⸺ croquet?"

"I adore it." She gave him a mischievous look. "I especiall⸺ adore smacking the ball with the mallet."

"Too bad it's played out of doors," he recalled. "You aren⸺ allowed out of doors. . . ."

"Yes, too bad," she agreed. "I'm in the mood to smac⸺ something."

This time Will let a smile slip out. "We can't have that." He thought about the options available indoors and within hi⸺ reach, searching his brain for a game similar to croquet. "D⸺ you by any chance play billiards?"

*"Billiards?"* Billiards was a man's game—played almos⸺ exclusively by men in their gentlemen's clubs and saloons, o⸺ the upper stories of their houses where women were no⸺ allowed, or were not able to navigate the narrow stairs i⸺ skirts and bustles. Julie had never seen the game played o⸺ known a woman to play billiards. The idea that a *lady* migh⸺ do so was scandalous. And Julie was instantly enamored o⸺ the idea.

"Yes, billiards," Will confirmed. "Pocket billiards, to b⸺ exact. It's an indoor game where one smacks a little ball wit⸺ a stick." He flashed his most gorgeous smile—the one where his dimple showed. "Similar to lawn croquet. I thought yo⸺ might enjoy it."

"It sounds delightful."

His smile broadened. Life with Julia Jane was anything but boring. "Is there anything else you'd like to play? Othe⸺ than tambourine?"

"Piano," she said softly. "I play piano."

"You are in luck, Miss Parham," Will said. "I happen t⸺ own a piano and a billiard table." He winked. "Now, I have work to do and more errands to run. If you're a good littl⸺

issionary and agree to wear your black wig and not to smash
nything, I'll pick you up tonight. After hours."

"I'll be the best little missionary you've ever seen, as long
s you let me go downstairs. . . ."

She was already the best little missionary he'd ever seen.
You've got a deal."

# Chapter Twenty-six

❧❧❧

*"If you must play, decide on three things at the start:
the rules of the game, the stakes,
and the quitting time."*
—CHINESE PROVERB

Y ou've been busy," Jack remarked when Will stepped inside the kitchen through the back door of the Silken Angel later that afternoon with an armload of packages, including another two-pound tin of chocolates from Ghirardelli.

"I had more errands to run." Will unloaded his packages, setting them down on the kitchen table.

"I see that." Jack couldn't keep the hint of amusement out of his voice.

"I had more people to talk to, more port authority officials to bribe. Chocolate works very well for that." He tilted his head to indicate the Ghirardelli tin. "And cash," he added. "Chocolate is a powerful inducement on its own, but it works a heck of a lot better when cash is added to the mix."

"But a gift always helps to open doors that might otherwise remain closed," Jack guessed.

Will shrugged his shoulders. "What can I say? Everybody expects a saloon keeper to be generous. It was either chocolates and cash or liquor. Chocolates were cheaper."

"I suppose I should be glad you chose chocolates," Jack teased.

"And cash," Will interjected. "Don't forget the cash."

"Especially since you might have just as easily given out okens for free drinks instead of going to Ghirardelli's, and worked me to death tending bar."

Will laughed.

"I'm sure you know word is all over town this morning about the Russ House changing hands, and that everyone is speculating about the identity of the buyer."

"It's a mystery to me how rumors like that get started," Will deadpanned. "And how the devil do you know about them?"

Jack's answer was smug: "Bartenders know everybody's dirty little secrets."

"They must," Will said. "God knows I don't have any secrets left."

"You still have one or two up your sleeves," Jack reassured him. "Like chocolate tins. You know, that might work once we return to Craig Capital. We can change the image of heartless capitalist bankers by giving every customer who opens a new account a tin of chocolates."

"A tin of chocolates won't ease the pain of rising interest rates," Will predicted.

"You never know." Jack walked to the stove and poured himself a cup of coffee from the pot he'd just finished boiling. "It might catch on." He lifted the pot so Will could see it. "Coffee?"

"Yes, thanks."

Jack filled another mug, brought both of them back to the table, and slid one across the surface to Will.

Will stared down at the dark, oily brew. "Did you know that you can buy chocolate-flavored coffee at Ghirardelli's?" He shook his head in bemusement.

"Who the hell would want to ruin good coffee by putting chocolate in it?" Jack shuddered in mock horror. "It's un-American."

"Says the man born and raised in the auld sod." Will chuckled.

"Look around," Jack invited. "America is full of Irishmen.

We may be poor and downtrodden, but we're not stupid. Every
Irishman knows an opportunity when he sees one. America's
one big, bright opportunity. In America, the son of poor Scots-
Irish missionaries can become a rich banker and buy himself
a hotel on a whim."

"A principle, not a whim." Will straddled a chair, propped
his elbow on the back, picked up his cup of coffee, and saluted
Jack with it. "And the note *was* overdue. What would you
have done?"

"The same thing you did," Jack told him, lifting his mug,
blowing on his coffee before taking a sip. "But I would have
done it behind closed doors and refrained from threatening
Palmer with the knowledge of it."

"That would have been ideal," Will agreed. "Unfortunately, Hammond and I were standing in the doorway of room
number eight facing the hall when we saw Palmer accosting
Zhing Wu. I reacted before I considered the ramifications.
Dammit, Jack, he was hurting the girl. He left bruises all over
her upper arm and elbow."

Jack raised an eyebrow at that. "You know this how?"

"I had Dr. Stone look at Zhing's arm before she left here
yesterday. When I paid her for helping Julie, I explained that
Dr. Stone examines all my employees when they start work."

It wasn't a lie exactly. Dr. Stone was the Craig Capital
physician on retainer. He was also the physician for the
employees of the Silken Angel Saloon. But Zhing wasn't an
employee of either business—strictly speaking. Jack supposed
Will was going with a loose interpretation of the rules of
employment. "And where did Dr. Stone conduct his employee
examination?"

"In my office."

Jack groaned at another loose interpretation of the
employee rules.

"Don't look at me that way. All he did was roll up her
sleeve, examine her arm, and advise her to rest."

"She's a laundry girl, Will. Do you really believe she'll
follow his advice?"

"No." He chuckled, remembering. "That's why I advised

he doctor to give her a dollar to pay an acupuncturist. That's
her tin of chocolates, by the way. A replacement for the one
our fierce Julia Jane dented." He fixed his gaze on Jack.
"Speaking of which, how *is* our other patient?"

"Whatever you said to her this morning worked. According
to our resident Pinkertons, she stopped her incessant pacing."
Jack looked over the rim of his coffee mug at Will. "And
they're grateful. Her walking up and down the hall was driv-
ing them mad."

"I'm familiar with the complaint," Will retorted dryly.

"Does she know they are staying down the hall from you?"

"She knows *I'm* staying in the room next door," Will
admitted, "but I have no idea whether or not she knows they're
here."

"She knows," Jack said. "Sorry. I accidentally let that cat
out of the bag."

"No need to apologize, Jack. She hasn't breathed a word
about it to me."

"Probably because she thinks she'll have to reimburse you
for their salaries, room and board, and expenses."

"How would she get a crazy idea like that?" Will took
another sip of his coffee and waited for Jack's reaction. Sometimes the man was honest to a fault.

"From the same person who let the cat out of the bag in
the first place," Jack confessed. "I was tired and frustrated,
and I'm afraid I spoke when I should have kept my mouth
closed. I've no excuse. I simply lost patience with her—"

"Easy to do," Will confirmed.

"And let it be known that her window smashing had cost
a great deal more than just the window."

Will set his mug on the table. "No harm done. I'm not
going to demand reimbursement from her for men for whom
we had already decided to send, any more than I'm going to
accept payment for the window or for Zhing's services." He
snapped his fingers. "That reminds me. I stopped in at Montgomery Street Glass. They've agreed to install the window
on Sunday, rather than Monday, so we can close."

*"Close?"* Jack raised one eyebrow.

"It makes sense to use it as an excuse, Jack. If we close on
Sunday in order for the workmen to install the storefront, we
can move the new girls early Sunday morning, and we won't
need to send for the old man until Monday night. . . ."

"When the theater is dark," Jack added. "And the actors
are idle."

"Right. And I changed my mind about the lettering on the
window and decided to make a slight change in our hours of
operation."

"I'm all for it," Jack told him. "Unless you're adding hours,
then I'm opposed."

"Not adding. Subtracting," Will told him. "No more staying open until four in the morning. From now on, we're closing at one on weeknights and two on weekends. I arranged
to have those changes made in the lettering we ordered."

"Thank God," Jack said. "I don't know how much longer
either one of us could continue keeping those hours along
with everything else."

Will winced. "It isn't all good news. Part of the reason I
shortened our hours of operation is the agreement I made with
Julie—or rather, the bribe I used to convince her to stop pacing like a caged animal. . . ."

"Do I want to hear this?" Jack knew the answer before he
asked the question.

"I promised to allow her downstairs, give her access to the
piano, and teach her how to play billiards."

"You're joking!"

Will was startled by Jack's reaction. "I'm afraid not."

Unable to contain it any longer, Jack burst out laughing.
"You're going to put a pool cue in that woman's hands and
give her free access to the downstairs. Are you daft?" He
didn't wait for Will to answer. "We're talking about Typhoon
Julia. The reason the window needs replacing in the first
place."

"She's going mad up there all day," Will informed him.

"And you're going soft. . . ."

"The opportunity to come downstairs is enough to keep
her on her best behavior."

"She promised to behave last time," Jack reminded him. "And look how that turned out." He glanced at Will. "Did you consider that you have an auction Saturday night? Are you going to allow her to have access to a pool cue once she hears about that? What if you return with girls? What if her missionary zeal returns in full measure?"

"If she plays 'Bringing in the Sheaves' on the piano, the deal is off." He would have to remember to tell her that.

"If she plays that song on the piano, she may wind up dead," Jack reminded him. "I hate to be the one to point this out, but, Will, the majority of the front of our building is glass."

"Frosted glass."

"That's true, but if you get close enough you can see through it. And what if she plays that song and somebody hears it? It only takes one person, and before you know it, the whole of Chinatown will know that she's not dead." He got up from his chair and began to pace. "And that she's staying here."

"I ordered shades for the front windows. They'll be put in right after the new window is installed. And she'll be in costume."

"You're serious." Jack was taken aback. "What's she going to be? A Chinese laundry girl working at the Silken Angel Saloon after hours?"

"I thought she might be an anonymous woman who was part of an auction. If she wears her black wig and the dress of a Chinese lady whenever she's downstairs, she should be safe enough after hours. Her disguise will protect her identity and add to the charade of our second-floor business." Will gestured toward several parcels wrapped in brown paper and twine. "I bought several more cheongsams for her to wear."

Jack conceded that the idea might work—that Julia might be able to leave the safety and secrecy of the second floor and live a relatively normal life as long as she pretended to be someone else. "You have given this a great deal of thought."

"I had to," Will admitted. "We can't keep her locked up once she's fully recovered, and we can't send her back to the mission as Julie Parham. The only way she could possibly go back would be as her cousin, Jane Burke, or under some other false identity."

"We could send her back to Hong Kong," Jack suggested halfheartedly.

"If only she would go." Will was torn between his desire to have Julie safe in Hong Kong, far away from the danger facing her in San Francisco, and his desire to keep her with him. "But the only way to get her to go back without finding Su Mi or finding out what happened to her would be to crate her up and ship her." He wasn't serious. He would never crate a human being and ship her on a cargo ship to a country seven thousand miles away. But there were people—men and women—on both sides of the Pacific Ocean who would do so without a qualm. There were men and women on both sides of the Pacific Ocean who shipped frightened women and girls in the holds of cargo ships from Hong Kong to San Francisco every month.

Su Mi had been one of those people. And Will thought he might have found a record of her arrival—or someone who remembered her arrival and knew something about what happened to her after she disembarked.

Before he knew it, Will was relating everything he'd learned to Jack.

"Are you going to tell Julie what you've discovered?" Jack asked when he finished.

"Not yet," Will said. "It's better to wait until I have more information than to disappoint her."

"I agree." Glancing at the clock on the wall, Jack asked, "When do you intend to put our new operating hours into effect?"

"No time like the present," Will said. "I made a date with Julie to escort her downstairs after we close tonight."

"We'll need signs to post alerting our customers." Jack was thinking aloud. "And we need to do something about our regular poker players—unless you're willing to trust them with the secret. . . ."

"I'm not." Will was adamant about that. He didn't doubt

for a second that the regulars could be trusted with the liquor supply above and below the bar. They could be trusted with the cash drawer and the kitchen larder, but he hadn't trusted them with the secrets of the second-floor business or the wine cellar. And Will didn't intend to trust them with the knowledge of Julie's identity. "I'm thinking the private dining room would work very nicely." The private dining room had never been used for its original purpose. "It's adjacent to both the kitchen and the bar, and furnished with a table and chairs. It's perfect for the poker regulars. It's close enough to the bar, the kitchen, and the facilities for their convenience, but far enough away from the billiard room and the piano that she should be able to grab a bit of freedom.

Jack nodded. "Especially if we screen the piano and the billiard room from the grand parlor and the bar." He took a few minutes to think everything through. "We should be able to make it work. I'll get started as soon as Luis comes in." He drained the last of his coffee and placed the mug in the sink. "Now that we've got that settled, you'd better get upstairs and surprise her with her packages."

"Is Zhing still here?" Will hefted the tin of chocolates.

Jack shook his head. "She left about an hour ago. She delivered your shirts, looked in on Julie, and left. Zhing said Julie was napping. You should think about doing the same," he reminded Will. "You're going to have another long night ahead of you."

# Chapter Twenty-seven

◆◆◆

*"You can discover more about a person in an hour of play than in a year of conversation."*
—PLATO, C. 428–348 B.C.

She was a ferocious competitor. She played billiards the same way she did everything else: with all her heart.

Will stared at her as she bent over the table attempting to line up a shot. The gold cheongsam Julie had chosen to wear from the dresses he'd left in her room pulled, cupping her bottom as she leaned forward.

"Am I doing this correctly?" she asked, measuring the angle from billiard ball to corner pocket, before stepping back again to reassess.

Fascinated by the play of silk over her rear end, Will didn't realize she was speaking to him until she poked him with the end of her cue. "Huh?" He glanced at the dot of chalk on the sleeve of his jacket. Jack was right about the pool cue: Giving one to a girl who wielded a parasol like a cricket bat was probably asking for trouble. But at the moment, it was worth it.

"Oh, sorry." Julie apologized for the chalk, not for poking him. "You aren't paying attention. . . ."

He was paying attention. He knew every shot she'd made, but he was a man, and at the moment he found the play of silk over her derriere a hell of a lot more intriguing than the angle of a ball to the pocket. "Problem?"

"The problem is whether or not I am lining this shot up properly," she repeated.

"Your form is excellent."

"Oh?" She paused to look at him, then beamed. "Jolly good."

"Your angle might be off slightly, but your form is excellent," he drawled.

He thought for a moment that she might swing her cue at his head as she turned around. "My angle is off?"

"Slightly," he admitted. "But as I said before, your form is excellent."

"Show me," she demanded.

Will stayed where he was, leaning against the adjacent billiard table, arms crossed over his chest, watching her, wondering how she expected him to show her that her form was excellent. It had almost killed him to show her how to hold the cue and approach the balls on the table the first time.

Will had demonstrated the proper way to rack and break the balls for a quick game of nine-ball first. Then he had handed her a cue and showed her how to hold it, with the object of the game being to knock the numbered balls into the pockets of the billiard table in numerical order. She'd scratched on her first attempt, nearly scarring the felt of the table, before he moved behind her, put his arms around her, cupped her elbows in his hands, and positioned the cue to make the shot, then helped her make it. But he hadn't counted on having her backside against his groin. . . . He'd made the billiard shot of his life by landing the first numbered ball in the pocket despite the feel of her soft bottom nestled against him, almost more than he could stand.

He remained where he was because he couldn't sit or walk without causing himself considerable discomfort or drawing attention to his burgeoning erection.

"Will!" Julie stomped her foot to get his attention.

"Yes?" He stalled for as long as he could, trying to recall every bit of information he knew about the game.

"You were going to show me how to properly align this shot so I can send it into the pocket."

The time for stalling had run out while he was busy battling the urge to take her upstairs and show her an entirely different sort of way to pass the time. "Was I?"

She frowned, puzzled. "I thought you were." She looked up at him, saw the color darken in his eyes as his pupils expanded to hide the golden brown irises. "We are playing a game of billiards, are we not?"

He gave her a warm, rather mysterious smile. "We are playing a game," he confirmed. "But I'm not sure what it is."

"Pocket billiards." She was nervous all the sudden and very much aware that she was out of her depth with Will Keegan. She knew he was attracted to her. She was deeply drawn to him, but she didn't know where to begin. "I'm a novice. You're the expert. And you're teaching me how to play the game."

He moved forward then, took her by the shoulders, gently turned her and her cue toward the table, and helped her carefully align her shot. "Now tap the ball into the pocket," he instructed.

She did. The ball rolled across the table and fell into the corner pocket. Julie was so excited she wanted to squeal her delight, but her bruised vocal cords wouldn't permit it. She whirled around and threw her arms around him. The cue hit him in the back of the leg. "I did it! I did it!"

"You did indeed." He smiled.

"I made my shot," she boasted. "I'm playing billiards with you. After hours. In a saloon."

"Yes, you are," he said.

"If we had champagne it would be perfect!" Julie exclaimed.

"We have champagne," Will told her. "It's a saloon."

She smiled up at him and Will smiled back, taking note of the stitches above her eyebrow and the bruising on her face that was beginning to turn from blue to greenish yellow. "I can make it perfect. Would you like me to open a bottle?"

"Could we?"

"Would that make you happy?" he asked.

"Yes, of course," she told him. "It's positively scandalous!" And she was almost giddy at the thought.

Will knew she was excited because she'd barely escaped being killed, had been badly injured, cooped up for days, and finally allowed a measure of freedom tonight. She was twenty-two. He was thirty-one and more experienced and should be the more circumspect of the two of them. He was a gentleman and had always behaved in a gentlemanly fashion, but tonight he was feeling a little scandalous himself. "I'll just be a minute."

He left the billiard room and went straight to the icebox beneath the bar where Jack always kept a bottle of champagne on ice. Will pulled the bottle out, grabbed two champagne glasses and a bar towel, and carried them back to the billiard room.

Julie gave a little start as the champagne cork exploded out of the bottle into the bar towel Will had wrapped around it. Streams of foaming effervescent wine poured out of the bottle and onto the towel. Tipping the bottle over Julie's glass, Will filled it to the rim before filling his.

Will lifted his glass in a toast.

Julie raised hers as well.

"Here's to you, Julia Jane."

She took a sip of her wine, smiling at the bubbles that tickled her nose and tongue. Her eyes sparkled. "This is the most wicked thing I've ever done!"

"*This* is the most wicked thing you've ever done?" Will wasn't overly fond of champagne, preferring a good Irish whiskey or a mellow Scots whisky to bubbly wine. The best thing he could say about champagne was that half the wine poured out of the bottle whenever you popped the cork. But he took a drink of it so she wouldn't be disappointed.

She took a sip of champagne, touched her bottom lip with the tip of her tongue, and nodded.

Will swallowed his gulp of wine, set his glass on the closest table, and stared down at Julie. "Does it hurt?" Reaching out, he touched her bottom lip with the tip of his index finger.

"Not so much anymore." She drained her glass.

"Good." Will's voice was low and husky and full of emotion as he took her glass out of her hand and set it beside his before dipping his head, touching his lips to hers. "Because I think we can be a bit more scandalous than that. . . ."

Julie would never have thought a kiss so gentle and tender could leave her breathless and wanting more, but his kiss did. His lips were cool and tasted of champagne, the touch of them a mere sweep against hers, like the brush of silk against her mouth. It was an exchange of breath—hers for his and his for hers—and the most erotic thing Julie had ever felt. Or dreamed of feeling.

Will knew he should pull away and put distance between them, but he didn't. He couldn't think of moving away when everything in him urged him to bring her closer. Will forgot about releasing her and allowed himself to luxuriate in kissing her. He touched the thread of the two stitches in her bottom lip with his tongue before he traced the seam of her mouth, entreating her to open it and grant him access.

She did.

Will broke the first kiss in order to change the angle of their mouths and kiss her more deeply.

Julie's heart pounded against her ribs so fiercely she was afraid her ribs wouldn't be able to take the abuse. She gasped at the heat and the pleasure his kiss gave her.

She was a complete novice. She tasted of an enticing mix of innocence and eagerness. Will knew that she had never been kissed before. What she lacked in experience, she more than made up for in warmth and enthusiasm. Will had kissed a number of women over the years, but he couldn't recall any kiss that affected him more than Julie's innocent one. Not even his first—a thrilling, heart-pounding, rather hesitant, wet affair with a girl named Eleanor from his father's church, who was a year older than he and more experienced.

Though it hurt to lift her arms for any length of time, Julie ignored the pain and placed them around his neck. He swept his tongue inside her mouth and began to taste its warm recesses. She gasped and he repeated the sweep—once, twice, three times—before nibbling on her bottom lip, careful to give nothing but pleasure and not to nip at her stitches.

Heat surged through Will's body as Julie moved closer. He wrapped his arms around her, cupped her bottom with his hands, kneading her beneath the silk.

Julie molded herself against him, enjoying the taste of his mouth, and the slight friction of his chin against the sensitive skin of her face, and the warm, clean, spicy scent of aroused male.

He groaned aloud. Julie pulled away from him, gasping for breath. Her shoulder was aching. She was light-headed, giddy, and completely immersed in the sensations his kisses created. She opened her eyes and found herself staring up into Will's brown ones.

She smiled at him, and Will leaned close to place a string of kisses from the two stitches in her bottom lip to the five stitches above her eyebrow. "Julie," he murmured. "Lovely, scandalous Julia Jane."

The look in his eyes was so warm, so tender, so caring, it almost hurt to see it. Closing her eyes, she whispered, "Gorgeous, sinful Will Keegan."

He tightened his arms around her, breathing in the peach scent of her soap. He wanted to bury his fingers in her hair, her real hair, but he remembered she was wearing her wig and caught himself in time. The importance of her safety far exceeded that of his needs.

She squeaked in pain and Will released her, reaching up to gently unwrap her arms from around his neck, stepping back to put some much-needed distance between them.

She looked at him and Will read the confusion in her expression.

"I hurt you." He was instantly contrite. "I caused you pain."

"No—" She started to deny it, but Will cut her off.

"Enough scandalous behavior for now," he said firmly. "We have a billiards game and a bottle of champagne to finish." He amazed himself by summoning the strength he needed to let go of her, when everything inside him implored him to hold on.

Julie pulled herself to her full height, straightened her back, and stiffened her shoulders. Draping herself in all the dignity she could muster, she lifted her champagne glass and held it out for a refill, sounding as regal as the queen of England and all her forebears. "Let's get to it then, shall we?"

Lifting the champagne bottle, Will refilled her glass and topped off his own. Gesturing toward the billiard table, he said, "I believe it's your second shot."

She took her cue, lined up her second shot, and missed. "Your turn."

He picked up his stick, drew a deep breath, and began to clear the table.

She stared at him, disappointed. "You won."

"I'm good at this game and I've had more practice. I'm the expert and you're the novice, remember?"

"But I thought . . ."

"That I would go easy on you? Allow you to win?"

Julie nodded.

"Why?"

"Because you're a gentleman, and gentlemen always allow ladies to win." She made the statement as if she were reading the rules of billiards and the rules of society to him.

"That would be demeaning to both of us," he said. "You couldn't expect to best me the first time. You had only made your first shot. I've made hundreds, even thousands of shots."

She was quiet for a moment, thoughtful. "Why would allowing me to win—to experience beginner's luck, as it were—be demeaning to me?" She took a deep breath. "I understand why losing to a beginning player and a female would be demeaning to you. And I understand that men object to losing in general, but I don't understand the other."

"I don't mind losing to a better player or a luckier player, male or female," Will explained, "because I always learn something from those losses. What would I learn from losing on purpose to a player playing her first game? Other than the fact that she expected me to let her win? Neither one of us would learn from the game or become better players. And I don't believe in insulting women by pretending I don't know they are as capable of mastering the game as any man. I despise that sort of hypocrisy. We are both Homo sapiens. We both have brains of approximately equal size; why shouldn't the female of the species be every bit as intelligent as the male? The only difference I can see in our proficiency of the game is experience."

"You believe it's possible that I might best you at billiards?" Julie asked.

"It's possible," he said. "Not likely, but possible."

"Let's play again," she said.

Will bit the inside of his cheek to keep from smiling as she accepted the challenge. She had the makings of becoming a talented billiards player. All she needed was practice, and incentive to play through her inevitable losses instead of quitting. If he had learned one thing about Julia Jane, it was that she didn't like to lose. She wanted to best him. And he would be happy to have her best him, as long as she did it honestly. A little incentive could be a powerful tool—and a powerful aphrodisiac. . . .

"What say we make a little wager?" he suggested.

Julie was instantly intrigued. "Wager?"

"Something to make the game more interesting."

"What would we wager on?" She frowned.

"Whatever you like," he offered. "How many balls you can sink? How many games I'll win? How many you'll win? How many colored or striped balls we sink? Whether I'll run the table? Whether you will? Whether you can beat me?"

Julie pursed her lips, discovered it hurt to do so, and frowned. "I should like to wager on whether or not I can best you."

That came as no great surprise. "Done," he agreed. "Shall we set a game limit—say, you will best me after ten games? Forty games? Or would you rather we set a time limit? In two hours of play, or five or ten? In one session—a session being the time we have to play between closing and opening? Or a dozen?"

"Sessions," she decided. "I'll wager that I shall beat you by our fifth session."

Will grinned. "I'll take that wager." He rubbed his palms

together in a gesture of supreme anticipation. "Now, what are we wagering?"

"Twenty dollars."

He frowned. "*Money?* Ah, Julia Jane, I hoped you might be more original than that."

She looked puzzled. "I don't understand. Everyone wagers money."

"That's right," he agreed, making the idea of placing bets for cash sound incredibly dull and passé. "Everyone wagers money."

"If not money, then what?" she asked.

"Pleasure."

She stared at him, and Will recognized the intrigued expression on her face.

"How does it work?"

"When you win, you demand something from me that gives you pleasure," he explained.

"Like champagne?"

"Like champagne," Will agreed. "If you win the wager, you could demand a bottle of my best champagne, or anything else that gives you pleasure."

She gave him a sly, calculating look. "Like playing the piano, or singing 'Bringing in the Sheaves' to my heart's content?"

"The piano, yes," he said. "But no 'Bringing in the Sheaves' in any form. Someone else might hear it, and that could put you in danger again."

"All right." Julie walked over to the billiard table and began placing balls in the rack. "What do you get if you win?"

"I get to demand something that brings me pleasure from you."

"Like kissing?" Her question sounded innocent, but the knowing look in her eyes wasn't.

"Whatever, wherever, whenever I want," he clarified.

"You know more about pleasure than I do," Julie told him.

"How do you expect to learn if you don't experiment?" he asked.

Julie picked up his cue and handed it to him. "Break."

\* \* \*

THEY PLAYED FOUR MORE GAMES BEFORE CALLING THE
session to an end. Julie was sagging with fatigue and too much
champagne, and Will was practically reeling from lack of
sleep and exhaustion. Will won every game, but Julie was
rapidly improving.

"I should have paid more attention to my geometry lessons," she grumbled, realizing he could calculate angles and
the force needed to sink the ball much faster than she could.

"You're improving." He complimented her play, then collected her cue, placed it alongside his in the holder mounted
on the wall, retrieved the rack and hung it up, then started
corralling the balls, placing them in a felt-lined leather box.

"Aren't you going to collect your payment?"

He had already collected three. He'd kissed her on the
pulse points of her left arm—the inner part of her wrist and
her elbow—for his first payment. His second payment had
been a kiss behind her right ear, which he stretched to include
the nape of her neck.

She'd shivered in reaction and expressed her surprise that
he was kissing her instead of demanding something from her.

He'd given her that wonderfully mysterious smile of his
and replied, "Kissing you brings me pleasure."

"That makes two of us," she retorted.

"I'm relieved to hear it." He gave a huge theatrical sigh.
"I'd hate to think my efforts were going to waste."

She had giggled, a rough, hoarse giggle that bore little
resemblance to her normal voice. "I get it now."

"What do you get, Julia Jane?"

"Pleasure. We both win," she realized. "Whether we win
or lose."

"Clever girl," he murmured, before he lowered his head
and claimed his third prize.

"Will?" she asked now, after he'd doused all but one light
in the billiard room and taken her by the arm to escort her
through the darkened rooms to the stairs.

They climbed to the second floor. "Yes?"

"Aren't you going to collect your last prize?" They were standing in front of her—his former—bedroom door. He reached around her and turned the doorknob and cast a longing look at his large, comfortable bed.

"Haven't you had enough kissing for one night?" he asked with a smile.

"No."

Her one-word answer nearly undid him. He thought for a moment that his knees would forget to support his weight.

Julie closed her eyes, pursed her lips, and waited.

Will stroked her battered face, sliding his palm from her temple to her chin in a supremely tender caress. He touched her bottom lip. "This is already swollen from my kisses. Dr. Stone will have my hide if I do any more damage. Your stitches come out tomorrow. I'll save my last prize until after that so we can both enjoy it."

Julie opened her eyes. "But . . ."

"Whatever, wherever, whenever I want," he reminded her, before adding, "Anticipation increases the pleasure, Julia Jane."

She groaned. If anticipation increased her pleasure, she would surely die from it. . . .

# Chapter Twenty-eight

"The billiards lessons must have gone better than expected," Jack commented as Will entered the kitchen late the following morning.

"Why do you say that?" Will covered a yawn as he headed toward the coffeepot on the stove. He had slept the sleep of the dead, despite the short, uncomfortable bed into which he'd folded his big frame. Grabbing a mug from the cabinet, he poured himself a cup of coffee and looked around for Julie's breakfast tray.

Jack anticipated Will's question. "She ate earlier. Zhing brought dim sum from Ming's and pastries from Kingman's Bakery on Stockton Street when she came to help Julie bathe and dress. Julie's been up for hours. Oh, I took the tin of chocolates upstairs so Julie could give it to Zhing. And Zhing was thrilled."

Will nodded. "Thanks for tending to business, Jack."

"Headache?" Jack waved an empty bottle and two champagne glasses he'd lifted from the baize surface of one of the tables in the billiard room.

Will gulped a mouthful of hot coffee and swallowed. It

burned all the way down. He didn't bother to respond to Jack's barb. "Sorry. I meant to retrieve those this morning before any customers arrived."

"Hard to do when you sleep late," Jack deadpanned, placing the bottle in the bottle collector's bin and the glasses in a dishpan of soapy water. "We've been open for forty-five minutes. Not that I blame you for sleeping late," he added. "Apparently you had a long and interesting evening."

Will looked at the wall clock to check the time, then smiled. "That reminds me: You need to replace the bottle of champagne you keep in the icebox behind the bar."

"I noticed." Jack glanced pointedly at the bottle bin.

"And you might want to add an additional bottle," Will said.

"Fond of the bubbly, is she?" Jack kept probing, hoping to get a scrap of information out of Will to satisfy his curiosity about what had taken place in the billiard room this morning. "Because I know you aren't."

Will was not forthcoming. He confided in Jack in matters relating to business, but he was notoriously closemouthed about his personal affairs. If he had a regular lady friend, Jack didn't know who she was. Or where she was. Or when Will visited her. And he and Will lived and worked in the same building. He shrugged. He had enjoyed being a detective, but he drew the line at meddling in his boss's love life, or lack of one, or whatever the case might be. Will was entitled to some secrets. . . .

"A gentleman doesn't disclose details of an evening spent in the company of a female companion," Will reminded his friend.

"Nor would I expect him to," Jack replied. "But—" He stopped abruptly, biting his tongue to keep from saying what he felt he needed to say.

Something must have shown on his face, because Will looked at him and uttered the words, "Go on, Jack; spit it out."

"It's none of my business . . ." Jack began.

"Probably not," Will agreed good-naturedly, "but that's never stopped you before. We've been friends too long for you to mince words. And we've been in this venture together from the beginning, so you might as well say what you're thinking."

"Be careful, Will," Jack cautioned him. "She's young and innocent and . . ."

"You're concerned that I'll hurt her," Will finished Jack's sentence for him.

"No," Jack corrected. "I'm concerned that she'll break your heart."

Will finished his coffee, stood up, carried his cup to the stove, and refilled it. "You know better than that, Jack." He turned from the stove and shrugged. "Ask any lady with whom I've kept company and you'll find that I don't have a heart."

Jack scoffed. "Says the man who's going back into the dragon's lair to rescue more helpless girls."

"Not this time," Will told him.

"What?" Jack was stunned. He couldn't imagine Will missing an auction when there was so much at stake. "You're not going?"

"I'm going. But not into the dragon's lair. This time it's at the Nightingale Song."

Jack shot him a sharp look. "It's always been Friday nights at the Jade Dragon."

"This time it's Saturday night at the Nightingale Song," Will said. "Send an unopened case of Irish whiskey there for me."

"I don't think that's a good idea, Will." Jack told him.

"I always have whiskey sent to the site of the auction, Jack. We don't need to bring suspicion on us by changing the routine now."

"I'll send it, but, Will, that place is in the roughest part of Chinatown. And it's closer to the waterfront than the Jade Dragon. They shanghai sailors out of the Nightingale Song. There could be all kinds of hoodlums and roughnecks about. The only good thing about the change is that we can move the girls early Sunday morning, instead of having to wait until the wee hours of Monday, when all the tradesmen are about."

He scratched his chin. "But the Nightingale Song . . . I don't like that at all."

"There isn't much I can do about the location, Jack. It's Li Toy's auction. She holds it where she feels the safest. My concern is that we be ready. I have no idea how many girls to expect, and even with the Pinkertons doubled up, we've got three fewer rooms."

"I've been giving that some thought, and I think you've already provided a solution to one of those problems."

"Enlighten me." Will set his mug on the table and began rummaging in the warming oven for something to eat. He found slices of ham and several sourdough biscuits in a pan. Grabbing a plate and a bread knife, Will sliced a biscuit in half and slipped two pieces of ham inside it, put it on a plate, and carried the sandwich to the table.

Jack opened the door of the pantry and brought out a tin of shortcake and a box of fresh pastries from Kingman's Bakery and set them on the table. "No dim sum. But we've got some grapes and cheese in the larder if you'd like some to go with your ham."

Will sat down and took another bite of his ham biscuit, then shook his head, but helped himself to a cream-filled pastry. "You were saying I might have solved the problem. . . ."

"You recently instigated a hostile takeover of a very nice hotel, Will. We can house the off-duty Pinkertons in the Russ House."

The impulsive decision to acquire the Russ House he and Jack had second-guessed had suddenly become an asset. Will slapped himself on the forehead. "We've got to decide who will run the place, Jack, and whom we're going to keep and whom we're going to let go."

"I suggest we bring a manager in from Craig Capital, Ltd. Pete Malcolm can help with that. He'll know the best man for the job," Jack reminded Will.

"I think Seth Hammond would be a very good temporary desk clerk." Will had given a great deal of thought to the staffing or restaffing of the hotel as well, but he hadn't taken the opportunity to discuss it with Jack. He had mentioned it to Seth when they'd left the Russ House, and Seth had liked the idea. It might help them find Julia Jane's assailant and would-be assassin.

"It stands to reason that a desk clerk might hear as much as a barman."

"What did Hammond think of the idea?" Jack asked.

"He has no desire to make the position permanent for any amount of money, but he has no objections to temporary employment, so long as he remains a detective for Mr. Pinkerton's agency."

"If the Pinkertons stay at the hotel, we will have freed up two rooms." Jack shot Will a mischievous look. "I'm assuming you will take care of freeing up the third one. . . ."

"Only if I bunk with you," Will retorted. "As you pointed out earlier, our upstairs guest is a young, innocent *lady—*"

Jack and Will recognized the voice of the doctor as he called out a greeting to Ben, who was on duty behind the bar.

"Who has an appointment with the doctor this morning, and if I'm not mistaken, he's arrived," Jack interrupted. "You'll want to be there."

Will stood up, set his mug and empty plate in the kitchen sink, brushed the pastry crumbs from the front of his waistcoat, and hurried out of the kitchen to intercept the doctor before he made it up the stairs.

Dr. Stone didn't use chloroform to remove Julie's stitches. He used a local anesthetic. He numbed her bottom lip by rubbing a paste made of cocaine over it until she could no longer feel it, then carefully snipped the knots on his sutures and gently pulled the silk threads loose. He injected a cocaine mixture in the area above her eyebrow with a hollow needle and glass syringe, then repeated the process, carefully snipping the knots of his sutures and gently pulling away the bits of thread.

When he finished, he held Julie's hand mirror up to her face so she could see the results. A tiny, thin line on her bottom lip marked the cut where she'd bitten through the flesh. The mark above her eyebrow was a narrow pink line with the slightest bit of scabbing to protect it. "Once it heals completely, the scar will be barely noticeable, if at all," Dr. Stone told her.

Turning to Will, who sat on a chair watching the procedure, the doctor added, "Satisfied?"

"Very," Will told him.

"I can hardly see them." Julie exhaled on a sigh of relief. "I'm not normally vain, but I admit to being afraid that I would be scarred for life."

"You are scarred for life, my dear," the doctor reminded her, examining the wound in her shoulder before turning to the other cuts and bruises on her face.

"Not that anyone will ever notice," she assured him. "I thought I might wind up looking like . . ."

"Mrs. Shelley's monster?" the doctor suggested.

Julie's laugh was strained and barely audible, but it was recognizable as a laugh. "I was thinking of Quasimodo."

"You're a far cry from Quasimodo." The doctor made note of the fact that her speaking voice was returning, but her bruised vocal cords still made laughing difficult. "And you can thank your friend over there for that. He stood at my shoulder, hovering over you, insisting that I make my stitches as small as possible."

Julie glanced at Will, but his face proved unreadable. "You did that for me?"

He didn't answer, but the doctor had no qualms about singing Will Keegan's praises. "Of course he did. Not that I wouldn't have taken small stitches anyway, but our Will here cannot bear the thought of females being mistrea—"

Will stood up, walked over to the doctor, and shook his hand. "Thank you for coming, Dr. Stone. Is there anything we need to do or know about her shoulder wound or her wrist?"

"All right, Will, I understand." Dr. Stone let go of Will's hand, then turned and began packing his medical bag.

"I don't," Julie protested.

"Keep your wrist bound until it no longer hurts. The sutures in your shoulder will have to stay in a bit longer, and it should stay bandaged. I'll be back to check on you next week."

"Thank you, Dr. Stone," Julie said. "I understand that. Now explain what you meant by the other."

Dr. Stone spared a glance for Will, then turned to Julie to explain. "It's simple. Our fellow Will is modest. He doesn't like anyone singing his praises—including me," the doctor said.

"He doesn't like singing," Julie grumbled.

Will laughed. "Come on, Galen; I'll walk you out."

The moment they were out of Julie's earshot, Dr. Stone began apologizing. "I nearly spoiled everything by not curbing my tongue."

"You didn't spoil anything," Will told him when they were halfway down the stairs. "She already knows what's going on."

"I am relieved to hear it." The doctor hesitated as they reached the bottom stair.

"Good," Will said. He clapped the doctor on the shoulder. "I may have need of you tomorrow."

The doctor had heard those words three times during the last few months, when Will had asked him to examine the young women he'd purchased at auction, many of them malnourished, beaten, starved, raped, and a few already showing signs of drug addiction, disease, and pregnancy from the sexual abuse they'd suffered on the journey. "Another cargo? So soon?"

"She's opening new places," Will told him. "New places mean more girls."

"Pray God it's not more cribs." The doctor shook his head in dismay. "I'm treating more and more young boys suffering from venereal diseases. Boys as young as eight and nine. And the girls . . . dear God, the girls . . ." It was enough to bring tears to his eyes. He'd spent his adult life battling death and disease, and, in the years since the loss of his wife, fighting for the right for women to be able to protect themselves from abuse, from disease, and from unwanted pregnancies. He had served time in jail for teaching birth control methods and had been condemned from pulpits for interfering with the rights of a husband over his wife. And it was never enough. Not when he was forced to battle ignorance and intolerance and inequality and greed. "Ninety percent of the Chinese sporting girls in this city are diseased."

The board of health and a city ordinance made it illegal for any young man under the age of seventeen to enter a brothel, parlor house, or the upstairs business in saloons, but for as little as fifteen cents boys of any age could visit the back-alley cribs where the poor, unfortunate, predominantly Chinese girls, whose average age was thirteen, were forced to entertain as many as thirty customers a day and were not allowed to refuse anyone.

"I do what I can, Galen," Will said. "I try to keep girls from reaching the brothels and cribs, but . . ." He held out his hands in a gesture of surrender. "I fear I'm fighting a battle I cannot hope to win."

The doctor nodded. "We have two very powerful forces working against us, Will."

"Time and money?" Will asked rhetorically.

Dr. Stone's shoulders seemed a little more stooped, as if the weight he carried was pressing down on him, bending him. "We have *four* very powerful forces working against us—a thousand-year-old culture that views women as chattel; greed; time; and the lack of money." He met Will's gaze. "If we had the richest men and women on earth working for our cause, we still couldn't buy all the unwanted girls in China— or anywhere else in the world."

Will sighed. "I know I can't save them all. But I have to try."

"I suspect that you and James Craig and I share the same motivation," the man who had once been a respected surgeon named Dr. Grandon Stonemeyer said.

"What motivation is that?" Will's question might have sounded cavalier to the casual listener, because the man played his cards close to his vest, but Dr. Stone knew better.

"Our failure to save the one who mattered most." The doctor knew Will had a good idea of his history. He knew nothing of James Craig's or Will Keegan's history except that it was shared. But failure had always been a powerful motivator, and the failure to protect human life was one of the most powerful motivators in history. Seeing the surprise on Will's face, the doctor added, "I've been a physician nearly half my life. I've seen more pain and suffering than I care to recount." He gave a little snort. "I never cease to be amazed at man's ability and willingness—no, eagerness—to destroy other men in unimaginably horrible ways. But I believe man's willingness to prey on the weak and defenseless is the most heinous crime of all. These girls did nothing wrong except have the misfortune to be born female and into poverty and indifference. For that they're enslaved and used in the worst possible way, and discarded when they're no longer wanted." He caught himself. "No, not wanted. These girls were never wanted; they were never anything more than something to barter."

Will met the doctor's gaze. "I'll do what I can tonight, Doctor."

"I know you will," the doctor said. "What time should I expect to hear from you?"

"Starts at nine." Will tried to calculate the time it would take to conclude the auction and get the girls back to the Silken Angel. "Before midnight if we're lucky."

"I'll be waiting."

## Chapter Twenty-nine

❧❧❧

*"In doing what we ought we deserve no praise."*
—LATIN PROVERB

The Nightingale Song was crowded with customers when Will entered the cellar shortly after eight o'clock. The basement was smaller than the one in the Jade Dragon or the Lotus Blossom. There were several tables and chairs, but the majority of the men and women present were forced to stand. The lighting was poor and the air inside dank and musty, smelling of pickled fish and brine and the city refuse along the waterfront. Everything about this auction was inferior in every way to the previous auctions.

The Nightingale Song was situated on the far edge of Chinatown in real estate occupied by the tongs between the area designated as the Barbary Coast and the San Francisco Bay. All around him were the sounds of the shrill, plaintive singsong voices of the crib girls calling out until late in the night the price they charged for looking, feeling, and doing.

It was deep into dangerous territory for a white man on foot without bodyguards.

Jack had wanted to send Seth Hammond along once again to watch Will's back, but Will had asked Seth and the other

Pinkertons to stay and guard Jack at the Silken Angel Saloon. *Guard Jack and Julie.*

Everyone in Chinatown knew the saloon was missing its glass storefront, and it was rumored that the gangs of young hoodlums who existed to terrorize the Chinese were looking to broaden their reach and had decided the Silken Angel was vulnerable.

Will wasn't worried about the Silken Angel. He knew it was well protected. His concern was for himself. If he survived the auction without being knifed or robbed, he had to make it home without being knifed or robbed—most likely with girls in tow. And although he had been raised in a household without them, he'd become proficient with firearms at university. In order to complete his education as a gentleman, he'd had to learn to hunt grouse and pheasant and stag on foot, and foxes on horseback. Hunting was part of being an English gentleman. Will hated it, but he'd learned to use the weapons—pistols, shotguns, and rifles—with a skill that was surprising in the son of nonviolent missionaries. He had hidden a pistol on his person tonight and prayed he wouldn't be forced to use it.

The hardest thing about this evening, other than getting here, Will thought as he made his way through the throng of people milling about, was canceling his billiards session with Julia Jane. He had used the excuse that Saturday was the saloon's busiest night, and with the new window being installed on Sunday morning, the place would be turned upside down to accommodate the workers. He made it a point not to lie to her. Everything he'd said was true, but he hadn't told her the whole of it. He couldn't. Not until he knew what he might find. He would be returning to the Silken Angel with girls. But he had no idea how many girls or in what condition. And he had no way of knowing whether Su Mi might be among them.

After, he promised himself. He'd tell Julie about all of it after the auction.

Now, waiting for Li Toy to appear and for the auction to

begin, Will made his way to the back wall. If he had to stand up, he preferred to do it with his back against the wall. Reaching it, Will elbowed his way to the brick surface and leaned against it, his shoulders touching the brick. He held on to his satchel containing the association ledger and pen and ink. He didn't dare bring his private ledger to a place like this, where it was in danger of being stolen. He had left it in his office safe and would have to memorize as many of the details about the girls as possible and record his impressions when he returned to the Silken Angel later.

"Keegan, what you doing standing up?" Li Toy had appeared at his elbow and sidled up to him while he was lost in thought.

Will gritted his teeth until his jaw muscle began to throb, in order to keep from jumping or showing any emotion. "Good turnout. The place is full."

"It not too full for Will Keegan to have table I save for him." She was wearing another lovely dress. It was gold and, if he wasn't mistaken, an exact replica of the one he'd bought for Julie after his meeting with Pete Malcolm on Wednesday. "Come with me."

Li Toy led him to a small table and urged him to set out his ledger and pen and ink. "I see you send box of your favorite whiskey from the Silken Angel here tonight. You sit down. Make yourself comfortable while I go fetch you your drink."

Fetch him a drink? That was new. Li Toy didn't fetch anything. She had servants to do it. Will watched as she toddled off to a makeshift table containing drinks, tea, and lemonade and one bottle of Irish whiskey. He furrowed his brow in concentration as he pulled the ledger and the pen and ink from his satchel and spread them out on the table in front of him. It was his brand of Irish whiskey. From the case he knew Jack had sent over from the Silken Angel. Will frowned again. He had never seen Li Toy like this, and that worried him. Whatever Madam Harpy was up to, it wasn't good.

He waited while she returned with a bar glass half-filled with whiskey and set it down on the table within comfortable reach. The glass was cloudy. "Thank you."

"You welcome, Keegan." She stood before him. "You try whiskey, see if you like."

Alarm bells went off in Will's head, and he wondered whether she'd coated the rim of the glass with poison or slipped it into the whiskey or both, and if she had, whether it was enough to kill him or just make him sick. But there was no getting around it. Lifting his glass, Will took a sip. He couldn't smell poison, whatever it was, but he knew in his gut that it was there.

"You not drink very much," she complained.

"Whiskey is meant to be sipped and savored," he told her. "You are meant to take your time."

She sighed, and Will realized that whatever she'd put in his drink wasn't going to be quick, but slow and probably painful. Li Toy twirled in front of him, showing off her dress. "You like dress?" she asked in her flirtatious voice.

"It's very pretty," he replied.

The look in her dark eyes changed, hardened, and her voice took on an edge. "I thought you must like, since you go to my dressmaker and buy three or four beautiful dresses like this to take home to someone else."

Will sat up on his chair. He was feeling very uneasy and decided the best course of action was to brazen it out. He had already sipped from the tainted whiskey. He was either poisoned or not. There was nothing he could do about it except stay alive as long as he could. "I liked your lavender dress so much I decided to send my sisters two dresses apiece as gifts."

"Keegan have sisters?" She eyed him suspiciously. "Where?"

"One in London and one in Dublin."

"Older or younger?" she demanded.

"Both older," he said, fighting off a sudden wave of dizziness, trying to focus. He couldn't tell whether Li Toy believed him or not. For all he knew she could be sharpening her chopsticks, ready to finish him off.

"What their names?" Li Toy seemed to be deciding whether he could be believed.

"Molly and Colleen." Knowing she was testing him, Will

decided on a test of his own and reached for the glass of whiskey. If she didn't call his bluff, he could be helping her commit murder by killing himself.

Li Toy bumped the glass out of his nerveless fingers. It bounced against the table and onto the floor, spilling its contents. "Li Toy clumsy." She looked at Will. "And Keegan ill." Reaching out, she quickly closed his ledger and shoved it into his satchel, followed by his pen and ink, then closed and buckled the satchel. She lifted her hands and clapped twice.

Two big burly bodyguards rushed to her side. "What are you doing?" Will barely managed to get the question out.

"Keegan go home to Silken Angel Saloon." Li Toy instructed her bodyguards, "Bring sedan chair. Hurry." She slipped her hand into Will's coat pocket and dropped a glass vial inside.

"What's that?" He was dizzy and feeling ill, but he still had some of his wits about him.

"Antidote. Mix in water and drink," she whispered.

"What about the auction?" he demanded.

Removing his wallet, Li Toy took out ten hundred-dollar bills and showed them to him so he would know she took only the thousand dollars. "You pay me for five girls at two hundred dollars a head. I send girls to Silken Angel after auction." She shrugged her shoulders. "Only two virgins this time."

"Why?"

"Li Toy jealous of Keegan's young lover. . . ."

"I don't have a young lover," Will said. "I don't have any lover."

"Li Toy believed gossip. She think you have lover. She think if her *special* friend, Keegan, need comfort, he should come to her, his *special* friend. Not Wu's laundry girl." She placed his wallet back in his inside jacket pocket and patted his chest.

Will's heart nearly stopped. He didn't know whether it was from his fear for Julia Jane or the poison he'd ingested. "Wu's laundry girl?"

His astonishment was genuine, and it must have convinced Li Toy, because she explained. "His son's widow."

*"Zhing?"* Will was furious but too ill, at the moment, to do anything about it. "What do you know about Zhing?" He didn't know what she would say or how he would answer, but whatever he said had to sound authentic. Madam Harpy had just poisoned him out of jealousy. What would she do to Zhing? Or Julie if she found her . . . ?

"Zhing Wu goes to Silken Angel every morning." Li Toy fixed him with a clever look. "And every night."

"She washes my shirts," Will bit out. "She collects in the morning and delivers in the afternoon, not at night. Our relationship is strictly business."

"Market Street Laundry does the Silken Angel Saloon laundry," Madam Harpy corrected. It was a point of honor for Market Street Laundry that they did the laundry for the newest and finest saloon in Chinatown, and everybody knew it. "Market Street has saloon business."

"Market Street does the saloon's laundry. Zhing does my personal laundry."

"Since when?"

"Since last week, when I decided I didn't like the way Market Street starched my shirts." He didn't have to pretend to be irritated by her interrogation. He was angry.

"You protect Zhing from hotel man," she accused.

"Why shouldn't I?" Will demanded. "The hotel had a 'no Celestials' policy. He hurt her because she went inside to collect laundry. Yes, I protected Zhing." He looked at Li Toy. "I would have protected any woman from a man of his size and strength—including you, madam."

The ruthless madam old enough to be his grandmother beamed. "You would give me a dollar for acupuncturist, too?"

"If you needed it."

Li Toy chewed on her thumbnail. "You do all these nice things for Zhing and you give her a tin of Ghirardelli chocolates and she not your girl?"

"No." Will shook his head, then wished he hadn't. He tried to bite back his groan. "Who told you she was?"

"Wu."

"Wu?" Will repeated the man's name, and it sounded to

his own ears as if he'd never heard it before. The word of
Zhing's honorable father-in-law would be hard to refute. He
shared a house and a business with her.

Li Toy nodded. "If Wu want to keep his laundry, he tell Li
Toy what she wants to know."

"I see." Everything became clear except his vision. He was
seeing two Madam Harpys, both of them blurred and fuzzy
around the edges. Will closed his eyes.

Li Toy patted his chest. "Go to sleep, Keegan. Not to
worry. Not die tonight. Just sick."

"I'm relieved to hear it."

# Chapter Thirty

Julie! It's Jack. Open up!"

Julie was roused from sleep by pounding on her bedroom
door. She turned the bedside lamp up, grabbed her robe, and
pulled it on as she hurried to the door. She swung it open to
find Jack struggling to hold Will upright. "What happened?"
she demanded. "What's wrong with him?"

"I don't know," Jack admitted. "I found him at the back
door." He walked Will into the bedroom and straight onto the
bed Julie had just vacated.

Julie stared down at Will, pale against the white sheets.
Something was terribly wrong. She leaned close. "Will?" He
was breathing, but it was shallow.

"Watch him," Jack ordered. "I've got to send someone for
the doctor, and I can't put him in the room next door."

"Why not?" Julie flipped the coverlet back to make room
for Will's legs, then bent to untie his shoes.

Jack shot her a disgusted look. "Because he's hurt or sick
or worse, and I'm not leaving him in a room alone and vulnerable and at the mercy of anyone who might slip past us and
get upstairs." He waited until she had his shoes off; then Jack

helped her settle Will onto the bed. "Lock the door behind me and don't open it for anyone except me. I'm going to get Hammond."

"Wait!" Julie stopped him. "There's something in his jacket. Help me get it off."

Jack lifted Will enough for Julie to remove his jacket. Jack watched as she struggled to get Will's arms out of his sleeves. Once she'd managed to get his arms out, the weight of his torso pinned the jacket beneath him. Reaching over, Jack grabbed the jacket by the collar, pulled it from beneath Will, and handed it to Julie.

She held it up. A slip of red paper was pinned to the right breast of his jacket.

Jack recognized it as a note written in Chinese characters. Notes like these were tacked to boards all over Chinatown. He saw them all the time, but he couldn't decipher them. He wanted to know what it said, who had written it, and who had pinned it to Will's jacket.

But Julie could read it. She glanced at the characters on the red paper and immediately reached into Will's pocket and pulled out a vial filled with dark powder. "Mix this with water. It's the antidote."

"Antidote?" Jack was mystified. "To what?"

"The poison." Julie didn't wait for Jack to react. Grabbing the water carafe from the bedside table, she filled a glass with water and poured the contents of the glass vial into it. She didn't have a spoon, so she stirred the powder into the water with her index finger, mixing it until it dissolved. She hesitated long enough to touch her finger to the tip of her tongue to taste the mixture. She grimaced at the taste. Julie couldn't remember what it was called, only that it was a powder the Chinese apothecaries sold to cure people who had been poisoned—accidentally or otherwise. Lolly had used it once when she and Su Mi had made a tea out of poisonous weeds as children.

"Help me give this to him; then send for Dr. Stone."

Jack was skeptical. "How do you know it's safe?"

"I had it when I was a child." She spared a look at Jack as

she began plumping pillows behind Will's back. "And I'm still here to tell about it."

Jack hurried over to help her, holding Will's mouth open so Julie could pour the mixture down his throat. When she finished, she covered his mouth and held his nose so he would have to swallow, the way Lolly had covered hers and Su Mi's.

"That's it," she said. "That's all we can do until Dr. Stone arrives."

Jack nodded. "I'll send for him and then I'll come back to check on Will." With one last glance at his friend, Jack left the bedroom and hurried downstairs.

WILL AWOKE WITH A START TO DISCOVER HE WAS IN BED and naked from the waist up. Mind racing, heart pumping, he looked wildly around, seeking a familiar point of reference, something to help him escape from his nightmare.

Squinting in the half-light of the room lit by a single low-burning lamp, Will recognized his surroundings. He was in his bedroom at the Silken Angel. In his own bed.

Someone was sleeping in the chair next to him. He moved his hand and his fingers brushed hers. "Julie."

"*Will.*" She breathed his name on a sigh of supreme relief. "You're awake."

He crooked his lips in a slight smile. "I'm alive."

She nodded. "Dr. Stone was here."

"I don't remember . . ." he began.

"You don't remember what happened to you?" Julie asked.

"I remember Li Toy poisoning me," he revealed. "I don't remember Galen Stone visiting me."

"You were unconscious. You slept through his visit," she told him. "But he's downstairs with Jack. He'll be back up to see you before he leaves."

"How did I get here?" Will asked. "The last thing I remember is Madam Harpy telling me not to worry—that I wouldn't die tonight but would be sick."

"Someone put the antidote to the poison in your pocket, along with this." Julie got up from her chair and walked over to the table to retrieve the note written in Chinese. Bringing it back to the bed, she turned the wick on the lamp up higher and held the note out for Will to see. She was going to translate it for him, but Will read it for himself, aloud. " 'Poison antidote in pocket. Mix with water.' " He looked at Julie. "Succinct and to the point, wouldn't you say?"

"I'd say you're very lucky to be alive. And lucky that I read Chinese characters." Her voice cracked.

"You found me?"

She shook her head. "Jack found you at the back door."

Will managed a ghost of his normal smile. "It's very lucky for me that you read Chinese characters, because I know for a fact that Jack can't. You saved me."

Julie felt compelled to defend Jack. He might not be able to read Chinese, but he had been worried enough about Will to go out the back door on his way to find him when he hadn't returned. "Yes, but he's allowed downstairs and out of doors. I'm not. His finding you allowed me to save you."

"You're right." He didn't try to argue the point. "You both saved me."

"What were you doing at the Jade Dragon—or was it the Lotus Blossom? And why did Li Toy want you dead?"

"I was at the Nightingale Song and Li Toy doesn't want me dead."

Julie wasn't sure she'd heard him correctly. "But you said she poisoned you. . . ."

"She did poison me," Will explained, "but she also dropped the antidote vial in my pocket." He thought of something. "Will you bring my jacket?"

Julie crossed the floor from her bedside chair to the armoire and removed his jacket from where she'd hung it, then walked to the bed and handed it to him.

Will pushed himself up against the backboard and the pillows positioned behind him. His vision had cleared and he wasn't feeling ill any longer, but he was surprisingly weak for a man in robust health a few hours earlier. Reaching inside his jacket to the inner pocket, Will pulled out his wallet and counted the cash. He'd gone to the Nightingale Song with five thousand dollars in his wallet. He counted four thousand. He was missing a thousand dollars. He looked at Julie. "What time is it?"

Julie rubbed her eyes with the heels of her hands and glanced at the mantel clock. "Nearly five."

Heart pounding again, he asked, "In the afternoon?"

"In the morning. Sunday morning."

He relaxed. "How long have I been out?"

"I don't know exactly, but Jack found you a little after eleven."

Will did a quick calculation. He'd arrived at the Nightingale Song before nine and had been there less than twenty minutes. He'd been unconscious for close to eight hours. "Was I by myself when Jack found me?"

Julie furrowed her brows, puzzled by his question. Had he been out with someone? A friend? Business associate? A *woman*? Someone Jack hadn't seen? Or found? Had he been paying a call on a lady friend? The thought that he might have been with someone other than her hurt like a physical pain, mixed with anger and disappointment. Julie realized she didn't like the idea of Will courting another woman. Teasing another woman. Kissing another woman. He was hers. And whether he knew it or not, she was his. He might as well get used to the idea. There wasn't going to be room for another woman, because Julie intended to take up residence in his heart.

Will was surprised by the ferocious look on her face. She looked the way she did when she played billiards. It was the look that said she intended to win. At all costs. No matter what . . . "Julia Jane? Was I alone when Jack found me?"

"I suppose so," she snapped. "Jack didn't mention anyone else to me." She glared at him. "Why? Were you with someone else when Madam Harpy poisoned you?"

He was astonished by her reaction. She was acting almost as if she were spoiling for a fight. . . . Or . . . Will looked at her again with new eyes. *Jealous. Green-eyed-monster jealous.* It was a thought that didn't seem as ridiculous as it should. Was it possible that she felt more than the first stirring of sexual attraction for him? Was there a chance? The idea burrowed into his brain, refusing to go away. "I was alone," Will said. "At an auction at the Nightingale Song. I was there to buy more girls. Li Toy took a thousand dollars out of my wallet to pay for five girls at two hundred dollars apiece."

Julie sucked in a breath, then went completely still. Her eyes lost their customary sparkle and her face paled. She looked completely stricken, and so utterly betrayed that Will feared he'd dealt her a mortal blow. He was glad she didn't have a parasol or a pool cue handy. "The Nightingale Song? Even the recruiters at the mission warned us not to go looking for converts or help in that notorious place. Sailors go in there and are never seen or heard from again. Have you lost what wits you possessed? You could have been killed! You almost *were* killed!"

"It's not what you think. . . ."

"What I think is that you went to an auction to buy girls from that . . . that . . . *monster.* From the person who hired someone to *kill* me. Who tried to kill *you.*" She didn't realize her voice had risen above a whisper, or that she was crying until the tears rolled down her face and she tasted the salt of them on her tongue. "Tell me it wasn't like that."

"It was and it wasn't."

Julie buried her face in her hands. "I know you rescue the girls and keep them upstairs until you can spirit them to safety. But, Will, don't you see that when you give that *monster* money it keeps her in business? It allows her to keep buying and selling *human beings*? And makes you something I know in my heart that you are not. . . ."

"Shh, shh." He turned, bunching the pillows beneath his forearm to support him as he reached over and pulled her to him, gathering her against him. Draping his arm over her waist, he held her until they were fitted together like spoons in a drawer. "Julie, don't cry. Shh, sweetheart, you're right. About everything." Will kissed the nape of her neck, then the side, and finally the hollow place behind her earlobe. His warm breath grazed her ear as he explained. "I understand that buying the girls from Li Toy allows her to keep buying other girls, but right now it's the best way. . . ."

She tried to turn toward him to argue the point, but Will held her in place. "Shh. I know it sounds barbarous—and maybe it is. But as long as they have monetary value, they're kept alive," Will told her. "When they lose that value, they lose their lives." He took a deep breath. "I know Madam Harpy will continue to import girls from China and force them to sell their bodies so that she can become rich." He snorted in disgust. "So that she and half of San Francisco can become rich. I can't stop that. I can't prevent parents in China from selling their unwanted daughters to people like Li Toy, and without laws to prevent it, I can't keep them from enslaving them here in California. There's not much I can do except try to buy influence from greedy politicians and city leaders who take money from both sides, who spout platitudes about the evils of 'yellow slavery,' but never enact legislation to stop it, because stopping it means losing a lucrative, if immoral, stream of income for them. It's all about money, Julie, and I've found that money is the most effective means of protecting the girls. . . ." His voice was hoarse. "God knows I would save them all if I could, but I can't. So I save the ones I can save. It may seem immoral to you—hell, it may be immoral— but I buy girls from the most ruthless bitch in San Francisco in order to keep her from using them up and throwing them away. And if that's a sin, I'll gladly burn in hell for it when the time comes."

"It almost came tonight, my friend."

Galen Stone stood in the doorway, medical bag in hand, Jack at his shoulder.

"Hello, Will. Julie," Jack drawled, humor and profound relief evident in his voice. "I see you're feeling better."

Julie squeaked at being caught in bed with Jack. She sat up like a cannonball shot from a cannon. She would have put distance between them, but Will caught a handful of her nightgown and held on. "Stay." He guided her back down so that she sat on the foot of the bed, while he pushed himself into a sitting position. "The cat's out of the bag, Julia Jane," he said. "We might as well let them see it."

"The fact that you both have nine lives? Or that you two can't keep your eyes—or your hands—off each other?" Jack queried, one eyebrow raised in mock horror and a smile playing on his lips.

"It's quite apparent," Dr. Stone continued in a similar vein, "that it's mating season. You two have been hissing and spitting at each other since you first met," he said. "What's equally apparent is that you're each down to eight lives."

"You were lucky, Will." Jack's statement was heartfelt. "The doc says that without that antidote you'd have died."

"I'm lucky you found me." Will looked first at Jack and then at the doctor. "And I'm lucky you arrived in time to give me the antidote, Doctor."

"I didn't," Dr. Stone told him. "Your lady did that."

Will turned to Julie, a question in his eyes. She'd told him she translated the note. She hadn't said anything about giving him the antidote.

"She mixed it up, tasted it to see if it was safe, and poured it down your throat while I held your mouth open," Jack told him.

"The administration was crude, but effective," Dr. Stone said. "For if they had not done it, you would not be here now." The doctor smiled at Julie. "You could not have done a better job, my dear."

Embarrassed by the praise, Julie deflected it. "I only did what the note told me to do."

"And thank the good lord that you could read it," Jack said.

Julie smiled at that. "Thank Lolly, our housekeeper, who began life as a peasant, but insisted that my father find someone to teach her how to read and write Cantonese so the shopkeepers and the butchers could not cheat her out of my father's hard-earned coin."

"I hope one day I may be able to thank her," Will said.

Julie pinned him with her gaze. "Help me find her daughter," she said. "Or help me find what became of her. That will be thanks enough for Lolly."

Will met her gaze and nodded.

"Speaking of daughters and what's become of them," Jack said, "Madam Harpy sent you five. They were packed into a shipping crate and delivered here a couple of hours after I found you."

Will closed his eyes and groaned, fearing the worst. "In a shipping crate? Are they dead?"

"No," the doctor assured him. "Alive. More alive than you were at the time. I've examined them," Dr. Stone said. "They are all malnourished and filthy, as usual. Two are suffering with dysentery and unable to travel for a few days, but otherwise appear to be in fair health. The three older girls are no longer maidens, but thankfully the two younger ones are. And now, for you . . ." Pulling his stethoscope from his medical bag, the doctor put in the earpieces and leaned forward to place it against Will's chest. He listened to the steady beat of Will's heart and the clear sound of his lungs and pronounced him alive and rapidly recovering from his ordeal.

"I'm as weak as a newborn, Galen." Will reached for Julie's hand. She placed it in his.

"The poison taxed your body almost beyond measure and the antidote purged it by purging you," the doctor informed him. "And you've gone without food for more than half a day. Once we get something in you, you should regain your strength."

"Well enough to continue the plan?" Will asked.

"In a few days, if you feel well enough to travel," the doctor told him. "I see no reason why they can't or you shouldn't—provided you and they can eat something and keep it down with no ill effects." Dr. Stone looked at Jack. "Send to Mr. Ming's for a large order of noodles, and ask Ben to scramble a few eggs."

Jack nodded.

"Wait a minute, Jack," Will instructed, before looking at the doctor. "What about her?" He squeezed Julie's hand, then lifted it so Dr. Stone could see their entwined fingers.

"What about her?" Galen asked.

"Is she able to travel?" Will asked.

"Will, are you sure about this?" Jack demanded.

"It's time," Will admitted. "She's trustworthy and she has a right to know all of it. She's living with us. We won't be able to keep things from her now that she's almost healed. And I don't want to." He smiled at Julie. "Our little missionary is a crusader, and instead of being at cross-purposes, we ought to let her know what we are about so we can work together."

"As long as you're sure," Jack told him.

"I'm sure." He had never been surer of anything in his life. Julia Jane had proven her courage and her loyalty to him and to Jack. She had a fearful temper, an unshakable sense of justice, and she was stubborn to a fault. She had sailed seven thousand miles to find her friend. She could be counted on to do the right thing as she saw it, and nobody could keep her from it. Will wanted her at his side as his ally, working with him, instead of as an adversary. Somewhere between the first verse of "Bringing in the Sheaves" and the smashing of his storefront window, he'd fallen madly in love with Julia Jane Parham, and if he was truly as fortunate as they all claimed, she felt the same way about him.

Still holding Julie's hand, Will faced her. "The day we met, you wanted to know about our second-floor business. If you still want to know, come with me and I'll show you."

"I want to know," she told him. "I *have* to know."

"All right with you, Jack?" Will asked.

"Looks like I'll be staying here to supervise the installation of Typhoon Julia's new window while she takes my place on the adventure." Jack tried to sound disappointed, but he was happy for Will and for Julie. A man like Will needed a help-mate. A man like Will deserved one. "Give my regards to the Treasures. And our two keepers of the Treasures."

"Thanks, Jack," Will said.

"You're welcome," Jack replied, a catch in his voice. "I'll take care of the details."

Will nodded. "And telegraph our friends?"

"I already have," he said. "Advising them that two of our guests were ill and that we will be delayed until they are well enough to travel."

"I knew I could count on you to carry on in my absence."
Will wasn't patronizing Jack. He genuinely meant it. If anything had happened to him tonight, Jack was fully prepared
to step into Will's shoes and run the operation.

"You're the boss." Jack saluted him, then turned and
headed for the bedroom door and the busy world
downstairs.

"Where are we going?" Julie asked.

Will smiled. "We're going to visit two of my oldest and
dearest friends and their family, and we're taking a few guests
along."

Julie recoiled in horror. "I can't meet your friends looking
like this." Her face had healed a great deal in a week, but it
was still marred by a collection of yellow-green bruises and
two black eyes that were a very unattractive shade of purplish
green.

"Not in your nightgown, no," Will agreed. "But your Chinese laundry girl disguise and your black wig will be
perfect."

## Chapter Thirty-one

In the three days it took for two of the five girls Li Toy had sent to Will in the shipping crate to recover from the worst effects of their dysentery, Julie thought she might go mad from boredom.

Postponing the trip meant a change in the routine of those who worked and lived in the Silken Angel—that included Julie and the five new girls. With Will installed in his suite of rooms once again, Julie had moved into the room he had previously occupied.

Still confined to the upstairs for her own safety, Julie was delighted when Zhing came to collect laundry. Days went by and her injuries healed. Her cuts and bruises faded a bit more each day. The marks left from the removal of her stitches were barely visible. She was the Julie of old, except that she wasn't. She was a woman in love with Will Keegan, and driven to discover what had happened to her best friend.

But this time she wasn't alone. Will was there fighting with her, searching for answers. He was still recovering from his poisoning, but he had kept his word to Julie and begun perusing each entry in his private ledgers, looking for any mention of Su Mi.

So far, he'd come up empty. He couldn't find a single entry with a mention of a girl named Su Mi from Kwangtung province, but that hadn't kept him from continuing the search. Chinatown was a relatively small community, and nothing stayed secret forever. Someone knew something, and Will was determined to find that someone who would lead them to Su Mi.

Despite his best efforts to quash them, the rumors that Will Keegan, owner of the Silken Angel Saloon, had taken the laundry girl, Zhing Wu from Wu's Gum Saan Laundry, as his mistress were rife in Chinatown.

Living at the edge of the area, Julie couldn't help but hear what was said about Will and Zhing in conversations among tradesmen and street vendors that drifted up from the streets. She ignored the rumors. Julie knew the truth. She had heard it from Will and from Zhing. Will Keegan *hadn't* taken a mistress, and if he ever did, she intended to make certain it was Wu's other laundry girl—Jie Li.

She smiled. In some ways she was still the laundry girl. Battling boredom, she'd implored Zhing Wu to bring baskets of clean laundry to the Silken Angel. Julia Jane Parham was learning to fold and iron. To that end, she and Will and Jack had turned the larger of the second-floor guest rooms into a laundry room.

"Not like that, Jie Li." Zhing laughed at Julie's clumsy attempts to properly fold men's shirts for wrapping in brown paper. "You do like that and Mr. Alcott's shirts be all wrinkled."

It was Wednesday morning, and she and Zhing had the saloon to themselves. Luis and Ben were downstairs in the kitchen and behind the bar, respectively. Will and Jack were meeting with Peter Malcolm at Craig Capital, looking to overcome more of the staffing problems at the Russ House Hotel—staffing problems Will readily admitted to creating when he'd instructed Malcolm to sack Mr. Palmer and begin reorganizing the hotel employees. As far as the San Francisco business community was concerned, it was business as usual at the Russ House; Iverson had lost the hotel, but the company that held the note on it was running it until a suitable buyer could be found. What they didn't yet know was that the owner of the Silken Angel had already bought the hotel. The *San Francisco Chronicle* had reported that the Russ House had changed hands, but had yet to report the identity of the new owner.

"Show me again," Julie replied. They were speaking a mix of Cantonese and English, with the emphasis on English, so Zhing could practice hers.

Zhing patiently unfolded Jie Li's effort and refolded it, showing her step by step how it should be done. "Here." Zhing pushed the shirt across the table. "Try again."

Julie did so and failed.

"Jie Li, you are hopeless." Zhing took the shirt, folding it quickly and efficiently before wrapping it in brown paper and scratching something on the packet in black grease pencil.

" 'Fat butcher on Fell Street,' " Julie translated. "So that's the way you remember everyone."

"It's good that you can read Chinese," Zhing retorted, "because you are one lousy shirt folder."

"Wait until you see me iron . . ." Julie shot back.

Zhing shook her head. "I don't trust you to iron yet." She took another garment out of her basket and pushed it across the table to Julie. "This one is easy. Try it."

Julie caught the garment, smoothed it out on the table, and froze.

"Jie Li?" Zhing's voice was filled with concern. "Are you all right?"

"Where did you get this?" Julie demanded.

"My laundry basket."

"No!" Julie spoke more sharply than she intended. "Where did you get it?" She'd recognized the exquisite embroidery on the tunic immediately. It was Su Mi's. "Which customer?"

Zhing looked at the tag on the basket. "This laundry came from the Nightingale Song."

"Did you collect it?"

Zhing shook her head. "No. No. Mr. Wu."

Julie clutched the tunic to her breast. It was Wednesday. She knew where to go to find the screeching little harpy and get answers about Su Mi. Glancing at the clock on the mantel, she saw she could make it if she hurried. Going to the armoire, she pulled out the dress and the accessories Seth Hammond had packed up from room number six and sent to Will at the saloon.

It was time Julie Parham, Salvationist missionary, came back from the dead.

"Bringing in the sheaves, bringing in the sheaves, we shall come rejoicing, bringing in the sheaves. . . ."

She announced her arrival with her tambourine and a song. Julie knew it probably wasn't the smartest thing she had ever done, but she was determined to end her search for Su Mi the way she'd begun it. She didn't make the mistake of going in the front door, as she had the first time she'd gone to the Lotus Blossom. She went around to the side entrance—the laundry entrance—and marched in determined to confront the madam and get the answers she needed.

There had been bodyguards standing at the front door, but there wasn't anybody to stop her at the parlor doors except the woman she'd come to see.

Li Toy stood up. "You!" she accused, her face pale, her eyes wide. "Missionary girl. You dead!"

Julie walked past her and locked the front door. "I'm the ghost of the missionary girl," she said in a native Cantonese dialect she knew Li Toy would understand. "And I've come for my friend Su Mi."

She had flown out of the Silken Angel in a white-hot rage, but Julie knew her mission was risky. Always too impulsive for her own good, Julie realized she should have listened to Zhing and waited for Will to return, but it was too late now. She was here and she owed it to Su Mi and to Lolly to do what she could to find her. She knew she might encounter Li Toy's henchmen before she found Su Mi, but she liked her chances.

If there was one thing Julie had learned from the last assault on her, it was that she was harder to kill than anyone expected. And Julie wasn't entirely on her own. She'd sent Zhing to find Will and Jack and to tell them where she had gone. No matter what happened, Julie had to believe that Will would find her

Will would save her.

"You come singing into my place looking for Su Mi when you should be dead." Li Toy rushed toward her.

But Julie stood a head taller than Madam Harpy and she stood her ground. "I'm harder to kill than you thought, you *murdering bitch*. You produce Su Mi and I'll leave with her and never trouble you again. Or you can keep denying you know where she is and I'll tear this place apart. Starting with you."

Drawing a chopstick from her hair, Li Toy gripped it like the stiletto it was and lunged, aiming for Julie's heart. "You want find your friend Su Mi? I help you."

Julie waited as long as she dared, then stepped to one side and swung her tambourine with all her might—right at Madam Harpy's evil head.


She awoke on a dirt floor and discovered she was alive. Alive and lying in front of a heavy wooden door. Pushing herself to her knees, Julie reached up and grabbed at the handle. A *locked* heavy wooden door. And she was on the wrong side of it in a room lit by a single tiny flame from a small oil lamp. She felt a warm trickle beneath her corset along her rib cage and recognized it as blood. She had been stabbed. Again. The wound wasn't as bad as it might have been, because she'd taken precautions: Julie had had Zhing bind her ribs and help her into her steel-boned corset beneath her Salvationist uniform. Madam Harpy's blow had been a glancing one, grazing Julie's ribs instead of penetrating her heart or lungs. It hurt, but not as much as the first knife wound had. As long as the chopstick wasn't poisoned, and she didn't die of infection or starvation or dehydration, she'd be fine.

Focusing on a pinpoint of light, Julie tried to stand up, but a wave of dizziness overtook her. She crawled on her hands and knees, exploring the room inch by inch, mapping it out. "Forty-eight, forty-nine, fifty." She bumped into the wall, changed direction, and crawled until she banged into a second wall. She gritted her teeth and began again. "Forty-four, forty-five, forty-six . . . Ouch . . ." She expected to make it to fifty, but she'd bumped into something protruding from the wall. Reaching out, she touched the edge of a wooden shelf. Relying on feel, Julie realized she had bumped into a raised bed of sorts—a shelf covered with what felt like a fraying woven mat. Her nose told her a slop bucket that hadn't been emptied in some time was close by. Julie gagged at the horrific odors, covered her mouth and nose by pressing her face into her sleeve. She alternately gagged and heaved as she felt her way along the shelf, making her way toward the light. Sitting back on her haunches, she reached for the tin lamp, lifting it off the floor and raising it high enough to get a better look at her prison.

For as long as she lived, Julie would remember the sight. The image was burned into her brain and branded on her heart.

There were three benches mounted a few inches off the floor. Two filthy rice mats. An empty tin cup. An equally empty tin bowl. And a girl lying on the middle shelf.

The hair on the back of Julie's neck stood on end, and her heart hurt so badly she thought it must surely explode. She put out her hand and felt cool flesh and crawling vermin.

Julie gagged.

The girl lying in her own filth was almost unrecognizable as Su Mi, but Julie knew it was her friend.

"*Su Mi.*" The high-pitched keening took Julie by surprise. She didn't recognize the sound as hers. Crawling to the shelf where her darling Su Mi lay, Julie brushed the tangled hair from her face, and gently laid her palm against Su Mi's cheek. "Oh, God . . . Su Mi . . ."

Su Mi didn't respond. Ignoring the filth, Julie placed her hand on her friend's chest. The rise and fall was barely detectable. "Su Mi . . . please . . . answer me. . . ."

"Julie?" Su Mi's voice was thready and weak, more a breath than a whisper.

Julie's voice cracked. "I'm here, Su Mi." She couldn't be sure in the darkness, but she thought she saw Su Mi's mouth turn up at the corner.

"He made me be a hundred men's wife, Julie."

"Shh, Su Mi, don't . . ." Julie forced herself to speak over the lump in her throat and the burn of tears threatening to choke her. It hurt so much to see her friend like this, to know . . .

"I cannot live"—her voice was slightly stronger, determined—"with the shame. . . ."

"Not your shame, Su Mi." Julie gave up the fight and let the tears flow. For her friend. "His."

"Julie . . ." Su Mi tried to lift her arm, but couldn't. "Madam put me here after the abortionist destroyed my baby and my womb . . ."

Julie took her hand. It was tiny, dehydrated, and reduced to skin and bone. Julie lifted it to her face and pressed it against her cheek. Six months ago, Su Mi had been a beautiful, healthy twenty-three-year-old woman preparing for her wedding, now she was skin and bones and a hair's breadth from joining her ancestors.

"Oh, Su Mi . . ."

"I knew you would come, Julie. I waited for you. Three months I waited."

"Don't, Su Mi, please . . ." Julie choked on her sobs. "I'm here. I've found you. I'll think of something. I'll get us out of here. I promise. And I'll take care of you. We're sisters. I love you. Don't give up. Please don't leave me. . . ."

"Julie . . ." Su Mi's eyelids fluttered, but she didn't have the strength to open her eyes. "I can't stay here. Let me go. . . ."

"No . . ."

"Please . . . Julie . . . I want to go home. . . ." Su Mi took a breath and then another and then she stopped. . . .

# Chapter Thirty-two

❧

*"The wise stand not in the way of lovers,*
*but let nature take its course."*

—ANONYMOUS

Zhing followed Julie's instructions. She waited until Julie was out of sight, then made her way from the Silken Angel Saloon to the Craig Capital, Ltd., offices in the heart of the financial district—where Julie had told her Will was in a meeting—running as fast as she could.

She burst into the building shouting Will's name: "Keegan! Keegan!"

"Here, girl, you can't go in there!" The doorman tried to stop her, but Zhing kept going, running up and down the hallway screaming for Will.

Hearing the commotion, Will got up from the table in the conference room where he was meeting with Peter Malcolm, Jack O'Brien, Seth Hammond, and several department managers. He looked at Jack. "That sounds like Zhing."

Stepping into the hall, he caught Zhing as she came running toward him.

"Keegan . . ." She was winded from her run through the streets. "Jie Li . . ."

Will took her by the shoulders to steady her. "What about Julie?"

"She left the Silken Angel singing 'Bringing in the Sheaves' in her missionary dress."

Will thought his heart turned over in his chest. It felt as if it were pumping molasses instead of blood. "Where is she going?"

"The Lotus—" Zhing gasped.

"Blossom," Will finished her sentence.

"Jaysus!" Jack swore.

Will looked at Peter Malcolm. "Send someone for Sergeant Terrence Darnell of the police department. Tell him James Craig recommended him. Send him to the Lotus Blossom. Jack, grab us a cab! Quick!" He hugged Zhing. "Take care of Zhing." Will called to Malcolm as he ran toward the door, with Jack at his heels.

"I'm coming, too, sir," Seth Hammond shouted, running to keep up. "My job is to watch your back."

They arrived at the Lotus Blossom to find the front parlor in disarray, Madam Harpy with a broken nose and screeching bloody murder. Will barely spared her a glance as he raced through the brothel, searching every room for Julie.

But Julie wasn't there.

He knew he was revealing himself to Li Toy, but it didn't matter. When this was over, Madam Li Toy was going to jail for two counts of attempted murder. If anything happened to Julie, Will would make sure Li Toy met her ancestors sooner than expected. Either way, the madam was out of business.

Will was exiting the brothel when one of the girls confined there ran down the hall after him. "You look for missionary girl?"

He stopped in his tracks and turned to face her. "Yes!"

"They take her to hospital."

"Saint Mary's?"

"Not white man's hospital. China hospital."

Will nearly fell to his knees. He'd never been inside one, but he knew what they were. There were dozens of them scattered around Chinatown. They were cellars hidden beneath buildings where madams like Li Toy sent troublesome prostitutes to die. . . .

*   *   *

JULIE DIDN'T KNOW HOW LONG SHE STAYED IN THE CELLAR holding Su Mi in her arms. It could have been hours or days. The lamp had gone out, and she lost track of time in the blackness. She knew only that she had to stay alive. For herself. For Will. But especially for Su Mi. If she died, who would take Su Mi's bones back to China?

Picking up Su Mi's tin bowl, Julie began to loudly bang it against the wooden shelf beside Su Mi as she sang. . . .


"LISTEN!" WILL STOPPED A FEW STEPS FROM THE ENTRANCE to Cooper's Alley.

Jack stopped next to him. "What is it?"

"Do you hear that?" Will demanded. "Or is it my imagination?"

They had been searching for Julie for more than six hours. Every man at Craig Capital who could search was searching. Every policeman Terrence Darnell had threatened, coerced, or cornered had joined in, as well as the San Francisco office of the Pinkerton National Detective Agency and the firemen from the local firehouses.

"I hear it." Jack grinned.

"I hear it, too," Seth confirmed.

It was a faint but steady rendition of a husky, slightly off-key "Bringing in the Sheaves" accompanied by the beat of a tin drum.


WILL, JACK, AND SETH KICKED IN THE CELLAR DOOR. ONE of the firemen handed Will a lantern. Will held it out in front of him as he crossed the threshold, illuminating a den of horrors.

Seated on the floor near a bench mounted to the wall was Julia Jane, holding a tin bowl in one hand, and the filthy body of a dead girl in her lap.

He had never seen or met Su Mi, but Will knew in his heart that Julie had found her. . . .

She looked up at Will, tears in her cornflower-blue eyes.

"Oh, my darling love, Julie." Will knelt in the dirt beside her. "Thank God I heard you singing that hymn. I couldn't bear to lose you. Not now. Not ever."

"I love you. I knew you would find me," she said simply. "I waited for you."


THERE WAS LIGHT AT THE END OF THE LONG, DAMP TUNNEL. Julie saw lamplight glowing in the fog as she followed Will and the five girls through the narrow, twisting tunnel a week after her rescue. The end of the tunnel opened onto an alley behind a warehouse where a closed carriage waited to take them to the San Francisco Ferry Building to board the ferry that would take them across the bay to the Southern Pacific pier in Oakland, where the Central Pacific Railroad terminal and a private railroad car awaited them.

Will led the way, carrying a lantern and wearing a knapsack that contained food and essentials on his back. The girls, ranging in age from eleven to sixteen, followed close behind him. The girls were a bigger surprise to Julie than the tunnel hidden in the wine cellar. Only two of them—Lan Chu and Gan Que—were Chinese. Two were Russian Jews from the same small village in the Ukraine, who had been sent by their parents as brides to young Jewish men, only to find that the arrangements had been an elaborate ruse to secure exotic prostitutes for bawdy houses in San Francisco. Julie didn't speak Russian or the Ukrainian dialect, but both she and Will spoke French, and Irina, the eldest of the two, spoke enough French for Julie and Will to learn their stories.

Li Toy's shipment was supposed to have been made up of Chinese girls only, but the rough ocean crossing and the horrible conditions belowdecks had cost the lives of twenty-seven girls—including three Chinese girls in Li Toy's shipment.

The broker had foisted three non-Chinese girls off on her.

Will figured that Li Toy had sent them to the Silken Angel

because she knew she could make a profit on them if she sold them to him. She knew Will wouldn't refuse to take them. Her other customers might.

The last girl was eleven-year-old Kathleen O'Flaherty, the blond-haired, blue-eyed, freckle-faced orphaned daughter of an Irish miner killed in a brawl. Kathleen had been placed in a workhouse, then given as a maid to the owner of a whorehouse in Sacramento before being sold to Li Toy. And like Julie, she was sporting a black eye and a battered face.

Julie brought up the rear of the little group as they trudged single-file through the tunnel. Just when she thought they would never reach the end, she was suddenly there, standing across the street from an empty gin warehouse, looking at the carriage. Julie tripped and would have fallen, but Will was beside her. He took hold of her arm and steadied her. "Are you all right?"

She stepped into the open and saw the lanterns hanging from the closed carriage. "I am now," she admitted. "You're here and we're out of that tunnel. I don't like confined spaces."

After what happened in the cellar with Su Mi, who could blame her? Will looked at her in the lamplight. She was pale and trembling, her eyes wide with fright. "Why didn't you tell me?"

"I didn't know we were going into a tunnel until we went into the wine cellar, and then it was too late," she told him.

"You could have told me." Reaching over, Will caressed her face. "I would have understood."

She took a deep breath. "You would have left me behind." She met his gaze. "And I couldn't have that."

"So you did something that frightened you instead."

"I wasn't frightened," she denied. "I was merely concerned."

Will grinned. "No need to be concerned any longer. You're safe." He ushered her into the carriage with the girls. "We're halfway there."

The carriage took them three blocks to the Ferry Building. At that time of morning, the building and the ferry were all but deserted. Will had paid for a private cabin on the ferry for the trip across the bay so Julie and the girls could ride in comfort.

He tried to sell Julie on the idea that she and the girls needed their rest as much as the privacy, but she knew he was worried about her. He'd been watching her like a hawk since he'd found her in the cellar with Su Mi.

Julie was in mourning and, following Chinese tradition, would remain in mourning for a minimum of one hundred days, and she couldn't seem to focus on anything beyond the next three months except helping Will rescue other victims. Su Mi. The memory of her emaciated body hurt more than both the stab wounds she'd suffered. Beautiful, perfect Su Mi reduced to skin and bones.

They had given her a first-class traditional Chinese funeral. She had been buried in a white cheongsam, with a yellow cloth over her face and a light blue one over her body. They had scattered ivory-colored papers punched full of holes during the funeral procession, since the Chinese believed the evil spirits must journey through each opening, keeping them occupied and confused; burned joss sticks; scattered ivory-colored paper called spirit money for the departed to use as currency in the afterlife; and had hired a Chinese band to help distract malevolent spirits.

Su Mi's temporary resting place was in the Chinese cemetery in the town of Colma, outside San Francisco proper. The voyage home to China took a minimum of three weeks, and since the Chinese did not embalm bodies, the dead were buried in temporary plots long enough for the flesh and muscle to fall off the bones so the bones could be interred in urns and repatriated to their homeland. When Julie returned to Hong Kong, Su Mi's bones would go with her.

Julie sighed. Taking Su Mi home to Hong Kong would not give her the justice she deserved. Madam Harpy had escaped punishment for Su Mi's murder and the attempted murder of Julie and Will. And while she had the local police in her pocket, she knew Will Keegan would not rest until she was punished. She had slipped out of the Lotus Blossom in the dead of night. She'd boarded a ship bound for China to escape

etribution for her sins and would retire from the flesh trade
.s a very wealthy woman.

"What's next?" Julie whispered, leaning close to Will as
hey sat in the cabin, safe from any prying eyes, sipping cups
f tea he had bought from the vendor in the ferry's dining
alon.

"When we arrive in Oakland, we'll board a private railcar
t the Central Pacific Railroad, and an hour or so later we'll
rrive at our destination."

"Are you going to tell me where that is?" she asked.

He smiled his mischievous smile. "You'll see for yourself
oon enough."

She glanced at the girls. Julie had spent the first few min-
tes of the ferry ride trying to assure them that she and Will
veren't taking them to work in another brothel. The Chinese
;irls were quiet and docile. They didn't offer any protests or
:omments on anything Will or Julie asked them to do, and
ad promptly leaned against their seats and closed their eyes.
The Russian girls, Irina and Chava, were nearly as coopera-
ive as the Chinese. After spending several weeks at sea with
.ailors who were encouraged to break them in for their lives
s prostitutes, and several days in the Nightingale Song, they
ad no hopes left of making proper marriages with nice Jew-
sh men. The best they could hope was a bawdy house where
he mistress didn't starve or beat them, and where Chava
vouldn't have to hide and Irina wouldn't have to accept every
nan who bought a token.

Eleven-year-old Kathleen was the sole exception. She'd
een quiet and subdued during the trip through the tunnel,
ut she'd chattered nonstop since then. For Kathleen, every-
hing was an adventure. "Isn't this exciting, miss?" She had
o be tired, but she was practically bouncing in her seat. "I've
ever been in a tunnel before, although my da used to go down
n the mines every day. After me mum died, it was just Da
nd me. . . ." Unshed tears sparkled in her eyes, but she
linked them away. "Then Da got stabbed in a brawl in Welsh
Charlie's bar. . . ." She shrugged her thin shoulders. "There
vas no one to take me, so the county put me in the workhouse.

I worked hard there, miss. They rented us out to the fine people in town who needed scullery maids and kitchen helpers and such." Kathleen took a drink from her mug of tea and looked up at Will. "This is ever so good, Will. Thank you. Until I came to your place I hadn't had tea with honey in it in a long time. Not since before Da. I've never ridden a ferryboat before. It's grand." Her stomach growled loudly.

"How long has it been since you've had a proper meal?" Julie asked, charmed by the little girl who refused to let the circumstances of her life dampen her spirit.

"Mr. Jack gave us chicken and noodles from Ming's. They were wonderful, but he wouldn't let us eat too much on account of having to go to the privy all night if you eat too much after not eating much at all." She beamed at Julie. "I didn't know about that." She sighed. "I haven't had too much to eat in a long time." She turned to Will. "Mr. Jack wasn't being mean. He promised that we could eat as much as we wanted when we got where we're going. He said that there would be cookies and cakes and bread and jam whenever we want. Is it true, Will?"

Will swallowed the lump in his throat. "It's true."

Handing Julie her empty mug, Kathleen stood up and flung herself against Will and wrapped her arms around his neck. "Thank you, Will. I'm so tired of being hungry, so tired of the gentlemen at those bawdy houses promising me something to eat if only I would . . ." She looked over at Julie and whispered, "You *know*. That's how I got my black eye. I wouldn't do it."

Will choked and turned it into a cough.

"One of the gentlemen callers at Miss Francie's hit me," Kathleen continued. "And Miss Francie beat me and sold me to Miss Li Toy for causing her bother. And Miss Li Toy beat me for not working hard enough and sold me at the auction and here I am. I reckon you know how it is, miss, seeing how you've got bruises around your eye, too."

Julie nodded.

"You didn't hit her, did you, Will?" Kathleen asked.

"Oh, no!" Julie protested. "Mr. Keegan would never hit a woman. He likes women."

"And little girls?"

"Yes," Julie assured her.

"In the good way? Or the bad way?" Kathleen wanted to know.

"In the good way," Julie said.

Kathleen hugged him tighter. "You and Mr. Jack are the only men who've been nice to me since Da died." And with that the eleven-year-old fell asleep on Will's lap.

Kathleen's revelations nearly broke Will's heart. He gave Julie a rueful smile. "I seem to have this effect on little girls."

"You mean girls have a habit of falling asleep in your arms?" she teased.

"Only after," Will answered.

"After what?" Julie asked.

"After I kiss them good night." Leaning over, Will brushed his lips against Kathleen's blond hair.

"*Oh.*"

Will smiled at her. "You look tired and sleepy."

"Do I?"

He nodded. "You look as if you could fall asleep in my arms."

Julie looked at him from beneath the cover of her eyelashes. "Does that mean I get a good-night kiss?"

"Would you like one?" His warm brown eyes twinkled with mischief.

"I'd like nothing better."

"Then I'll do my best not to disappoint you." Shifting Kathleen in his arms, Will leaned closer to Julie.

Closing her eyes, she met him halfway. "You could never disappoint me. . . ."

An hour and a half after they left the ferry and boarded the private railroad car, the train chugged into the small town of Coryville, California.

A carriage waited at the depot as they departed from the train. Julie followed Lan Chu and Gan Que off the train. Will followed Irina and Chava. He carried Kathleen, who had slept through the train ride—probably her first, and one she would have enjoyed ever so much.

He smiled at the thought. There would be more train rides and more excitement for her from now on, and none of it involved having lecherous grown men attempt to violate her innocence. Unless he missed his guess, he would bet that Kathleen would soon become a member of the Craig household, and if she didn't, Will swore he'd make a good home for her himself. And he'd see that the other girls got the education and the training they needed to be successful. Or, if they wanted, he'd see that they were returned to their homelands. He and . . .

He stared at Julia Jane's back as she walked ahead of him. He and Julia Jane . . . He and *Julie* . . .

A short while later, the closed carriage that met them at the Coryville railway station deposited them at the rear entrance of the home of the owner and president of Craig Capital, Ltd., James Cameron Craig.

James and his wife, Elizabeth, met them at the back door.

"Will!" Elizabeth rushed forward to hug him as he passed the little girl he was holding off to James. "Welcome home! We've missed you!"

*Home?* Julie stared at the exterior of the beautiful house, with its lovely landscaped garden and paved terraces surrounding the back. This was his home away from the saloon? She glanced over at Will and her heart nearly turned over in her chest. She had known he was a gentleman, had known there was more to him than simply being the owner of the Silken Angel Saloon, before he'd explained that in addition, he and Jack worked for Craig Capital, Ltd., but she hadn't expected him to have a family in a town like this.

Will hugged Elizabeth, inhaling the scent that was unique to her. Once the smell of her perfume had the power to make him ache with longing, just as he had ached with longing for Mei Ling all those years ago.

Five months ago, he'd left Coryville because he'd been afraid he was falling in love with James's second wife the way he had fallen in love with his first one, but now all he felt for Beth was the deep abiding love for a dear friend. There was nothing romantic in it. He didn't desire her. What he felt

or Elizabeth Sadler Craig paled in comparison to the love
nd desire he felt for Julia Jane Parham.

James shifted the sleeping child to his left hip with the
ase of long practice and offered his right hand to Will. "Good
o see you, Will."

Will shook James's hand, then retrieved the sleeping Kath-
een. "Good to see you, too. I've missed you both. And the
Treasures." He glanced around. "Where are the little
darlings?"

"Upstairs in the nursery with Delia," Elizabeth said. "It's
nap time. Oh, Will, wait until you see Diamond. She's
walking."

"And talking," James added.

"Diamond?" Will was clearly surprised. "When I left, she
was babbling gibberish and still crawling."

"She got tired of being left behind." James laughed. "One
day she simply stood up and walked. Now she talks and fol-
ows the others everywhere, much to Ruby's dismay." He fixed
his attention on Julie. "I beg your pardon, but we seem to have
forgotten our manners." He'd thought, at first, that she was
Chinese. She was dressed in the clothing worn by Chinese
peasant girls: a white cotton tunic and black trousers, with
white stockings and black cotton shoes. Her hair was braided
into a neat queue and hung down her back. She had been
careful to keep her eyes downcast except when she looked at
Will. James noticed right away when she did that her heart
was in her cornflower-blue eyes. He'd lived in Hong Kong
most of his life, and he'd seen many strange things, but he'd
never seen a Chinese woman with cornflower-blue eyes. "I'm
James Cameron Craig and this is my wife, Elizabeth."

"James Cameron Craig of Craig Capital, Ltd.?" she asked
in a crisp British inflection that was almost identical to
James's.

"You've heard of us?" James inquired.

"Of course," Julie answered. "I grew up in Hong Kong."

He glanced over at his good friend. "You've been remiss
in introducing us, Will."

Will nearly laughed at James's rebuke, because it sounded

exactly like one of his mother's. He made formal introduction even though James had already made informal ones. "Mis Julia Jane Parham, may I introduce you to my very dea friends, James Cameron Craig and his wife, Elizabeth Sadle Craig."

"Parham?" James inquired. "Commodore Parham' daughter?"

"The same," Julie replied.

"What on earth are you doing here dressed like that?" James asked.

"Helping Will Keegan deliver precious cargo." She smiled "May I present Lan Chu and Gan Que from Hunan province and Irina and Chava, late of the Ukraine, who have yet to reveal their surnames, and the sleeping beauty, Miss Kathleen O'Flaherty of the Strawberry Mining Camp?" She turned to the girls and translated. "Mr. and Mrs. Craig."

The Chinese girls bowed respectfully, and the Russian girls curtsied. Kathleen slept undisturbed. Julie reached ou and touched the toe of her scuffed, too-big brogans.

"Shall we go inside?" Elizabeth invited, turning to lead the way into the house by way of the kitchen.

She led them through the kitchen and up the stairs to the nursery, where Will left Kathleen in the capable hands of Delia, the governess's helper, and the new governess, Miss Kittredge, a teacher from the same Providence school where Elizabeth had been a teacher before moving to California and meeting James Craig.

"I thought you might be tired after your journey and would like to freshen up before luncheon," Elizabeth said to Julie "We'll get the other girls settled into their rooms and I'll show you to yours."

Julie looked at Elizabeth and frowned. "I'm afraid I've nothing else to wear."

Overhearing that part of her conversation with Beth, Will handed her the knapsack he'd carried on his back since they left the Silken Angel. "I think you'll find most of what you need in there. If there's anything else, ask Beth. She'll see that you have everything."

Julie took the knapsack. "Beth?"

Elizabeth laughed. "Me. Everyone calls me Elizabeth except Will. He's always shortened my name to Beth."

Julie joined her in the strained laughter that was all she could manage these days. "Everyone calls me Julie except Will. He usually calls me by my full name, Julia Jane."

Will looked over and met her gaze. Heat sizzled between them. "Because you introduced yourself to me as Julia Jane Parham the first time we met. I thought it suited you."

"Not as well as your other name for me," she teased.

"Oh?" James quirked an eyebrow in query, his curiosity piqued by this new side of Will and the reason for it.

"Typhoon Julia," she said, laughter evident in her throaty voice. "He and Jack named me Typhoon Julia behind my back."

"Affectionately, of course," Will added.

"Of course," she confirmed, before she waved to the gentlemen and followed Elizabeth as she led Lan Chu, Gan Que, Nina, and Chava to guest rooms down the hall in the nursery wing, where Miss Kittredge and Delia had their suites of rooms.

# *Chapter Thirty-three*

❦

*"Accept the things to which fate binds you,
and love the people with whom fates brings you
together, but do so with all your heart."*
—MARCUS AURELIUS, A.D. 121–180

Y ou've been busy," James said as he and Will lounged on
comfortable leather chairs savoring whiskeys in James's
study. Elizabeth had shown Julie to the suite of rooms connected to Will's suite, in the wing opposite the one she and
James and the nursery occupied, and Julie had retired to rest
and bathe before luncheon.

Will smiled a cat-that-ate-the-cream smile. "Jack said the
same thing to me yesterday."

"Jack usually knows about which he speaks."

"That he does," Will commented agreeably, as he sipped
a very fine Scots single-malt. He savored the smooth feel of
it as it burned its way down his throat.

"His telegram was quite informative."

"I'll bet," Will retorted. "It's been an eventful few weeks."

It was James's turn to laugh. "Tell me all about it. And let's
start with the Russ House Hotel. I hear you called in the
overdue note and purchased it with your own money instead
of the firm's."

"That's correct," Will told him. "And I'm prepared to offer
you equal shares in the venture if you're interested."

James considered. "I may be. But before we discuss that, may I ask what possessed you to buy the hotel and fire the manager?"

"I caught Mr. Palmer mistreating a Chinese laundry girl who had gone to the hotel to collect laundry from a guest."

James frowned. "I've never been overly fond of Palmer or he of me—especially after I kicked my bedroom door in when Elizabeth locked me out of it last year—but the hotel runs smoothly, and I believe he's reasonably competent, if not good at his job."

"Have you ever taken the Treasures there?" Will answered.

"No." James shuddered in mock horror. "I don't want to think about the chaos that might ensue. They're far too young to be trusted to behave in the manner the hotel expects and the guests require."

"Did you know the Russ House has a 'no Celestials' policy?" Will posed the question in a calm, matter-of-fact tone of voice and waited for James's reaction.

*"What?"* James was clearly surprised.

"The Treasures wouldn't be allowed inside the front door—or the back, for that matter. That's one of the reasons I called in the overdue note," Will explained. "The hotel was enforcing a policy that barred Chinese from the premises. Not to mention the fact that their security left a great deal to be desired. Julie was a registered guest there when she was attacked by an unknown assailant." He clenched his fists in helpless frustration at the memory. "She escaped before her attacker succeeded in killing her. He damn near accomplished his task as it was. The only reason she escaped is that she managed to brain him with a two-pound tin of chocolates, head-butt him, and kick him in the knee."

"So that's what happened to her face," James said. "I wondered."

"If you think it looks bad now, you should have seen it a fortnight ago," Will told him. "And her face is not the worst of it. Her body is a collection of healing cuts and bruises. She has a sprained wrist, bruised ribs, and two stab wounds."

"Ouch!"

"Ouch is right," Will continued. "She's wrapped from her waist to her chest. Wearing dresses that require a corset and petticoats is out of the question."

"Hence the Chinese peasant costume," James concluded, taking a sip of his whiskey.

"She wore the tunic and trousers because we were traveling through the tunnels, but the fact is that until a few days ago, tunic and trousers and Chinese cheongsams were the only things she could wear. And then only while wearing that hideous wig."

"Wig?" James looked puzzled. "That's not her hair?"

"No. Her hair is a glorious dark red, but there's a bounty on her. Li Toy paid a policeman to kill her. That's why she was attacked at the Russ House. Li Toy fled the city for China, but she didn't cancel the contract. Julie's not safe in San Francisco. She has to wear the wig because she's too easy to recognize with her shining hair, but she refuses to leave until she completes her mourning for her friend Su Mi."

"We got your letter and were very sorry to hear about her friend," James said.

Will nodded.

James got up from his chair, walked to the sideboard, and refilled his glass from a crystal whiskey decanter. He held the decanter up so Will could see it.

Will shook his head. "I'd better not."

"That's right," James remembered. "According to the telegram I received last week, you also had a close call at the hands of Madam Harpy."

"If she wanted to kill me I'd be dead," Will affirmed. "It was a strange sort of warning. Li Toy was letting me know that she considered me to be her special friend."

"I don't want to think about that abomination for fear of losing my breakfast," James replied.

"How would you like to be the object of her affection?" Will posed the question.

"It doesn't bear thinking on." James looked at him. "I'm just so glad that you're alive. And so obviously happy."

"Crazy, isn't it?" Will said. "I ran from Coryville to San

Francisco as fast as I could because I was dreaming about your wife—your wives—and was afraid I was falling in love with Beth." He looked at Jamie. "And the strangest thing happened. A Salvationist missionary girl invaded my saloon, my life, and my heart. I'm not sure quite how it happened, but suddenly I find myself in uncharted territory for the first time in my life."

"I can see that," James said.

"I've dreamed of Mei Ling for as long as I can remember, and the dreams became more real after she died. When she started to transform into Elizabeth in my dreams, it scared the hell out of me. To think I could make the same mistake twice . . ."

"And now?" James asked.

"All my dreams—sleeping and waking—are filled with Julie." He smiled at the thought. "I love her, Jamie."

James knew how much it had cost Will to make that admission. "From what I've observed, the feeling is mutual."

Will shot him a smile.

"You should see how she looks at you when you aren't aware of it," James said. "Now why don't you tell me how you met?"

Will complied, telling him everything that had happened since Julia Jane Parham had marched into the Silken Angel Saloon singing "Bringing in the Sheaves" and banging her tambourine. Since she'd barged into his place of business and left with his heart.

"I thought I would die when Zhing Wu told me Julie had left the safety of the Silken Angel to confront Madam Harpy," Will said. "And my heart skipped a beat when I walked through the door of that hellhole of a cellar and found her."

James leaned over and clapped Will on the shoulder. "I'm afraid your condition is incurable, my friend. I feel the same way about Elizabeth."

"I never knew love could be so overwhelming or so completely terrifying," Will said. "The thought of losing Julie . . ."

"Is enough to drive you mad—if you let it," James told him.

"How do you survive?"

James laughed. "You don't survive. You live with it." He looked Will in the eyes. "Living with it is the key. For better or for worse. And I promise you it's worth it. All the pain, all the terror, all the chaos are nothing compared to the love and the joy and the pleasure and the deep sense of belonging they give us. And that feeling is the holy grail and the pot of gold at the end of the rainbow all rolled into one. It's what we spend our lives searching for, why we fight dragons and tilt at windmills and rescue the damsels in distress. We give them our hearts, Will, and they give us the world and all its endless possibilities."

THE CHILDREN HAD EATEN LUNCHEON IN THE NURSERY. THE adults and the older girls had taken advantage of the unusually mild day and had eaten on the terrace. James and Elizabeth, Will and Julie had watched as the girls all got acquainted.

Delia did her best to put the Chinese and Russian girls at ease as they scampered across the lawn chasing the Treasures, James and Elizabeth's adopted Chinese daughters—Ruby, Garnet, Emerald, and Diamond—who, upon seeing him, had run to him at full speed shouting, "Will! Will!"

When they reached him the three oldest Treasures had flung their arms around his legs and hugged him, while Diamond had lifted her arms in a gesture demanding that Will bend and pick her up so she could love him.

Ruby had demanded treats. "What you bwing us, Will?" And they had been rewarded when Will magically produced penny candy from his waistcoat pockets. Kathleen had stood off to one side watching the scene, until Will beckoned her closer by dangling pieces of candy from his fingers to tempt her. Soon she was caught up in the thick of things, demanding treats like the other little girls, following six-year-old Ruby's lead, learning how to play like a child again.

James, Elizabeth, Will, and Julie joined the girls in fierce games of lawn croquet. The Treasures were veterans of family lawn croquet tournaments. The new girls had never seen the game, but they were eager to join in, and the game proved to be the miracle necessary to bridge the cultural and language barriers.

It was a glorious Sunday afternoon. Julie had forsaken her wig after her bath and donned the sky-blue cheongsam Will had packed in his knapsack for her.

When they tired of lawn croquet, the girls had played tag and hide-and-seek in the late-afternoon sunshine; the young ones had hidden and the older girls, led by Delia, had gone in search of them. And then they'd reversed the procedure. The wide expanse of back lawn was filled with the laughter and squeals of ten girls.

And when Elizabeth clapped her hands and rang a silver dinner bell, the girls had come running to find an elegant dessert table filled with cookies and cakes prepared by James and Elizabeth's housekeeper, Helen Glenross, along with the vat of ice cream James and Will had taken turns churning.

Kathleen O'Flaherty, blue eyes sparkling and face flushed with color, had run to Will and flung herself at him. "Oh, Mr. Will, this is the most wonderful place and the most wonderful day in my whole life! Thank you for bringing me here!"

Will's eyes had shimmered with unshed tears, and it had taken him long minutes after Kathleen scampered off to inspect the dessert table to regain control. He was standing on the terrace, almost overcome with emotion, when Julie slipped her hand in his to let him know that she understood how much this afternoon meant to him.

Supper had been soup and sandwiches, and everyone had pitched in to help with the cleanup. It was a traditional Sunday afternoon at Craig House, with the entire day devoted to family and friends.

"I DON'T BELIEVE I'VE EVER SEEN WILL HAPPY," ELIZABETH said as she sat at her dressing table brushing her hair in preparation for bed.

"It's been a long time," James agreed.

"I like her," Elizabeth told him. "She's exactly the sort of woman he needs."

"What sort of woman is that?" James was eager to hear Elizabeth's assessment.

"The sort who will challenge him, who will keep him on his toes and love him with all her heart."

"Do you think that's the case here?" James asked.

"I know it is," Elizabeth told him. "Because Julie looks at Will the way I look at you."

James smiled and pulled his wife down onto his lap in front of the fire, where he'd sat watching as she'd brushed her hair and readied herself for bed. It was a shame she had gone to so much trouble to find the perfect nightgown, because he was about to dispense with it in order to make love to her. "It's a shame she and Will are relegated to separate rooms."

"They're not."

"What?"

"I put her in the suite that connects to Will's in the bachelor's wing." She looped her arms around her husband's neck. "We didn't observe strict proprieties before we married, and I wouldn't deny either one of them the pleasure of this." Leaning forward, Elizabeth planted a kiss on James's mouth. Seconds later, he untied the drawstring ribbon at the neck of her nightgown and shoved it over her shoulders, past her waist, and eventually over her hips and down her legs, where it puddled on the floor, forgotten.

## Chapter Thirty-four

*"We are well matched, you and I,
perfectly suited to one another."*
—ANONYMOUS

Will had shaved and was soaking in a tub of hot water, leaning his head against the rim, when he heard a noise that sounded like pacing coming from the suite of rooms connected to his.

Stepping out of the bath, he didn't bother to towel off, but pulled a dressing gown on over his wet body and padded barefoot from the bathroom to the door that connected his bedchamber to the one next door. Lifting his hand, he knocked on the door. "Julie? Is that you?"

"Yes," she whispered.

"Can't sleep?" He'd felt rested and relaxed in the bathtub, dead tired and yawning broadly, but at the sound of her husky whisper, his body reacted in the predictable manner, and he was hard and aching with desire.

"No."

"Aren't you tired?" he asked, hoping she'd say she wasn't.

"Very," she admitted, "but I can't sleep. I don't quite know what's wrong with me. I'm restless and achy and out of sorts. . . ."

"Would you care for some company?" he asked.

"I don't know if I would be good company right now."

He begged to differ. In fact, he was about ready to beg, period. "I'm willing to risk it if you are." Will held his breath as she turned the key in the lock and opened the door.

They were dressed alike, both wearing dressing gowns and nothing else. The difference was that Will was wet. His dressing gown clung to him in several places.

*"Oh!"* She stared at the damp wedge of hair on Will's chest, visible through the opening in his robe.

"I was afraid I was underdressed," he teased, "but we appear to have had the same idea."

Julie warmed to the twinkle in his eyes, emboldened by the way he looked at her. She felt brave and a little shy at the same time. "The nightgown Elizabeth loaned me was too long. I couldn't walk without tripping on it, so I took it off." She thought now would be the time to act coy or mysterious, but it was beyond her.

"I'm delighted to hear it."

He was such a gorgeous man—in every sense of the word. He was handsome and brave and generous and strong, with the most direct moral compass of any person she had ever known. She loved the way he spoke . . . and she couldn't take her eyes off his chest.

He noticed. "Feel free to explore," he invited.

"I-I . . ." she began. "You haven't claimed your last prize," she reminded him.

He didn't pretend not to know what she meant. "I haven't, have I?"

Julie shook her head. "I've thought about it all afternoon. Worried about it, really. You see, we played lawn croquet for prizes"—bits of colored ribbon they'd worn pinned to their clothing like medals of honor—"and it occurred to me that I still owed you a prize from our wager at our last game of billiards and that I had forgotten to remind you to collect it."

"And you can't sleep unless you get that failure on my part off your mind?"

"Something like that." Julie looked up at him. "As a missionary, I consider it my duty to look out for your soul."

"Just my soul, Julia Jane?" He sounded disappointed.

"Well," she drawled, "I am partial to other parts of you as well."

The air seemed to thicken around them. Julie was suddenly hot, the silk robe almost too painful to wear. Her skin had grown incredibly sensitive to the scrape of the silk whenever she moved. She had unbound her breasts while she was preparing to take her bath this morning, and left them unbound when she'd donned her Chinese dress. Now she could feel the bounce of them every time she moved. The silk of her robe teased them, and the tips of her breasts were standing firm and straight at attention, like two soldiers standing watch. And the sensitive area between her thighs seemed heavy, engorged and damp and tingling.

Julie had the sudden urge to fling her robe off and throw caution to the winds. She wanted—no, needed—to feel the cool air against her overheated flesh. She inhaled sharply, taking in the scent of him, the spicy soap he used that gave him his unique smell. She wanted to bury her nose in the hair on his chest, wanted to feel the texture of it and see just how much of him it covered. She wanted to touch him and taste him and have him touch and taste her as well.

Some of what she was thinking must have shown on her face, because Will asked, "Feeling scandalous, Julia Jane?"

"Yes," she murmured, hoping he would understand. "But I don't know how to proceed."

"We could wager," Will suggested, knowing Julie couldn't resist a bet.

"I don't have a billiards table in my room," she told him. "Is there one in yours?"

There was one downstairs in the parlor that opened into Jamie's study, but he doubted Julie was willing to make good use of it. She was, after all, a lady. Will chuckled. "There are other ways to wager, Julie."

He stared at her, his light brown eyes seeming to bore right through her to discern her innermost thoughts. "What ways?" she wondered.

"We could cut cards."

"How?"

"Follow me," he invited. "I have a pack in my room." He had a deck on the bedside table. He'd placed them within reach in the event that he found it hard to fall asleep. He could entertain himself with a few hands of solitary card games until he felt tired.

Julie followed him into his bedroom and to the bed. "Have a seat," he invited, patting the top of the coverlet.

She sat, gingerly perching on the side of the bed until Will taunted her by saying, "You can do better than that, Julia Jane. Live dangerously."

She recognized his baiting for what it was and smiled. She had a bounty on her head and was forced to wear a disguise in order to protect herself from men who would take money to kill her. She was already living as dangerously as she possibly could. Except . . .

Will Keegan knew how to issue the perfect challenge for her. He knew her. Knew she couldn't resist the twinkle in his eye when he dared her to try something scandalous. So she wiggled her way to the center of Will's bed and sat crosslegged, something she'd never done in the company of anyone except Su Mi, and then only when they were children. But she did it now, covering the private part of her with the ends of her dressing gown.

"Very scandalous." Will nodded approvingly, wondering whether she realized that her sitting position drew his attention to the place she had modestly covered with the tail of her robe. He slit the seal on the pack of cards with his thumbnail, discarded the jokers, and shuffled the deck.

When he completed the shuffle, he placed the deck of cards facedown on the bed, then lay down across the coverlet, propping his head on his hand, angling himself so he could focus on the part of her anatomy she'd carefully covered. "The rules are simple. Cut the cards like so." He demonstrated by cutting the deck, then placed his cut portion back on top and reshuffled it. "Ladies first. Aces are high, and high card wins."

"What do we win?" she asked.

"Let's make it interesting. . . ."

As if sitting on a man's bed in the middle of the night wearing a dressing gown and nothing else wasn't interesting . . . "All right."

"High card wins. Loser takes off his or her robe."

"What happens when both our robes are off?" She was excited and breathless with anticipation as she asked the question.

"Pleasure. Just like before. Winner gets to do anything that will bring him or her pleasure. With the caveat that if I do something that makes you uncomfortable, you can call a halt to our game with no hard feelings."

"It's a deal." She stuck out her hand.

Will shook it, then let it go and said, "Your cut."

Julie cut the deck and turned her card up. "Queen of diamonds."

Will took his cut. "Ten of clubs." He looked at her, his gaze hot and hungry. "Congratulations, you win." He placed his card back on top of the deck. "Do you want me standing or on the bed?"

Julie moistened her lips with the tip of her tongue. She wasn't quite sure what wanting him entailed, but want him she did. Now. On the bed. At the moment she would wager that he was the most wanted man in California. "Bed."

Will felt his body react to her one-word reply, spoken in that low, husky whisper that he'd come to associate with Julie. He shifted his weight against the mattress, untied the belt at his waist, peeled his robe away from his damp body, and tossed it on the floor.

Julie sucked in a breath. He was more gorgeous than she could have imagined. His shoulders were broad, his chest well muscled and covered with thick, curly hair. She followed the pattern of chest hair with her gaze. It disappeared when it reached his stomach—a stomach that was remarkably taut and rippled with rows of muscles—and reappeared below his navel as a little trail that led to a thatch of thick hair surrounding . . .

Julie blinked. "Oh, my . . ."

She didn't realize she'd spoken aloud until he gifted her with a naughty smile.

" 'Oh, my,' is it?"

She blushed to the roots of her red hair.

"Are those your words for it?" Will teased.

His playfulness loosened her tongue. "It isn't as if I've never seen a naked man before," she protested. "I've seen plenty. After all, I've been in most every brothel in San Francisco. . . ."

Will traced her nose with his index finger. The twinkle in his eyes darkened to something that smoldered. "So you're a young lady of some experience. . . ."

Julie frowned. "Only *visual* experience . . ."

Leaning over, Will planted a kiss on the corner of her mouth. "Do you think you might enjoy a more *tactile* experience?"

She nodded.

Taking her hand, he placed it not where he most wanted it, but on his chest, so she could explore at her own pace. Even if it killed him.

Julie loved the feel of his skin, loved the warmth he generated, and the rough hair on his chest. She threaded her fingers through it and followed where it led, across his muscles, over his firm, flat nipples, over his abdomen, around his navel, through the thick hair at the base of his shaft and up to the velvety soft tip. "And what do *you* call it?" she taunted as she gently caressed him.

"I call it sheer bliss." Will barely managed to get the words out. "But you're welcome to call it anything you like. . . ." He sighed in pleasure.

"Does it hurt?" She moistened her lips once again.

As he watched her tongue slip through the seam of her lips, Will's penis jumped in reaction. He groaned. "Only if you stop."

Julie leaned closer to him to get a better look at the drop of liquid glimmering on the head of his penis. "Is it always like this?"

"It is when I think about you."

"Only me?" she asked.

"Only you," he answered, hoping he'd be able to keep himself from imploring her to do more.

Julie touched the pearl of liquid with the pad of her index finger. The feel was incredible. It was like warm wet silk. She smoothed the little drop over the head and watched Will's reaction.

He tried to smother his moan of pleasure, but Julie surprised him by moving closer, scrambling across the mattress, dislodging the deck of cards, scattering them all over the bed.

It was impossible for her to keep her distance. Every instinct she possessed urged her closer—and Julie followed her instincts. Leaning forward, she kissed him on the mouth.

Reaching up, Will tangled his fingers in her hair and gently pulled her down, holding her pressed against his chest as he deepened his kiss, tightening his embrace, sliding his hands to her back in a smooth, fluid motion that sent her senses spiraling. His kiss was everything she'd learned to expect from his kisses. It was everything she hoped for. It was soft and gentle and tender and sweet and enticing and hungry and hot and wet and deep and persuasive at once. It coaxed and demanded, asked and expected a like response, and Julie obliged.

She parted her lips when he asked entrance into the warm recesses of her mouth, and shivered with delight at the first exploratory thrust of his tongue against hers. She met it with her own, returning each stroke, beginning a devastatingly thorough exploration of him.

Will was torn between bliss and frustration. He was fighting to keep the promise he'd made not to rush her. He was going to be a considerate lover and allow her to set the pace of their lovemaking—no matter what it cost him. With that thought in mind, he let his arms fall to his sides and abruptly broke contact with her lips. He drew in several ragged breaths and leaned his forehead against the top of her head, struggling for control. God, he loved kissing this woman!

"Will?"

He was gratified to discover that Julie's breathing was nearly as labored as his own. "Yes?"

"Would you mind very much if I stayed here with you tonight?"

He bit back his groan. "I'd like that," he said. "On one condition . . ."

"You have conditions?"

"Only one."

"What's that?"

"Remove your robe." He rubbed his hands up and down the silk of her dressing gown, sensitizing her skin even more.

She smiled. "Concede without cutting cards? I don't think that's fair, do you? I mean, you lost. I didn't."

His smile matched hers. "I wouldn't say that. But I understand your point. You are a woman who enjoys a wager. . . ."

"I enjoy wagering with *you*," Julie amended. "Ordinarily I'm not the wagering kind."

Holding on to her, Will gently rolled with her onto their sides, then reached around her for one of the cards scattered about. He lifted it and grinned. "Ace of diamonds . . ."

Julie reached down and plucked up the card that was sticking to his muscular thigh. She looked at it, then held it up for him to see. "Seven of diamonds."

"Lucky seven," he said, "but not as lucky as my ace."

"I wouldn't say that," she threw his words back at him as he untied the knot at her waist. She shrugged out of her robe as he reached up and cupped her breasts.

"Clever girl." He dipped his head and sucked one luscious little nipple into his warm, wet mouth.

She reacted instantly, arching her back, turning and pushing her breasts into his face. She sucked in a breath at the wonderful sensation. Desire gripped her. Eager for more, Julie reached up and threaded her fingers in Will's thick brown hair, and held his head to her breasts. "Again," she ordered.

Answering her demands, Will rolled to his knees. Leaning forward, he continued his erotic exploration, touching and tasting, gently nipping at the hard bud with his teeth. And then he suckled her, and Julie thought she might die of the

pleasure as her nerve endings became gloriously alive and
sent tiny electrical currents throughout her body, igniting her.

"Touch me," he told her. "Please."

"Where?" she whispered.

Will took her hand and guided it between their bodies to
the place he wanted it most. "How about the not-so-subtle
part of me standing erect and dying for attention?"

She laughed, then gently wrapped her hand around him.

Will quivered with pleasure and came very close to spilling
himself in her hand as Julie stroked him without shyness, but
with a gentle enthusiasm that had Will thinking that he must
have done something right to find a woman like the one who
held him. He swallowed a lump in his throat, then paused in
his tender ministrations to her breasts to ask her one question:
"Still want to stay the night here with me?"

Julie glanced down and looked him in the eye. "What I
want is you, Will Keegan."

"You understand the consequences? What it means?"

"I live in San Francisco. I've seen what goes on between
men and women in the boardinghouses and cribs," she told
him. "I'm not as innocent as you think."

"You're every bit as innocent as I think," he said between
kisses. "But if you stay the night here with me, you won't be
innocent in the morning." He kissed her again, deeper this
time.

"I don't want to be innocent in the morning," she clarified.
"I want to be your lover. I want you to be mine."

Mindful of her injuries, Will ran his hand down her side,
to her waist. Keeping one hand over her flat belly, he moved
the other one to the triangle of red curls between her legs.

Slipping his finger between her soft folds, Will discovered
she was wet.

He rubbed the moisture over her, spreading the liquid
honey over and around her labia to the hard little button at
the center of her and massaged.

She sighed and squirmed and dissolved into a world of
unimaginable pleasure as he worked his magic against her.
She grew hot and achy and tense. She called out his name in

wonder, in need, and finally in complete surrender as he gifted her with a magnificent release.

Opening her eyes, Julie gasped. "I didn't know. . . ."

"And there's still a lot you don't know." He smiled at her.

"Teach me, Will. Teach me all there is to know about pleasure. About pleasuring you."

He kept his word. He took his time, following the path his hands had taken with his lips and tongue, offering her more pleasure when she climaxed a second time and then a third as he tasted the essence of her. And then, when she was quivering and on the cusp of a fourth incredibly intense release, Will positioned himself between her legs and carefully pushed inside her.

The effort cost him. His arms were shaking from the strain of holding himself back and easing himself inside her warm, tight opening. Will leaned forward and rested his forehead against hers, giving her time to adjust to the size and feel of him inside her.

Just when he believed he might die from the wait, Julie put her arms around his back and urged him on, lightly squeezing his tight buttocks. His muscles bunched and rippled under her hands as Will held her tightly, half lifting her off the bed as he ground his hips into hers and rocked his throbbing erection deeper inside her. She scored his buttocks with her fingernails in a little bit of pleasure-pain that telegraphed her need.

"Wrap your legs around my waist," he instructed, kissing her cheek, then her eyelids, and finally her mouth. He kissed her gently, tenderly, reverently, and held her as if she were precious and fragile.

Julie shifted her hips experimentally and whimpered as the pleasure began to build once again. She shifted her hips and Will understood. He fought to go slowly, fought to maintain control. His body strained with the effort. Julie tightened her hold on him. She put her arms around his neck and held on as he began to move within her.

Gently, slowly at first, then faster.

Julie matched Will's movements until they began to move

in tandem, developing a rhythm of sex that was uniquely their own. She kissed him as they moved together—kissed his arms, his shoulders, his neck, his chin, the corner of his mouth. And she trusted him to lead her to that place that seemed just beyond her reach—the place where she became him and he became her. . . .

The place where the two of them became one.

Then Julie felt it as Will shuddered, shouted her name, and spilled himself deep inside her. She screamed his name and let herself go with him to the spot where there was only Will and the almost unbearable feeling of pleasure spiraling inside her.

# Chapter Thirty-five

꩜

*"One word frees us of all the weight and pain of life:*
*That word is love."*
—SOPHOCLES, 496–406 B.C.

Julie woke up some time later to find that Will had pulled back the coverlet, placed her on the soft sheets, and crawled in next to her. She was on her left side. He was behind her, and she could feel him stirring against her bare bottom as she nestled closer to the warmth his big body offered. She liked the feel of him, his large body curved protectively around hers, his face pressed into her neck, his warm breath brushing her ear, his arm draped over her waist, his hand possessively splayed over her abdomen, the tips of his fingers touching her red curls.

She pressed against him.

"Wriggle at your peril, my sweet," Will whispered in her ear.

"Am I in peril?" she queried.

"I fear you may find yourself sheathing my sword at any moment."

Instantly intrigued, Julie asked, "Is that possible from this angle?"

"Not only possible, but about to begin." With that he slipped inside her from behind and rocked them both to the stars and beyond. . . .

* * *

LATER, SHE LAY CRADLED AGAINST HIS CHEST, LISTENING TO the steady beat of his heart. His arm was wrapped around her, holding her close. "Will?"

"Hmm?"

"Are you asleep?"

He gave a little snort of laughter and Julie felt his chest rise and fall with it. "Are you insatiable?"

"Yes," she admitted. "I can't seem to get enough of you."

He hugged her. "Then I'm not asleep."

Julie giggled. "Thank you."

"You are very welcome," he said, the leer clearly evident in his tone of voice.

"Not just for the lovemaking," she told him. "Thank you for trusting me with your secret, and for bringing me to Coryville with you to meet your friends. I like them very much."

"The feeling is mutual," he told her.

"How do you know?"

Will took a deep breath and gave up on sleeping. "I've known Jamie a long time. I know when he approves of someone and when he doesn't. He approves of you." He pressed his lips against her hair. "He told me so."

"How long have you been friends?"

"More than twenty years. We went to school together, then university in London, and then we returned to Hong Kong and started work at Craig Capital, Ltd. I'm a year older than he is, so I started work first and was his boss when he began."

"But that changed?" She phrased it as a question, but she already knew the answer.

"Yes. As it should have. I'm second in command at Craig Capital. James's father turned the company over to James on his twenty-fifth birthday. Jamie offered me forty-nine percent of the business if I would help him expand it and to branch out from Hong Kong. I accepted the deal, and Jamie and I became partners. We run the business together and share in the profits. I took over the San Francisco office five months ago and built the Silken Angel Saloon as a front for our rescue operation." He smiled in the darkness. "It's turned out to be far more profitable than either one of us expected."

"I'm amazed you could leave Coryville behind to go to San Francisco. . . . Craig House and its grounds are like a fairyland." She began sliding her hand up and down his arm.

Will took another deep breath and slowly exhaled. "Jamie built Coryville in honor of Cory, his little girl who died. He wanted it to be the perfect place for children to grow up."

"I didn't realize he and Elizabeth had lost a child." Julie didn't see how either one of them could bear the loss.

"Elizabeth and James married last year. Cory was Jamie's daughter with his first wife, Mei Ling. She died before we left Hong Kong." Will surprised himself with his sudden willingness to talk about Mei Ling and Cory and the life James had had back in Hong Kong, because he'd never talked with anyone except Jamie about any of it. "She's the reason we left Hong Kong. Jamie nearly went mad from the grief."

Julie was silent for a moment. "What about Mei Ling? What happened to her?"

"She died, too." Will's voice was hoarse. "Shortly after Cory died."

"How awful! That must have been devastating for James."

"It was devastating for both of us," Will told her. "I was madly in love with Mei Ling, too. I had been since I was seventeen. Watching her die was horrible. It nearly tore us apart." He pulled Julie closer to him and began caressing her upper arm, running his palm up and down over it. He pressed another kiss against her hair. "She starved to death."

"Like Su Mi."

"In a way," he said. "The difference was that Mei Ling starved herself to death. And it was a bloody wretched way to die. I'll never forget the sight of her. After." His voice broke, and Will had to take a moment to compose himself.

Julie gasped, hearing the pain in what he didn't say. She had seen Su Mi. She knew what starvation looked like. And she would never forget the sight either. "Why would she do such a thing? Was she grieving for her little girl?"

"Who could tell with Mei Ling?" It was easier to talk in the darkness, easier to tell her when he could hold her in his arms. "You grew up in Hong Kong," Will said. "You've heard of the practice of 'bathing the infant'?"

"Oh, no." Bathing the infant was a Chinese euphemism for drowning unwanted babies—usually girl babies, but sometimes male babies were drowned, too, by their parents or the midwife or another family member. It was a horrid practice. Newborn infants were drowned in basins and bathtubs, or often taken to the country or to the ocean and left in bodies of water to float until they sank. Julie's heart hurt at the horror of it.

"Mei Ling left Cory in a pond while Jamie and I were away on business." Will sucked in a ragged breath, remembering. "Mei Ling starved herself to death because Jamie wouldn't—couldn't—forgive her for what she did."

"And you, Will?" Julie asked, her heart aching for him, for his pain. "What about you?"

"I forgave her," Will whispered. "I just never forgave myself for not being able to save her."

*"Oh, Will . . ."*

"There's more," he warned her. "Let me get it out while I can."

"All right." She lifted his arm from around her waist and placed his hand on her cheek.

"I left Coryville five months ago because Jamie refused to accept the resignation I tendered. I had decided to return to Hong Kong to help take care of my father, because I believed I was falling in love with Elizabeth."

Julie gasped once again and tried to roll away from him, but Will held on. She lay quietly in his arms for a long time before she whispered, "Do you still love her?"

"As a friend," he answered honestly. "But I'm not in love with her."

"You're not?"

"No," he affirmed, turning Julie so he could see her face, so she could see his. "There's only room in my heart for one woman. I'm in love with you, Julia Jane."

"And I'm in love with you, Will Keegan." Julie hugged him.

"And just so there are no misunderstandings, let me say that I want to marry you, Julia Jane Parham, and make you my wife."

Julie tightened her arms around him. "You are all I've ever wanted."

"You're certain?"

"As certain as I've been of anything in my life," Julie told him. "I'd love nothing more than to be your wife and to have you as my husband."

"When?" he asked.

"As soon as possible."

Will grinned. "There's just one thing. . . ."

"Oh?"

"Before we get married, I need to know what you plan to do about your missionary work," he said.

Julia blinked.

"I'm not going to be a Salvationist missionary any longer," she confided. "I'm giving it up."

"That's a shame," he said. "Some of my favorite people were missionaries. They've always held a special place in my heart."

She snorted. "I suppose you paid them not to sing 'Bringing in the Sheaves' in your presence, too?"

"No," he said. "My mother would have boxed my ears if I'd been impudent enough to try."

Julie looked up at him.

"Didn't you know, Julia Jane? My mother and father were missionaries." There was a twinkle in his eyes. "The joke was on me from the moment I met you. I suppose it couldn't have been otherwise. I was meant to fall madly in love with a flame-haired missionary."

She smiled at him, and this time the twinkle was in her eyes. "Can we sing 'Bringing in the Sheaves' before the ceremony?"

"Of course." He surprised her. "It's always been my favorite hymn."

"Since when?" she demanded.

"Since you walked into the Silken Angel singing it . . ."

# Epilogue

※※

*"I love thee with a love I seemed to lose*
*With my lost saints—I love thee with the breath,*
*Smiles, tears, of all my life!—and, if God choose,*
*I shall but love thee better after death."*
—ELIZABETH BARRETT BROWNING, 1806–1861

William Burke Keegan and Julia Jane Parham were married at the Coryville Presbyterian Church by the Reverend Simon Winston later that evening, surrounded by the friends they cherished.

James Cameron Craig stood up for the groom, and Elizabeth Sadler Craig stood up for the bride. The Treasures—Ruby, Garnet, Emerald, and Diamond Craig—were allowed to stay up past their bedtimes to witness the ceremony and feast on cake. Delia, Miss Kittredge, and Helen Glenross were there as well, along with Lan Chu and Gan Que, Irina and Chava, and Kathleen O'Flaherty.

The newlyweds spent another two days honeymooning at Craig House, then bade the girls and James and Elizabeth good-bye.

Mr. and Mrs. Will Keegan returned to San Francisco, rented a house on Nob Hill, settled into a blissful married life, and continued rescuing girls from the horrors of slavery and prostitution—not just in San Francisco, but throughout California. Li Toy was gone, but the tongs and other madams and procurers were eager to fill the void she'd left. Will and

Julie's work would endure as long as crime and corruption ruled the city and the government turned a blind eye to the plight of the Chinese.

And on a beautiful sunny day eleven months after their wedding, Will and Julie Keegan and James and Elizabeth Craig, the Treasures, Delia, Miss Kittredge, Helen Glenross, and Kathleen disembarked from a steamship in Hong Kong into a crush of relatives. Will's father, Reverend Francis Keegan; his sisters, Molly and Colleen, and their families; James's parents, Julia and Randall Craig; and Julie's father, Commodore Lord Nelson Parham, home on leave from the Royal Navy, and Lolly were all there to greet them

Will and Julie had kept Julie's promise to her friend. Su Mi had brought them to each other, and to the families they had left behind in Hong Kong. And they had brought her home to her mother and her ancestors.

Julie had given her heart, and then herself, to Will Keegan, the man who loved her and would cherish her and keep her safe.

As she would do for him.

Until death did they part, and beyond . . .